# the chocolate ship

**Also by Marissa Monteilh**

MAY DECEMBER SOULS

# the chocolate ship

A NOVEL

MARISSA MONTEILH

AVON BOOKS
*An Imprint of* HarperCollins*Publishers*

**This sophomore title is dedicated to my big, handsome brother Claude Jay McLin III, who is cruising in heaven. Thanks for being my protector, my friend, and my rock. I miss you, Big Mac!**
**"Loving You"—Sis**
**R/I/P 6/27/93**

Poems "I Miss," "All There Is," and "One Last Tear, One Last Kiss" written by Paul Bennett.



HarperCollins books may be purchased for educational, business, or sales promotional use. For information please write: Special Markets Department, HarperCollins Publishers Inc., 10 East 53rd Street, New York, NY 10022.

FIRST EDITION

*Designed by Rhea Braunstein*

Library of Congress Cataloging-in-Publication Data

Monteilh, Marissa.
The chocolate ship / Marissa Monteilh.—1st ed.
p. cm.
ISBN 0-06-001148-3 (alk. paper)
1. African American women—Fiction. 2. Ocean travel—Fiction.
3. Cruise ships—Fiction. I. Title.

PS3613.O548 C47 2003
813'.6—dc21 2002032880

03 04 05 RRD 10 9 8 7 6 5 4 3

# ACKNOWLEDGMENTS

Praise to God always and in all ways! I took a leap of faith and He caught me!

With much appreciation to my three heartbeats—my children—for making my life complete: A-Dub, Big Play, and Cola. La-u! And to my new, gorgeous, dimpled granddaughter, Alexis—you are my heart! Love, Grammy.

Much love to my big, hunk of a brother Greg and my cutie niece, Mony. And to my handsome nephews—Shannon, Spencer, and Eddie. Auntie is crazy about you!

My supportive bevy of foxy friends: Vanessa, Ollie, Vicky, Almeta, Annette, Tami, Mary, Victoria, Lori, Kevin, Pamela, and Terry. They say if you have one friend, you're lucky; if you have two, you're lying. Well I have many and I tell you no lie!

Thanks to the first readers of *May December Souls* and the first book club members, especially Special Thoughts Reading Group in Los Angeles—Andrea, Janel, and the rest of my lovely ladies! Also the It's All About Us Book Club in Palmdale, California—my new friends Joyce, Vee, and all of the other awesome members who welcomed me and made me laugh.

The bookstore owners and employees who encouraged and embraced me: Pam at Barnes & Noble in Palmdale, bold and beautiful Bernard at Alexander's in San Francisco, Feron at Phenix in San Bernardino, Marie and Grover at 2000+ Books in Long Beach, Carly at Waldenbooks in Palmdale, and Charles at Smiley's in Carson.

Fellow authors Victoria Christopher Murray, Zane, Nancey Flowers, Cydney Rax, Alicia Clark, Gabrielle Pina, Maryann Reid, Beverly Clark, Lois Lane, Lolita Files, Vanessa Davis Griggs, and C.F. Hawthorne—I'm proud to be connected with a group of such talented and gracious authors.

A shout-out to the online interviewers: BookRemarks.com, RawSistaz.com, NubianChronicles.net, Authorsontheweb.com, and SisterDivas.org. Deep gratitude to Pam and Mary at Pageturner.net for the unforgettable cruise and for my pretty purple website.

A special nod to my fellow L.A. Black Writers' members, especially Ericka, Yolanda, Gabrielle, and Sonia. Thanks for having my back!

Many thanks to the HarperCollins family: Carrie Feron, Gena Pearson, Lisa Gallagher, Leesa Beltz, Donita Dooley, Diana Harrington and all of the other dedicated employees who work so hard to get my titles ready for release and beyond.

RC, my talented agent, for your genuine concern that allows me the freedom to exhale. I am very thankful for your undying support and enthusiasm.

A special thanks to the talented and wonderful Paul Bennett for writing the steamy poetry in Chapter 18. You will no doubt have the ladies looking for you!

And to all of you who've been kind enough to pick up this book, I'd love to hear from you after you've taken a ride on this fantastic, soulful voyage called *The Chocolate Ship.* Please email me by visiting my website, *www.MarissaMonteilh.com*, or be so kind as to post a review on amazon.com.

Gotta go complete the next one! Until then, write on!

# WHEN FIRST THEY MET

***Three years ago***

It had been over six months since Mia had sex. She broke up with her boyfriend of two years nearly seven months ago, but they did get together one last time after that. She did it just to see if the thrill was gone . . . and it was.

Perhaps she'd lost that loving feeling because she found out he'd slept with her co-worker last summer. She knew he was eyeballing this chick with a little too much intensity at the Reebok employees' Christmas party last year. But she had no idea they would run into each other again at the mall and embark upon an affair behind Mia's back.

He was an airline pilot, so needless to say he was out of town quite often. Actually Mia's mother had hooked them up after taking a flight a few years ago. She bumrushed him after the flight once the stewardess informed her that he was single and lived in Los Angeles. She gave him Mia's number and he called that same day.

The particular week Mia had busted him with her co-worker, he was supposed to be on a flight from Los Angeles to New York.

Mia went to dinner with her sister-friend Bianca at their favorite Italian restaurant in Westwood, and *bam,* there was the happy little couple sitting amongst their own intimate laughter just across the elegant dining room on the other side of the bar. Before Mia and Bianca could even be greeted by their regular tuxedo-clad waiter, Bianca stopped in mid-sentence and her eyes directed Mia's vision toward the skin-crawling sight. Mia dropped her eggshell cotton lap napkin onto her empty white ceramic bread plate. From the sheer strength of her emotion, she effortlessly pushed her fancy cane seat away from the table to make room for her own departure to the sound of the rounded chair legs scooting along the hard floor.

"Excuse me for a second," she told her best friend, with eyes fixed on target.

She stood tall, adjusted the stretch fabric of her skintight blue-jean jumpsuit around her ba-du-ka-dunk hips and placed one foot in front of the other, hearing only her quickened heartbeat and the sound of her burgundy spiked heels clacking upon the roman tile flooring. She stopped within two inches of their table and shifted her weight onto her right leg with her hands clasped behind her.

His eyes met her waistline, and shame prevented him from looking up toward her face, but he knew either by her familiar sturdy build or the familiar scent of Escape, mixed compatibly with her chemistry, that he was busted. Her co-worker cracked a painted-on smile about as fake as a three-dollar bill as though the two simply managed to hook up because maybe he decided to interview her regarding a stewardess position, only holding hands across the table was perhaps a way of testing her mile-high people skills.

Mia looked through him from the top of his sweat-beaded, tobacco-colored bald head and said, "Take a good, close look at this plump rear end as I walk away because you're never going to get it again. Have a nice evening." She nodded to her co-worker, almost giving the girl permission to continue her tryst, and after a runway pivot, Mia switched the hell out of her size thirty-eight hips, picked up her wine-colored leather purse, and motioned for Bianca to follow her out of the door. Mia and Bianca went to a cozy, much more private Thai restaurant down the street. She asked Bianca to never mention another word about it.

After he'd placed fifty million "Oh, baby please" phone messages and in spite of her idle threat that he was never gonna get it again, Mia thought she would just lay the bomb nana on him one last time, just to give him a taste of what he'd be missing.

After Mia tossed and turned deep into the wee hours of the morning, she showed up at his apartment wearing nothing but a coal black trench coat and scarlet Charles David high heels. She stepped one foot in the door, dropped her coat to the floor, and as he pulled her inside, she let him go down on her with her back flat against the closed door. But the thought of the very tongue that was pleasing her giving pleasure to that woman turned her stomach. The idea of him inside of someone else's body brought tears to Mia's eyes. Or perhaps it was just the feeling of betrayal. So with a tear forced down her left cheek by the repeated blinking of her bloodshot eyes, she forced him to wear a glove and got it over with, him taking her from behind while she stood against the door, high heels and all, and even without an orgasm on her part. More tears continued to flow down her cheek as the palms of her sweaty hands repeatedly pressed against the wooden inlaid door in conjunction with his last-ditch effort at pump-mania. He got off like he'd never gotten off before.

"Please, Mia. I need you so much, I . . ." He lost his words in his manly explosion.

Mia simply put on her coat and left.

One thing was for sure, when Mia was done with a man, she was done for good. She changed her phone number and rejected every attempt he made to contact her.

Today, Mia forced her heavy eyelids open to the unwelcome light of day peering through her maple-colored plantation shutters. It seemed as though she had only bonded with her slumber for fifteen minutes. Actually, it had been more than nine hours. She laid still upon her canary yellow cotton bedding, flat on her back in the exact spot she'd awoken alone, somehow feeling as though the bad girl was in her.

As her brownish green eyes adjusted to the illumination of the first morning light, she rotated her neck in the direction of her pine nightstand and gave her attention to a ruby red bottle of coconut-scented body lotion staring back at her. As she lay on her back, Mia elevated her lower body and pulled off her cherry thong. She took hold of the fancy octagon-shaped bottle, stretched her legs straight in front of her, removed the round, gold cap, and poured a generous amount of lotion—about the size of a nickel—onto her fingertips.

As the nutty aroma met her nostrils, Mia rubbed the lotion onto her right upper thigh, spread her lips apart with her left-hand fingers, and taking just enough gel-like cream onto her right fingertips, smeared the coconut scent over her caramel jewel. She massaged it back and forth, inserting her right middle finger inside, and rubbed her lips in a circular motion. Mia shut her eyelids and imagined a tall, handsome man with dark, deep, sexy eyes, standing at the end of her bed, just watching her, unable to please himself because his hands were cuffed behind him. Her momentum grew and she started to moan and moan and moan, louder and louder as the vision seemed so real that she began to focus on the direct hit of her center, as if this person would still be there when she opened her eyes. She felt her blood rushing up and down her legs and at the very point of her peak she yelled, "Aaah!" as she felt her vagina throb in response to her very own maneuvering.

Out of breath she said, "Damn Mia, you're good." After all, no one knew her better than she knew herself, and she knew this was the epitome of safe sex. "But you need a lover, girl," she said out loud.

"Hello," she panted after reaching over with her left hand to answer her phone. She adjusted the cordless between her chin and left shoulder. "No, Mom. I'm just waking up. Yes, I'm alone. No, I wasn't running to the phone, I told you I just woke up. No, I have not heard from him. What's up, Mom? I know Monday is your birthday. I bought you something you're going to love. I've got to get up and take a shower now. I'll talk to you later. I love you too, Mom."

She wondered if her mother had ever masturbated. Surely she had if she'd raised a freaky daughter like her, she thought. Mia's mother had been alone for the past fifteen years. She never remarried after the rigors of being the wife of a military husband took its toll. "I know Mom gets her swerve on," said Mia, rising from her bed of solo love. "That was a good one. Who was that man, anyway?"

Actually, Mia had lied to her mother; she had not bought her mother a gift. She had forgotten that her mother's birthday was the coming Monday in the first place, and she was certain that her mother knew it, too. Mia knew she'd better get to the mall and then off to the post office to ship her mother's package to San Diego before they closed at one o'clock. Otherwise her mom was going to disown her.

After her hot, steamy shower and sweet, black coffee, Mia hurried to brush her wooly, light brown hair into a ponytail, only to throw on an old Lakers cap from the Magic Johnson days, a faded gray GAP sweatsuit, and the latest version of Reeboks as she ran out of the house in a major rush.

It was a banal, gloomy, early Saturday morning, which did not help Mia get into a decision-making mood as she went from store to store. After hours of indecisiveness, Mia picked up a one-hundred-dollar gift certificate from Nordstrom's and rushed off to the Inglewood post office. She thought she looked whipped as she caught a glimpse of her casual, hurried reflection as she whisked past the double glass doors of the post office. And she was right.

Miles sauntered into the lobby not more than three minutes

later to buy some postage from the stamp machine. He looked in Mia's direction, which was to the left of the machine. His eyes locked upon her casual image just as her extended tongue was smack-dab in the middle of a quick shellac to moisten the flap of an envelope. Mia spied him checking her out. Her tongue froze at the sight of him.

*He looks familiar,* she said to herself. Somehow, her brain was too busy—making sure her bulging, bugged eyes didn't pop out of her head—to tell her tongue to retract back into her waterless mouth. Finally her brain told her to pull in her tongue to produce enough saliva to lick her dry, lipstick-less lips and resume sealing the envelope.

*Damn, he looks good,* she thought as the theme from *Shaft* came to mind. He dwarfed her average frame by a mile, so he had to be well over six. He had a slender build and was wearing all-black Iceberg gear.

*He must be Shemar Moore, the actor,* she supposed. He had a black, well-groomed curly fade and a perfectly trimmed goatee. *Or maybe he's the man in my fantasy from this morning. He is the spitting image of that fine, sexy brother.*

He strolled over nonchalantly and stood next to her, just as she rotated her back away from him to reach into her purse for that spare tube of hot cocoa lipstick she'd noticed last week under her checkbook, spare change, and crumpled ATM receipts. She turned back around and took a step toward him with the discovered lipstick in hand, looking down only to realize that without a Q-Tip, she wasn't going to be able to scrape enough gloss out of that depleted tube anytime soon. She rested the weight of her body against the counter and attempted to strike a Madonna-like pose, hoping she would look chic enough to distract him from her plainness.

Next to her he had the presence of a movie star. He had a four-inch, diamond-cut sterling silver cross hanging from an eighteen-inch, *S*-link chain around his neck. His platinum Swatch watch had to be a high-end model and his diamond studs must have been two carats each. The only piece of jewelry Mia was wearing was her gold hoop ring studded through her now rock-hard nipple.

Miles spoke in a calm, polite tone as she watched his brownish-reddish-pinkish lips move. "You know, I read a recent e-mail that warned of cyanide-laced envelopes and stamps in Black communities."

Mia smiled as heated blood rushed to her cheeks. "Oh, really?" she replied, wondering if he was always that smooth. She wondered if he was wanted by the authorities as the post office Mack Daddy.

Miles nodded his head in affirmation. "Yes, I just read it last night on the Internet. You really should use the pre-moistened envelopes or use a sponge, lovely lady."

*He must be blind under those Maui Jims,* she thought as he lowered his lenses past the bridge of his nose and gave her a look she perceived to be that of a player begging to be reformed. *Yes, those are the deep, dark, sexy eyes of the man in my fantasy.*

He asked suavely, "Would it be okay with you if I were to take your telephone number just to make sure you don't die in your sleep tonight?"

"That would be very chivalrous of you," Mia replied, thinking he was both original and a little morbid.

He extended his hand to offer a rust Montblanc fountain pen between his thumb and forefinger while she removed her business card from her wallet.

She smiled and took the pen with a welcoming glow. "Thank you."

Writing her home number on the back, she swirled a heart over the *I* in her name, handed the card and pen to him with one hand, and pulled the visor of her cap down farther to cover her mascara-hungry eyes with the other.

"My name is Mia White. It's nice to meet you."

"And my name is Miles. Miles Lewis. You know, you have very beautiful, light eyes," he complimented, leaning down toward her face for a better glimpse. He kept her hand after taking the card and gave her a gentle, provocative squeeze instead of a shake.

"Thanks," she said, making every attempt to look away.

"I'll talk to you later tonight." Confident, he gave her hand back and headed for the door.

She watched him promenade out of the door and past the post office window just as she found herself following him, preparing to exit as if she actually forgot what she came to the post office for in the first place. Miles never got his stamps either.

That evening they talked on the phone for more than four hours. Mia could not believe how sexy his voice was. It was as though Don Cornelius was on the other end of the phone, yet he looked like a fashion model.

"Have you been in a relationship lately?" Mia asked, getting right to the point.

"No. I was in one for about a year, but I ended that two years ago."

"Are you looking for short term or long term?" she inquired, remembering to clear this up early on.

"Perhaps long term. I enjoy the monogamy of a relationship," he admitted.

"I heard that," Mia said. He had given her the million-dollar reply.

Mia wanted everything that went along with having a man. Traveling together, cuddling, sharing your day, waking up together, talking on the phone three times a day, and rocking each other's world, regularly.

Within one month, Mia no longer had a reason to embark upon self-pleasure. Miles took matters into his own hands. He was handling his stamp-licking business so tight that she wondered how she ever got by without him.

# THOSE SAME OLD FEARFUL FEELINGS

A year later, those same charms had Mia wracking her brain trying to understand the disappointing fact of why she did not see or hear from Miles even on a semi-weekly basis, why they did not talk three times a day, did not travel together, and did not always wake up together, even though he was rocking her world.

Some nights she would go out with other men just to pass the time or to test his reaction just in case he took time to notice. But after all, they weren't actually "committed." Uh-oh, there's that "C" word they'd discussed before. Other nights, when she realized she wasn't going to hear from him, she'd just hang out with her girls at the Hot Spot. They'd party and dance and drink and catch and meet and mingle and mix and laugh and smile and indulge in all that player-type big-headed crap. All of that empty behavior that boosts the ego but does nothing for the heart and mind if you're not emotionally connected to the very men who scope you out in an attempt to get whatever for the night. Mia never was a believer of the "If you can't be with the one you love just love the one you're with" philosophy.

* * *

Mia just couldn't take it anymore. She had to take her lovesick butt over to his house to ask him what was the real deal. After all, they were screwing royally. Maybe that's why she was so in love.

One evening after work she showed up unannounced. Not late enough to really interrupt anything, just in case he'd planned his evening's entertainment. As she pressed her manicured index finger against the tiny, round doorbell, she heard his size-thirteen footsteps approaching from the other side of the door and the faint sounds of the play-by-play of a tennis match, as well as his muffled good-byes to whomever he was talking to on the phone. He pulled the door open wearing nothing more than brown-and-blue silk gingham boxers with his cordless phone in his hand. He extended his other hand to move in for a hug.

With his perfect collection of curly black chest hairs staring her in the face he said, "Hey, baby. This is a nice surprise. Come on in."

Mia backed up and stood at the doorway with her peach leather purse dragging from her limp hand along the floor. She was wearing a burnt orange short skirt and a matching blazer, which was why Miles lovingly teased, "You look like a juicy mango melon. Get yourself in here and out of the doorway."

He grabbed her arm to pull her into his warm, familiar, cozy living room that always smelled like Coolwater incense, only illuminated by the subtle glow of the television, and closed the door. Surely he was able to tell that she was in no mood for his usual cute wisecracks. Before she could take two steps inside, the question just propelled itself from her mouth as she turned toward him.

"What's up with us?" she asked with an observable lack of patience. The dim lighting in the room transposed itself according to each flashing scene radiating from the tube.

He looked at Mia as if he was considering his words with prudence. And then he casually returned her blunt inquisition with an inquiry of his own, which turned into a volley that definitely did not end up in LOVE. "You tell me. What's the problem?"

She gave him a direct stare. She was tired of playing games. "I want to be your lady, Miles."

Miles tried to seem cooperative. "I'm flattered. And in some ways you are my lady and I am your man. Mia, we've talked about this before. I'm just not ready to be fully committed. I told you I'm checking you out much like my dad checked out my mom when he was my age. But, I'd understand if you decide to move on. I just hope you don't."

Mia wrinkled her nose, trying to think of a way to clarify her intentions. "I'm not moving on just yet. You'll know when my glass is full. In the meantime, let's just keep wearing those condoms, because your sexual behavior is irresponsible."

He turned his head, looking to the side as he replaced the cordless in the cradle. "Let's have a seat," he offered, hoping to divert the flow of conversation.

"So, I am your lover, right? Am I your only lover?" Mia asked as she plopped down on his dark green leather loveseat with her arms crossed under her chest.

"I didn't say I was a saint. I won't lie to you."

Mia's squinted eyes gave a clear indication that she took offense. "How many women *are* you checking out and making love to?"

"Mia, now stop this," Miles requested, making his way to the video closet to pick out a movie for the evening.

"Okay, Miles the saint. I'll stop all right. I won't be a saint either," she cautioned as he continued.

"How about if we watch *Two Can Play That Game*?" Miles spoke in fun as he popped the disc into the DVD, chuckling all by himself.

# THEY BE CLUBBIN'

Mia and Miles were creeping up on three years together, yet Mia was once again spending her summertime Saturday nights at the Hot Spot with her girls. Through the years, the Hot Spot, a trendy little nightclub up on the Sunset Strip in Hollywood, had been called everything from Nick's Fish Market to Bar One and more.

Mia and Bianca drove up to the valet. Before Bianca could move her gearshift into park, the attendant opened the driver-side door, reaching out his hand for her keys. She looked at him for a moment, shut off the ignition, and then took her time to point her ebony leather spike heel out onto the street. She dropped her keys into his hand, taking the stub and filing it in her teeny, tiny black satin purse. With comparable grace, Mia exited the passenger side of Bianca's brand-spanking-new midnight blue Cadillac truck. Before she could close her door, the valet tried to put the car in drive, prepared to speed away at a breakneck pace.

"Hold it," Mia clamored, closing the door with a frown.

Bianca looked back at her fading license plate as if her baby had been jacked. "That boy has lost his mind."

Mia glared at the other attendant. "You all really need to watch yourselves," she warned, looking out for her girl's property.

But rolling up in a high-class–type luxury car like Bianca's Escalade helped to impress the decision makers—the bouncers. Mia and Bianca strutted toward the long roped-off line of partygoers.

Mia peeped the scene. "I realize that after all these years I'm still in awe of this game we play."

At the Spot, where all of the ballers and high-rollers hang out, it would be nothing for these guys to buy a woman a damn drink. Hell, these guys could buy the whole damn bar. Patrons can't get on a guest list or make reservations for the Southern–style cuisine in this trendy hip-hop–type environment. All they can do is stand in line looking as fine as possible, as sexy as possible, and as nonchalant as possible. The eager beavers do not get in. Patrons can't look desperate or as though they are in awe. Dress to impress is the order of the night.

Speaking of dressed, Mia had poured herself into a backless, liquid quicksilver micro-mini and hot-ass platinum mid-calf open-toe boots. They matched her metallic number to a T. Bianca was dressed a bit more conservatively in a black linen pantsuit she'd bought at The Limited last week. Obviously she decided to go subtle-sexy this night, because she left the blazer partially unbuttoned to reveal a soft, ice-pink, sheer front-clasp bra coyly peeking from underneath her tig-ol-biddies.

Mia looked Bianca up and down. "Bianca, you're a closet freak."

"You've got your nerve. You need to go back in the closet and pick out the rest of your outfit," Bianca joked. "You're always showing too much skin. You'd never know you even had a man."

"That's true," admitted Mia.

Mia and Bianca converged upon the packed line of party people as the hunky Michael-Clarke-Duncan–looking bouncer immediately flagged them over.

"Ladies. You in the silver, come on in," he invited, lifting his head toward Mia.

"He flagged you down as if I am invisible," Bianca told Mia in frustration. "Oh well, whatever works," she added under her breath.

They peeled their way through the frozen stares of people in the front of the line who obviously had been waiting long enough to get an attitude.

"Excuse us, excuse us." Mia threaded her frame sideways past the immovable bodies, with Bianca at her back. "Thanks, Darren," Mia said to the buffed bouncer as they approached the door.

Darren talked to her legs. "You're welcome, ladies. Just slip me those digits on your way out."

"And you know that hero," Mia teased. She knew he didn't really want it and he knew he was never going to get it anyway. It was just part of the game.

"Okay, cut the cuteness and niceties and move it," announced the girl at the window with the gruff voice. Mia looked at her with an on-again, off-again smile and cut her eyes.

Bianca gave an abysmal exhalation. "I don't know why we come here anyway."

They handed over their twenty dollars each and entered at their own risk. The room was dark yet airy, catch-action classy, sophisticated yet fresh. Every aspect of the décor was a rustic mahogany and deep burgundy mix. The bar itself was maybe fifty feet long with five suited-up bartenders scurrying around in busy mode. The surrounding VIP tables were roped off by three bodybuilder–type guards. The circular black-lacquer tables were always are on a first come, first serve basis and you could scratch that idea if it was after nine o'clock. It was already after eleven. They walked into the crowded, smoke-filled VIP room. They strutted inside, diva-like, making sure that each footstep exactly matched the beat of the extreme bass blasting through the speakers.

Everywhere they looked, there was nothing but Hollywood–type people looking like they belonged, hoping to be seen, and making sure they were flossing something. Flossing asses, tits, ice, their honeys, their gear, their dollar-dollar bills. Just flossing and being seen.

* * *

Since Mia was in a monogamous relationship with Miles, she was not even tripping. She only had eyes for her baby, but she and Miles agreed they should go out with their buddies every now and then just to appreciate what they had at home. And this place could truly make one appreciate her significant other.

Tonight Mia just wanted to hang out with her girl Bianca and Bianca's friend Megan Barnes. Megan befriended Bianca last year while they were all up at the Spot.

Megan, a White girl with ash blonde shoulder-length hair, large icy-blue eyes, and tanned skin, always seemed to be the flavor of the month, every month. Her twenty-something frame towered over Bianca and Mia and she was as thin as a starving cat. She loved color: colorful clothes, colorful men, colorful cars. Megan just lived a colorful life. And she was crazy about some Black men. Last year alone she dated Dennis Rodman, Dave Justice and Ken Griffey, Jr. Groupie, you ask? Does Jennifer Lopez have much booty? Mia thought Megan was just using Bianca to be Black friendly. Bianca and Mia battled over the subject much more than it was worth.

"You ladies want to sit here?" offered a young Black man who barely looked twenty-one, standing up and leaning in toward the ladies to slice through the loud rumbling sound coming from the five-foot-high speakers.

Mia looked pleasantly surprised. "How gentlemanly of you. We would really appreciate that."

His fine friend sat in silence for a minute and then stood in slow motion with a brilliant smile. This guy looked sexy Italian, maybe late forties and dressed in what could have been a Dolce and Gabanna Italian suit.

Megan winked with her long, fake eyelashes. "I smell money."

"He is handsome," said Bianca, looking at the older gentleman.

"I'm talking about Mr. Bad Boy in the Phat Farm gear." Megan wanted the young brother of color.

Mia smiled at both of them. "Thanks. Let us send you both a drink," she offered the gentlemen.

The Italian Stallion gave a hip, smooth, appreciative grin. "We wouldn't think of it, Foxy Brown."

Mia admitted to her buddy, "Bianca, I could get in a lot of trouble up in here. This has to stop."

Both men extended their arms and waved their hands toward the table with an "After You" gesture and then they walked away toward the bar.

Mia, Bianca, and Megan made a pretty fine threesome. That was until the twins, Yanni and Lexi, came over to their table to add to the trio, looking like adorable matching Lil' Kim bookends.

"Girl, there's nowhere to sit up in here. Can we join you?" asked Yanni, sounding frustrated, adjusting her micro-mini.

Mia responded, "Of course, grab a seat."

Lexi and Yanni were of medium height and complexion. Yanni seemed to prefer the shorter version of outfits and Lexi usually wore pants. Mia had met them in college at UCLA. They were both extremely intelligent and very studious.

Both had perfectly toned bodies, high ghetto booties, long, curly chestnut brown hair, and could easily be members of the IBTC—ittie-bittie-tittie-committee, but they still showed off their breasts with pride. They always wore high heels, even when going to the supermarket. But there was something about their individual demeanors that made them as distinct as Venus and Serena. They definitely had minds of their own.

To Mia they were cool, but it was Mia's main girl Bianca whom she shared her deepest and darkest secrets with. Bianca and Mia had been friends since elementary school. People always said they sort of looked alike. They were both five foot six and maybe one hundred thirty pounds or more. Bianca's hair was very short and curly, sort of a saucy beige, sugar-cane color, and Mia's was now long, light brown, thick, and flat-ironed straight ever since she bought into the relaxer fad. Also, Bianca's maple-syrup complexion was a couple of shades darker than Mia's. Mia had been told she looked like Vanessa Williams, which was a complete opposite look from Bianca's. Perhaps it was their keen features, high cheekbones and thick lips that were similar, or maybe they'd just been around each other for so long.

They lived across the street from each other through middle and high school and their moms used to go out and party together just like they were doing now.

Bianca had grown up without a father because he died right after she was born. Mia's father lived out of the country most of the time because he was in the service and she'd only see him every now and then. Eventually, her mom had divorced him.

They'd been through it all together. Especially when Bianca got pregnant when she was only sixteen. Her son, Corey, was almost thirteen years old and he was Mia's heart. He called her Auntie M. She said it made her sound like the Aunt in *The Wizard of Oz* but she loved it. Corey had been pretty sick when he was born because he was premature, and he still suffered from asthma attacks regularly, even as a budding teenager. Mia had been there every step of the way. She had not yet had any children of her own, so she tried to make sure she was there to help Bianca out, being that she was a single parent and all.

Tonight the five of them were just hanging out drinking Mai Tais, when Yanni decided they were not getting noticed.

"We need to stand up so the guys can see us. It'll never happen back here in this corner in the dark."

Bianca said, "I figure if they don't like what they see from the waist up, then they're only all about the booty anyway."

"No!" Megan replied, "It's just that you should want them to see the whole package. Shoot, I'm five ten, I don't want any SDs to come walking up to me asking me to dance."

Mia looked to Bianca and Megan with a question-marked face. "SD?"

"Short dog," explained Megan, cracking her own self up amongst everyone else's silence.

# BLACK PEOPLE CRUISE?

Just then, Mr. SD himself approached the table. Brandon Wick was the comedian who emceed the comedy showcase theater on BET. He was also rumored to be in development with Warner Studios for his own television series. Brandon was known for dressing to the nines, sharp as all get out, pretty much always wearing a designer suit no matter what. He had a perfect, three-inch Afro that looked to be freshly trimmed by a private barber each morning—not a hair out of place. He had a permanently flared nose and extra thick lips. He smelled like he bathed in Bijan for men. And he spoke as if he was from down South.

Megan jumped up from the table in her banana yellow leather skin-tight cat suit and purred all the way up into his very being. Suddenly his being an SD didn't matter to her.

He made an announcement and an inquiry at the same time. "I know you ladies are coming to Nassau later this month for the Soul Cruise, right?"

"No, what is that?" Mia asked.

"It's the jamminist, baddest, hippest going-on event of the year. Where have you ladies been?"

"I've heard of it, Mr. Wick, but I'm not interested. After all, Black people don't go on cruises," said Yanni.

"Oh, who said?" Brandon replied, "And don't call me Mister unless you gonna' call me Daddy!"

"Okay, Brandon," she said showing a faint dimple that went previously unnoticed. "But I hear last year's cruise was a bust and that the cruise line refused to give the promoters the entire ship, so there were only really maybe five percent Black folks on the cruise."

He corrected Yanni. "Wrong! See why we are always lookin' for an excuse to not have fun. Rumors will get your gossiping ass left behind. Some people are always exploring what's around the block instead of having an around-the-world mentality. Anyway, so what? . . . Even if that was true, why would that alter yo' desire to see the world and have fun?"

"Yeah, I'm ready to go!" Megan blurted out, only to follow up with the true motivation for her support. "I know Brandon's gonna hook us up with free tickets!"

"You ain't earned that yet, Miss Banana Boat. This ain't no get-in-free club pass like at the Garden of Eden," Brandon remarked, looking at Megan's long legs. "Here," Brandon handed Lexi a business card, "you ladies call this number and get more information fo' yo' selves. And, you all had better hurry up. We set sail in less than three weeks."

" 'Set sail'—sounds like the Love Boat," Lexi said, eyeballing the card.

Brandon announced, "I'll tell you one thing, It is 'exciting and new.' This is a pioneering event. This is the first Black–owned cruise ship, called the *Chocolate Ship.* Delmonte Harrison, who owns Black Bottom jeans, bought this ship. He's also gonna be having a fashion show onboard to promote his line of clothing. Celebrity models and performers will be there, including myself, I might add."

Megan's eyes expanded. "I'm there."

"Is Delmonte married?" Yanni asked with a gleam in her eye.

"Girl, stop. Who else is performing?" Mia asked.

Brandon gave more information. "The female rappers Ebony and Ivory; the group from the sixties, El Dorado; and the rapper Big Mack. And ladies, don't forget the football players, Bo Richardson, Rasheed Harper and Deshaun Reed are scheduled to model. They are also doing a shoot for Mr. Harrison's *Big Black Male—BBM* magazine startup. I gotta go, ladies, call that number. And you," he peered at Megan. "What was yo' name again Miss Peel and Eat?"

Megan moved in closer. "Megan."

"You call this number. See all you lovely ladies later. Bon voyage!" He handed Megan a folded napkin and walked away, shaking hands with the crowd with every step.

"Okay . . . I'm there, Mia, let's go," said Bianca with an excited vibe.

Mia was not as ecstatic. "I don't have any time off from work. I cannot make an impulsive decision like that. We don't even know the itinerary or how much it will cost."

Yanni took the card from Lexi and exclaimed in an anxious tone, "Well, I'm going to use my mobile to get more of the four-one-one, because he said Deshaun Reed, and I'm there."

Yanni dialed the number, as they all stared at her as if they were disgusted by her eagerness, yet impressed.

Yanni repeated the recorded message. "Seven days . . . the end of the month, the twentieth through the twenty-seventh . . . departing from Fort Lauderdale, Florida . . . fifty percent deposit was due two months ago . . . full payment ranging from twelve hundred to twenty-three hundred dollars, excluding airfare, is due by next Monday, only a few spaces left." Yanni ended the call.

Megan nodded in confirmation. "I'm there."

"Me too, I've had the money from my dad's life insurance just sitting around, earning interest for years. Hell, I could die tomorrow. I'm in," Bianca stated.

"Where are we going to get that kind of money so quickly?" Yanni asked Lexi, placing her cellphone back into her macramé bag. "We don't have enough money to take a boat to Catalina, let alone airfare and a weeklong cruise."

"Speak for yourself. I have some money saved from my last few paychecks. I might have half of the money on my credit card. I know, let's ask Mom and Dad," said Lexi. She stared at Yanni for a second. "Okay, bad idea."

Yanni gave her a look of hope. "Actually, I think Dad might spot us for a part of it if we say we're thinking about getting into the cruise business."

"Like your dad is going to believe that. How do you get into the cruise business?" asked Bianca.

"You start promoting cruises like that big travel company does. It could happen," Yanni said.

Lexi corrected her. "I think there's more to cruising than promoting one."

Mia continued to mull it over. "Well, I have the money, but I could never go away alone, without Miles, on a cruise ship, with men all around, drinking day and night, pajama parties . . . He would never let me go."

"Let you go? Damn, Mia, he never asked you if he could go to Cabo to go fishing, did he?" Bianca reminded her.

Lexi gave a wow face. "He goes to Cabo to go fishing?"

Bianca answered for Mia, "Yeah, and he comes back without fish. He goes for the snapper at the strip clubs. And what about when he went to Martha's Vineyard, without you? Did he ask you?"

"No, that was to go play in a golf tournament," Mia corrected Bianca.

"And when he went to Hot-lanta for two weeks?" Bianca asked as if she had been taking notes.

Mia explained for him, "He was visiting his family and . . . What *was* he doing?" She searched for recollection while gazing up at the ceiling and scrunching her eyebrows.

Bianca tried to straighten Mia out. "Mia, we are going, I'm taking Corey with me, and you are calling Miles tomorrow to TELL him you are going on a cruise, without him. He's been on one before. Isn't he moonwalking away from you right now anyway because he needs time to work on himself?"

"That only means he'll come back even closer when he's done," Mia said, as if she had no problem with it whatsoever.

Bianca gave Mia a fortune-teller–like prediction. "Well, while he's working on himself you'll be working on yourself from the waters of the Atlantic Ocean."

Suddenly, a well-dressed man who had to be seven feet tall walked up and asked Lexi and Yanni to dance. They both leaped up and obliged, each grabbing an arm, sandwiching him onto the dance floor.

A very informed Megan gave them the 4-1-1. "That's the new guy who plays for the Sacramento Kings, Karl Watts. They're in town to play the Lakers tomorrow. He just signed a forty-five-million-dollar deal for six years. I don't even think he's old enough to be in here."

Just then Megan marched off to the dance floor to make it a foursome. Karl Watts was surrounded.

Bianca took one foot off the footrest of her barstool and leaned toward the dance floor. "If you go out there I will kick your butt," Mia threatened.

"You just start rehearsing your speech to that tired-ass Miles," Bianca said, running off to give Karl the booty clap. Mia collapsed onto the table with her hands to her face. Suddenly her cut came on, "Danger" by Mystical.

"I'm about to make it a six-some," she said, running off to join in.

# BREAKING THE NEWS

That next Monday morning Mia sat at her teakwood desk, staring across the towering glass buildings of picturesque Century City from the tinted windows of her twenty-fifth-floor office. In a trancelike state, her fingers dialed Bianca's work number from her speakerphone.

Mia still stared out of the window, leaning back in her chair. "Are you going on this cruise for sure, girl?"

"I have already booked the cruise for me and Corey," said Bianca.

"But what travel agent are we supposed to use?"

Bianca answered as though Mia was tripping. "Girl, Delmonte Harrison owns his own travel agency, Harrison Travel. Just call the same number Brandon gave us. What's wrong with you?"

Mia asked another question without answering one. "Can I stay in the same cabin with you?"

"No, Mia. Corey and I had to get a double to ourselves. Why don't you call Megan? She needs a roommate."

Mia declined, saying, "That girl will have me sleeping in the hallway waiting for her to finish getting her groove on the whole week long."

"I don't know why you have such a low opinion of her. Guys like her because she's energetic and pretty darn attractive. And besides, she likes the attention just like we do. Are you having a problem with her being White?" Bianca asked straight on.

"Oh yeah, considering that Miles is biracial and my mother is half White. I don't think so. I just think she's loose. Besides, once Miles finds out I'm going and sharing a room with her he really won't trust me."

Bianca paused and then asked, "He doesn't know yet?"

"No," Mia answered, swiveling her gray, high-back desk chair toward her computer, expecting Bianca's tongue-lashing.

Bianca was ready to read Mia. "Why not?"

"I haven't been able to reach him. I paged him earlier. I'll try again when I get home," Mia said, letting her know she was on the case.

"He's not worried about you, so you need to stop worrying about him, Mia. Get with it! Call that number."

Almost at the same time that Mia realized she was sorry she'd called, her other line rang. "I will. I've got to go. That's my other line."

"I just got back today. Were you trying to reach me?" Miles inquired, as if he didn't know that her messages meant just that.

Mia took a deep breath and again swiveled back toward the highrise view as she exhaled through her cranberry-glossed lips. "Miles, I just wanted you to know that I'm going out of town for a week or so toward the end of the next month."

"That's fine, where?" he responded like it was no big deal.

"To the Eastern Caribbean on the Soul Cruise."

"With whom?"

Mia stared without blinking. "Bianca and Megan."

He suddenly seemed to need more information. "What brought this on?"

Mia played it down. "Nothing, I just need to get away."

"I doubt if it will be a relaxing getaway, a lot goes on during those cruises."

Mia rocked in her seat. "Like what? You tell *me.*"

Miles explained himself, "Like . . . nothing. Thanks for telling me. Actually, I'm going also. I was going to tell you. Scott is taking Kelly for their one-year anniversary and he paid for me to go along."

A feeling of repulsion rose in Mia's chest as she prepared for her reply. "When were you going to tell me? Around the same time you told me you were going wherever the hell you were this past weekend?"

"Mia, calm down. I'm not going *there* with you."

She felt herself wanting to really get into it. "And, I'm not going *on the cruise* with you. Just act like you don't know me, Mr. Bachelor, fun-loving, single . . ."

"Single what? Mia, I was going to ask you to go with me," he said, switching gears.

"You were what?" she replied as if her ears were deceiving her.

"I was going to ask you later this week, when it was confirmed. But, I just found out last night. So, I can pay for you and we'll both go, like a two-for-one."

"Miles, are you sure you're not just saying this because now you know I'm going?"

"I'm telling you now because you ruined the surprise. I think the getaway would be good for us both. Plus, I think this will be a real special week for us," he stated.

Mia replied, still semi-skeptical, "For the better I hope. Our lives, or yours?"

"Ours, Mia. So, what do you think? You didn't book it yet, did you?"

"No."

"Then it's on. We're going. And tell Bianca and what's-her-name, Sharon Stone?" Miles kidded.

"Megan!"

Miles instructed her, "Tell them they're on their own."

Mia wondered if maybe she really just wanted to get away with the girls, freak all week and get in some serious "revenge fucking," as Miles always said. He believed anger toward each other could cause them to be weak and get in subconscious revenge through screwing around with other people. Not that he'd ever done that, mind you.

A big part of her wanted Miles to take her on this cruise so that they could have the time of their lives together—bonding, realizing, renewing, screwing, doing, loving, breathing, and engaging. *Heck*, she thought, *Miles had better have thoughts of asking me to marry him on that dang ship. Otherwise, it's over.*

Needless to say, Bianca was pissed off because Miles was going also. She thought Mia needed time away on her own. In Mia's opinion, Bianca just seemed to put all of her time and energy into her son, Corey, and never took time for herself.

When Bianca got pregnant more than thirteen years ago, she and Corey's dad, who was only sixteen himself, thought about getting an abortion. They decided they wouldn't tell their parents and they'd just go to a local hospital, using Bianca's medical insurance provided by her mother. After they arrived to receive the exam, the hospital called Bianca's mom's employer to verify eligibility and that sparked an investigation by her mom to find out why Bianca was there. They scheduled the procedure for one week later, but the day before, her mother came home from work, mad as hell, just as Bianca had laid out on the sofa eating Neapolitan ice cream and black licorice.

Bianca's mom wasted no time in getting to the point. "What the heck is going on with you, young lady? You're pregnant?"

Bianca played dumb. "No, Mommy. Of course I'm not pregnant."

"Oh really? You just showed up at the hospital to piss in a cup and schedule an abortion, right?"

"Mom, it wasn't me," Bianca said, sticking to her denial.

"Then who was it?" her mom asked, standing over Bianca, just waiting to see if she could come up with a good one.

A voice in Bianca's head commanded her to lie. "I let my friend use my medical card. She's pregnant."

"Who? What's her name? I know it's not Mia."

"If I told you, you'd call her parents and . . . I just can't tell you," Bianca said, going into the kitchen to put the ice cream in the freezer. Her mom was hot on her heels.

No fool, her mom said, "I can tell you one thing. If you think I buy that crock of bull, you have lost your damn mind."

Later that evening, Bianca's mother called her into the living room. She had gone through Bianca's purse and found the paperwork, signed by her.

Her mother held the paperwork in her hand. "Your dad would not want us to be struggling this way. Perhaps it was his angelic message that caused me to find out about your pregnancy, Bianca, but I am here for you. You are seventeen years old and I cannot imagine what you're going through. But you should have told me. I would have understood."

Bianca gave in. "Mommy, how do you tell your parent that you're having sex when you're just sixteen?"

"It's a lot better than going through the stress of hiding it. I want you to know that you are not alone. I wish you hadn't gotten yourself into this situation, but you did. And now we must deal with it together. You are not going to have an abortion. And that's the final word on that. It's time to pray on this."

Bianca and her mother got down on their knees, holding hands, and asked the Lord to show them the way. Her mom prayed, "Lord, through you all things are possible. We know that there are no accidents in life. Everything happens for a reason. Your divine order is acknowledged and accepted. Amen."

Bianca and her boyfriend decided they would hurry up and get married, get jobs and work through everything. But one day, her boyfriend suddenly disappeared and moved back East with his grandmother. His parents refused to talk to Bianca or her mom, even accusing her of having slept with someone else.

By the time Corey was six years old, his dad had tried to call and come around. Bianca was able to keep him away when she lived with her mother, but once she got a place of her own, she started letting him stop by and spend the night. Before long, they were a couple again.

Soon he started staying out late, sometimes all night. He would hang out with his boys at strip club after strip club, sometimes even inviting Bianca to go. But her only priority was Corey, who was now seven years old and who sometimes suffered attacks in the middle of the night. Bianca would do what she had to do all by herself, whether it was soothe him herself or take him to the emergency ward.

Bianca had dated maybe three guys since the days with Corey's dad. Mainly they had been really young guys who were just looking to have fun. Even Corey worried about his mom.

"Bianca, come on, let's go," Mia said, standing in Bianca's mocha-and-peach–themed living room. "There is going to be a long line to get into Loehmann's this morning for their sale. And I am in the mood for some bikini buying, sexy lingerie selecting, big hat choosing, suntan lotion pickin', and hoochie outfit grabbin' shoppin'," Mia said, dancing around in a circle with her hands in the air.

"I'm right with you," Bianca replied with cooperation.

"And you know we have to pick up some traditional African outfits for the farewell party."

Bianca stated, "I already have an outfit that I wore to an event the league gave a couple of years ago, I'll just wear that, but I need to get something for Corey." She yelled in the direction of Corey's room, "Corey, we're about to go. We'll be back later."

Corey walked into the living room. "Okay, Mom. Hey, Auntie M. Mom, where did you put my Reebok socks that Auntie gave me?"

"In your sock drawer, where else would they be?" Bianca answered.

With respectful irritation, he said, "Okay."

She added, "Did you even take a minute to check and see if they were there, or do you just expect me to put my finger on everything?"

"Mom, last time I saw them was in a bag in your room. Sorry."

"Where are you off to anyway?" Bianca asked, grabbing her purse and fumbling through it.

"Kevin and his dad are going to pick me up so we can go hit some balls on the driving range," Corey said.

Bianca peered at him and asked, "Were you going to ask me?"

"I was going to. I didn't know you were leaving so soon. Dang," he said, sipping on the tiny straw of a Capri Sun cooler.

"Dang? Show me the word *dang* in the dictionary," Bianca said, while Mia looked at her as if she could second Corey's emotion. "Corey, I'm sorry. I'm just trying to get everything ready for our cruise and I've been working late so that darn woman who is supposed to be filling in for me doesn't set the WNBA back five years."

"No problem, Mom."

"I'm going to pick up some things for you, too," Bianca told him.

Corey replied, "Just anything Nike is fine with me."

"Hey, watch it with that," Mia said, as if he had spoken of the enemy.

Corey caught himself, remembering that Mia worked for Reebok. He quickly clarified his request. "Or Reebok of course."

"I'm not buying designer labels. You need some shorts and swimming trunks and cool, light clothing like that," Bianca said.

"Can't I pick it out?" he asked.

"Do you want to come with us now?" she responded, already knowing the answer.

Corey declined, "No, Kevin's dad is coming in an hour or so."

"Then if that's your priority, you'll have to deal with whatever I pick out. Okay?" Bianca asked, standing in place, trying to trace her steps in her mind as to where she could have left her keys.

"Ah-right. It'll be cool," he said in surrender.

"So, what does Kevin's dad look like?" asked Mia.

"Girl, that man is married. I'm not thinking about him," Bianca said, checking behind the cushions of the couch.

"No, he's not, Mom. I told you before that they got divorced last summer," he reminded her. "By the way. Here, Mom. See, I've got your back too," he said, holding up her keys as she walked up to him.

"Thanks, Corey, but the fact that he's divorced still doesn't matter," she said, walking past him as she took the keys and then opened the door.

Corey followed her. "Mom, he's nice."

"I know he's nice. But nice isn't everything. Besides, I like Kevin's mom. I wouldn't date her ex-husband. Give me a hug, baby, we'll see you later," she said as Corey put his arms around her and then walked back into his room. "And make sure you take your inhaler with you, son."

"You are mighty cranky with him lately. That ain't nothing a nice hard one won't cure," Mia teased her friend.

Just as Mia thought, the stores were packed on a glorious, sunny afternoon for the fifty percent off, post-summer weekend sales.

"Hey, watch out," Mia said as one woman bumped into her without even looking back. "You'd think they were giving this stuff away."

Bianca was too busy getting a rush. "Look at this tangerine tankini. Even this blue-and-citrus-colored one is cute. I know I'm getting one of them."

Mia held up a black swimming suit. "I think I'll go for a more conservative one-piece, something less loud."

"Look who's talking about less loud. You rarely cover up when you go to church, now you're going to get conservative on a cruise ship. That's a perfect excuse to show it all," Bianca said, surprised.

"Yeah, but Miles won't like that."

"Well Miles isn't taking you on this shopping excursion, so I say you buy what you want for once. Anyway you've got the body for it. I'm the one who needs to cover the stretch marks on my belly."

"You need to show more skin than I do. You're the one who needs to meet a man on this ship," Mia said as though Bianca should be on a mission.

"Mia, I am so tired of you always suggesting that I'm some sex-starved old maid who needs a man to save me."

Mia searched through the racks of wrap skirts and tops. "I know you're not sex starved. You just don't talk about the men you get with. I'm talking about someone who you can bring home to meet Corey and start a real relationship with. All you do is work and take care of that young man."

"I'm doing just fine, thank you very much. I'm going on this cruise to have fun. I'm buying what I like and not what I think is going to turn on some tired brotha who probably has one thing in mind anyway. This is nice," Bianca said, checking out the white DKNY string bikini with tiny pineapples on each cup and on the ass.

Mia told her, "Now, that will get you noticed."

"I mean for you. This is exactly what you'd pick out if Miles wasn't coming. I'm buying it for you," Bianca said, placing it into her cart.

Mia and Bianca hit several more stores in the Fox Hills mall and then rampaged the shops on Venice Beach for all of the other items. By early evening, they returned as exhausted as could be, yet still on a shopping high. They fell backward onto Bianca's peach-colored sofa.

"See, we leave in one week and we're done already. I say we did an excellent job," said Mia.

Bianca leaned forward to peak into her bags. "That was invigorating to say the least. Did they put Corey's shorts in your bag or mine?"

"I made sure everything is there. All of my stuff is in the trunk."

"Oh, except for this pineapple thing I bought you," Bianca said, tossing it at Mia.

Mia held it up for examination. "Thanks, but feel free to borrow it whenever the freak in you comes out. Hopefully it will."

"I hope Corey likes these," Bianca said raising her head from the bag and placing a pair of flowered Roxy board shorts and a pair of shoes on her lap. "And these thong sandals. He's going to puke."

"He'll find out he needs them once he steps onto that hot sand." Mia realized it was getting late. "Oh my goodness, I still need to go get the African outfits for Miles and me. I've got to go." Mia stood up, stretching her hands high above her head for a tension-relieving yawn.

At that moment, Corey walked in, turned and waved good-bye to Kevin and his dad from the doorway. "Thanks. Okay, hold on a minute," Corey told Kevin's dad. "Mom, Kevin's dad wants to say hi."

Bianca pointed to him. "Corey. You are in trouble."

"He just wants to wave hello to you," Corey assured her.

Bianca leaned only her torso into the open doorway. "Hi. How are you both?"

"Fine, Bianca. How have you been?" Kevin's dad asked.

"Just fine. Thanks for taking Corey to play golf."

"No problem, he's really good. He's got a knack for it. I'm encouraging him to keep it up."

Kevin suddenly got out of the car and ran through the door, right past Bianca and into Corey's room.

"Did Corey summon him in here?" Bianca asked Mia, who was peeking through the window curtains.

"He's cute, sitting all up in that spaceship-looking black Lexus," Mia told Bianca.

Kevin's dad called from his car, "Do you mind if I come in for a minute?"

Bianca clenched her teeth. "No, not at all."

"Girl, I'm going to go. You have a good time and lighten up. There's nothing wrong with that man. Give me a hug," Mia said as Bianca left her hanging. "Oh, you're not going to show me any love?" Bianca looked past her as Kevin's father exited his car.

Mia took the front stairs down to the walkway, past Kevin's dad who was maybe five foot seven himself. Mia knew her girl Bianca was not into SDs, as Megan called them. *No wonder she said she didn't like him*, she thought.

"Have a good evening," he said to Mia as they passed each other.

"You too. Good-bye, Bianca," Mia said, turning around as Kevin's dad took the stairs up to her perturbed friend. Talking to herself aloud Mia said, "He is definitely not her type." As Bianca shut the door, hopefully with more puissance than she'd intended, Mia pulled off in her brand-new platinum Mustang. "She's got to get with someone that she finds attractive and who is nice to Corey. She needs a man of her own," Mia said, popping in her Alicia Keyes CD.

# SO HAPPY TOGETHER

Mia picked Miles up from work early Friday evening so that they could go to her house and get a good night's sleep before their flight to Fort Lauderdale early the next morning. They were to set sail late Saturday afternoon.

Miles worked for a dot-com company near downtown Los Angeles. He had a bachelor's degree in information technology from USC and worked on a contract basis as a web designer, earning an hourly rate that some people take years to achieve, and he was only thirty-three years old. With three sisters, Miles was the only son of a mixed couple. His father was Black and his mother was White. They had come to Los Angeles from St. Louis when he was three years old. In St. Louis, his family had lived in an upscale, mainly White community where his father was an executive at a local bottling company. Most of Miles's friends were White, even today.

All of his sisters were married with daughters, and his parents, who believed in the sanctity of marriage, looked to him to carry on the Lewis name. They wanted him to settle down, now that he was making good money and owned his own home in Baldwin

Hills. They wanted a grandson. His dad in particular put a lot of pressure on him to get married. They kept telling him he'd better grab Mia up quick since she was creeping up on twenty-nine. "Make an honest woman out of her," they'd say.

Miles appeared happy living on his own. He owned a brand-new pewter Expedition and had two garaged Corvettes as collectors' items, just for fun. He also collected black art and chessboards. Chess was his passion. Any kind of chessboard: marble, wooden, antique, contemporary. Chess was a mental escape for him. He was very complex and very intelligent.

Miles worked out almost every day and played golf every weekend. Mia's biggest complaint was that he was a loner.

They never discussed Mia moving in with him, but she supposed that once they got married, she'd be the one giving up her place.

Mia rented a one-bedroom apartment in Hawthorne. She was a marketing manager for Reebok, so she kept everybody hooked up in the latest, tightest gear.

"Baby, I love your place. It's so bachelorette-ish," Miles said jokingly while snuggling into her pale yellow and camel chair-and-a-half. "If you don't mind, Scott is going to stop by to bring me my ticket," he said with his feet propped up on the ottoman while channel surfing.

"You haven't gotten the tickets yet?" Mia asked.

"No. But I have yours, don't worry."

"That's cool," Mia said just as Scott knocked at the door. Miles got up and opened the door, still glancing at the Fox Sports Channel.

"Hey man, what's crackin'?" Mia heard Scott ask as she took a seat at her pine and white tile dinette in the kitchen to go over a checklist of last-minute things to do.

"Okay, man, so thanks a lot, dude, I really appreciate it," Miles said without closing the door and before Scott could even take a seat.

"Where's Mia?" Scott asked.

"She's here. Mia, Scott is here," Miles yelled to her as he shut the door, already knowing she knew Scott was there.

Mia rose from her chair and stood at the kitchen doorway. "How are you, Scott?"

Scott was the Blackest White boy Mia had ever known. He made Eminem look like Beaver Cleaver. He talked cool, dressed with the sagging ROCAWEAR jeans, always wore headbands or do-rags, and had every pair of Jordans ever made. One would not believe he was thirty years old.

"I'm cool. I'm feeling your place. Yo, Miles, that's a smooth picture," he said, referring to a large, framed picture over the fireplace of Mia and Miles taken at Glamour Shots last year. Miles was seated in the shot and Mia was standing behind him. Her arms were draped around his shoulders and her hands were clasped near his chest.

"That's me and my king all right," Mia said.

"Where's your queen?" Miles inquired.

"Kelly's at home getting ready for tomorrow. She's really excited."

"Tell her I said I'll see her tomorrow. And thanks for giving Miles a ticket. That was very nice of you," Mia said with a quarter smile.

Miles looked in the envelope, glancing at the ticket. "Yeah, I really appreciate that, dude." Miles slipped what looked like two envelopes into his gym bag.

"Okay, man, well I'm about to break," said Scott giving Miles daps.

"Thanks for stopping by," Mia said, heading back to her seat to resume reviewing her list, shaking her head.

Miles closed the door, headed to the refrigerator for a cold can of Miller Genuine Draft, and took a seat next to Mia.

"So, I see you've got everything covered," he said, popping the top and then rubbing her palm with his thumb.

"It looks like it. I'm all packed, you're all packed. All we need to do is show up. You do have your birth certificate and identification, right?"

He took a big swig and answered, "Yes, ma'am."

"I'm just checking."

"That's what I like about you. You're always on top of things," he complimented her.

That night, they lit aromatic sea-breeze and rain candles and sipped Martini and Rossi Asti Spumante to celebrate their decision to set sail together, lounging in Mia's living-room chair.

"My body is aching and drained from the last two weeks," Mia said with her eyes half closed.

"Baby, why don't you go ahead and take a shower so we can get ready for bed? I'll take one in the morning."

"Okay, I know you like morning showers. I'll be right out." Mia got up slowly, adjusting her step from the champagne buzz just as Miles lovingly popped her on her bodacious butt.

Once Mia was done, she proceeded to her bedroom and collapsed facedown on top of the khaki fitted comforter of her bed with just a damp pink towel adorning her waist section and mid-thighs.

"Just relax, baby. You deserve this," Miles said in a low voice. He rubbed her down with toasted hazelnut body lotion and lightly massaged the back of her head, shoulders, neck, lower back, spine, hips, rear end, the backs of her legs, and her feet until Mia fell fast asleep.

At three thirty in the morning Mia opened one eye to find herself naked under the covers with an unclad Miles in a deep sleep, emitting a wide-open-mouth snore right behind her. That, to her, could have only meant that he was fatigued too.

*I'll surely get mine on that ship,* Mia thought to herself as she resumed her slumber.

As they prepared to land at the Fort Lauderdale airport, Miles took Mia's hand.

"I love you," he whispered to her.

Mia planted a peck upon his cheek. "I love you too, baby. Thanks for this vacation."

How freely it seemed that they extended the three-word kiss of death. They'd come a long way.

# TO SAIL WITH LOVE

"I salute you, Captain Douglas. Good Luck," Captain James J. Douglas said to himself upon releasing a stiff right-handed salute to his own massive full-length mirrored image.

Mr. Delmonte Harrison, the owner of the cruise line, had chosen the stylish crew uniforms and requested that they coordinate with the ship facilities colors of medium olive and chocolate brown.

James Douglas stood with pride in his summer-white, double-breasted captain's waistcoat, khaki trousers, dark brown vest, white shirt, and taupe bow tie. The rank insignia of four chrome diamonds adorned his collar and cuffs. And his branch-of-service colors of gold and black were stitched along the nineteen-inch collar of his crisp, freshly starched dress shirt with two rows of gold piping braided along each sleeve.

He glanced at his white, navy blue, and gold military hat with the black patent leather brim hanging from the coat rack and thought, *No. I'll take the nay side of that option*. His low cut pepper-with-a-little-bit-of-salt Afro was freshly cut and reeked of distinction.

The captain's muscle-clad chest poked out like a proud young father on the very day of the birth of his first-born child. If he'd had wings, he'd have been a proud eagle, with the girth of his chest poked out for the world to see, flapping his wings in preparation for a flight unlike any other he'd ever taken. Preparing to soar to new heights and new opportunities.

Over the P.A. he could hear the scripted captain's bulletin he'd recorded from the bridge earlier that long-awaited morning, which was scheduled to be repeated many times over the next couple of hours.

*Ladies and gentlemen, Harrison Cruises and I would like to welcome you aboard the maiden voyage of the new and pioneering superliner, the* Chocolate Ship—Caribbean. *I am your Captain, James Douglas, and I am honored to have you as guests on this magnificent floating hotel, as I like to call it. You won't find shuffleboard on this ship. You'll find wine tasting, fashion shows, golf chipping, Internet cafes, skeet shooting, motivational lectures, movies and the opportunity to chow down to your heart's content. On the* Chocolate Ship *we want phenomenal cruising to be the rule, not the exception. As you've noticed, this cruise is considerably more affordable than most, yet the level of service and accommodations are first class. Cruising is no longer for the elite. More than fifty percent of passengers' incomes are under sixty thousand dollars per year. Yes, things have changed quite a bit since the nineteen seventies when* The Love Boat, *which was filmed aboard a real Princess cruise ship, represented a glimpse into the world of cruise travel. The cruise industry has enjoyed a nine hundred percent growth spurt in the number of passengers over the past twenty years. Five and one half million North Americans cruised on ships owned by U.S.-based cruise lines last year. It seems no matter what happens in the travel industry overall, cruising is booming again and we want Harrison Cruises to be your first choice when you decide to return. It is our goal to see to your every need, because you're worth it. From our cruise director to our ship doctor, we are at your service. So, whether you are a family cruiser, a novice cruiser, a relaxed cruiser or a dancing cruiser, you will find that we've covered every base to make certain that your experience is an unforgettable one. I look forward to meeting each and every one of you. Thanks again for choosing Harrison Cruises.*

So how did Captain Douglas arrive at this opportunity of a lifetime? The opportunity to take charge of thirty-two hundred passengers and a crew of twelve hundred on the first and only Black-owned cruise ship in the world?

Ocean water was in Captain Douglas's blood. One would think he inherited it. Normally, navigating the mammoth oceans was a skill handed down from one generation to another, but that was not the case with James Douglas. His father was a West Point graduate who had spent more than twenty years in the military. So when James accepted a scholarship from the U.S. Naval Academy right out of high school, his stern father did not take it too well. Mind you, to serve your country in any way was indeed the right thing to do, but he had wanted his son to follow in his footsteps and become a career army man. The navy was a dirty four-letter word to his old-fashioned father.

Four years later, he was assigned as the executive officer for the fifth fleet. After receiving his master's degree, he completed his commercial captain's certification. He had known back then that he wanted to become one of the great seagoing navigators docking in and out of Florida, which was a big dream for a Black man in the navy.

He resigned his commission from the navy after ten years of service to pursue his lifelong dream. He worked as a staff captain on the *Windblade Voyager* for two years, which was an adventure expedition ship that held less than one hundred passengers. He went on to work in Houston, Texas, as the first Black chief engineer of a roll-on, roll-off ship, which carried vehicles and equipment to support U.S. humanitarian and combat missions.

Later, he received his first command and was made captain of a research ship in Antarctica, which was owned by the Indian government. He spent fourteen weeks on duty and fourteen off. There were very few areas of the world that he had not traveled.

About two years ago he'd met Mr. Delmonte Harrison while attending a captain's dinner out of the port of Long Beach to Mexico. Mr. Harrison was a well-known business mogul who owned several franchises, magazines and lines of clothing. Financially, he was one of the most successful Black men in the world, if not one of the most successful men, period.

"Captain James J. Douglas," Mr. Harrison said. "I'm about to secure a few ships that were part of a canceled purchase from Royal Caribbean's fleet."

Captain Douglas had just taken over Royal Caribbean's *Western Songbird,* his first commission as captain aboard a luxury cruise ship.

Delmonte Harrison told him, "They had a freeze order on their fleets just when I was contracting with a builder for my first ship. They had an order for three, so I paid a discounted rate and redesigned the ships once they were one third of the way into the process. One day, I'd like you to be the captain of my first ship. It will be an event unlike any other. It will be a historical moment in the African-American community. These premiere ships will soon grow into a fleet of twenty within five years."

Three months passed, and Captain Douglas had supervised the building of this magnificent floating wonder. He saw to every detail from the navigational system, to the décor, to the hiring and training of the crew. He claimed to love the technical part of the ships best of all, but he enjoyed the galley as well, because food was another love of his, especially on the soul cruise. He also loved the design of certain amenities, like the grand theaters, massive rock climbing wall elevations and the magnificent tri-level malls. They took delivery of the first *Chocolate Ship* class vessel in the late summer.

* * *

Now it was show time. Time to meet and greet his passengers and see to it that his entire staff was on the job, ready and prepared to make this launch as stellar as the ones to follow.

With one more straightening of his tie and proud pull of the bottom of his coat jacket, he stepped through the threshold of his spacious cabin and closed the door behind him. The sight of the aqua blue-and-cinnamon carpeting in the hallway took him back to the day he had selected it. As he stepped his size-fourteen black leather shoes onto the plush starburst pattern, he noticed his new, young cruise director on the job during embarkation, greeting arriving passengers with a friendly smile.

He took what he surmised to be a hidden position behind the wide-eyed young couple she was welcoming, waiting his turn to wish her well. But, Captain Douglas's presence was far too overpowering to ignore.

He noticed the rays of hormonal steam raging from the couples' scantily clad frames. With that, he was reminded that part of his mission was to ensure that everyone had fun on this "city on the sea," and to make sure no one overstepped the boundaries, turning it into a "sex on the sea" saga.

# WILL YOU GET A LOAD OF THIS?

In the port of Fort Lauderdale, Florida, as the sun prepared to set after delivering its post-summertime warmth through a light blanket of low dissipating clouds, the five-star fleets of state-of-the-art cruise ships were docked and lined up like shiny, virginal new race cars in an upscale showroom. They appeared ready and eager to whisk you off to a fantasy island somewhere. These massive vessels were enormously oversized, yet amazingly able to skim the crystal waters of the Atlantic, floating thousands of passengers to another place and time like magic.

One of the distinctive, handsome, and powerful cruise ships was labeled the *Chocolate Ship,* its name gracing the bow of this magnificent three-football-field-long wonder. It was a deep, dark brown color like a chocolate bar, and the funnel-designed smokestacks of stainless steel were backlit by regal blue neon lights and emblazoned with the name of the cruise line: Harrison Cruises. The ocean liner had twelve decks, two basketball courts (one being a full court), four pools, seven Jacuzzis, a bowling alley, a shopping mall, a waterslide, a chapel, a driving range, a miniature golf course, a rock-climbing wall, an ice-skating rink, a barber shop, a beauty shop, coffee bars, a cigar lounge, a tri-level theater, and three nightclubs.

There were new, charcoal black lifeboats along the port and starboard sides of the upper hull of the ship. The aft section of the hull was kissed by an ebony-hued image of the continent of Africa. But this ninety-ton, nine-hundred-room ship was not headed for the motherland. It was about to embark upon a round-trip adventure on the crystal blue Eastern Caribbean, visiting such exotic ports of call as Labadee, San Juan, and St. Thomas, with a final stop in Nassau, the Bahamas, including Harrison Cruises' own private island.

The enormous ticketing area reserved for checking luggage and showing identification was a large, barren, hangerlike room with a few dozen attendants to check in passengers. There were about ten or so border officials and security guards who kept an eye on things, what with all of the terrorist activity that had gone on since 2001.

"Thanks, sir," said the attendant as Miles handed her his ticket. "And your birth certificate and driver's license, please."

"Here you go," he replied with an accommodating tone.

She checked her list. "Yes, Mr. Lewis, here is your room key and ticket stub. Have a great time."

"Thanks. We will," Miles replied.

"Hello, ma'am, do you have a ticket?" the woman asked Mia.

"Miles, do I have a ticket?" Mia looked at him as he shuffled through his organizer full of papers.

Miles told the woman, "Her reservation is ticketless. I booked it over the Internet."

"Did they send you a confirmation slip?" she asked.

"No. It was a last-minute booking," Miles said.

"May I have your birth certificate and driver's license, please?" she asked Mia.

Mia looked down into her purse to remove her wallet and handed the attendant her identification, keeping one eye on Miles.

"I don't see a Mia Lewis on the list," the woman informed Mia.

"My identification is Mia White, if you'll notice. I am not Mia Lewis, ma'am," Mia corrected her, two seconds away from a panic.

"Oh, I'm sorry. I thought you had the same last name. My apologies. You're both in room S224. Enjoy your cruise," she said, handing Mia her key and printed receipt.

Miles gave a sigh of relief. "Thanks."

"She had me worried there for a minute," Mia said to Miles as she returned her I.D. to her wallet. "I thought you'd be going on this cruise by yourself after all."

"Baby, I've got you covered. You should never doubt me," Miles said with a nod as if he had everything under control.

Just as they prepared to step onboard, a photographer asked them to stand in front of a huge life preserver setup with an enormous brown anchor over their heads.

"Smile," he said as Mia and Miles grinned from ear to ear, hugging each other around their waists. "You can pick up a copy in the photo lounge at any point during the cruise."

"Thanks, sir," Miles said.

"Did he give you a ticket stub?" Mia asked, sounding inexperienced as they stepped away.

Miles replied, "I think we'll be able to find our own picture."

She went on to say, "You're right. How silly of me. Well, that is one shot we're going to have to get."

Miles said, "And I'm sure there will be a lot more pictures taken before we're through."

As Mia and Miles crossed the bridge for embarkation, the cruise director, who looked like she could compete in the Miss Fitness America pageant, greeted them with a cool mint smile. Talk about shipshape, she had legs of polished steel. And she was the deepest shade of earthy brown they had ever seen, almost like well-done toast. Her almond-colored hair was freshly braided into carefully parted cornrows with tiny, sparkly, powder blue-and-silver butterfly clips at the base of each braid. She was wearing the same chocolate-brown shade outfit as all of the other crewmembers, but her top was low cut and her skirt very, very short.

"Welcome to Brandon's Soul Cruise aboard the *Chocolate Ship—Caribbean.* Mia and Miles, is it?" she inquired with an energy that could light up the Las Vegas strip.

"Yes, you are correct," Mia replied.

"My name is Tangie Watson, and I'm your cruise director. I know your cruise will be one of the most memorable times of your life," she said with a confident voice that could sell an Eskimo woman a brass bra. "Here are your name tags." She handed one to each after checking their names off of her list. "Feel free to wear them if you'd like, of course they are optional. Your bags will be delivered to your stateroom shortly. If you require any assistance, please do not hesitate to contact me. I am constantly at your disposal. Enjoy!"

"Thank you, Tangie," Miles said with an approving smile.

As they headed toward their room, they both looked back to eye Tangie as she greeted the next group of passengers. "It looks like Delmonte Harrison definitely hired the right person to make a great first impression," Mia commented, as if to read Miles's mind.

"Uh-huh," Miles nonchalantly replied, turning forward again to regain his sense of direction.

Mia continued to stare back as her eye caught a glimpse of a dapper looking, gargantuan gentleman who walked up next to Tangie just as her trio of passengers walked away.

She imagined correctly, *That must be the Captain, James J. Douglas.* He looked like a cross between Billy Dee Williams and Colin Powell. He was a good six inches taller than Tangie and she was no midget. He was manly and colossal, maybe two hundred eighty pounds at the least. *He's looking all good in his uniform,* she thought to herself, also deciding to keep an eye on where she was going before her admiration was discovered.

They turned down the passageway and headed for the all-glass elevator near the nine-story atrium. Spellbinding mirrored columns etched with elaborate African designs surrounded them.

Next to the elevator was a giant angular lion statue in polished black lacquer, spotlit by laserlike beams.

"The eyes look so lifelike, it's as if that statue winked at me," Mia commented.

"I can't blame him. He probably did," Miles joked, gazing at her ample rear end as she stopped to admire the king of the jungle.

"This is so symbolic of our people, Miles. Strong and magnificent," she said, turning in a circle as if she were Dorothy in *The Wizard of Oz,* taking a moment to look around at every detail of the ship's design. "I can't help but think how amazing it is to see all of these Black people . . . cruising. Taking time out to do something once thought of as an adventure only explored by the White world. Putting our money together to get our butts onboard a Black-owned cruise ship with Black employees, black carpeting, black leather furniture, Black art, Black soul food and Black drinks like Alizé, Hennessey, Seagram's, Olde English, Sex on the Beach, Long Island Iced Tea, and Miller Genuine Draft, and some Cristal too," she said on a roll.

Miles added, "With Black folks' games like bid whist, spades, and let's not forget dominoes, and some activities not thought of as Black friendly, like golf, skeet shooting and ice skating. Black music and Black entertainment, like jazz and comedy. Black hosts, Black booties, Black lips, and Black hairstyles," Miles continued, sounding like a cruise director himself.

"Now this is what I call Black–owned here," said Mia with a happy face.

"Auntie M!" Corey yelled just as Mia snapped out of her trance. Corey's youthful, pimple-free, coffee-bean skin radiated with energy and anticipation.

"Hey, Corey," she said, standing on her toes to give his long, thin body a hug. "Boy, you're almost as tall as Miles. Hey, Bianca."

Bianca was wearing the hell out of her zebra-print short set with a matching hat and bag.

"Hey Miles, what's up? And you, Mia, looking like a ripe banana," Bianca said, as if she'd never seen Mia's outfit.

She was referring to the long, lemon yellow, tie-dye skirt Mia had bought last week at Venice Beach with the matching strapless bikini top, oversized straw hat, and clear thongs. Miles was sporting his new ivory-linen Bermudas with a pineapple yellow-and-navy blue surfer-type shirt.

"Bianca, I can't believe we're here. And Corey, you look so handsome in your Hawaiian print shorts," Mia said, still giving him a one-armed hug.

"My mom made me wear these," he said with a puberty-ridden frown. "I hope no one my age clowns me."

"Corey, I have the same pair in my bag, so we'll get clowned together," Miles told him in a comforting tone.

"I think our staterooms are down the same hall. Ours is on the Sienna deck," Bianca said, looking at her arrival envelope.

"Ours too. The decks are called Sienna, Tawny, Ebony, Cocoa, Mocha and other shades of color. How cute!" Mia stated.

"They should have named the decks Mandingo and Kunta. That would have been better than all of these feminine names of colors," Miles said with a chuckle. Corey laughed with him.

They reached Bianca's room first as she handed Corey their key card to open the door. "We'll catch up with you two later," Mia said.

"Okay, girl. We'll see you at dinner," Bianca said as she and Corey stepped into their room.

Halfway down the hall Mia and Miles reached room S224. Miles took his backpack from his arm and searched the small front pocket for his key.

A high-pitched voice rang out from behind Mia. "Girl, is this cool or what? Is this Miles? We've never met, but I've heard so much about you," Megan said. She rambled on as she ran up hugging Mia like they were old buddies from way back just as Miles swiped the room key card through the slot. "My room is right next to yours." She was wearing a tiny periwinkle sundress.

"Miles, this is Megan," Mia said. "I've told you about her."

"Yes you have. How are you, Megan?" He greeted her without even turning around to give her eye contact.

"Just fantastic! This is going to be the best time ever. Hold on tight to your woman, because I hear there are a lot of sharks on-board," she cautioned Miles. "See you two later."

Miles then gave Megan the head-to-toe once-over and walked into the room. He sealed the look with a fake smile as Mia walked in behind him and closed the door.

"She's the shark I've got to watch out for. That scrawny girl looks like a dyke," Miles said with a deep, exaggerated, vertical frown line between his bountiful eyebrows.

"Well, she's far from that," Mia assured him.

Every time he made one of those juvenile, insecure comments, Mia remembered his telling her about his borderline attempt at just ending it all when his ex-girlfriend admitted she was gay. Because of that, it was Mia's opinion that he believed all women to be one drink away from licking stamps.

# 9

# GETTING SETTLED IN

Mia and Miles's stateroom was elegant and very contemporary-looking. Most of the interior design was a Black and leopard theme and the drapes, which were the same neutral beige as the silk velvet sofa and love seat, had leopard-print tiebacks. There were freshly cut deep orange marigolds and bright lemonade-colored sunflowers in a gold-plated and onyx vase on the maple nightstand. The smell of African musk oil from the brass diffuser on the noir lacquer coffee table lingered in the air from the moment the door was opened. Several strawberry votive candles outlined a dish of floating honeydew candles. To Miles's delight, there was even an Egyptian hand-painted chess set made of ivory and brown soapstone with a black walnut board.

"Mia, check this out," said Miles, picking up a few of the pieces. "The king is a pharaoh, the bishop is a priest and the castle is a pyramid."

"And the queen is Nefertiti, let's not forget about her," Mia noticed.

"Now this board is going to get a lot of use," Miles guaranteed her.

"I hope this mattress gets a lot of use," Mia said as she bounced up and down on the king-size bed enveloped in a black, soft, velvetlike comforter trimmed in a sand color with tan and rust animal-print pillows. In the middle of the bed was a silver tray of individually wrapped chocolate-chip cookies shaped like tiny cruise ships.

"Miles, this is too much. They have pulled out all the stops," she said, looking wall to wall.

Miles was frozen in place as he looked out of the sliding glass door onto the veranda, admiring a view of nothing but the magical charm and brilliance of aquamarine water, water and more water, as far as he could see.

"I suppose the days of portholes are over," Mia commented, standing behind Miles, looking over his shoulder.

The floor-to-ceiling, beveled, ocean-view doors were tinted in a dark gray smoke and emblazoned with the initials "CS" trimmed in gold.

"I've got to go out here and check this out," Miles said eagerly.

"Open the door, baby," Mia said, jumping up and down behind him like a child on Christmas morning.

The private veranda was complete with black and white gingham lounge chairs and a black-leather wet bar. The half-moon–shaped balcony looked directly out onto the never-ending azure seas.

"Now this is what I call a patio. I could hang out here just reading and sipping on a piña colada all week," Mia replied.

Miles set his focus upon the view, losing himself in the visual splendor. "I've never seen anything like this before in my life."

"I'm going back inside to check out the rest," Mia said, stepping back through the doorway.

The stateroom was carpeted in a butterscotch gold tone Berber with dark brown trim. The desk was black marble with a black leather chair. The royal suite came with a refrigerator, microwave and coffeemaker. And the Roman tile fireplace was ready to go, with clear glass folding screen doors and a week's supply of matchlight pine mountain logs.

"This is what I call the lap of luxury," Mia yelled to Miles, who was still looking out toward the Atlantic.

Speaking of lap, there was even a laptop computer next to the bed. The ethnic tone was sealed with Ernest Watson and Banana Tree artwork garnishing every inch of the wheat cloth-papered walls. Hard-shell Afrocentric gourd vases tied in the culture and heritage of the décor.

"I'm wondering how much Mr. Harrison had to fork out to have this done first class," Miles said, now stretched out on the lounge chair as Mia made her way back to the veranda.

"Bianca said he hit the lottery, but I heard he's just an intelligent man who made some awesome real estate investments," Mia said, facing Miles and straddling him as he lounged. "Here, close your eyes and open your mouth," she instructed.

"What are you up to?" he asked with caution.

"Nothing. Just close your eyes and open your mouth," she insisted. "Trust me."

Miles kept one eye open and said, "There's no telling what you'll put on my tongue with your oral fixation self."

Mia slipped the miniature cookie into his mouth and leaned in to take a bite herself. "Let me have half of it."

"No," he said turning his head and chewing it as quickly as he could. "That's nasty."

"It is not. I was just trying to be romantic," Mia said, removing herself from Miles's lap by raising one leg high over his head.

"What was that? I saw nothing but pubic hair," Miles said in surprise, wiping his mouth while still chewing.

*Ladies and gentlemen, this is your ship steward. For your safety, the Coast Guard and SOLAS require that we conduct emergency lifeboat drills within twenty-four hours of leaving port for cruises seven days or less. In the next few minutes, please go to the reporting area located on the listing on the back of your cabin door. Also, you will notice we have supplied life vests in the overhead compartments above your closets. Each passenger must bring a vest to the reporting area immediately. This drill is mandatory and has been organized for your safety. We look forward to seeing you on deck within ten minutes. Thank you very much for your cooperation.*

"Mia, what are you up to?" Miles asked, standing up from his chair.

"Nothing, Miles. Let's just go report for the drill." Mia went back inside and grabbed a life jacket for each of them. "Here," she said, tossing Mile's jacket as he came in.

"Thanks," he said, barely catching the jacket, which landed on the bed. "Look at you," he added, looking at the top of the comforter. "You took your panties off while I was out there? You're just asking for it."

"I thought we could get in a little straddled sex before things got going around here. But it's cool."

"You're just dying to be the first passenger to get some, huh?" Miles asked.

Mia shook her head side to side while looking down to strap on her vest.

Miles said, "Oh, you're going to get it. I want to know what it's like to do it on a ship too."

"You've never done it on a ship before?" she asked.

"No, have you?"

"No, but you're the one who has been on cruises before," Mia said.

"Well, if you haven't been with me then I haven't had sex, Mia."

"Okay," Mia said, rearranging her mouth and then popping her lips. "I was talking about before you met me. Let's go."

"Don't you start anything with me. I'm going to wear your butt out tonight."

She put her hand up to his face as they exited the room and said, "No, you missed out on your chance. Acting like I'm the freaky one of the duo." Mia closed the door behind them.

They took two steps. "Mia, go back in there and find out where we're going," Miles said as she made an about-face to check the listing. "And put on your damn draws, too."

The Sienna deck near the wraparound pool was where Bianca, Corey, and Megan reported, as well as Mia and Miles.

Bianca said, "Are these rooms something else or what? Everything in our room is dark brown and spicy rust."

"I used to think you could spread your arms out and touch each wall of a stateroom. The bedroom in our cabin is bigger than my bedroom at home," said Miles.

"These are the ugliest vests I've ever seen," Megan noted.

"I don't think they're meant to be a fashion statement," Bianca told her.

"What is your room like, Megan?" Mia asked.

"I'm in a single room, thanks to Brandon. He really gave me a good deal. My room is every shade of blue from powder to midnight," Megan said.

"You're going to owe him on that one," said Mia.

Changing the subject, Bianca told them, "So, Corey joined this teen group of thirteen- to fifteen-year-olds who get involved in these Camp Chocolate programs. They have a lot of different activities so he can spend time with his peers."

"That sounds like fun," said Mia.

"Yes, it sounds cool. Anything's better than hanging out with grown-ups all day long," Corey admitted.

"I understand that," said Miles.

"Not that you wouldn't be a lot of fun to hang with, Mom."

"Oh, son, please. Nobody wants you to enjoy yourself more than I do," Bianca told her son without doubt.

*In the event of an emergency, you will hear this sound over the P.A.*—A piercing, whistling alarm went off as Corey and Megan covered their ears—*This sound means that you are to report to this area after you have proceeded to your room to gather your life vests. Please put on your vest before leaving your rooms and wear them until you are told to take them off. A trained crewmember from the steward department will muster everyone right where you are and give you appropriate instructions for boarding the lifeboats, if necessary. We do not anticipate an emergency as this ship is state of the art, however, rest assured that the total capacity of lifeboats and survival craft far exceeds the total number of passengers and crew aboard. So please remain in your area until a staff member checks to make sure that your vests are donned and adjusted properly. At that time, they will clear you to proceed. Thanks for your cooperation. If you have any questions, please do not hesitate to ask.*

"That sounds pretty serious," Corey said.

Bianca replied, "It's just precautionary."

"Yes, this is the boring part of the cruise, but the most important. But, we'll get this out of the way and then enjoy our vacation," said Miles.

# 10

# CHRISTENING

The christening ceremony likened itself to that of a celebration for kings and queens. A local news helicopter flew high above and several news vans with live satellites lined up near the dock. Spectators were yelling, holding up bon voyage banners and leaning over the railings of the pier, trying to catch a glimpse of the festivities.

The mayor of Fort Lauderdale, the chief of police and local council people were standing with the captain as he prepared to speak. Reverend Ray Smith said a quick prayer for the event and for their journey.

"Please bow your heads. Thank you. Be with us now, dear Lord, over the sea's entire massive domain, bringing light to this maiden voyage of the *Chocolate Ship*. We thank you, Lord, for this vessel, this opportunity, this vision brought to fruition by your will, your divine wisdom and your saving grace. We pray to you for the safety, health, well-being and abundance of every person here today, Lord, and all over the world. We thank you because we know that through you, all things are possible. We know that it is all you, all God, and for that knowledge we do give thanks, and so it is. Amen."

The crowd repeated together, "Amen."

The heavyset, designer-suit-wearing Reverend Smith gave Captain Douglas a hug and a handshake, exchanging places with him. "Thanks, Reverend Smith," said Captain Douglas. "Yes, this is all God. When I was a young man I dreamed of becoming the captain of a cruise liner and that day has come. But never in a million years did I envision that I would one day become the first captain of a Black–owned cruise ship. What we are witnessing today is a piece of history. This is so much more than just a few privileged passengers embarking upon a fun-filled vacation to another part of the world. This is the witnessing of a major purchase by a major Black man who is as powerful in our community as he is intelligent."

The captain went on, "This is about a Black man who owns major corporations left and right and who has made it without sports, without acting, and without handouts. Mr. Delmonte Harrison made a major expenditure of upward of a billion dollars to see his dream become a reality. Mr. Harrison is a self-made billionaire who is able to empower our community. He is providing jobs, opportunities and hope for our people and for all people. He has the ability and desire to give other people a shot at becoming millionaires themselves. We need more African Americans who are able to finance and support other individuals so that they too can say that they earned major dollars from a Black man or woman. Statistics show that Whites pay ninety-eight percent of African American salaries. Every African-American I know has made their money from White America. While that's all good, it is time for that to change. It is my hope that Mr. Harrison serves as an example to all entrepreneurial people to share and empower and educate so that we too shall rise. Ladies and gentlemen, I present to you, the founder and owner of Harrison cruises, my boss and your host, Mr. Delmonte Harrison."

The crowd applauded and leaned over the starboard-side railings, as Mr. Harrison was supposedly standing below, just toward the front of the massive ship.

"Can you see him?" Megan asked, stretching her neck to get a glimpse.

"No, can you?" Bianca asked too, looking downward.

Mr. Harrison began to speak. "Well, Captain Douglas, that was very impressive. I truly appreciate your more than kind words; however, I want to give you a hand for becoming the first Black captain to head up our first Black–owned cruise ship, the *Chocolate Ship—Caribbean*." The onlookers applauded as Captain Douglas took a humble bow. "But I would like to thank all of the passengers who decided to join us by booking a reservation and taking time off from their busy schedules for this momentous occasion. You are a very special part of the success of this venture and it would not be possible without you. We booked the entire ship the first time around. Not a charter and not a section of the ship, the entire ship. So to you, and all of the other many people who came out today, I present the first ship in our fleet, the *Chocolate Ship—Caribbean*."

The sound of a bursting bottle rang through the speakers as the crowds of people cheered.

He continued, "And this is something I've always dreamed of doing as a send-off to my first ship. Hit it, DJ."

The opening beats from *Mothership Connection* began to play over the speakers as Mr. Harrison continued, "Well all right, Starchild, citizens of the universe, recording angels. We have returned to claim the pyramids."

The passengers began hooting and hollering to the old school cut, and some were even singing along with the ship's owner.

"Partying on the Mothership," he continued as Mia and Miles gave each other a high five while the screams intensified.

"Getting down in 3-D. Light year groovin'. Well all right. Everybody now, sing," he encouraged, to the sound of his popping fingers. "If you hear any noise, it's just me and the boys. Hit me, you gotta' hit the band."

"Mr. Harrison has really started something here," said Miles, screaming the lyrics in between clapping his hands and bobbing his head.

Mia agreed. "I've heard of rocking the boat, but this is crazy."

Captain Douglas could be seen near the bow of the main deck dancing with Tangie, his cruise director.

"Come on, shake your booties for a successful brotha, now," said the newly-arrived Brandon as he grabbed Megan. They ran off to dance on the basketball court.

Corey was dancing with his mother, and Mia and Miles were doing the bump.

"What do you call that, Corey?" Mia asked.

"It's called the c-walk," Corey replied, doing his thing.

"Show me," Mia said as she stood next to him, lined up for instruction. Corey proceeded to get his hop and skip going and Mia stopped, looking lost. "Wait now, how did that foot get over there so fast?"

"Forget it, Corey, I can hang. Let's show them how it's done," Miles said as he and Corey did their walk back and forth while Bianca and Mia watched, dumbfounded.

"I'm going to stick to the bump," Bianca said as she and Mia bumped with each other.

"Ain't nothing but a party y'all," Mr. Harrison yelled into the microphone again.

The spectators along the dock were rocking their butts off, as well as Reverend Smith and the politicians. The Mothership Connection had landed.

The champagne reception just sort of blended into the christening, with dozens of waiters passing around large trays of Chocolate Ship souvenir glasses filled to the rim with brut extra dry champagne.

"I still have not actually seen Mr. Harrison," said Bianca. "But that voice was killer."

"I agree. Even the captain sounds like Darth Vader himself," Mia said.

By now, the passengers were groovin' to the sound of P-Funk.

"I want my funk uncut," Miles said, walking back up to Mia, Bianca, and Corey.

"Where did you go?" Mia asked.

"Just thought I'd look around to see if Scott and Kelly were here yet. If not, they're about to get left behind."

Mia asked, "Do you want to get in that long line to meet the captain?"

Miles declined. "Heck no. We'll run into him."

"I say we go get a good spot near the front of the ship so we can catch the full effect of setting sail," Mia suggested.

"Let's go. Check you two at dinner," Mia said to Bianca and Corey.

As the ship prepared to embark upon its journey, the beautiful northernmost image of the burnt orange sun aligned with the horizon of the royal Atlantic. Within another ten minutes, the sun would fade behind the massiveness of the ocean, only to shine its light upon another part of the world.

Mia and Miles lined up along the railing of the main deck to prepare to set sail to the sound of the sterling, new and powerful foghorns. The fresh, warm evening breeze blew past them in slow motion. Mia and Miles embraced, cheek to cheek, in an exhaled hug and waved good-bye to the States. After all these years, they were finally traveling to an intimate corner of the world, together.

*By the end of this soul cruise,* Mia imagined as Miles stood behind her, holding her around her waist, *I'm sure to be sporting an engagement ring.*

"Well, we're on our way," Miles stated while looking out onto the vast, dark topaz waters.

"Let's go, baby. I want to take a hot bath before dinner," Mia said, walking hand in hand with her other half.

"So, Corey, what do you think so far? Do you like it?" Bianca asked.

"Yeah, it's pretty cool."

"What do you think you'll want to do first?"

"Probably just walk around and see everything. This ship is huge."

"Yes, it is. I'm glad we came together," Bianca admitted.

"Thanks for paying for me to go, Mom. I know this was not cheap."

"No, it wasn't, but it's worth it. Corey, do you ever wonder about your father?"

"Wonder about what?" he responded as if he wasn't getting her point.

"About what he's doing and why he doesn't come around as much as you'd probably like him to."

"No, I know he's working and trying to get his finances together, like he told me before."

"But what about when you see other kids with fathers who are not as absent as yours? How does that make you feel?" Bianca asked.

"Mom, there are a lot of my friends whose fathers are not around. Kevin is probably the only one who lives with his dad. It doesn't feel different because I'm used to it," he said, walking slowly, stride for stride with his mother.

"Who do you really look up to as far as a male image?"

"Probably my volleyball or basketball coach. And Kevin's dad is cool to talk to."

"Do you ever wish I'd gotten married?" she asked.

"No, Mom. Do you?"

She replied as if this had been on her mind for quite a while, "Sometimes I do, just so you'd have a man around to teach you how to be a man. In my opinion, it's hard for a woman to teach a boy to be a man. There are just certain things I can't show you. Like mechanical things and what it's like to be a Black male and what it must feel like to have testosterone-filled thoughts."

"You mean like to talk to about girls?" he guessed.

"Yes."

"Mom, you do a fine job at teaching me how to treat females, I'll say that much. You've always been there."

"That's nice to hear," Bianca told him with a pleased face.

"But no, just having any old man around the house would not have been better than not having one. I want you to get married when you meet the right person and when you're ready. I'm fine, Mom. Really. Are you?"

"Corey, I will tell you, there are times when I get pretty lonely. You know I go out every now and then, but meeting men is not easy. Especially meeting a family man who is spiritual and trustworthy."

"Maybe you need to start doing different things instead of going out with Auntie M to the club. Maybe you should start doing more things like this. There have to be a lot of guys on this ship," he said.

"I've thought about that," she admitted.

"And I know one thing, I'm not going to be hanging on you the whole time. I'll make sure you have your space."

Bianca responded, "Oh, is that your way of telling me you'll give me space or your way of asking me to give you space?"

"The first one, Mom," he said, to discourage her from feeling that he did not want to hang with her.

"Corey, I know it's not cool to have your mommy with you all the time. There are surely enough things to do on this ship to keep me occupied. Just look at this rock-climbing wall." They both stopped and looked up to the highest point.

The wall looked like an authentic outdoor rock with cracks and pockets and edges that resembled textures and designs by Mother Nature herself. The steel gray rock was maybe twenty-five feet high, with four individual routes.

"It even feels like real rock," Corey said, rubbing his hands along the surface. "What's the age limit on this?"

Bianca read the posted sign. "We'll have to find out. It looks like they only have certain times of the day."

Corey was already farther down the deck than his mom, admiring the Olympic–size pool, looking up at the domed roof.

"Look, Mom, the sky dome to the pool opens up and closes like a huge claw. This is where I want to be tomorrow," he said, walking toward the steps of the pool. "I miss when I used to go swimming with Dad at Grandma's house. We would just lay out and barbecue and swim during the summers all day long on Saturday and then wake up early on Sunday and do the same thing."

"Yeah, you with your dog-paddling self. He wanted you to take lessons, but I thought you were too young and we just never got around to it."

"Well, Dad taught me by throwing me in one day. I remember that time I went swimming with Dad at Grandma's house. We laid out, ate barbecue, and swam all day long."

"No, he didn't!" Bianca said protectively.

"Oh, Mom, don't get mad. That's how I learned to just let go of my fear and go for it. He was right there keeping an eye on me."

Bianca said, "Okay now. See, that's just an example of the kind of things he used to do that would make me scream."

"Uh-oh, Mom. They have a Chocolate Chip Cookie Dessert Bar. Now this will be another one of my hangouts."

"We'll have to check that out after we eat. Right now we'd better get ready for the captain's dinner at seven," she suggested.

Corey said, still focusing on the many amenities, "And then I want to go to the video arcade. I hope they have the cool games like Madden 2003 and NBA Street 2003."

"I have a feeling that Delmonte Harrison has made arrangements for the best of everything. Let's go get dressed," Bianca told Corey as they walked to their room with his protective and loving arm across her shoulder.

# 11

# THE CAPTAIN'S DINNER

With a plush snow white towel wrapped around her head, Mia leaned back on the chartreuse bath pillow, basking in the luxury of a sea-salt glow in the oversized crystal white oval Roman tub with powder blue ceramic tile and ocean blue grout. The grout had hand-cut inlays of red hearts and silver mirrored triangles throughout. Mia briefly opened her eyes and noticed the tiny silver stars and half moons painted high above on the opulent circular ceiling with the midnight blue background.

"Miles, this is what I call heaven. Do you want to get in here with me, baby? There's room for four up in here," Mia yelled through the open bathroom door over the faint sound of an Erykah Badu CD.

"No, baby. You know I'm checking out my chess set here. Besides, that seaweed or mineral oil thing you've got going would not agree with me. It smells like medicine in there," Miles said.

"It's called aromatherapy, Miles—rosemary, eucalyptus, peppermint and chamomile. You should try it. And it's even better with two people. There's enough room."

"That's okay. I'm in heaven right here," he said, moving the opposing pieces as if developing a strategy.

"For the first time we'll be able to see Mr. Delmonte Harrison in the flesh," said Mia, exiting the bathroom with one towel wrapped around her body, tucked in between her breasts, and another around her head. She removed the towel from her head, shaking her hair and running her fingers through her leftover curls. "I wonder if this hair is going to last all week."

"It looks great, baby," Miles said, still looking down at his chess game. "Anyway, I saw Mr. Harrison earlier while I was walking around the ship. I thought he had this elusive attitude, like he was too cool to be seen. He had a couple of guys with him who looked like bodyguards."

"Oh, really?" Mia said, even after she brought it up, as if she could care less. "I know what I'll do tonight. I'll just throw this baby up into a bun and forget it. Come on, Miles. We need to start getting dressed. We have reservations for the main seating."

"I'm not going to take as long as you. Go on ahead and work on that bun," he said with eyes glued to his game.

Mia brought the dark green evening dress Miles had bought for her on New Year's Eve. Miles had laid out a black Armani tux with a silver-blue bow tie.

The enormous Egyptian Ballroom beckoned the passengers to step back in time to the splendor of the Egyptian pharaohs. It was lavishly decorated with sweeping columns carved with deep red, beige and black ancient art. The room itself looked to be two hundred by two hundred feet, as if it could accommodate two thousand people easily. The roof of the teakwood-domed ceiling opened up to a mezzanine that exposed four floors of inside cabin verandas on each side. High at the very top of the ceiling was a large skylight with decadent, intrepid blue and fire red stained glass.

Lining the floor of this breathtaking room was pile carpeting with a blue-and-red zigzag pattern. The border was earth green with tiny hieroglyphics images throughout. Two hundred or so circular tables draped with ornate silver stenciled cloths were surrounded by ten chairs each, all lined up in front of a grand stage, which was closed off, for the moment, by deep brown velvet drapes. Narrow gold columns lined each side of the stage and huge brass urn vases stood guard at the steps leading to the stage. High above the stage, looking over the room, was the seal of the great pharaoh Ramses.

Mia and Miles sashayed inside, looking all around, gasping at the splendor and yet looking as though they always dined this way. They were seated at table number eighty-four with all of Mia's girls, just as Mia had requested.

The table itself was graced with place settings for ten of white china with the gold *CS* crest in the center of each plate. Even the crystal water glasses, wineglasses, and platinum flatware sported the emblem. The centerpiece was made of pale green fruits and vegetables, like whole apples, cabbage and artichokes, all mixed in with tall, cream-colored candles and icy white irises.

The headwaiter placed a glass pitcher of chilled melon martinis on the table for the captain's toast.

Bianca, who was wearing a short-sleeve fuchsia sequin top and black pants, tried to include her teen in the toast. "I'll order some sparkling apple cider for you, Corey."

"I just want a Coke," Corey said, fidgeting with his black bow tie as the waiter walked by with a tray of sodas. Corey grabbed one in each hand.

"You two actually persuaded your daddy to foot the bill for this little soiree?" Mia asked, looking at Lexi and Yanni.

"Lexi talked him into it," said Yanni. Both of the twins had decided to wear knee-length halter-top dresses. Yanni's was sky blue and Lexi's was topaz blue.

"Plus I got a bonus from the hospital last week, so I actually paid half of it back already," Lexi explained.

"Bon appetit," the captain said to everyone, raising his champagne glass as he stood up to take a bow, signaling that it was okay to begin ordering dinner.

Everyone lifted their glasses and said, "Cheers," taking a sip in unison.

The menu was every bit as soulful and Southern as if their moms had taken over that galley and proceeded to cook up all of their favorite dishes. The choices were smoked turkey with giblet gravy, smothered chicken and smothered steak, chitterlings, fried chicken, fried catfish, ox tails, garlic meatloaf, hot links, macaroni and cheese, fried okra, potato salad, brown sugar baked beans, sweet creamed corn, black-eyed peas, candied maple yams, collard and mustard greens, sweet-potato pie, sock-it-to-me cake and peach cobbler.

"Lord have mercy," said Miles. "This is just like going to M & M's soul food restaurant without pulling out your wallet. And they feed you until you're full."

The headwaiter came over to take everyone's main course order. The popular choice was the smothered chicken, but Corey and Miles ordered fried chicken.

"Thanks, man," Miles said to the well-dressed waiter in a crisp, new bolero jacket. "I should have known Delmonte Harrison would hook us up like this."

Mia asked him, "Yeah, and where else can you eat soul food and feel like you're sitting in a royal palace?"

"They did not spare any expense, that's for sure," Bianca agreed, still admiring her surroundings.

"Whoever designed this room knew exactly what they wanted. This has to be the most expensive spot on the whole ship," said Miles.

Corey reached across the table to the white ceramic bowl of cornbread muffins and dinner rolls and pulled back the burgundy cloth napkin, exposing the swirling steam and soulful aroma rising from the freshly baked breads.

"Boy, don't reach over across Mia. Where are your manners?" Bianca said, lightly popping Corey on his upper arm.

He retreated. "Auntie M, I'm sorry. Can you pass the bread, please?"

"That's better. I didn't raise you to do that," she said, trying to whisper toward Corey's right ear.

"He's just excited," Mia said, passing the bowl to him.

Miles reached over in front of Mia for a pad of butter in anticipation of when he'd be able to get his crack at the bread.

"Miles, now you know better than that," Mia said, beating him to the punch at retrieving the butter. "Here you go," she said, handing him the tiny plate.

"Don't try to be funny and front me like that," he told Mia.

"Oh, I'm just kidding," she said with a forced smile.

"Corey," he said looking to his right, "grab that bowl and reach around behind your auntie and hand me that bread. Will you?"

"Don't you do that," Bianca said, semi-laughing but giving Miles the eye.

Corey snickered and said, "Here Auntie M, Can you pass this to Miles?"

Mia took a muffin from the bowl and passed it on to Miles.

"You all had better lighten up on this ship. I'm letting down my hair and having fun," said Lexi.

The waiter served dinner salads to everyone but Corey. "Lettuce has no taste at all," Corey complained.

"That's why I drown it with ranch salad dressing," said Mia, pouring the rich, thick dressing from the silver tureen dish. "Where is Megan?"

"She's seated next to Brandon, the promoter. Look at her over there at the captain's table, like she's somebody," Yanni remarked, giving Megan an investigative stare.

"The captain is attracting women like flies," said Lexi.

Yanni agreed. "It's as if they're all circling around him to get a whiff of his money."

After Megan gave the captain a seductive wink, she caught Mia eyeing her. She motioned for Mia to come over. Mia dropped her fork full of ranch salad, springing to her feet. She took a couple of steps and then remembered to say, "Miles, come on."

"Captain Douglas, this is my friend Mia and her guy Miles," said Megan, standing tall and proud in her short, lively green mini, showing her long, thin, toned legs.

The captain stood up and said, "Hello, glad you could come aboard."

Miles shook his hand while Mia smiled, taking a bow as if the man was royalty.

"The ship is beautiful. You are an inspiration to a brotha," Miles expressed, also glancing over at the rest of the passengers at the captain's table.

The captain said, with appreciation of the sentiment, "It's all for you to enjoy. The owner of this floating wonder, Mr. Harrison, is the one to compliment. But, I am your host tonight and I look forward to seeing you both later."

"Thanks, Captain. It's nice to meet you," Miles replied.

Mia just smiled and did the moonwalk back to their table.

"Baby, did you see Big Mack, the rapper, and El Dorado, the group from the seventies, sitting there? Big Mack isn't as big as I thought," Miles said, starstruck.

"I didn't see them. There were so many people at that table," Mia replied, like she really noticed anyone other than Captain Douglas. *You go, Megan,* she said to herself.

Scooting herself into her chair with Miles's assistance, Mia thought, *I'm not going to look at that man again for the next week. Even though it's not like I'm attracted to him. I mean, he's old enough to be my father. Maybe I'm just in awe of his position and status. Good thing Miles is here. I always say it's okay to read the menu, just as long as you don't order anything. But the menu looks pretty appetizing.* Mia replaced her napkin in her lap and took a sip of her drink.

"Who was speaking of appetizing?" asked Bianca, giving her a look of warning, like she'd better lay off the martinis.

Mia placed her empty glass on the table. "Never mind," she said, picking up her fork to finish her salad.

The waiter returned with the main course orders, serving the ladies first, and then Miles and Corey. Very little was said as mouths were stuffed with tasty side dishes and chicken. Miles ordered seconds as everyone else started on his or her desserts.

"Corey, slow down," said Bianca as he picked up the sock-it-to-me cake with his hand.

"If I keep eating like this, I'm not going to be able to fit in those tiny outfits I brought," said Yanni.

"I know I'll be on a diet when I get back," said Mia, patting her little pooch of a stomach and leaning back in her chair.

"I don't care what this peach cobbler does to me. I am grubbing the entire week like every day is my last day," said Lexi.

"I'm with you on that," Miles admitted as his second plate of fried chicken was served.

After dinner, the fashion show began next door on the stage of the Ebony Theater, which was like a mini-Greek amphitheater. The rows of lavender velvet theater-style chairs, maybe thirty in each, were three sections wide. The walls were painted black, with pictures of colorful, animated, unknown, ebony-faced African Americans distinctly lined up in straight-across rows from the left to the right, all around the theater. Their faces were jovial and carefree as if they too were happy to be a part of this experience.

Strutting down the one-hundred-foot runway were three atomic-looking, six-foot-plus bionic women. Three professional football players, Rasheed, Bo and Deshaun escorted the female models down the runway. Yanni and Lexi were already having orgasmic convulsions as these brothers modeled Delmonte Harrison's new line of Black Bottom jeans, made of stretch knit to show and hug every pulsating muscle. And every muscle was indeed showing. Deshaun caught a glimpse of Yanni bouncing while seated as he walked to the beat of Q-Tip's "Vivrant Thing." He exited the stage, made his way over to her wearing those "Bad Boy" Iverson cornrows and gyrated in her face as she sat in her front-row seat. He gave her enough personal attention that one would swear she was getting a lap dance.

"I don't think this show was intended for minors," Bianca said, turning around to talk to Mia and Miles in the row behind her and Corey.

A studly, dark and handsome man walking up overheard her and laughed. "I just said that to my kids also, but perhaps the worst is over," the man said, glancing at Deshaun, who had made his way back onto the stage. "My name is Omar Young, and these are my kids, Logan and Dillon."

"Nice to meet you. My name is Bianca. And, this is my son, Corey."

"Can we sit next to the two of you, Mr. Corey?" Omar asked, pointing at the few seats next to Corey while holding on to his daughter's hand.

"Sure, I'm cool with that," Corey replied with a smile.

Bianca turned to glance at Mia as if she'd struck gold. Omar did look like quite a catch. He was the color of fudge, baldheaded and athletic. While his kids took their seats he stood tall and proud, looking like he could be one of the models in a beige dress shirt, spice-colored bow tie around his manly neck and a toffee brown tux jacket hooked on his finger and draped over his shoulder. He appeared to be a few years older than Bianca, but Mia thought that was what she needed. Usually it was the scrubs who came a-calling.

As he took a seat four spots away from Bianca, Omar said, "I didn't realize the performers would start already. I thought the entertainment would take place on the island in Nassau."

"I didn't either," Bianca replied with a girly voice just as the legendary Ms. Ashley Isley herself came onto the stage. Ms. Isley had to be fifty, but she looked good! She was coke-bottle curvy, golden brown and wrinkle free. She worked her way over to Omar and serenaded him with her rendition of "God Bless the Child."

A camera crew videotaping the happenings came over to shoot some video. Just then, Omar jumped up and hurriedly corralled his kids, disappearing from the Ebony Theater as quickly as he'd come.

"What the heck was that about?" Bianca said as she and Corey sat with their mouths wide open.

"You'll see him again. He can't get away from you on a ship sailing the Atlantic. Where's he going to go?" said Mia, leaning in from her seat behind them and putting her hand on Bianca's shoulder.

Miles raised one eyebrow, trying to figure it out. "That was weird."

"Maybe his pager went off," Mia explained unconvincingly.

"Oh, please. That was just an out-and-out bad first impression. I think that was rude," Bianca admitted.

Mia told Bianca, "He'll show his face again, girl. Just keep an eye out for those kids, because you know they'll be running him wild. Shoot, if push comes to shove, you can always ask Tangie what room he's in and call him. He did say Omar Young, right?"

Bianca blew a slight bit of air through her pursed lips. "I'm not going to chase after him and call him. He'll have to find me if he's interested."

Mia realized she was hitting a nerve. "Okay, I'm just trying to help."

Bianca continued, "Besides, I didn't come here to meet a man. And if I did, there are a whole lot of other big Black men on this big Black ship."

Mia looked at Miles as Corey turned around rolling his eyes and twisting his lips. Mia whispered to Miles, "She came here to meet a man!" Mia and Miles departed from the theater, leaving Bianca and Corey to continue checking out the show.

Just as they were coming out of the theater, they noticed that the photographer was set up for more passengers to take pictures in their elegant, formal attire, alongside an antique chair with a black velvet backdrop.

Mia looked around at the setting and the sample portraits. "Let's take more pictures, Miles. Please."

"Baby, we'll have many more chances. That line is too long," he said as he continued to walk by.

Mia stopped him, taking hold of his arm. "Miles, how many more times are we going to be dressed like this, though? Please, honey. This is a very special evening."

His voice dropped. "All right, Mia. Let's get it over with."

Mia examined the frown line between his eyes. "Are you sure?"

He motioned for her to precede him. "Come on. The line is getting longer as we stand here."

Within maybe twenty minutes, it was Mia and Miles's turn.

The photographer directed them. "Okay, you sit down and your lady can stand behind you. How's that?"

"That's fine," Mia answered for Miles.

The photographer took three shots. Mia grinned from ear to ear and Miles gave full lips with no teeth. They were done within no time and the photographer moved on to the next group.

Mia was pleased. "See, that didn't take long. That's going to turn out nice and we'll be glad we waited."

Miles wanted to move on. "Let's find that gambling table."

Mia realized that she just had to understand that her man was impatient. He liked to do things and he liked to have fun. She'd hoped there would be enough fun to satisfy him for the entire week. Of all of the times to be cranky and ruin a vacation, this, she was determined, would not be one of them.

The Safari Casino was reminiscent of the exotic jungle, with giant fishnet designs angled in each corner and framed pictures of giraffes, zebras, and exotic birds covering every inch of the walls, along with lifelike pictures of nomadic cattle herders and beautiful close-ups of village children with painted faces and ornamental costumes.

The clamor of silver coins falling into the waiting steel trays in response to lady luck rang throughout the room along with the sound of bells accompanied by flashing red lights, signaling those fortuitous souls who had beaten the odds.

Hopeful cruisers taking a shot at the toss of the dice or shuffle of the cards surrounded the roulette, baccarat and blackjack tables.

"You know craps is my game. Come on over here with me and be my good luck charm," Miles told Mia.

"Okay," Mia said, even though she was dying to take a spin at the dollar slot machine that she was always so lucky on when they went to Vegas.

Miles noticed Mia's turned head. "Don't even look over there. Remember that time you hit the mega-bucks and only had one coin in?"

"Don't remind me."

"We'll do much better over here. I'm feeling lucky up on this ship," he said taking his place at a five-dollar craps table. He gave the main dealer fifty dollars and received his chips, betting six dollars on the pass line. Miles would always bet with the shooter. The shooter, a young White gentleman with enough chips lined up to buy a convenience store, rolled the dice. He rolled an eleven and Miles doubled his money.

Miles cracked a smile. "Hey, girl, I told you I feel lucky. I'm going to try the Big-6 and see what happens."

"What is that?" Mia asked.

Miles appeared happy to explain. "That means I have to hit six before they roll a seven."

"Come on lucky seven," said the shooter, blowing on his dice. He threw the dice across the other end of the red felt table and they bounced off the left side of the wall.

A three and another three. "That's six," said the dealer. Miles had won again. He'd won twelve dollars in three minutes.

"Baby, I just want to try the dollar machine once, I'll be right back," Mia said as if the corner machine near the change booth was calling to her like an old lover.

Miles agreed, still focused upon his game. "Okay, go ahead. I'm on a roll anyway."

Mia kept an eye on Miles for the next hour or so from across the room. He was still gambling, so she assumed he was winning. Mia had now demoted herself to the nickel slots, hoping for just a two-dollar win so that she would feel as though the casino hadn't gotten the best of her ninety-eight dollars.

She saw Miles walking toward her. "How did you do?" he asked, looking at her empty tray.

She downplayed it. "Oh, okay. I lost a little but I'm going to just finish up these nickels. How about you?"

"I stopped at my fifty. I'd tripled it but couldn't hold off. These casinos always see us coming."

As Mia stood up from her stool, she suddenly realized Miles

was without his running buddy. "Hey, where in the hell are Scott and Kelly? After all, aren't they responsible for you being here?"

"Mia, they are celebrating the one-year anniversary of the honeymoon they never had. I doubt if they'll be leaving their room anytime soon."

A thought popped into Mia's head. "Are you thinking what I'm thinking?" she asked with hormones raging.

"I'm there," Miles replied, as if she'd taken the words right out of his mouth.

# GETTING NAUGHTY ON THE HIGH SEAS

Miles glided up alongside Mia's left ear and decided he would play horse and master with her. "Hey, lady. You want a ride to your room?"

Mia's face blushed. "Yes, sir. That would be nice."

"Hop on," Miles said, turning his back toward Mia. She jumped on, wrapping her arms around his neck and her legs around his waist.

He trotted along down the hall while an older couple glanced at them, smiling as they moved aside to make room for the lovebirds.

"Thanks," Mia said to the couple while spanking Miles on his butt. "Getty-up."

"I'm going to be getting up soon enough."

They reached their cabin door and he turned his back so she could slide the key card. He pushed the door open with his foot.

They crossed the threshold of their beautiful, cozy room, where Mia jumped off, turned him around, and hugged him with her head to his chest. Mia then gazed up at him.

"It's so good to be away from it all with you. This is a first for us and I don't know why we haven't done it before, but I . . ."

Miles placed his index finger over her lips, looking deep into her eyes as if she should hush. He stared at her face with a focused, investigational look toward her upswept hairdo and down to her chin.

"Hold on a minute." Miles backed away to put on a Babyface CD. He bounced and snapped his fingers to the beat, walking toward the dimmer switch and turning it as low as possible. He bent down to light the fireplace log.

Mia walked over to him and leaned over to mumble in his ear. "I'm going to slip into something more comfortable." She briefly pressed her lips to his forehead.

"Me too," he said.

While Mia was in the bathroom, she smiled in response to hearing Miles sing "Whip Appeal" as if he was onstage at the Apollo.

After she changed, she stopped and posed in the bathroom doorway, looking into the dimly lit living area, wearing a tea green silk robe, tied at the waist.

He checked her out from head to toe. "Damn, look at you, girl. Come to me, baby."

Miles had lit the fireplace and votive candles on the coffee table so the whole room smelled like strawberries and cream.

"So, this is your more comfortable look, huh?" she asked, staring at his bare, protruding member and taking slow, seductive steps to greet him.

He bounced toward her, meeting her halfway in his birthday suit. "You know it." And what a suit it was. Mia's man's abs were cut like an ice sculptor had chiseled and carved their way into his belly, seeking perfection with every shaving. His aesthetics were grade A, with legs as muscular and strong as they were long. Mia often told him he had a butter-pecan ass, like that of a triathlon-runner in training for the Olympics. She gazed in admiration at the man she'd caught and loved for so long.

"Come with me," he said, taking her hand and backing up toward the off-white bearskin rug in front of the fireplace.

He opened her silk robe to give light to her hot pink and green G-string.

"Damn, baby. Is that all for me? Here, lay down for Daddy."

She dropped her robe and Miles laid her on her back on top of the shaggy, soft rug. She spread her legs while looking up at him as he faced the opposite direction, standing over her.

"That'll do it," he said as he moved to the beat, straddling her head. Mia looked up at his magnificence, loving every moment of it. She rotated her hips in a grinding motion in anticipation of his next move.

Miles lowered himself to one knee, bending down to kiss her mouth, upside down. *Kissing upside down is erotic as hell,* she thought as he swallowed her intoxicating kisses. The tops and bottoms of their tongues rubbed and slid about while he took her entire tongue into his mouth like he was sucking his thumb.

Miles moaned at the sight of Mia. "You look so good, baby." He lowered his other knee and leaned down toward her breasts, kissing each aroused nipple tenderly and pointing his tongue to flick her nipple ring back and forth. Mia sighed.

Now she could see his abs up close and personal. She licked each ab separately, tracing the outline of his six pack with her wet, warm, welcoming tongue.

He moved down to her belly button, sticking his tongue inside while framing her navel with his puckered lips, then flicking his tongue on down to her hairline.

This upside-down view was now providing Mia with a direct connection to a glorious eyeful of her baby's most private part, his perfect partner, first rubbing it against her forehead, her nose and right into her wide-open, waiting mouth.

She attempted to give attention to his testicles by kissing and blowing with a slight pucker, tickling his skin from the scrotum and on back to his anus.

"Umm, Mia," he responded to her technique, contracting his gluteus repeatedly in a sudden, sporadic jerking motion as if this little trick was too much for him to bear.

Just as she brought one hand up to assist in guiding him to

her northernmost lips, Miles found her southernmost lips and took them in his mouth with a suckling that caused her legs to shake involuntarily. He kissed her with his generous lips as if they had just been reunited after thirty years. And the upside-down view of the shape of his goatee as it framed the exact shape of her opening produced juices that he'd be sure to notice. *Oral sex in this position can be distracting as a motherfucker,* Mia thought.

She felt the vibration of his voice as he asked, "Can I taste your sweetness?"

"Uh-huh," Mia responded in unrelenting pleasure. She still felt butterflies in her stomach in response to their passions blazing in unison. His touch always made her skin tingle.

Miles suddenly explored her hole from just around the sides. He licked his way inside, tasting her soul like she was a chocolate ice-cream cone. With a combination of his tongue within her and his chin rubbing against her tiny muscle, Mia squirmed as her warmth liquefied. She saw the love juices gleaming all over his mouth and chin while he worked his magic as only he could do.

Mia could not see his face from his fully engorged member blocking her view. She proceeded to take him into her mouth with one hand. Her other hand was on his cheek, maneuvering him fully into her hot, wet mouth, tickling his tip with her tongue, stroking his shaft with her right hand and sucking him like a Tootsie Pop with all of the deep throat expertise she knew drove him crazy.

Miles had more in store. He was now focusing on her jewel while he placed his hands under her butt. Mia moved her hips, taking on his face as if she was making love to it, with total whip-appeal action. He was groaning the words of the song in pleasure from this cruise-ship blow job. It was as if they were one, as Baby Face sang about whippin' that sweet sad lovin' on him.

Yes, Mia and Miles were butt naked in a sixty-nine to the flickering flames and crackling sounds of the wood-burning fireplace.

Ten minutes later, Miles brought himself around to lie behind Mia, spooning her as he lovingly pressed kisses upon her fatigued back to seal the moment. Exhausted in climactic ecstasy, they fell fast asleep gently cradled by the smooth, subtle, romantic sway of the *Chocolate Ship*.

# 13

## THE WEEK'S ITINERARY

The next morning, Bianca and Mia walked over to the Freedom Café for a buffet breakfast. The bright room, with its floor-to-ceiling windows provided a view of every inch of the ocean and land within miles. The all-you-can-eat bar was covered by a blue canopy and surrounded by black marble rectangular tables aligned along a walkway of pine flooring around the circumference of the café.

"It looks like we'll be at sea all day today," Bianca said, perusing the seven-day itinerary. Aside from studying the daily activities, she appeared distant, as if in deep thought. A few minutes later, Megan made her way over to the table, led by a flirting Jamaican waiter.

"I'm never going to let you go home now. You have no choice but to live on the ship with me," said the smooth, fine, toffee-colored, Mr. Lover-Lover brotha in his strong Jamaican accent. It was obvious he had not mastered the English language.

"Bianca, do you see what I see?" Mia asked as they both looked down at the waiter's bulging crotch.

Bianca mumbled with full-on eyes, "Oh, that cannot be possible. It has to be the length of a water hose and it's running straight down his leg."

"My name is Olandi. Olandi Townsend. And you are what?"

"I am whom? I am Megan."

"Then you are now Megan Townsend," he said, serious as a heart attack.

Megan played along. "Wow, Mr. Townsend, I'm game."

"So we are on our honey, what? How do you say, by the moon?"

"Honeymoon," Megan said.

Bianca joked one-on-one to Mia, "This girl has only been here for one night and has a husband already. She can't handle that pipe."

Megan missed the comment but leaned in to whisper, "If his thing can get as deep as his voice, this could be my future ex-husband right here."

Olandi and Megan continued their mutual admiration rap groove.

"Oh, that's some weak-ass rap," Miles commented on the down low, looking at Olandi, obviously having overheard him. "No sight of Omar yet, Bianca," he said, after receiving a cheek kiss from Mia and an unwelcome stare from Bianca.

"Why would you bring that up? I'm not thinking about him," Bianca replied in denial.

"Where's Corey?" Mia asked Bianca.

Bianca answered, once again perusing the cruise schedule, "He went on a kids' retreat to play games and go rock climbing."

"Maybe he'll run into Omar's kids," Mia said, realizing that Bianca was about to bitch slap her as she cut her eyes. "Okay, I'm sorry." Mia retreated, holding her hands up in surrender.

Just then, Kelly and Scott came over to greet Miles. Mia's perception of Kelly was that she was cool, even though she thought Kelly sort of knew all of Miles's goings-on because he and Scott were so close. But Kelly never let on. For a while Mia was mad at her because she felt Kelly might have been betraying the sister bond by probably letting Miles bring girls over, or not sharing information with her. Now, Mia realized that Kelly just wanted to stay out of it. Or maybe there was really nothing to tell in the first place.

Kelly was Black, but she was Whiter than Shirley Temple deep down. She had been called an Oreo cookie for the longest. She was the exact opposite of Scott's hip-hop ass. She wore her jet black hair in dreads that just barely reached her shoulders. Her skin was black-coffee black and she never wore makeup. Perhaps that was why her skin looked so flawless. She wore a silver nose stud, had a pierced tongue and at least six piercings in each ear. Kelly was fairly short and pleasingly plump and round. Scott joked about Kelly's ghetto booty and how he liked to spank that ass.

Mia still could not figure out why Scott needed Miles to go with him everywhere all the time. It was like he was Scott's bodyguard, or something.

Mia stood up from the table and hugged Kelly, patting her on the back. "Hey Kelly, I haven't seen you in ages. Where have you two been hiding?"

"Like up in our room, okay?" she said with a valley-girl flair. "So, when Miles told us he decided to bring you along, we were like just so thrilled. We can't wait to get our fun started in St. Thomas."

"I was thrilled too. Believe me," Mia said, turning to Scott as he reached for her. "Hey Scott, what's up?" Mia asked as they exchanged left-to-right smooches.

He kept his hand on Mia's shoulder. "See, man, this girl has got to be your soul mate. She's even starting to look like you. You'd better pop that question before she gets away. Then we can both have chains to go with our balls—I mean, wives."

Kelly chuckled. "Oh, Scott, don't kid around like that. I mean, come on."

Miles pulled Mia close to him. "I know. I'm not letting her get too far away." He realized Bianca had not been introduced. "You both know Bianca, right?"

"Hey, you two." Bianca leaned over to speak into Mia's ear opposite Miles, "If Miles is not careful, Captain Douglas just might jack him right under his nose."

"Couldn't he, though?" Mia mouthed in response. "And you both know Megan, right?"

"I don't think we've ever met. I would have remembered," Scott said, taking a step toward Megan's table as if Kelly were invisible. "My name is Scott."

Kelly took a step forward as well, as if Scott simply forgot to mention her. "And my name is Kelly. I'm his wife." Kelly extended her hand and gave Megan a dainty shake with her fingertips.

"Nice to meet you," Megan said, keeping both eyes on Scott and blushing beet red as she released Kelly's hand. Olandi returned to her side and mouthed a few intimate words into her ear to earn her focus. It worked—after a few seconds of eyeing Scott she giggled her attention back to Olandi.

Miles tried to distract Scott from making a fool of himself. "So, I say we get some grub."

"I'll get mine later," said Bianca, sort of daydreaming out of the window as Megan and Olandi continued to talk between themselves.

"Mia, like so what have you been up to?" Kelly asked as she walked to the buffet line with Mia.

"Just working hard and keeping an eye on Miles."

"Oh, my gosh, no need for that. We've got some totally good men, girl," Kelly assured Mia.

After they joined in the long line of breakfast seekers, they made their selection from the hot, fresh and steaming Belgian waffles, chicken sausage patties, fried chicken wings, grits, salmon patties, banana fritters, and scrambled eggs with cheese and onions.

Mia suggested to Miles, Kelly and Scott, "Let's go over to the bar and get our early drink on while we eat."

The young, skinny, curly-headed, vanilla photographer who had taped the fashion show the night before was sitting at the bar talking to the bartender.

"Hi, you all. My name is Dante," said the bartender as they

grabbed their stools. "Dante Tyrell Shaquille Willis the Fourth is the name, making drinks is my game."

Dante looked barely twenty-five and was the deep, rich color of the very bourbon he served. He had beautiful, expressive eyes with long lashes. He had bushy, dark brown eyebrows and wore a thick mustache. His head was clean shaven and he was stocky yet all muscle, as though his fat ratio was zero. He had long, strong, clean, bare fingernails that he would point toward you when he talked, particularly his pinky finger.

Dante placed napkins next to the plates, which were piled high with enough food to feed the entire nation of Islam.

Mia took a bite of her toast. "What should we call you?"

"Tell your man to call me tonight," Dante said, giving Miles the Betty Boop pout and stare.

Miles did not even smile as he turned his back to the bar.

"Call me Dante if you'd like. You may not want to turn your back to me, though," he warned Miles in jest.

Miles looked at Mia as if he was questioning if this guy was for real or not and then gave Dante a kick-ass narrowing of the eyes to indicate that if this fool kept tripping, he was going to get a fist to his jaw.

"Oh, lighten up, I'm just kidding. I've got a man. Don't want you to sue the cruise line for sexual harassment or nothin' just because I'm trying to be a charming boy," he said, placing a glass of water next to Miles's plate, pinky extended. Scott and the cameraman laughed.

"Hey, everybody. My name is Justin," the cameraman said.

Everyone introduced himself or herself to Justin while Dante took Justin's hand and gave him a special greeting.

"Hi, Jus. Mind if I call you Jus?" asked Dante.

"No, that's what my sister calls me, actually." Jus definitely did not seem to mind.

"What can I get you, Jus, and all of you of course?" Dante inquired while wiping the bar.

"Another bartender," mumbled Miles.

"I'll have a Moet Mamosa," Mia stated on the heels of his last word, loud enough to drown out Miles's reply.

"We'll have Sex on the Beach," said Kelly. "And no jokes," she quickly said to Dante just as he opened his mouth.

Justin explained to Mia, "I work with Winter Jackson, the news reporter you saw earlier. We're here to cover the events of the first ever Black–owned cruise line for our station in Fort Lauderdale, KMIA."

Just then Winter walked up with Tangie, the cruise director. Miles immediately stood with his plate in hand and offered his seat to either of them. At that moment, Mia was able to count every filling in his mouth. Mia shook her head and took a bite of her sausage link.

Winter made Sally Richardson look homely. She had it going on from manicure to pedicure. She was nearly six feet tall, her weight was in proportion to her height, and her breast size was at least a dozen inches greater than her hip size. She had a forehead that was more like an eight head. In spite of that fact, she wore her copper-colored hair off her face with pride, in a straight, shoulder-length bob cut. Her complexion was like golden honey. Yes, she was the Queen Bee, and men buzzed around her sweet sticky thing like they'd gladly pay for a shot at her hive.

Tangie gave the group the rundown for the rest of the cruise as Winter took Miles's vacated seat.

"You'll have the ship to yourselves all day because we will be at sea until tomorrow morning. You can swim, play tennis and basketball, go bowling, play cards, enjoy seminars and aerobics classes, lift weights, peruse the art gallery and Black book exhibit, or whatever. Obviously there are tons of activities. Tonight we have an electric slide competition and seventies' night in the Blue Room. We should arrive in Labadee, Hispaniola, early tomorrow morning, Monday, for a day of sun and fun on land or enjoy the poetry reading and dominoes tournament. Later tomorrow evening we'll enjoy Part Two of Brandon's Soul Cruise, which is the comedy portion. After the comedy you can get your boogie on again at the cha-cha marathon competition, take salsa lessons in the Chocolate Bar, or just hang out and dance on deck.

"On Tuesday we'll arrive in San Juan by noon for our day of shopping, snorkeling, scuba diving or just plain old sunning on the beach. Later we'll board the ship again for the pajama party and karaoke night. Wednesday will be the big evening beach party in St. Thomas. That's our late night, when we hang out on the island until midnight. We'll set sail again all day Thursday. That evening is the final event for Brandon's Soul Cruise. That's the rap portion with Big Mack and Ebony and Ivory. On Friday, we arrive in Nassau for a peek at Delmonte's privately owned island, called the Fantasy Island, so you can either hang out in Nassau or take the shore boat over to the island. Kids are not allowed because it is a nude beach, optional of course."

"Damn, now that's an itinerary," said Scott.

"That's not all. After boarding the ship on Friday evening, we'll change into our African attire for the African-American Heritage evening in the Egyptian Ballroom. We'll serve a late farewell dinner and the DJ will mix the cuts all night long. We arrive back in Florida early Saturday morning."

"When is El Dorado going to perform, that's what I want to know," asked Dante.

"Tomorrow night in the theater," replied Tangie. "El Dorado will open the show for Brandon's comedy act."

Pointing at her choice of vodka, Winter said to Dante, "I'll have a cosmopolitan with Skyy, baby. Tangie, can I do my live shot from the theater as well as from the island?"

"Your satellite will pick up every minute," Tangie said with confidence.

"I want to know where the captain is. That man is fine. Is he married?" Winter inquired, horns protruding from her head.

"Girl, no, he's not. But get in line," said Tangie.

"Well, the line forms behind me," Winter said with a cocky, confident head roll as Dante placed her drink in front of her. "Thanks, baby." She took her glass and spun around in her seat to ask Tangie another important question. "What about Delmonte Harrison? I saw him earlier and he is all man." By now, Scott and Miles were shaking their heads, peeping her mission.

"He's such a workaholic that you won't see him too often. I'll tell you who is a good man and available," Tangie said, peaking Winter's curiosity.

Suddenly, Lexi and Yanni came running up to the bar at the sound of that music.

"The ship doctor, Steven Taylor," Tangie said. "Dr. Taylor is a 'mighty good man,' as En Vogue used to say."

"But from what I heard, not a mighty hard man," said Dante with his arms crossed along his midsection.

Kelly said, "Dante, do you, like, always reinforce the stereotype that all bartenders are gossips?"

"Just the facts, ma'am . . . Don't get all up in my stuff," he said, flailing his hand in a circle around his head.

Tangie interjected, "Dante, there's one more event I forgot to tell you about."

"What's that?" he asked, all ears.

Tangie informed him, "There's a worship service going on in the Skylight Chapel. You should check it out." Kelly and Mia snickered under their breath.

Dante made the sound of a skidding car and shoved his flat, flexed hand within an inch of Tangie's face. "*Errrrrk,*" he imitated with attitude.

"You really should go," Tangie suggested, fearlessly leaning in toward him.

"Whatever!" Dante replied. "Anyway, everybody, strap on your seat belts, 'cause this is going to be on and cracking."

# SUN, FUN AND THEN . . .

The main pool area with the sky dome was a glorious sight to behold. Rows and rows of buff-colored deck chairs encircled the Olympic-size, neoteric pool with swimmers and waders and dog paddlers jumping around to take a dip into splendor. Along the edges of the pool, fun-loving vacationers were seated just to get their toes wet or gradually gaining momentum toward taking the full plunge. The ninety-degree water welcomed every inch of one's body from head to toe.

Sienna complexions basked in a row to tan or just to relax, looking like they simply decided to surrender to the power of the enormous sun and the protection of the endless azure sky. A neatly folded root-beer-colored *Chocolate Ship* towel rested upon the foot of each deck chair, and beyond three rows of lounging passengers was the panoramic window view of the romantic Atlantic as far as the eye could see.

The groups of glistening tawny-toned bodies of every hue of the chestnut realm blended well with the caramel-colored umbrellas that stood guard over the lounge chairs. At the Stingray Bar, men, women and children were all seeking the bartender's attention to order a bit of liquid to cool down from the full effect of the blazing sun.

Sun, fun, lounge chairs, and oiled-up sweaty bodies. Nothing better than Black folks tanning. Chocolate bodies all greased up with Coppertone and Bain de Soleil. It only took a few minutes of Banana Boat oil and brothas and sistahs were three shades deeper into their blackness. The scene was paradise.

"Oh no, Miss Ashley Isley did not decide to wear a bright orange thong bikini up on this ship with some T-strap, sling-back espresso heels to boot. Some people just need to leave the unseen a mystery," said Bianca in her tangerine tankini.

"You're just mad because she has on the same exact color you're wearing. I think that lady has a body like Thelma on *Good Times*. She still looks good after all these years."

Corey was swimming and leaping around in the pool like a frog.

Bianca commented with a smile, "He is having the time of his life. What a good young man." Then she noticed Corey with another teenager, holding their breath underwater for what seemed like an eternity.

As he came up for air, Bianca called out, "Cut it out. Your eyes will pop out of your head and get stuck if you keep that up." Corey looked embarrassed by her close supervision.

Bianca and Mia laughed, sipping on their strawberry banana coladas as the Jamaican waiter with the WWF Smackdown body sprayed their sweaty bodies with cool, fresh Evian water while they wiggled their French manicured toes in the sun.

"We are queens of the Nile," Mia exclaimed, holding her drink high above her head.

Scott and Miles began to approach Mia and Bianca, wearing floral shorts and matching ribbed wife-beaters, but were interrupted by two lounging lovelies.

"No, Yanni and Lexi are not stopping them asking for help putting suntan lotion on their backs," said Mia.

Miles looked at Mia as he gracefully, intelligently, *busted-ly* declined. Scott appeared elated at the chance.

Bianca stated, "The twins should just be naked if they think those strings are covering anything."

Lexi was wearing tropical peach and Yanni had on red-hot red. They actually had matching booty art on each cheek. Each had the tattooed image of thick lips smacking a kiss on her left cheeks, and on the right was a hand-scripted *Y* and an *L*, respectively.

"They are just inviting trouble if you ask me. What am I going to do with my girls?" Mia said as Scott continued to rub down the twins as if he were earning frequent fucking miles.

Bianca commented, "Kelly shouldn't let him out without a leash."

Miles came up splashing Evian water on Mia's hair, jacking up her just-laid hairdo. It had taken a five-hour beauty-shop visit to get the roots right. He knew Mia hated that.

"Mind if I sit here, ladies?" he asked, standing in between the queens as if the king had now arrived.

"If you stop playing water games," said Mia, patting her head for a water check.

"Mia, where did you get that Band-aid bikini?" he asked, referring to her pink tourmaline two-piece.

"It's not as bad as some I've seen up here. At least it's not a thong," Mia said, pulling her bikini bottoms down to cover her backside.

"Don't get me wrong, it looks tight," he asserted with glee. "I'd better sit down here and keep an eye on you."

"Miles, you look pretty good yourself in those Bermudas, baby," Bianca said, laughing.

Miles stopped for a second to pose and then lay down on the chaise next to Mia. "You *should* like them. They're the same ones Corey has. Where is he, anyway?"

Bianca turned to point to Corey and said, "Yeah, but he's only . . . Corey? Where did Corey go? Corey?" Each mention of his name was louder than the first.

Bianca jumped up, tipping over her drink as she forced herself to move in closer, only seeing a faint reflection of an image in the water. A kid next to the steps of the pool was pointing down toward the bottom. Bianca screamed and stumbled over her chair as she ran toward the pool.

Just then a man rushed over and jumped in. He quickly pulled Corey's pale and limp body from the water. He placed Corey on a towel, which Bianca had laid out on the deck, and began to give him mouth-to-mouth. Miles and Mia ran over to try and help. Justin grabbed his camera and caught the rescue on tape as Corey began to cough and abruptly spit up water. The man who saved Bianca's son's life was Omar Young.

Dr. Steven Taylor, the ship's doctor, came from out of nowhere to take over. Omar's children clutched their daddy's leg as he stood back, almost amazed at what he'd done.

Bianca, with tears streaming down her face, asked the doctor in panic, "Is he going to be okay?"

"Yes, ma'am, he'll be fine. It appears as though he passed out and then got water in his lungs," said Dr. Taylor, placing his hands behind Corey's back to help him sit up.

Bianca handed him Corey's inhaler. "He has asthma, Doctor."

"I thought so. He'll be fine, ma'am."

Hearing the grand news, Bianca turned to Omar, placed her hand on his upper arm and said, "Omar, thank you so much. I can't believe how quickly you reacted to save my son. I am so grateful."

Winter, the news reporter, came rushing through the vortex of the crowd with her microphone and yelled out with excessive energy to the onlookers, "Who saved this young boy's life?"

The crowd pointed to Omar, who shook his head to affirm, "It was nothing!"

"Surely it was, Mister . . . ?" asked Winter, prompting him to finish her sentence.

Omar's daughter replied, "Young, Omar Young."

"Mr. Young, what made you react so quickly, and what did you see?" Winter inquired with a microphone all up in Omar's mug.

"Nothing, it was just an impulse, I have kids of my own," he answered modestly.

Winter continued her questioning. "Obviously you've had training or been through this before? Correct?"

"No, like I said, I have children too." Omar grabbed his kids by the hand and rushed them off toward the lobby. Winter began interviewing other passengers to get their eyewitness accounts.

Dr. Taylor removed the blood pressure cuff and tiny flashlight from his bag.

"I can help," Lexi offered with desire. "I'm a nurse."

"Okay, Nurse," he said without even looking up at her, "you check his pressure and I'll test for responsiveness."

Lexi wrapped the cuff around his arm and pumped the rubber ball of the pressure machine, focusing her attention on Corey's reading. She then took his pulse, checking the second hand on her nautical watch.

"His pressure is one twenty over ninety. His pulse is a little low, though."

The doctor instructed, "Let's get him into the medical facility as quickly as possible." He grabbed his bag, stood and tucked his supplies inside.

"I'll take that," Lexi proposed, grabbing his bag just as he closed it.

"Thanks," the doctor replied, finally taking a moment to look her in her eyes with a quarter smile.

Dr. Taylor then scooped Corey's long, thin body into his arms and Lexi watched, standing behind him, keeping an eye on one or the other of the doctor's flexed, hairy forearms or his wide back. Lexi grabbed Bianca's hand as they hurried off to the infirmary. Lexi's bouncing tattooed booty jiggled all the way down the hall.

Mia said, sounding worried, "I'm going with them, Miles. Keep an eye on my things, okay?"

Miles asked, "Do you think I should come too?"

"No, I think we're going to have enough people as it is. Too many of us and we'll just get in the way," Mia stated as she turned away and ran to catch up to the others.

* * *

"What did you see?" Winter asked Miles with a notepad in hand.

"Just what everyone else saw. We all looked over toward the pool and Corey was gone. His mom realized it just before we did, but as she ran toward him, that gentleman was already on the case."

Winter stared at him, tucking her pen above her ear and looking him up and down. "What is your name? I know you were at the breakfast bar earlier."

"My name is Miles Lewis."

"Like Miles Davis?" she asked, attempting a mixture of seductiveness and humor.

"Like Miles Lewis. Is that something you need to know for your story?" Miles inquired, definitely not amused.

She moved in closer as though admiring his impeccable face. "No, that's something I need to know for me."

"Well, then maybe you need to know my baby's name, Mia White," Miles replied, making his woman's presence known.

"Mee-ya. Like see ya?" Winter asked, still attempting to be comical.

Miles heard her, but suggested her comment was inappropriate by asking her to repeat herself. "Pardon me?"

"Because that's what you're going to be saying to her by the time this ship docks back in Fort Lauderdale. I guarantee you!" she said with unbroken certainty.

"Sorry, Ms. Jackson, but I don't think so!" he replied, looking down toward his lounge chair.

"Oh you'll go for it," she said, her eyes torn between the view of Miles's chest or his crotch area, pouting her sugar-plum lips. "You'll go for it for sure. See ya," she said, deciding the crotch area would be the best focal point. She did a one-eighty, grabbing her cameraman who stood nearby, and they dashed off to discuss the story.

Miles slowly lowered his body to his chair, laid on his back, crossed his legs at his ankles and covered his eyes with his forearms. "Damn, why me?"

* * *

As Mia headed back to the pool area, she noticed that Miles looked to be a shade darker in less than an hour. Megan and Yanni had graciously sandwiched him in between the two of them. Between Yanni's red bikini with rhinestones and Megan's red mono-kini with gold chains linking the sides, it was hard to tell if Miles's tan was from the sun or the two-alarm fire on each side of him.

"We were looking out for your man. We're just soaking up the sun," Megan informed Mia as she walked up.

"You two *are* the sun. Will one of you move over so I can lay next to my man please? Actually that's my seat," she said to Megan with a cranky, no-nonsense edge.

"Excuse me, Mia, dang. What's wrong with you?" Megan asked with an attitude of her own as she started to get up.

Mia spoke right back, in no mood. "My best friend's son could have died, that's what's wrong. Get up."

"I am. Don't you see me moving?" Megan asked, taking a chair next to Yanni.

"How is Corey?" asked Miles, more concerned about Bianca's child than their estrogen battle.

"He'll be fine. It seems he had an asthma attack while holding his breath," Mia informed him.

"Just typical kids playing around. He's all boy," Miles said, taking a sip of his cold, blended Soul Kiss.

"Yes, well, he'll be cooling it for a while, and so will Bianca, knowing her," Mia added.

Across the pool, three of the football players and female models strutted around the deck, modeling Mr. Harrison's new line of swimwear. One of the football players leisurely walked over to Yanni.

"And what do we have here?" Yanni asked.

"This is the DH line of knit drawstring shorts," he said, turning his bare chest around for her to get a closer look at the all-black, knee-length surf shorts.

Yanni only noticed his dark, muscle-bound back. "Miles, why don't you buy some?" Yanni asked, keeping both eyes on the model.

"I already brought what I need, bro, but they're cool," Miles acknowledged.

"Can I get a closer look?" Megan asked.

"They are such tramps," Mia said to Miles.

Megan sat up in her chair for a better view. "What's your name?"

"Bo," he answered after giving Megan a male model turn.

"Nice to meet you, Bo. I'm Megan. You are wearing the hell out of those, I'll say that much," Megan complimented, licking her lips and dousing herself with a water fan.

Bo, with his molasses-colored, Tyrese-looking self, made his way back to Yanni and inquired, "And your name is?"

"Yanni."

"My boy and I saw you earlier in the Ebony Theater. You were sitting in the front row, right?"

"That was me," she responded, happy to be remembered.

"You look like you were dipped in chocolate, baby, laying there gleaming under the sun."

Yanni melted. "Dipped in chocolate? Now that's a really great way to describe me. I'll just say thank you."

"No, thank you. Well, Yanni. I'll see you later, okay?" Bo all but promised her.

"I hope so," she conveyed, as if she'd have it no other way.

"And don't bake that beautiful skin too long," he said, staring at her thick, shapely legs.

"I won't," Yanni said watching him walk away to the next group of sunbathers. "Damn, he is fine. Talk about eye candy. I know who my shipmate is going to be."

"From what I saw in the medical facility, I think Lexi's shipmate is going to be that available doctor," Mia commented.

Yanni replied, still staring at Bo, "I noticed that too, but he's too old for her."

"I don't think so. You should have seen her in his office. She was acting like he was her lord and master. She's never really been the one to lose her cool and be that obvious," Mia mentioned, free of doubt.

"Well, good for her. I'm just keeping an eye on what Bo knows. I get delicious vibes from him," Yanni said, as if she could taste her desire.

"I thought you wanted to meet the other model with the braids," Mia said, recalling a previous conversation in the theater.

Yanni salivated. "Either will do."

# 15.

## REAL GIRLFRIENDS CHECK UP ON EACH OTHER

Bianca was in no mood for any electric slide competition or sock-hop. Corey had been sleeping for the past few hours and Mia knew for sure that he could use a few more after all he'd been through.

Corey was knocked out on the balcony while Mia sat on the off-white sofa in Bianca's room.

"You know, Megan stopped by earlier to check on us," Bianca said.

"That was sweet," Mia replied.

"She was with that Olandi guy."

"She's in for a real ride, I guess," Mia deduced.

"I guess so."

"Don't you think you should call Corey's dad and tell him what happened?" Mia asked, trying to keep her voice down.

Bianca responded without pause, "For what? His tired butt wasn't around during the most dangerous, trying, risky, important time of his life—his birth!"

"He should know what his son has gone through. I thought he was trying to have a tighter relationship with Corey over the past couple of years," Mia asked, flipping through an *Ebony* magazine.

"Mia, you of all people know he only comes around every now and then just to shoot around with Corey and then he's off. That is after he hits the strip joints."

"He's still into that? Whatever happened to the stripper he lived with?" Mia asked, looking up as she turned the page. "I mean, dancer."

"I heard he's still with her," Bianca said, as though it was nothing.

"Anyway, maybe to him shooting around is bonding," Mia added, trying to be impartial.

"Shooting around so that Corey will have the skills to be in the NBA one day and take care of him."

Mia still tried to weigh both sides, saying, "I know he doesn't think that."

"He not only thinks it, Blackey Carbon himself actually said it. He told me to keep him ballin' so we can get paid! He told Corey to never go anywhere, not even to the bathroom, without dribblin' a damn basketball."

"Who the hell is Blackey Carbon?" Mia asked.

Bianca informed her as though she should know, "His black butt!"

Mia looked outside to make sure Corey was still fast asleep. She suggested, "Bianca, you'd better stop clownin' that man about being so dark. Next thing you know, Corey will have a complex himself. Besides, you need to encourage Corey to keep playing golf or volleyball and diversify his athletic abilities. Better yet, get him into computers or the stock market. Time to shake 'em up like all the other Black entrepreneurs, like Delmonte Harrison, or at least like Tiger."

"And, what you need to do is diversify yourself right on over to that Blue Room to get your dance on and stop worrying about Corey's tired dad," Bianca said, shutting down the laptop and heading for one of the queen-size beds. "All I'm thinking about is my baby and what could have happened to him today. I'm going to be right here with my child."

"Good, then I'll just hang out here with the two of you and chill for the rest of the day," Mia said, resuming her read and putting her feet up onto the sofa table.

Bianca lay back on the bed after fluffing all four pillows. "No, Mia, I'm not having it! You and Miles are here to bond and do things that man has never taken the time to do with and for you. Don't let him slide on putting one hundred percent into showing you a good time."

"He's drinking with Scott and Kelly anyway. They'll be whacked in another half hour."

"Good, then go get whacked with them. One thing's for sure, you don't need any designated drivers on this big, bad ship. Relax and enjoy," Bianca said, closing her eyes.

Mia stated, "Bianca, I don't know."

"This is all part of being a mother. Now go keep an eye on Don Juan, girl!"

"Aren't you even slightly interested in Omar's whereabouts?" Mia asked, standing and placing the magazine on the coffee table.

Bianca spoke with her eyes closed. "Not even slightly. Mind you, I owe him one for his heroic deed, that's for sure. He saved my son's life. I do plan on letting him know exactly how much I really appreciate what he did. I will before Saturday, don't worry. But, I'm done for the day. This has been a hell of a trip already."

"Okay, I'm going to check on you in a few. If you change your mind you know where I'll be," Mia said, grabbing her purse.

"And go ahead and do something with your hair," Bianca said, peeking one eye open with a smirk.

Mia ran her fingers through her hair as she walked to the door. "Thanks to Miles for jacking up my hair with his water-drop game."

"Go back to your room and put on that tuff straw number you bought. That hat makes you look like Josephine Baker and stuff," Bianca said, rising from her comfort to walk Mia to the door.

"All right, I'm on my way to my room to hook things up. Why you gotta cap on your girl? Can't you just suggest things nicely?

Don't you know how to be subtle? But I guess I should say good lookin' out or something like that. I'm out!" Mia said.

Bianca stopped Mia as she opened the door. "And, Mia . . . thanks for looking out for Corey and me, I love you, girl!"

"You know what?"

"What?"

Mia turned Bianca around to check out her neckline. "Your kitchen could use some heat too. I call those worry beads."

"I'd say I've had enough reason to worry. Get your nappy headed, brotha' tolerating, nymphomaniac self out of here before you wake up my baby!" Bianca told Mia, with more head action than before.

They embraced as Mia patted her on the back and asked, knowing it would strike a nerve, "What if I see Omar?"

"Get out!" Bianca said, pushing Mia down the hall.

Mia yelled while turning to get a door closed in her face, "I'm off to plug in my curling iron."

# 16

## GET YOUR GROOVE ON

Miles walked in smelling of Johnny Walker. It was obvious to Mia that he and Scott and Kelly had their threesome at the Stingray Bar.

"Is Corey feeling better?" he asked, heading for the closet.

"He's all right, but I'm not thrilled about leaving Bianca in her room on our second night. I feel a little guilty going out without her," Mia said, standing near the bed, half dressed.

"This will give us a chance to shake our butts like we used to. Just the two of us. She'll be fine," Miles said, holding up two blazers. "Which one, baby? The tan or the money green?"

"I like the tan. It works with your skin. And the other one is army green, not money green."

"Whatever," Miles replied, irritated until he glanced at Mia's never-ending legs extending from a sheer, black, short dress. "I know you're not wearing that out of this room. I can see your panties creeping up your ass in that dress."

"This is not a dress, it's a long top that goes with my mini-skirt. It just happens to be about the same length," Mia said, wiggling her womanly hips to try to close the stubborn zipper to her skirt. "Help me out, please."

Miles walked up behind her. "Are you going to be comfortable in this?" he asked, pulling the fabric with his left hand while pulling the zipper upward with his right.

She answered, exhaling with all of her might, "Yes. I will. Besides, if it creeps, it creeps, but I am wearing my new outfit to show off all the hard work I put into working out over the past few weeks."

"Showing off to whom?" he asked, walking back to the closet.

"To you, me, anyone," Mia said.

"You can show me right up in here in private," he corrected her.

"You know what I mean. I just like looking good," Mia said, pulling her top over the skirt as she slid each foot into her black, strappy, high-heeled sandals.

"You are one sexy thing, Mia, I'll say that much. I'm not letting you out of my sight tonight."

"Hopefully you won't let me out of your sight any of the other nights either," she said with a foreboding tone as she pulled her hair back and put on her elegant straw hat.

The Blue Room was set up like a disco from back in the day. The dance floor was smack-dab in the middle of the room so everyone could gather around and check out the dancing kings and queens. The enormous disco ball, high above, appeared to be the size of a Volkswagen. And the multicolored, flashing beam lighting pulsated to the exact beat of the music. A few people, Yanni included, went way out and brought Afro wigs, bell-bottom pants, and platform shoes, but Lexi dressed conservatively.

Mia said upon spotting them, "You look like porno cheerleaders, with the pleated shirts, and stiletto heels."

Yanni said primly, "Being cute takes precedence over being comfortable. We've only got a good decade left of jamming our toes into these pointy shoes. I'd better look cute while I can."

"Yeah, that's pretty kinky-looking. It works though," Miles added as a compliment. "And Lexi, you look beautiful too," he said.

"Yes, you do," said Dr. Taylor as he appeared behind the group wearing dark jeans and a blue plaid shirt. The doc was a redbone with skin so fair you could see a few scattered freckles around his nose. He had a faint moustache, a tiny shadow of hairs on his dimpled chin, and his curly hair was neatly trimmed to a fade. He was maybe a few inches taller than Lexi, so he had to be barely six feet. He looked maybe early forties and had a slight beer belly even though he was average weight. His eyes were sad like a puppy dog, sexy and deep set.

Miles extended his hand in a brotherly greeting. "Hey, man. I hear Corey is going to be just fine."

"He just needs some rest. He'll be good as new by tomorrow," Dr. Taylor responded back. "Hi, Lexi," he said taking her hand in his and planting a soft kiss on her wrist. He continued, speaking to Mia. "She made a great assistant."

"You made a great teacher, Doctor." Lexi purred like a contented kitten.

"Call me Steven."

Lexi agreed, flattered. "Okay, Steven. And this is my sister, Yanni."

"Hey, Doc."

"Nice to meet you, Yanni."

"He looks like he can get it up to me," Yanni said to Mia, talking out of the corner of her mouth.

"Hi, Steven. I'm Mia and you've already met Miles."

Miles commented to the doctor, "I see you don't believe in that all work and no play rule."

"No, that makes Steven a dull boy," he responded, returning his attention to Lexi. "What are your plans for tonight?" he asked.

Before Lexi could reply, Bo and Deshaun rushed over to grab the twins, just as Aaron Carter's "Outstanding" started to bump.

"Oh, no. I'm cool," Lexi declined as she shifted her focus to the doctor. "Would you like to dance, Steven?"

Steven's face beamed. "Let's do it. Are you two coming?" he asked Mia and Miles.

Miles nodded in affirmation. "We're right behind you."

Hand in hand, the four of them rushed off to the dance floor. Yanni grabbed both Bo *and* Deshaun and joined in.

"Girl, you knock me out! Let's do this," Miles said as he focused on getting his count right before he made his move. He always got behind Mia when they would do the electric slide. He said he liked to watch her rear end sway but Mia knew it was because he didn't know the first few steps. By the time they'd hit the third turn, she was usually able to examine his skills for real. It had been a couple of years since they'd done the slide anyway.

"Ooh, you're looking sweeter now," everyone shouted as though rewound in time.

The seven of them rapidly turned into twelve people and twelve turned into twenty and within a couple of choruses it looked like fifty people were shaking their butts on the dance floor.

"Baby, it doesn't even feel like we're on a ship," Mia said to Miles as they made their kick, step, turn. "It feels like we're on land at the Hot Spot. This is the life. All that's missing is Bianca."

By two o'clock in the morning, Lexi and Yanni were shoeless and Mia was wishing she hadn't worn her short-ass skirt. It just kept on creeping and she just kept on pulling on it.

Yanni and Steven caught her yanking her skirt from the bottom as Miles said, "Man, I told her not to wear that micro-mini, but she wouldn't listen."

"She looks good to me, man." Steven heard a familiar beat. "Hey now!" he said, running off with a twin on each arm just as the next cut geared up. Bo and Deshaun just chilled and watched from the sidelines, keeping their eyes on Yanni.

Mia commented, "Miles, I'm cool, I don't know what you're talking about. I'm shaking my thing more than you."

"Yeah right, and I know your stuff is sweating," he said in fun.

Mia responded, fanning herself with a napkin, "Will you leave me alone and worry about those sweat stains under your arms? Maybe you should have worn that darker color."

Even through their usual bickering, Mia and Miles's ears perked up to the intro bursting through the speakers. It turned out to be "Let's Stay Together" by Al Green.

They danced with their hands in the air, bellowing in accord, "Good, bad, happy or sad, come on," sounding like Al's backup singers.

Before they could get through the first minute of the song, Miles wiped his dripping sweat from the side of his face with his shirtsleeve and said, "Come on. Let's get some fresh air. I had a hangover before we even started out tonight. I'm dead," he told Mia. He then looked to everyone else. "Bye, everybody. We'll see you tomorrow."

"We're going to cut out too," said Dr. Taylor, grabbing Lexi by the hand.

Yanni had resumed her dancing with Bo and Deshaun.

"So tell me about yourself," Dr. Taylor said, later that evening as he and Lexi walked along the deck. Its wooden planks creaked under their footsteps in the still, cool midnight air. The moon set the mood.

"Believe me, there's not much to tell. I was born and raised in Los Angeles, I'm the oldest of fraternal twins by three minutes."

"I thought so. I don't think the two of you look that much alike."

"Oh yeah? What's different?" she asked, taking long, carefree steps, trying to match his every stride, interlocking the fingers of her left hand in his.

"Well, you're a tad bit shorter, I think. And you have bigger eyes, your skin is just a little bit darker than hers, and you have that sexy little mole just to the side of your left eye," he said, looking at her face with approval.

"Oh, you noticed? Yes, I have the mole and Yanni has the dimple," Lexi replied, placing her middle fingers of her right hand over the barely noticeable nevus on her skin. The faint sounds of disco music echoed in the background.

"Oh yes, I noticed," he said, as if he had not missed much. They stopped near a corner section railing and faced the pitch black ocean water, lit only by the flickering moonlight in the near distance. "And you definitely don't seem as though you try to dress alike," he said, admiring her black knee-length, backless evening dress.

"Sometimes we do, but for the most part we gave that up in high school. We even make a point of wearing our hair differently every day. Even if one starts to wear her hair the way the other wants to, we won't," she said, reaching behind her to grab the curly ponytail extending down her back.

"Why is that?" he asked.

She answered as if she'd thought about it before. "I think we're both seeking some sort of individuality."

"I've learned that does happen after a while with identical twins because they have such similar personalities and tendencies that they branch out to make their own identity known. Fraternal twins are no more genetically similar than siblings born apart, because they are formed from two separate eggs and fertilized by two separate sperm," he explained, while she focused on his every word.

She agreed, "I can attest to that. Yanni and I are very close, but we are like day and night."

"In what way?"

"First of all, I'm a southpaw and she's right-handed. She likes to horseback ride and I'd like to race cars one day. She's a night owl and I'm a morning person. She likes hip-hop and I like jazz and even country. But we do look out for each other and we feel when something is wrong. Maybe that's from being together so much of the time. We have an older sister who is married with three kids already," Lexi informed him.

"And your mom and dad are still together."

"Oh, yes. They travel all the time and go visit my sister in Canada so they can wear their grandparent hats. They're really cool. Deep down, they're just fairly radical hippies who can't stay in one place too long."

The doctor went on to tell about himself. "They sound a lot like me. That's why I've contracted my services with cruise ships over the past few years. I used to watch the cruise ships lined up at the port of Miami when I was a kid and dreamed of one day stowing away on a one-way journey to a faraway land. You know, it is not a requirement that most ships have doctors onboard but it is for one this size. Captain Douglas hired me because I worked for him years ago, aboard one of his other ships. He made certain that the medical facilities here were an important part of the ship's design and had all of the equipment we needed, just like a small hospital."

"That's amazing," she responded. "It seems as though you are really living the life in this capacity. Where did you go to school?"

"I graduated from Xavier University School of Medicine in Louisiana. I knew I wanted to pursue a career in the health-care profession right out of high school after my father, who was an oncologist, died of the very cancer he studied. So, I started my first year at Xavier and took up biology pre-med. I know this is boring stuff."

"No, not at all," she said in reply. She continued to ask for more information. "Where did you receive your advanced degree?"

"I received my Ph.D. from UCLA in 1988 and my M.D. from Xavier back in 1991. I also spent my residency at UCLA Medical Center in Westwood."

Lexi stopped and leaned her head back as though she could not believe the coincidence. "That's where I work as a pediatric nurse."

"Really? I know all of those doctors over there. One of my best friends is Dr. Gary Williams, who heads up the functional neurosurgery unit."

"I've heard of him," she said. "Wow, you're big-time, Steven. I guess you never know who people are and where they come from until you take the time to find out."

"I guess not. Sounds like we have a lot in common, though," he claimed.

Lexi smiled. "So, I suppose you are much happier doing this."

"Yes. I can't tell you how much longer I will do it. But I do get a chance to have six weeks off in between, and the pay is pretty darn good. On day I'll settle down and decide where I want to live and set up practice there." He stared down the side of the boat as if losing his train of thought for a moment. "You know, it's amazing that you can't really see the water right alongside the ship, but you can smell it and hear it and feel it. It's kind of like life. It's all right there in front of you and you can miss it if you don't take the time to smell the coffee, as they say."

Lexi took a deep breath through her nose, taking in the aromatic, cleansing sensation, then prolonged the release through her mouth. "I see what you mean. And it's right next to you." She switched reels. "You've never been married?" she asked, as if the answer would help her put two and two together about this deep brother.

The two were silent for a moment, again looking out over the darkness. "I married my high-school sweetheart right out of college, but she stayed in Miami and the distance was just too much strain on our relationship. Plus I was so focused on school. That only lasted less than one year. And you?" he questioned in turn.

"Oh, no, I've never even been engaged. Yanni was engaged in high school but he broke it off after he went off to college. She was pretty devastated because she never heard from him again, just like that. We both agreed we'd get our professions going and then think about all of that."

The doctor asked, as if the answer didn't matter anyway, "Well, you're pretty young anyway, aren't you?"

"Pretty much. I'm twenty-eight," she said with directness.

"Wow, that is pretty young," he commented, suddenly realizing that her answer made him feel pretty old.

Doing the math, she said, "I take it if you got your B.A. sometime in the eighties then you're in your forties."

"Yes, Lexi, I'm in my forties. I'm old enough to be your dad," he stated, trying to put the age difference into real terms.

"Barely. I've dated men your age before," she admitted as though it was no biggie.

"I've never dated anyone your age," he informed her, admiring the innocent look on her attentive face.

The night was still young. With twilight in her eyes Lexi said, "I say we talk about it further tonight. Do you want to hang out?"

"I'd like that."

"You like this pussy, don't you?"

"Oh, yes. I like it all right," the captain admitted with a groan and a deep breath.

"What does it feel like?" asked Winter, the sound of lust rolling off her tongue.

The captain answered like he had no fear in putting the sensation into words. "It feels like a deep, wet, warm, tight cave for me to explore."

"And am I moving my hips well enough for you?" she asked as he lay on top of her, following her lead.

"Oh, yes, you are," he replied, not afraid of her aggressiveness.

"You know you don't want somebody just lying there like a dead fish, right?" she said as if he should appreciate her hard work.

"Oh, no. I wouldn't want that," he agreed.

Winter kissed the captain deep and slow like she had the ability to tongue kiss a piranha. Just when he started to get a rhythm going, she stopped. "And how about if I let you hit it from the back," she offered with a tease. "Would you like that?"

He cooperated, slowing down in preparation for the position switch. "Oh, yes, I'd like that."

"Well, not tonight. Tonight I'm going to give it to you just like this. I want you to feel my swollen lips envelop you until you release inside of that condom like a fire hose. So, I'm going to count to ten. And by ten, you're going to let it go for me, okay?" she asked as he resumed his stroke.

"Oh, no baby, I want you to get off first," he said as he focused on keeping up with her.

"Oh, I'll get off just fine by feeling you and hearing you and watching you get off. Now I'm going to count backwards, okay?" she asked again.

"Okay, baby," he acquiesced in ecstasy.

"Ten," Winter said with her sweaty back pressed upon her butter-cookie-colored satin sheets, pushing her hips toward him in a deep, repetitive jerking motion and then to the left and back upward. "Nine," she said, jerking again but to the right this time.

"Slow down, baby. Just take it slow," Captain Douglas said as if the momentum was too intense to last.

"Eight, seven, six," said Winter, ignoring his request and milking him with a provocative crescendo of thrust. "Five," she said as he moaned as if he was trying to fight it. "Four, three."

The captain felt her thrust grow in rapidity with a straight up and down momentum as he started to bury his face in her neck.

"Two," she began to push his chest upward with her right hand, going straight for his left nipple, sucking it as if it were the tip of an ice-cream cone.

She paused for a minute as he said in an intense swell, "See what you've done to me."

"And one," Winter yelled in an X-rated wave of loss of self-control. She suddenly released his nipple from her moist mouth as she too felt her flow rushing down from her head to her midpoint, and they expelled together in a rapturous trance of exhalation.

As the captain lay upon her slippery chest he felt himself panting in honor of his new freaky woman. He dabbed the sweat from his forehead, paused to give her that post-incredible-sex look and then raised his body upward. He lowered his hand to grip the base of the condom and pulled out from her wetness as he fell to his back.

"You are one bad woman," he confessed, resting for a moment to calm his racing heart before disposing of the love glove.

"And don't you forget it," she said as her long, lean frame sprang from the bed, cool, calm and collected as though she'd barely consumed any energy. She swung her pale yellow silk baby-doll robe around her, sliding her arms through and tying the belt at her tiny waist. "Yep, don't you forget it," she said as she made her way out onto the balcony, pouring a glass of water from her crystal decanter and lighting up a Benson and Hedges 100.

# WHAT A FEELING!

Mia and Miles had a joint morning shower ritual that they engaged in quite often, but not frequently enough as far as Mia was concerned. Miles always said if they were not getting along, they should just rip off their clothes and yell, "The last one in the shower is wrong!"

It's funny how Mia would usually let out a loud uncontrollable scream when it was about to happen . . . It was about to happen.

Mia pressed her hand flat against the ivory-and-sapphire oversized shower for fear that she would fall and break her groove and her neck. Her other hand was grasping the nape of Miles's head, which was embedded deep into her feminineness. She would usually tighten up her rear end muscles as she gradually built up momentum in response to the circular sucking motion that made her cherry quiver with fright and ecstasy at the same time. His tongue was licking and penetrating and flicking as fast as a butterfly's wings.

Years ago, Miles used to blow inside of her like he was blowing up a balloon. She often wondered who he'd been with before her that enjoyed that little trick. She often thought how he could have killed her. Now, however, all she could think about was his expertise.

This was his occasional good-morning hello for Mia. He was on his knees pleasing his woman while the soft penetrating spray of the sauna-like shower greeted the top of his curly head. They agreed that standing and receiving was such an intense, stimulating feeling of being given to. And Miles was usually the one doing the giving. Mia's thighs and calves were in on the pulsating muscle tightening while her blood flowed up and down from her toes to her booty like a stock exchange. "If a woman only expels one tenth the orgasmic force that men do, then damn you brothas are lucky," Mia said as Miles moaned in agreement.

"Ahh, ahh, ahhh, Miles, I'm cuming, it's, it's, ohh!" Her post-release deep breaths were like those of a parched pit bull panting from the heat of a hot summer day.

She reached down to help raise him to his feet and took his tongue into her mouth to taste herself. This kiss was an erotic gesture of full acceptance and appreciation.

"Your turn will come tonight as soon as you walk through that door, baby. I promise you that," she told him.

He knew what Mia meant because that was just the kind of shenanigan that bonded him to her in the first place, when he used to come over her apartment after they first started getting intimate. She would always greet him at the door on her knees with a blow job from heaven.

Miles stepped out of the shower and exited the bathroom, wiping his chest and stretching the extra-long bath towel back and forth along his back. "I suppose the ship has dropped anchor. Even though the movement is minor it seems like it's more of a side-to-side motion. Did you notice?"

Mia went into the bedroom and slipped into her white cotton undies. "I didn't notice much besides that quake in the shower."

"Very funny. Isn't this the day we're in Labadee?" he called, walking back into the bathroom.

"Yeah, baby. We are in Haiti out on Dragon's Point, I read. Apparently the beach will be set up with lounge chairs so we can lay out, jet ski, snorkel, or whatever else we want to do. I know Tangie mentioned a poetry reading and a dominoes tournament."

"Dominoes, now that's what I'm talking about," he said with jubilant gaiety.

"I know you're not going to blow me off for a dominoes tournament, are you? Pardon the pun," she said, continuing to get dressed. Mia threw on a short garnet wrap dress and raisin brown, tri-strap sandals.

"What the hell would I look like at a poetry reading?"

"Have you ever been to one? Obviously not, because you'd know that men like poetry too," she said to enlighten his horizons.

"Shoot, I'm getting back in the shower by myself. You made me forget what I got in there for in the first place," he replied, tossing his towel onto the sink and reentering the stall.

"Go ahead on and clean your dirty self. I'm going to check on Bianca and Corey anyway. I'll catch up with you later. Maybe we can hook up back here again to get ready for the luau," she suggested as she stood up from putting on her shoes.

"Now that's more my speed."

"Bye, Miles," Mia called out to the sound of the shower and her contented man humming "Here and Now" by Luther.

"That's always going to be our song," she commented under her breath as she stepped through the doorway. "Oh, excuse me," she said as she closed the door and bumped head-on into Megan, who looked like a roughed-up zombie. "Are you just getting in?"

"Don't ask," Megan said, cupping her hand over her mouth to shield her morning breath.

Mia could tell right away that somebody had rocked Megan's world but good. "You were with Dolomite, huh?" Mia teased.

With no response, a bloodshot Megan traipsed into her cabin, slamming the door behind her.

Mia stood still for a quick beat and then proceeded. "I know she's tired if she gave him oral sex. That would be what I call a blow JOB. And she was walking funny too," she said to an empty hallway.

* * *

"Bianca, are you two all right up in here?" Mia asked as Bianca opened the door half dressed in a carrot-colored, leotard-like swimsuit.

"We were just about to get up and get some food. Corey is going stir crazy."

"Hey, Auntie M," Corey said, looking as good as new.

"Hey, Corey. Are you the same kid I saw passed out yesterday?" Mia asked, almost wishing she hadn't decided to joke.

"Don't remind me," he said, still embarrassed.

Bianca looked at her like the comment was inappropriate. "Mia!"

Mia tried to correct herself. "Sorry. Corey, just make sure you don't underestimate the amount of energy you think you have. I think you should stay around the room for another day or so. The sun cannot be good for you."

"Dr. Taylor checked him out earlier. He's okay. He should be running around with all the other kids by tomorrow," Bianca told Mia as she tried on a few pair of shorts.

"All right. Mother knows best. Do you want to check out the poetry reading at eleven this morning?" Mia asked Bianca.

Bianca kept her focus upon deciding between the kiwi green or bright white cargo shorts. "No, I already read the advertisement. It must be X-rated, because they do not allow minors. I'm just going to take it easy with Corey. They even have an AMC movie theater on this puppy, maybe we'll check that out." She slipped into the pale green ones.

Corey sat on the couch playing a video game. "I don't want to watch a movie, Mom. I just want to be with the other kids. They'll think I'm a punk or something."

"Kids," she said, tying the drawstring of her shorts. "Corey, you'd better stop worrying about what people think and take care of yourself. You'll be more embarrassed if you get out there and faint or something. And make sure you have your inhaler." She slipped into her thongs.

"I'm not going to faint," Corey corrected her as if he was no weakling.

"Corey, sweetheart. I am not asking you. I am telling you that you will take it easy today and you're just going to have to deal with me. Like Mia said, don't take what happened too lightly. Now let's go and get something to eat," she said, grabbing her bag and then opening the door.

"Mom!" he said taking slow, heavy steps.

"Corey! Go!" Bianca said, pointing down the hall.

# A POET AND DON'T KNOW IT

A small section of the Chocolate Bar was set up like a lounge with just a microphone and a few dozen chairs. The bar was intimate and quaint with a large circular bar in the middle and tobacco-colored chairs all around. There was a tiny stage in the far corner, maybe seven feet by seven feet.

Captain Douglas approached Mia as she sat at a front-row table for four and asked, "Can I get you something to drink, Mia, is it?"

"Yes, please. Baileys on the rocks would be fine. Thanks, Captain."

"No problem," he said with a need-to-please smile.

"Hey, baby! I'll have cognac with a water back," Winter called out, taking fast-paced steps, bare heels slapping against the inside of her crimson high-heeled slides. She approached them with a fake smile directed Mia's way. Wearing a ladybug bikini top and sheer green short skirt, she ceased her pace as she reached Captain Douglas. Even though out of breath, she offered a less than casual peck on the lips. It was obvious that she had her hooks in him already.

"Sure, I'll be right back," he told her, breaking from their hug.

"Wow, I thought I'd be late," she said, sliding her small scarlet cloth Chanel bag under her chair without even asking if she could join Mia's table. "I was told the reading started at ten thirty."

"It is kind of early for poetry, huh? I've never been to a morning reading," Mia said, realizing that Winter smelled of Poison by Christian Dior. "When did you catch the big fish?"

"It happened last night while he was checking out some books in the bookstore. I was all sweaty from my aerobics class, but I had to check out his taste in reading. It turns out that we both like Christian fiction."

"Oh, really?" Mia asked.

"Shit, yeah! He was checking out the book called *Joy* by Victoria Christopher Murray and I was surprised. I told him I had the book in my cabin if he wanted to read it while I took a shower and then we could talk about it at the bar. Turns out he picked up his own copy but he came to my room anyway. We never made it to the bar. He didn't leave until this morning."

"Winter, you do not waste any time, do you?" Mia commented, as though it were a compliment.

"I had to snag this one early, girl."

"I guess so."

"Here you go, ladies," the captain said, placing their drinks on the round bar table and turning to proceed onto the stage.

"Thanks, Captain," Mia said just before he stepped away.

Winter swirled her cognac in the snifter as she watched him step away. "You can call him Jim, right Jim?"

"Yes, you can. I'll be right back," he said, rubbing Winter on her back.

"He's all right, but he's a little square. I like the bad-boy types. Where's that stud of yours? Miles, right?" Winter asked, as if she had a true need to know.

Mia answered, not oblivious to Winter's tone, "Yes, it's Miles. He's off doing whatever involves competition."

"That means he has an ego, I'll bet," she asked, sounding extra concerned.

"You guessed it," Mia said, taking a gigantic sip of Baileys to chase down her slight irritation.

"He is fine, girl. I'll be honest with you. He'd have women lined up if he were here alone."

"Well, he's not," Mia stated for the record.

"I hear you," Winter replied, applying more burnt sugar lipstick without a mirror, as if she'd memorized every curve and crevice of her luscious lips. She swigged her cognac like it was in a shot glass.

"The theme is love, folks," Captain Jim explained as he opened the show. "So, I hope you came with love-appropriate poetry. Believe it or not, I'll start off."

Mia asked Winter, "Did you know he was going to read?"

"No, I didn't," she said, trying to get the attention of the waitress for more cognac.

"This little poem is called *I Miss*," the captain said, feeling his comfort zone. "I wrote this at a point in my life—well, I'll just recite it from memory. I wrote it years ago and know it very well."

*I miss the sun's rays glistening off your soft smile,*
*I miss the moonlight's reflections from the passion-smoked depth of your eyes,*
*I miss the night stars dancing to the undulating concert of your giving,*
*I miss lightning's flash of penetration, and the acceptance,*
*I miss soft moans of your longing as rhythm and flow marks our union,*
*I miss rising moans crowned and awaiting my lips,*
*I miss knowing your sweetness in the night,*
*I miss your touch, the fragrance of your being, your woman's essence,*
*I miss our intimacy and the depth to which it searches, it needs,*
*I miss the euphoria of our passion's crest, its crescendo and culmination,*
*I miss the contentment of our completion. Your warmth holding me and mine you,*

*I miss the reality, and the anticipation of its renewing,*
*I miss the tenderness of being close searched out by me and made it we,*
*I miss your caress. Your kiss verified my life when doubt shadowed my knowing,*
*I miss not being able to say I love you. But then I was never good at it,*
*I just hoped you knew.*

"Oh, please! Who whipped him?" replied a condescending Winter. The crowd of poetry aficionados began to applaud.

"Ahh, that sho' was sweet," teased a hidden Brandon who had been sitting at a corner of the bar. He was seated with Nona Fox, the ivory portion of the Ebony and Ivory group.

The captain responded to the appreciation. "Thanks. And now you are all welcomed to come up and read. And let's be sure to show the readers our love. This is not an easy thing to do."

A lady in a pink sundress, maybe in her mid-thirties, slightly heavyset with her hair in a stiff, post-black-woman's-been-swimming ponytail, took the stage.

She said in an extra-girly voice, "Thanks, Captain. Hey, everybody. I didn't know we'd be having a poetry reading, so this is a nice surprise. I write poetry as a hobby, usually about the one thing I know about most, men."

One woman in the audience said, "I heard that!"

The reader went on, "I just happened to have my little journal with me, so I'd like to share one with you. It's called *All There Is.*" She opened a tiny notebook with a sunburst yellow-and-blue laminated cover.

*Love is giving all that you are freely,*
*All there is to share without reservation,*
*All your dreams, your hopes, your ideas,*
*All your strength, all your weakness and tenderness,*
*Your happy tears, your sad laughter,*

*Your sense of humor and profound seriousness,*
*Your thoughtful intentions, deliberations, impulsive flings,*
*All your fiery lust, sweet sensuality and consuming passion!*
*All the seed that is your essence that recreates you when united,*
*All that makes you vulnerable to love allows you the same,*
*All your anger, and too, your forgiveness,*
*All your calm in the storm of outrage,*
*All your insight in the face of uncertainty,*
*All your wisdom in the midst of confusion,*
*All your indignation, tempered with mercy,*
*All your pride softened by reason,*
*All your pain, and too, your joy,*
*All your trusts and doubts,*
*All your can-bes, and maybes,*
*All that was you and is you,*
*All that you were not,*
*All that you will be,*
*All the you that is you,*
*And the moods that make you someone else,*
*All that you imagine you are,*
*All that is real, and hopes to be,*
*All there is to give,*
*All there is to share,*
*All the love in you,*
*And finding a way to give more.*

Brandon yelled out again. "I guess all us brothers should take note, huh?"

"It couldn't hurt," blurted the lady in pink as she closed her journal and returned to her seat.

In spite of Brandon's condescending remark, the audience showed its admiration for her warmth and talent with intense applause.

As the praise faded to a hush, a handsome man made his way to the microphone with a multi-folded piece of clean white notebook paper in one hand. He took the microphone with the other.

"Hey, everyone. I'm Omar and I wrote this poem last year. It's the only poem I've ever written. I've just kept it in my wallet and thought I'd share it with all of you tonight. There are no children in here, right?" He set his sights on the faces in the room, looking around past the first row, blocking the spotlight from his eyes with a saluting hand, making sure the crowd was of legal age.

Winter commented with peaked interest, "That's the hero for the day who saved that boy."

"Uh-huh. That's him," Mia replied.

Omar carefully unfolded the paper, almost as if he were taking enough time to spark a second thought. With apparent reservation, his hands shook slightly. After looking around again and hesitating for a moment, he composed himself, cleared his throat, looked down and began to read.

**One Last Tear, One Last Kiss**

*Clouded vision, heartbeat crying I watched,*
*Her memory strong in my body, my sense of loss,*
*Her face captured in the eternity of my soul,*
*It lived beyond the years of my imagination.*

*The whisper of her kiss still teases me,*
*Then I taste the salt of my own tears. I miss her,*
*The one we were. Should have stayed. Is no more,*
*I let her go without a fight. With what could I fight?*

*How could I explain a betrayal unintended. Yet was.*
*Could she forgive? Would she forgive?*
*I wanted to forget what no longer was,*
*The reflection of her in my mind would not fade.*

*I could not get enough of her. Loved even her shadow.*

"Damn, that's deep," said a perky Winter along with the sound of muffled moans in the room. Several women shifted their glances to one another, offering affirmative headshakes like they might want to garner a consensus to devour him on the spot.

*I held her close. We fit together our bodies matched,*
*Height, length, points of pleasure touch, as they should,*
*I tasted all of her. Drank of her essence, and she mine,*
*Yet my thirst was not quenched. I needed more,*
*The drive too strong and I yielded and she was appeased.*

*The wine of her intoxicated me,*
*Succulent southern lips flavored with honey future,*

"Hey," a lady in the back remarked.

*The wings of the butterfly tempted their moistness,*

"Hey, hey, hey!" she remarked again.

*Captured the treasure crowning their entrance,*
*She creamed de la crème, and screamed.*

"Ooooh, girl," someone yelled.

*A rumbling wave from the depth of my beast raced its length,*

"Did he say its length?" Mia whispered to Winter.

"He did indeed," Winter replied, raising her hand as a stop sign to tell Mia not to interrupt again.

*Spewed forth silken syrup exploding within her lusting darkness,*
*Her moans, throaty, uncontrolled . . . complete. Filled us.*

*Muscular waves caress the beast within her enveloped him in*
*that cream of creams. It mingled with my syrup,*
*There is sweetness. We are one.*
*Our bodies fit well together.*

*I was without will, save the craving for more,*
*The need for her was without reason,*
*But we are no more,*
*My heart moans in silence.*

*I miss her so much screams dare tempt my lips,*
*But I am a man, so silent torment shakes the core of me,*
*I mask the anguish of my pain. My loss too deep to measure,*
*My eyes open to a dream and no love.*

*What do you do with a dream and no one to share it with,*
*Yet the dream is all there is.*
*So I slipped back inside her,*
*For One Last Kiss, I cried One Last Tear.*

Silence greeted his last word. With a quick smile he said, "Thank you."

# STICK TO COMEDY, PLEASE

The lady in pink who read the previous poem stood and clapped with two-second intervals in between. Her friend stood up, and the lady next to her, the lady behind her, the lady in front of her, the lady to the left of her, and finally, the lady in the back started to applaud with eardrum-piercing intensity. Mia leaped to her feet along with every woman, standing and applauding in celebration of the possibility that there could be a man on this earth with such sensitivity, eroticism and emotion. Hesitating for a moment, Winter stood up and gave Omar a piercing, two-finger, sailor's whistle, chorusing in conjunction with cheers from every woman in the room.

"I love even your shadow, baby," one woman yelled out, as if she'd memorized every word.

"That's a wet-panty poem there!" Winter roared, even though Jim was within earshot. He stood and clapped briefly and made his way to the stage, all the while gazing at Winter in disbelief.

"Well, brother Omar. That was well written and well read. Thanks," the captain said.

Omar had already headed out the door, nodding his head in gratitude as he made his way down the hallway.

"Hold up everyone, before you chase that brother back to his room! We're not done yet," Brandon exclaimed, walking to the stage and taking the mic into his hand. "I've written an example of the true essence of poetry. What's up with all of you brothas trying to get sensitive on us dudes? Are poems used to get coochie credit, or what? Especially you, Cap. I've got a poem for your ass, literally. I memorized this one too, Captain." Captain Jim reservedly stood off to the side.

Brandon said, "I wrote this poem called *Joy*. Like to hear it? Here it goes."

*I met this girl named Joy. She promised me no pain,*
*Her quote was she'd bring me sunshine, no rain,*
*I bought her dinner and took her to a show,*
*She returned the gesture with a kiss and straight showed me to the do',*
*I said baby I thought your name was Joy. Won't you show me some?*
*She said just have patience baby boy, and one day you'll get to cum,*
*Oh Joy my love, it's been three months, surely you can show me yours,*
*I don't want to see no one else little lady, see I don't love them ho's, I mean whores,*
*Okay Brandon, she said I'll let you see it but you can't touch it—you promise?*
*I said Joy, you would being me if you'd do that and grant me one small wish,*
*Once I see it, can I stick it in? I'd just like to see if it fits,*
*Maybe if you watch me masturbate first and show control I'll let you suck my tits,*
*Well then hey little girl, let's get it on, I'm ready for any part of you,*
*Okay now if you stick it in now Brandon, I'm telling you we're through,*

*She pulled down her panties and laid on her back and her legs she started to spread,*
*I'll be dog-goned if instead of a coochie, Joy had a clit like a head instead,*
*I said I can't see your snatch your clit is so massive how do I get to the hole,*
*She said reach behind my clit and a little further back you'll see a hole once an exit right next to a mole,*
*Oh hell, that's a dick that ain't no clit, girl you know I am scared of you,*
*She said don't be afraid, I'll stick you too now baby, it'll just be a rear view,*
*Oh Joy, you're my pain, no sunshine, no rain, how did I ever let you fool me this way,*
*She replied since you're playing it off and stroking your thing, could it be maybe you're gay?*

"Now that's a poem, ladies," he said as if to tell them something they needed to know.

The ladies waved him off and stood up to gather their purses, even though they appeared amused enough to give a chuckle or two, either laughing with him or at him.

"That was crass. Where did Omar run off to?" said Winter, who made a mad dash toward the door.

"Come on, man, play and stop talking," Scott said, taking a long drag on a cigarette.

"I'm not talking to you, I'm talking to myself," Miles replied.

"That's some crazy-ass shit. You take too long. I could have jacked off waiting for you," Scott said.

"I'm sure you could do that by the time I blink, with *your* quick-draw behind."

Scott tried to clarify Miles's statement. "You don't know me. I gets mine and I gives too."

Miles joked again, "Yeah, but not when it's just you and your own hand. I'm sure you get right to the point."

"Shoot, my hand is my best friend. Who else is going to let me hit it from the back without talking shit? Surely not Kelly," Scott remarked, taking another puff.

"Hey, Mr. Miles. How are you?" Winter said, pleasantly surprised, almost passing him by but coming to a halt upon seeing him.

"I'm all right," he replied without giving her any eye action.

"I see that. Are you winning?" she asked, pulling out a chair next to Scott.

"So far, yes," Miles answered, forcing himself to concentrate.

She offered her hand to Scott as she sat down. "My name is Winter."

Scott dropped his dominoes from his right hand and shook her hand with a boyish grin. "We met in the Freedom Café the first morning. I remember you."

"Well, I can't stay. I'm going to get back to the poetry reading. You know your girl is in there shooting the breeze with the captain. I'll tell her I saw you," said Winter, trying to cause concern where none was due. She parted her sunkissed legs while rolling her feet to the side, pointing her knees outward. Miles's eyes were immediately drawn to her never-ending, toned, brown-sugar thighs. Scott, who sat across from Miles, looked at him and followed the direction of his visual interlude. He dropped his jaw at the thought of the view that Miles must have had. Winter's very bare, clean-shaven vagina was the color of a Sugar Daddy and it was staring Miles square in his scarlet-blushed face.

Winter supposed that his eyeball feast had lasted long enough, so she leaned back for a second before leaning forward and pressing her body to a standing position.

"I'll see you later," she said, patting Miles on the back of his sweat-beaded neck.

He said nothing.

As she sashayed away, again Miles stared at her as if forever traumatized by his discovery.

"Man, did she just pull a Sharon Stone on you or what?" Scott asked with envy.

"I think so," Miles replied, trying to snap out of it. "I could have sworn that thing winked at me. It was as bare as a peach, man. She's purposely walking around without bikini bottoms. That's a real freak, there."

"Yeah, and if that wasn't a personal invitation to tap that ass, I don't know what would be. Damn, I'd've paid to see that," Scott said, taking the last hit from his cigarette and smashing it into his empty glass. "I'll bet that tastes like a Cinnabon."

"Oh, she's just tripping because I'm not available, that's all. Women always want what they can't have," Miles said as if he had the situation peeped.

Scott replied, "She can't have you, huh? If she told you to meet her in her room tonight at midnight and you knew Mia wouldn't find out and she opened the door butt naked, you wouldn't hit it?"

"No, first of all I wouldn't show up," Miles said.

"Okay, what if Mia wasn't here?"

"If Mia wasn't here would I go for it? Good question. I'd be tempted," Miles remarked, again focusing on his dominoes.

"Why are you frontin', man? Dude, I can read you like Helen Keller reads braille. You know you'd be flexing the latex all up in there."

"Scott, can we concentrate on this tournament? I'll bet the other team hired her to distract your butt and now we're all tripped up. Play."

"You are one lying Negro," Scott remarked, not buying Miles's innocent act.

"That was a great idea, Jim. I had no idea there was so much talent on this ship," said Mia.

"I didn't either," he replied, looking over toward Brandon, who was departing with the lady in pink and her friend.

"I don't mean to pry, but what's up with you and the reporter?" Mia asked.

"You don't mean to pry? Well, you are," he replied with a warm smile.

Mia attempted to clarify the reason for her inquiry. "Okay. I guess I do mean to. I think you really like her. I apologize."

"She's an elegant, energetic lady. Yes, I like her," he said plainly.

"I'm not sure that she's as focused as you are, but you're old enough to know if your interests are requited or not."

"Yes, I am, Mia. Thanks for your concern. On a different subject, are you coming onto the beach for this luau we've been planning?" the captain asked, searching for a different topic.

Mia understood. "I wouldn't miss it."

"I'll see you there. I've got to get going to check on things. I'm glad you enjoyed yourself. Poetry is an acquired taste, so I thank you for coming and supporting."

"It was interesting. I'll see you later, Jim," she said as they started to walk away in different directions.

Winter returned to the bar. "There you are, baby. I'm ready to go shopping now," Winter purred suggestively. "Oh, did I interrupt?"

"No, I was just leaving," Mia replied.

Captain Jim responded to Winter, "Baby, I have to check with Tangie to make sure everything is in order."

"Oh, let's just run over to the shops first. Come on, Boopie," she said with a persuasive wave of feminine charm.

"Good-bye," Mia said, holding her departing glance just long enough to hopefully hear the anticipated henpecked response.

"Good-bye, Mia," he said with a wry grin. Mia got a last-minute glimpse before turning the corner and exiting the bar. She saw Winter jumping up and down through her giddy hug. She'd gotten her way.

# THREE'S A CROWD

The luau started at three in the afternoon on the beach in Labadee. There was no sign of Miles, so Mia threw on a snow white brushed-suede bikini and a zebra-print wrap skirt and made her way to the boat for a ride to the island.

When Mia arrived, she saw Lexi and Yanni. Lexi was joined at the hip with Steven again.

"Hey, Mia," Lexi said. They were standing near a row of large, royal-blue-and-white-striped lounge chairs and matching beach umbrellas, lined up to protect everybody from the powerful rays of the tropical sun. The island had one of the premiere beaches in Haiti.

"This island is beautiful," Lexi remarked, looking all around.

Steven replied, "Yes, I hear this is where Dr. Martin Luther King, Jr., wrote his acceptance speech for his Nobel Peace Prize."

"He's so smart," Lexi said while holding on to his arm.

The scenic, secluded island had a very laid-back atmosphere, with its blue waters crashing along the rocks. There was not a cloud in sight.

Out in the vast tepid waters there were paddleboats, sailboats, banana boats and swimmers galore. On the shore there were people playing volleyball and dancers performing traditional songs and dances as they did over two hundred years ago. And just inland a way were the shoppers making sure they came away with some Haitian art or a souvenir from the Dominican Republic.

"Lexi, I have to get going, but I'll catch up with you later if that's all right with you," Steven said just as Lexi was about to pick her favorite spot.

She answered, "That's a great idea. I'll see you later." They embraced with a friendly hug.

"Good-bye, ladies," he said to Mia and Yanni.

"Good-bye, Doctor," said Yanni, looking down with a pouted lip as she placed her beach bag next to the second chair in the row.

"Hey, you," Mia greeted Yanni with anticipated excitement.

"Why the long chin, Yanni?" Lexi asked as she and Mia took a chair on either side of her.

"Bo and Deshaun tried to pull a train on me last night," Yanni said with shame.

"What? Why didn't you tell me?" asked Lexi with anger and concern.

"I would have if you'd come home last night," Yanni replied with a blank look.

"I was with Steven," Lexi took a second to say.

Yanni's response was, "Uh-huh."

"And nothing happened. We fell asleep on top of the covers. Forget about that. What happened to you?" Lexi questioned her sister.

Yanni started to explain. "Bo and I were hanging out on deck after the dance and then we went to the Stingray Bar on the main deck. We drank Long Island Iced Teas until maybe four in the morning. He was charming, funny and smart and he looked so damn good, I just remember watching his dark lips move with every word he spoke. Before I knew it, those dark lips were in between my legs, right there at the bar. I thought I was dreaming. My head was spinning and spinning and that, mixed with the suddenly annoying sway of the boat made me sick to my stomach. I remember Deshaun stretched out on a lounge chair across from us, just watching. I don't even remember a bartender or any other passengers. Before I knew it, I was in my room sitting on the couch, with Bo, once again, eating me out."

She continued, rubbing her forehead and taking a deep breath, "He started to lay me back and spread my legs and then I felt him put his raw thing inside of me, no condom or nothing. And then, Deshaun comes over to the side of the couch, pushing my head toward his little pecker, which was peaking through the slit in his shorts like he wanted me to suck him off while Bo did me. I got up and ran to the bathroom and threw up to the smell of vodka for what seemed like hours. When I woke up I was on the bathroom floor, naked from the waist down. By then, it was almost eleven this morning. I haven't even seen their asses since then. They just left me in there."

Lexi said in shock, "Girl, they could have given you a date-rape drug. And, that fool Bo could be HIV for all we know."

"I take the blame for drinking myself into a fog. I had enough to wipe me out even without being drugged," Yanni admitted.

"Lexi, when did you get back to your room?" Mia asked.

"I haven't been back. I packed my overnight bag before midnight," Lexi told Yanni. "And I left you a message on the phone."

"I didn't check a thing. I've been at Starbucks for the last three hours," Yanni said, dragging her words.

"Dang, man. I mean you hear about this stuff happening, but you never think it will actually happen to you," said Lexi.

"We've got to report them, Yanni," Mia suggested.

"Yeah. And I'm telling Steven," Lexi said.

Yanni begged in a low-pitched tone, "No, don't do that. I put myself in that situation. I don't want anyone else to know, especially Daddy. Oh, my God, Daddy would trip out!"

"Yanni, do you think you got raped, or are you blaming yourself?" Lexi asked.

"I think I contributed to a freaky scene that they thought I was down for."

Mia remarked with deep concern, "If they cared they wouldn't have left. And if they thought you were down for a threesome, why did they have to sneak Deshaun in on the side?"

"He didn't get any. I'm cool. I just want to forget about it," Yanni said, lying back on her chair.

Mia continued, "Oh, heck no, Yanni. They need their asses kicked. What if they try it with someone else? You have to say something."

Yanni disagreed. "And what is the cruise line going to do? Lock them in their rooms? They'll just deny it. There are two of them and it's my word against theirs."

"Hey, ladies, what's up with the huddle?" asked Miles, wearing his long, baggy, camouflage drawstring trunks. "You're hanging over the side of your chair trying to get deep into that conversation," he said to Mia.

"There you are, baby. How'd your tournament go?" Mia asked Miles, trying to calm down.

"Scott and I came in second," Miles said.

"Hi, Miles," said Lexi.

"What's wrong? Since when does Yanni look like that?" he asked as he prepared to lie down next to Mia.

Up walked Olandi and Megan, who was wearing a sheer sarong that was the color of her skin and made her look naked underneath. "I smell a party brewing," said Megan. "Has everyone met Olandi?"

"Oh, my God!" Yanni said, looking straight on at Olandi's private parts.

"Don't say it," Mia mouthed to her, placing her finger to her lips.

"We'll be over there," Megan said, pointing to the bar and walking away, hugging her catch.

"I swear there are some queer brothas on this cruise. Why does everything have to be so damn tight on grown-ass men?" Miles mumbled under his breath. "I'm ready for some fun."

Lexi said, "Well, Steven has to work, but I think between the four of us, we should be able to have some fun this afternoon. Aren't we going to roast some pig or something and do the limbo?"

"I think so," said Yanni reservedly.

"Then come on. Last one to the bar is a rotten egg," said Mia.

"Don't say bar," said Yanni. "I'll just wait here. I'm going to die if I drink any more alcohol."

Mia offered, "Then come with Miles and me to the shopping area. Maybe picking up a couple of trinkets will make you feel better."

"No, I don't think so. I just need to chill," Yanni stated, closing her eyes.

"We'll be right back, you two," Mia said, walking away with Miles.

Miles asked, "What happened to her?"

Mia and Miles approached a solo Kelly, wearing a grape one-piece, sprawled out on a red, flamingo-print beach towel along the shore.

"Hey, girl. What are you doing all by yourself? We're going shopping. Do you want to come?" Mia offered.

Kelly said, "No thanks, I'm just catching up on some reading and getting some sun, as if I really need some. I'm sure my sepia skin agrees."

"Are you sure?" Miles seconded the offer.

She still refused. "I'm sure, she said, holding up her book. I've been trying to read *Casting the First Stone* by Kimberla Lawson Roby for the past year. Now I can finally get to it. Just me, my book and my water bottle."

"We'll be back soon to check on you, okay?" Mia said.

"All right, but I'm fine, really. Have fun, you two," Kelly said, adjusting her chair back.

"Kelly, I'm sure Scott will be over here soon. We just got through playing dominoes, so he's on his way," said Miles.

"It's cool. He's always playing something. I don't even trip, so don't you trip," she said, opening her novel to the bookmarked page.

"See you in a minute," Miles said, realizing he should wave the white flag and give up the concerned-friend routine.

As they walked away to continue their conversation, Mia said, "Kelly can take care of herself. So, Yanni had a damn train run on her last night."

"And she's complaining," he said.

"It was without her consent," Mia said with a hint of annoyance.

Miles commented, "Yanni didn't give her consent? Mia, that would not have been a first for her, or for Lexi for that matter."

"Miles, did you hear me? She didn't give her consent," Mia said again for explicitness.

"I understand, I'm not trying to be insensitive, Mia. I just know these things happen on a ship."

"Well, it shouldn't happen anywhere. I don't want it to happen again to someone else."

"Who was it?" he asked.

"Those two guys from last night, you know, the football players."

"Those guys are in the league. That's a big risk for them," Miles admitted.

Mia slowed down and said, "Yeah, and?"

"And—I can't believe they would be that stupid," Miles replied.

"Is this a guy thing? I can't believe they would think *she* was that stupid," Mia said, resuming her pace as they walked.

"Was she drinking?" he asked.

Mia slowed down again. "Okay, now I refuse to talk about this with you," she said as she turned to him.

"You have to think about these things because, unfortunately, that's how the system will examine it," he said, trying to sound sensible.

"I'm not going to put any more thought into it until Lexi and Yanni decide to report it. Let's not ruin our day, because I can feel myself getting irritated," she walked ahead of Miles.

Miles joked, trying to pull her in, "Oh, you just need a morning shower."

"If I don't kill you before then," she said as she exhaled.

Miles hugged Mia only to receive a less than willing, stiff return. Mia eventually put her arm around his waist as they approached the shopping area.

# HOW MUCH FOR THAT?

The merchants on the island of San Juan were locals who made a living selling their wares. They were lined up with dollar signs in their eyes, hoping to sell their ceramics, leather goods, glassware, tons of jewelry, knickknacks, artwork and clothing. Each individual hut had a grass roof and counters made of redwood.

Miles decided to run down his bargaining strategy ahead of time. “Okay, here’s the trick. Never pay full price. Just offer half, and then walk away. They’ll call you back,” he told Mia as if he were an expert.

“Okay. Never pay full price. Now that’s a new one,” Mia said facetiously.

Miles had his eye on a pair of designer sunglasses. He picked them up and examined them carefully, checking for a brand name. “If these are Nike, my name is Tom Cruise.”

Mia managed a chuckle and moved on to another table. “Oh, look, baby. These puka shells are nice. Let’s buy matching ones for our ankles,” Mia suggested.

Miles reacted, “Ankles? I might wear it around my neck, but I’ll be damned if I’ll wear an anklet.”

"Why are you so homophobic? Everything has to be an indication of femininity to you," she claimed.

"Mia, don't start with me. Go ahead and buy the damn things. How much?" he asked the older lady with the dark green turban.

"Ten doulla' each," she replied with a raw Haitian accent.

"How about two for ten?" Miles negotiated.

"No, two for eight-tan," she countered, fully understanding his English.

"Two dollars off. Forget it," Miles said as he walked away.

"Two for twelve," Mia said to her.

"Two for fif-tan," the lady replied.

Mia walked away with Miles.

The lady called to her, "Okay, two for twalf."

"Two for ten," Miles shouted on Mia's behalf.

"No, man, two for twalf," the woman said.

Mia agreed, "Okay, I'll take them."

Miles shook his head and said, "Oh, woman, please. You bargained her into a low that was two dollars higher than mine."

"Miles, can we just buy the necklaces?" Mia asked with a long breath.

He snatched the ten from his wallet. "You pay the other two," he said, holding out the ten while Mia grabbed it.

Winter and the captain walked by as if they were suddenly deaf and blind. Winter's smirk said it all.

Mia pulled two dollars from her waist pouch and paid the lady.

"Thank you," Mia said to the woman, who nodded while looking down to count the money.

Mia turned to Miles and asked, "Miles, what's up with you?"

"What is up with you?" he replied, looking at the three-for-ten T-shirts.

"All of that over two dollars?"

"It was the principle of the thing. I told you what the deal was, but you've always got to be in control."

"You know what? I'm going to hang out with the twins. I'll see you later," Mia said.

Miles replied as Mia took a step, "Good, maybe I can buy these shades without you looking out for their profit instead of mine."

"Good-bye, sweetheart," Mia said sarcastically as she walked away.

After a second thought, Mia casually walked back to him, all the while looking down in her bag.

"By the way, here's your necklace." She opened the clasp and placed it around his neck, closing the clasp while her arms encircled his neck. "I love you."

"I love you, too. Thanks," he said.

"You look good in those," Mia commented.

He took a peak at himself in a small, round standing mirror on one of the counters. "I look like a light-skinned Taye Diggs."

# HOW LOW CAN YOU GO?

The luau was as authentic as it gets. The cruise line handed out brown-and-yellow leis and grass skirts, and the female waitresses passed out blue curaçao margaritas by the tons and offered icy pineapple treats of blended fresh fruit cups. Captain Jim was running around, much too busy to keep an eye on Winter, which was cool because she was working as well. Winter and Justin were doing a story for her final piece on Delmonte Harrison, which included the luau portion of the cruise.

"Justin, do you want to stay away from the bar long enough to get behind that camera," Winter rudely interrupted, as Justin leaned over the bar to talk to Dante. Megan and Olandi lovingly played with each other at the end of the bar.

"I'll see you later," said Justin with a wink meant for Dante.

"Okay. Don't work too hard," Dante said, winking back.

Justin ran away with Winter, kicking sand behind him with every hurried stride.

"Hey, Dante," said Mia.

"Hey, girl. I wonder how he deals with that wicked witch," Dante said, watching the two get back to work.

"I suppose it's a job," Mia replied.

"Where's that guy of yours?"

Mia looked over at the merchant's area. "He's shopping. He'll be right back."

"Is he always uptight?"

"No, not all the time. How do you know if he's uptight? You've only seen him once," she stated, thinking he had some nerve.

"No, I've seen him around more than once, but he was rude enough the first time as it was."

Mia tried to clear up what she thought was Dante's unwarranted image of her man. "First of all, Dante, you were a little bold with your comments the first time we met you."

"Do you always make excuses for his behavior?"

"No. And I'm not doing that now," she said.

"So let's change the subject. What can I get you?"

"Nothing. I'll just go get one of those blue curaçao deals over there," Mia answered with a frustrated edge.

"Okay. Are you all right?" Dante asked, wanting her to not take his observation the wrong way.

Mia got up to walk toward Miles, who was coming back to the beach area. "Yes, Dante, I'm fine."

Mia and Miles found a small table near the luau pit where a massive pig was being roasted with sweet juices made from honey and hickory maple spices. The aroma was smoky and fruity all at once. The captain sliced generous portions of roast pig as everyone lined up along the twenty-foot-long buffet table in the sand, making sure to get the sides of roasted teriyaki beef steak, rum baked beans, sweet and sour chicken, greens with tomatoes, salmon macaroni salad, coconut chocolate cake and banana bread, while Justin videotaped the happenings.

Yanni was still lounging with Lexi. Steven joined them and it looked as though the three of them were clowning around. Winter actually took time out from working to chum it up with, of all people, Omar. But Omar walked away, totally uninterested, to take a seat at the bar. Before long, another woman walked up and sat down next to him. Omar was suddenly very popular. Mia watched, thinking she could not wait to give Bianca the rundown on his hot poetic skills. Within two seconds, the woman walked away, shoulders slumped and head hung low.

"What's up with you, man?" Dante asked Omar.

"Not much. I've just got a lot on my mind," Omar said.

"Join the club. Can I get you anything?"

"Just a stiff shot of Hennessey. Make it a double."

"You've got it," Dante said, breaking the seal on a new bottle. "If I could join you I would," said Dante. "Aren't you traveling with a couple of kids?"

"Yes, my son and daughter. They're with the other kids, having a ball, enjoying their carefree lives."

"And you? Aren't you having a ball?" asked Dante.

"Man, I'm just wondering how and why things happen the way they do. One day you're doing something that you enjoy and life is good. The next day everything just blows up in your face and all hell breaks loose."

"I take it this is about a woman?"

Omar replied, "My kids' mother and me. We definitely do not belong together, man. So I guess that's cool."

Dante placed Omar's drink on the rattan bar in front of him. "Coming to that understanding is half the battle," he said.

"But coming to terms with the fact that your life is changing as far as raising your kids with that person is rough. And understanding it is inevitable that each of you will move on with other people is also a little difficult," Omar admitted.

"I'm sure it takes time. Especially when that someone was your other half for so long. You need time to disconnect and fall out of love and de-bond from that person," Dante said, sounding like an advice columnist.

Picking up his shot glass, Omar asked, "My question is, why do we make such dumb-ass decisions in the meantime?"

"It's called emotions. Sometimes they get the best of us."

"I guess so. Emotions are a trip. All rationale just gets overshadowed by emotion."

"So has she moved on?" Dante asked.

"Oh, yes. She'd moved on long before I knew she did."

"When are you going to move on?"

"I already have. I think," Omar said, leaning his head back to gulp down his double swallow of hard liquor.

"You think?"

Omar slammed down the empty glass and responded as if he had swigged water. "Yes, I'm headed in a totally different direction and I refuse to look back. Full speed ahead, right bartender?" he asked. "I'll have another."

Dante again grabbed the Hennessey and poured. "Full speed ahead. There's no better place to be to get your mind off of things than on a cruise vacation, that's for sure."

"I agree with you on that one," he said, raising his glass.

"Check out what's going on over there," Dante said, keeping an eye on what was happening behind Omar.

They both turned and perused the beach area, with its rows of never-ending umbrellas, island drummers playing, the sun shining in all of its glory, dark, oiled bodies lounging, the smell of BBQ pits smoking, volleyball games, people snorkeling, dancing, hugging and having fun, fun, fun all around them.

"Now that's where you should be. Having the time of your life and picking out one of those honeys," Dante advised as Omar leaned back against the bar, basking in the postcard-like scenery.

"It's time for the colorful native limbo dance, or the *under the stick* dance as it's called. If you're not game, get the hell off the island. How low can you go?" asked the captain, snapping his fingers to the beat. "Are you game?"

The trio of bongo players continued to pound a beat that made the passengers want to strut their stuff and shake their asses and show off what they were working with. Especially after the island drinks kicked in to lower their inhibitions.

Winter the extrovert was the first to exchange her wrap skirt for a grass skirt. The waitresses wore long grass skirts, bra cups that looked like coconut shells, red circular hats, and white and blue leis. Suddenly they took on the role of dancers, and began to instruct each lucky person who moved down the line. The crowd was growing, leaving behind whatever it was they were into and running over as they heard the music. Winter now had a crowd around her and she was working it but good.

"Oooh, I'm about to go down now," she yelled, taking her lei from around her neck and swinging it in wild, reckless circles in the air. She leaned back and hopped her way under the pole, looking over at Big Mack, who had walked up with Brandon. "Don't you want to go down with me? Come over here and get to this!"

"I'm right here, baby," Big Mack yelled, cheering her on.

He stood in front of her and prompted her to him. "Scoot it on through," he said. He abruptly plopped down to his knees onto the sand and leaned back with his tongue hanging out of his mouth, ten inches from her pubic bone.

Winter parted her grass skirt so that he could get a better view of her blueberry colored bikini bottom, leaned back farther and screamed in exhilaration, "Here I come, baby!"

She made her way under the stick and slowly stood up with Big Mack still on his knees in front of her, shaking his shoulders in yearning of more teasing. She turned around and shook her ass in his face, strutting away to the beat of the drums.

Brandon leaned in to Big Mack, offering to help him up while grabbing him under his arm. "Get up, man. You've been played."

Big Mack looked around, brushing the sand off his knees and dancing to the beat to play it off.

Before long, Megan shook her hot hips and bent backward, barely making it under the bamboo stick. She was followed by the wonderful Olandi, who only had to follow his head to make his way under. Oops, his head hit the pole. That had to have hurt.

Mia ran over to grab an unwilling Kelly and said, "I'm not hearing no, girl. Come on."

"Okay, Mia, I'll do it. Don't like yank my arm off," Kelly said, tossing her book onto the blanket.

Mia replied, now grabbing even harder, "Get your lazy butt over here."

It was quickly discovered that Kelly had a little freak in her. Girlfriend was acting like this was a strip contest.

"I don't need a skirt," she yelled to the waitress who held one out for her. And, obviously, she didn't need any lessons either.

"Dang. Work that body," said Big Mack. Even Olandi was checking her out as if he wanted to know where she'd been hiding, while Megan gave Kelly the evil eye.

She got as low down as everyone else, damn near breaking her back. Her vagina almost scraped the pole and her head was bent back even lower than her waist. Her dreads were dragging in the sand as she hung her head backward, still with room to spare. And she still kept going long after she cleared the pole.

"Kelly, you can come up for air now," Mia yelled over the bongos.

Kelly stood up, bouncing and laughing, and then proceeded to get back in line. Suddenly Scott appeared and took his place behind her as if he'd seen all of this before. She turned around to hug him, yelling and laughing as if he'd been there the entire time.

Mia and Miles barely made their way under. Mia leaned back and scooted her way under with a hopping motion. Miles was on her tail. Their bodies were curved backward in synchronization but Miles cheated by ducking his head under, coming to a quick stance.

"My back is killing me," Mia said, rubbing her butt as she stepped away from the pole. "I think they lowered it on us."

"That's not even as low as it gets," said one of the waitresses.

"Then I'll just watch from here," Mia told her, taking careful steps back to their seats.

Miles decided to throw his body down on the sand and Mia

joined him, sitting between his legs. They laughed as Lexi and Steven tried to make their way under together, both falling down on their butts.

"It's obvious that you won first prize in the *Chocolate Ship*'s first-ever limbo contest," the captain said to Kelly, handing her a brass limbo trophy of a lady bending over backward with a pole across her belly. "Congratulations."

"Thanks," freak-of-the-week Kelly said, taking the small statue and walking back to her space in the sand.

Winter approached Kelly. "You looked pretty talented out there," she said, looking at Kelly's upper-thigh area.

"I'm just limber, I guess," Kelly responded with a smile.

"I guess," said Winter, staring at her as she walked back to her spot.

Scott was busy taking lessons from two of the Playboy Bunny-looking hula dancers.

# KEEP US IN STITCHES, PLEASE!

The comedy show was scheduled to begin onstage in the Ebony Theater at any moment. Brandon had asked the sea of audience members to wear white linen, but there were a few definite exceptions here and there.

The event promoters made sure to seat the finest women with the shortest skirts and the firmest legs around the front tables onstage. Of course Lexi and Yanni had been chosen. Perhaps the crewmembers decided to get some work in because Lexi was without Steven tonight. Even Megan was without her hung one, Olandi. Megan was seated at the head table with Big Mack, Ashley Isley, Winter, the captain and Tangie. Megan always broke the rules when it came to attire and tonight was no different, as she was clearly one of those white linen violators. The girl was wearing a teal blue, velvet one-piece hot-pants set. She even had on a pair of matching teal stripper-style platforms with a wide, clear strap. Obviously she was working it for purposes of getting noticed.

"Bianca, I didn't expect to see you here. You even missed dinner on the island," Mia said as Bianca took a seat next to her. Bianca was wearing the hell out of a white, short, fringe dress with a wide, red leather belt tied tight at the waist and thin-strapped red mules.

Bianca's curvy hips filled her seat as she placed her white clutch in her lap. "I had to get away from Corey for a couple of hours. His depressed butt was driving me crazy. I just told him I'd be back in a few and he continued playing video games."

"I'm glad you did. You need to relax. Laughter is the best medicine," Mia assured her.

"Yeah, yeah," Bianca almost mocked Mia, making her sound corny. She looked all around the theater, certainly not looking for Omar. "I hope Brandon doesn't start clowning the audience. I think that's so tacky. Tearing down the very people who pay to see him."

Mia moved in closer, remembering to share the news. "Girl, I've got to tell you about Omar at that poetry reading today. That man is a true freak, I promise you."

"I cannot imagine what you have to tell me about the elusive Omar Young. I'll pass on that bit of information," Bianca said as though she could just yawn.

"I think Corey's attitude rubbed off on you. Or maybe it was yours that rubbed off on him," Mia remarked, sitting up straight.

Anyway, Mia and Miles were too sharp, decked out in matching white-linen pantsuits. His pants were sagging and hers were skintight, as usual.

Scott and Kelly sat to the right of them, both dressed casually in blue-jean outfits and short-sleeve white shirts. Speaking of clowning, they were sure to get the jungle fever jokes.

The captain began his introduction. "Please take your seats, ladies and gentlemen. Welcome to our first annual *Chocolate Ship* Soul Cruise Comedy Show. I'm Captain James Douglas and I'm proud to see so many of you coming out to see Brandon Wick and his opening act, El Dorado, perform. And here we are. All of you are looking so good," he said, eyeballing the audience.

"You're the one who is looking good, Captain," one woman with a smoky voice yelled from the front row.

"Thanks, ma'am. I appreciate it," he said with a bow of his head.

"So on with some serious entertainment. To open the show, please welcome the incomparable, renowned, sensational group, El Dorado."

He returned to his seat next to Winter, who was wearing painted-on, cream-colored Fendi capri pants and a matching knit midriff top. She looked over at Mia and Miles and gave a wave like a Rose Bowl queen, kind of rotating her hand at the wrist from side to side without bending it. Mia smiled and Winter nodded in reply. But she continued waving . . . at Miles.

"Miles, Winter is trying to get your attention," Mia whispered through the loud musical intro.

Miles looked forward. "I see her out of the corner of my eye, but you just want to make it obvious that I do. Well, I don't see her, okay?"

"Okay, damn, that's rude. What's up with you?" Mia inquired, turning to look at the side of his blank face.

"Nothing, she's just a little too friendly for me," he admitted.

"To ignore her is not necessary. Just wave back."

Miles looked at Mia with irritation written all over his face. "Mia, she came on to me twice already. And you still encourage me to give her attention. You sistahs be trippin'. If we try to hide something you say just be honest. And then when we're honest you say it's just our imagination. Forget I even said anything."

"I did not say it was your imagination. Some things we women just know in spite of what you tell us. I'm secure with you."

"So why should I tell you anything then, since you're so secure?" Miles asked, again looking forward. "You weren't so secure when your ex ran off with your co-worker now, were you?"

The pleated, deep-brown velvet drapes separated and the lights dimmed just enough to vaguely reveal the silhouettes of three cool cats dressed in loud, red double-breasted three-piece suits with matching suede shoes.

Mia started blinking as though a direct wind were in the room aiming its wrath upon her face. She tightened her jaw as she spoke. "It is not necessary to bring that up. I will still trust you no matter what I've been through. I will not run off all insecure every time a woman looks at my man. Anyway, Miles, unless you have a mutual admiration that you're trying to deny, you can surely wave back at the woman."

"Do you mind letting me be a man here? Shit, Mia, you judge everything I do! Now drop it," Miles said, crossing one leg over the other at the ankle.

"Oh now we're going to argue the evening into the fucking trashcan?" After no reply, Mia just stared straight ahead.

Winter continued to look over at them as they folded their arms in disgust of each other. She smiled, showing off her pearly whites, no doubt proud of the ruckus she'd jump-started, and proceeded to watch the show.

The music to "Backstabbers" started to play and El Dorado began to blow it up. Mia looked over at Winter, who was bouncing in her seat while she and Miles sat like mannequins with their legs crossed, facing away from each other.

Mia warned herself about Winter. *Maybe the words about fake smiles and taking people's place are apropos in this case. I do plan to keep an eye on her lanky ass. But I refuse to check every woman who flirts with my man. I will learn to trust him and be more secure if it's the last thing I do.*

After nearly an hour, and in spite of the voluminous screams begging for continuation, El Dorado exited the stage and Brandon came running out wearing a double-breasted, pinstriped, black-and-chalk Hugo Boss tailored suit with a taupe and olive silk tie and a black brim hat. He clapped and urged the audience, "Give it up for El Dorado! Come on now. Give it to them. They took us way back." The applause grew and then slowly subsided. "I'd say we're ready to laugh. What do you think?" The crowd hooted and hollered in anticipation of the stomach-contracting laughter that was sure to fill the room.

*"Here we are on the dang* Chocolate Ship. *Just think about that for a minute. They've even got chocolate chip cookies shaped like boats and shit.*

*"Black folks cruising. Ain't that something? Now that's a new one because I know for a fact that Black folks are not into three basic things: Cannibalism—we are not going to kill you and eat your ass no time, no how. Skiing—we don't like cold, so snow and ice are out. If it's seventy degrees outside we think it's cold as hell. Now don't get me wrong, you'll find Black folks' ski clubs all over the world, but we're just trying to be cute and catch. I cannot tell you how many fine women join those clubs. And men know it. Everybody laying out around the fireplace or sporting a new, loud-ass ski suit, ain't thinking about getting on that lift chair no time soon. I see Delmonte Harrison did not put an ice-skating rink or bunny slope on this puppy. Oh, yes, that's right, he* has *an ice-skating rink on the ship. Well, that was for you White folks. I guarantee you it will be the least popular spot on the boat.*

*"And we don't like water unless we're washing our asses. So swimming, waterskiing and diving do not excite us. And that also means boats are out. I'm not going to get too deep into slavery humor but one thing is for sure—we've taken too many one-way trips being sold here and there and whatnot. I won't even go into that. Actually, I wasn't going to announce this, but I heard that a threat was made to hijack this very ship, what is that? It turns out it was George Bush trying to navigate all three thousand of our asses back to Africa. And if any White folks happen to be onboard, oh well. That's your punishment for mingling with the minorities. Oh, you all like George Bush now that he's acting like a gangster president against the Taliban. I don't blame you. He actually told Bin Laden, you can run but you can't hide. Wasn't that a song by the Dramatics a while back? G. B.'s got soul after all. I know he'll get my vote next term.*

*"But really, watch out for those White–owned cruise lines that get too friendly about accommodating a ship full of Negroes—that's why Harrison cruises was born. Mr. Harrison makes sure this is a round-trip adventure with all of the festivities we love.*

*Am I right, Captain? Yes, now you can make sure the ship you sail upon is owned by an African American. If that ain't something. But really, I salute you, my brother. You must have worked your butt off, because this is one bad ship. I mean that sincerely.*

*"This is the kind of cruise O. J. needs to book. Doesn't he live right over there in Florida? He'd find himself in Chocolate City for sure. Shoot, all of these sisters up in here, he'd have no choice but to come on home. Hell, I love me some Black women. But, I think O. J.'s crazy ass would try to get funky with a Black woman and end up getting his dick thrown overboard. Sisters do not play like that, O. J., so just stay over there where you are. Actually, I don't care what color you are, just as long as I can get my whiskey on ice and my women on fire. And this is definitely the place for that.*

*"Okay, now I'm gonna get nasty so if you don't want to hear it, go play Ping Pong or climb a rock, because it's gonna get ugly up in here.*

*"You all hooked up with any freaks yet? You have? Good for you, man. All the brown bathing beauties I saw laying out on that deck, you all had better get on that. I got some on the first night but I gave up after that. Shoot, I'm on sabbatical until I get back home. 'Cause you never really have time to get to know the person in such a short period of time. At least wait until the fifth day or something, but not the first night, I don't know what I was thinking.*

*"Man, I was hitting it good and I had to go and ask a dumb-ass question. I asked, "Whose pussy is this?" And girl had the nerve to answer, while I was on the downstroke, mind you: "You don't know him." I was like, oh no, you didn't. Made me mad, I thought about stopping but I just said well let me go ahead and handle my business with this stuff I don't even know. But I wore my jimmy hat. Gotta wear those jimmy hats in the Y2K.*

*"When you really think about it, everybody's stuff belongs to*

*someone other than you, I guess. I don't even know why we ask that. Why do we ask that stupid question? I think we saw it in a movie or something and it looked exciting to put some ownership on it and hear her or him tell you it's yours. It's not mine even if she had said it was. Even your wife's good stuff is not yours. It's her stuff. It goes everywhere she goes, and, ladies, his magic wand goes everywhere he goes. But that's what I get—shut your mouth in bed.*

*"Another thing I noticed. Have you ever broke up with someone and then once you got back together with your stuff, they talk out loud in bed and give themselves away. I know I did. Man, I missed my girl so bad, especially after dealing with a few stragglers along the way, that I just hung myself with my own noose. We were getting into it and I said, wow, I miss your long legs, and it seems like your titties got bigger, and damn, did your ass get tighter? Now you know she knew that I had been with a short, flat-chested, loose-ass chick that only made me miss her even more. Then, after we were through and she went to get us some cold juice to cool our asses off, she said, damn, baby, did your dick get smaller? That truly meant that my stuff, who don't forget now, is never really yours, had been with some hung pimp all the while. I call that the invasion of the booty snatchers. I looked at her and said, no, it's just that your stuff got looser. She agreed. That's just one bit of advice—don't get back with anybody you've been missing and open your big mouth, brothas. I deserved that comment, though. Let's just shut the hell up in bed. I ain't saying another word.*

*"But, back to cruising, I guess there is some sort of sailing etiquette that we should be aware of, but it's no different than when you're at a nightclub. But on a ship, it's like you're just in that club for a week. Ladies, I promise you one thing, those same brothas who have been checking you out across the ship since we set sail will get a lot friendlier as time goes on. It's almost like when you're in the club and a brotha in the three-piece suit and Jherri Curl is trying to be cool all night, just*

*staring at you like he's gonna use your visual image when he goes home and jacks off in your name. But right around two forty-five he rolls up thinking he's gonna try to get lucky.*

*"That's what's going to happen around here right about the last night—everybody's gonna start getting extra friendly so they can say they did it on a ship when they get back home. You single people can't go home saying you didn't get you some cruise pussy and dick. You've got to do it on the ship, on the ocean waters just so you can say you did it. Actually it didn't feel any different on land than when I was getting some the other night. Especially after she just dissed my ass with her comment. "You don't know him"—girl had lost her mind. Just shut your mouth in bed.*

*"Man, I heard there's a couple who met on the Internet and this is their first date. Where are you? Man, have you lost your mind. Fool—you know you can't leave—what kind of shit is that? You'd better be glad she looks good. What would have happened if you didn't like each other? What would you have done? Where would you have gone? At least if you met somewhere in Inglewood you could have hopped on the 405 and made your getaway. Damn, people. What are you thinking?*

*"Hey, dude, how are you doing? Tell me something. What's your old ass doing? Is this tenderoni your lady? Man, that is statutory like's a mug. Has she had her period yet? I'm telling you, a few more nights of that nookie and you're going to need a pacemaker. There's no way you can keep up with her, man. No, I'm just kidding, man—you two make a nice couple. She looks like a sweet child, I mean girl. Oops, you dropped something. Right there under your chair. Let me get it for you.*

*"What does this pill say? V—I—A—G—R—A all up in there. I thought so. You a bad brotha. Are you rich? No. You've got a big dick? Ha, she said no. He what? He eats pussy right. Oh that's it? She said yes—that's it—You're like KFC—you do pussy right, huh? Well you look like a Negro Colonel Sanders—*

*What's your name? Kenny? KFC—Kenny Fucking Coochie. Go ahead, Kenny, I can't even catch that kind of girl—But see, that's because I don't be eating no pussy.*

*"See, that's a whole nother topic. Like that woman who told me her stuff belonged to someone else. See that's another reason why I don't go down. I'm not putting my mouth on 'You don't know him's' coochie.*

*"To me, that's gay. Men don't lick, brothas . . . we stick. I'll leave that to the women. My woman can have a woman come over and eat it—all the prelims are just unnecessary. I don't care. I guess I'm a foreplay hater and I admit it. See I'm just interested in closing the deal once they're done. I think oral sex all around is woman's work—especially sucking dick. It just makes sense that a woman should master the act of giving head. Giving head is a nurturing function. Even though you really don't know where our dicks have been either, so I'll understand if you say no. Our job is to enter and destroy. Buck all that oral, putting things in your mouth and shit. I had this girlfriend who used to masturbate after I got mine. I just put one hand on her thigh and had one hand on the remote. Go ahead, girl, and bust a good one. You deserve it.*

*"See the lady over here is now cutting her eyes at me. What's wrong, you lazy woman, what did I say wrong? Would you rather have your coochie licked all night or a big stiff one up in ya? Both—well, that sounds like a threesome to me.*

*"If you're not down—cool. Just don't look at me like I just put an end to your good time. Get you some dick over the next few days—just not from me. I am not the one, no, I am not.*

*"What's up with you two? Oh, you're twin sisters. Thanks for clearing that up. I didn't think you were twin brothers. Well, nowadays you never know.*

*"Twin sisters, huh? Hey now freaky-deaky. Come on now, the two of you have never ever gone down on each other out of curiosity or just out of being lonely? Please—with your lying asses—I know you have.*

*"I'd probably do that if I were a twin just to see what it would be like to fuck me. What are your names? Lexi and Yanni—you all even have freak names. And you both got those big, thick lips—oh yeah. You two are not fooling me, no, you are not. No, really, you two are some beautiful sistahs. Both fine as hell!*

*"Dang, my breath stinks. Anybody got some gum or something? You all know the best way to check your breath is to lick the inside of your wrist and then sniff it. Look at you all trying it. I'll bet the only ones who checked it are the new couples. Once you've been with somebody for a while you don't care. Just wake up in the morning talking dead-on into their face. Even when in the beginning we used to at least cover our mouths and give a morning nod from the opposite side of the bed. Now we're just all up in your grill saying the worst two words for people with bad breath . . . good morning. We'll even eat some corn chips and then try to stick our tongues in your mouth, won't we? We are some nasty brothas.*

*"Thanks, baby. What's your name? Megan. You are one brave white girl. No, I know her, she's cool. Not only did you volunteer to hand me the stick of gum—you had the nerve to stand up after you violated my dress code request. Yeah, I saw you as soon as I walked out. What's your story? You don't have one. Megan, read my lips. Why didn't you wear white linen like I had asked? You wanted to be different. Well, you are that. And you weren't a bit afraid to come up on a Black–owned ship with your white ass?*

*"What? You say you're Black on the inside? I'll bet you are, all the Black dick you've probably had. I ain't mad at you. The world needs more White people like you. Give her a hand.*

*"Speaking of White, man, you got you a real Black woman sitting next to you. Is that your lady? She looks good. What's your name? Scott. Damn, that's a white name all right. Oh, that's your wife. What's her name? Kelly? That's a White name too. A Black woman named Kelly, what's that all about? I thought your name would be Kacheena or Taniesha, a real*

*Black name. Kelly, huh? So, Scott, have you always dated Black women? I'm not mad at you. Once you go Black you never go back, right? Or have you gone back? You didn't answer. Okay, we won't go there. And you, Kelly, once you go White you get it eaten right? Is that it? I'm just asking because I heard White men love eating pussy for hours. Oh, it's just a myth? Yo, I think she's punking you, dog.*

*"But it's cool, because I guess there are a lot of myths going on, because not all Black men have big peckers either. Just like this ship, it's not the size that counts; it's the motion of the ocean that can rock your world. Hey, I'm not going to lie. Mine is more than adequate. I'll swab the deck with your ass. But you know what they say about breasts? I say it about dicks. If it's more than a mouthful it's enough. So ladies, give a brotha a break about the size of his penis. Until you learn how to suck it right, all the way and cut out that gagging, I don't want to hear it.*

*"And what's up with you two beige people. You just blend right on in with the white-linen thing. What are your names? Mia and Miles—Damn, you two have a baby and she'll be transparent and shit. But, I'm with you—at least you both followed the rules—unlike Megan. No, the two of you look good together. You are together, right? What's wrong, does he have corn-chip breath or what? You all sitting away from each other. I bet by three in the morning you'll be having that intense make-up sex and he'll be hitting it from the back. That's why they call it make-up sex. Folks be making up shit to argue about so they can make up.*

*"What are you looking at? I saw you turn your nose because I picked my ear. My ear itched, dammit. See, you ladies make no sense. Why do you ladies let men talk to you anyway they want to in bed, and then get ready to kick his ass when he says, 'Hey, ho', make me some dinner'? You were his ho' last night when your legs were spread from west to east. But like I said—just shut your mouth in bed.*

*"First you lick us in places only our mothers would wipe—like sticking your tongue in our waxy ears . . . and then you think it's nasty when we rub and scratch those places in front of your friends. Come on now, ladies. Give us brothas a break.*

*"You all can get mad at me if you want, but I'm just keeping it real. I can't believe that girl said, 'You don't know him.' What kind of crap was that? Just shut your mouth in bed.*

*"Before I go, I just have to tell you to make sure you continue to support Harrison Cruises and thank you all for coming out. Stay out of trouble on this big, Black ship, and keep cruising. And remember life is too short to take things too seriously. Do yourself a favor and keep laughing. And remember my advice—just shut your mouth in bed. Peace out!"*

# WHAT TOO MUCH ALCOHOL CAN DO

After the comedy show, Miles walked with Mia to the casino. As she played the slots for a moment, it was obvious to Mia that the machines were in on his little attitude. The machines did not show her any love whatsoever. Pissed-off mates never make good gambling companions.

Mia asked a silent Miles, "Do you want a drink?"

"Sure," he said looking around the casino to catch a glimpse of anything but her face.

"Sure? What do you want to do? Do you want to try the cha-cha marathon or call it a night?"

He looked down at the floor and answered, "I'm going to catch up with Scott and take in a game of chess. I'll be up later."

"Fine. I'll see you, Miles," Mia said just as he'd already begun to make his way around the corner. *How could one night take such a complete turn from the one before?* Mia thought. *Maybe he would have been happy if I'd kicked Winter's butt. Oh well, I'll just call it a night.*

Mia knew that Bianca had returned to her room for the evening, and there was no telling where the twins were by now.

Mia's slow trek down the hall toward her cabin was interrupted. "Mia, help me get Megan's drunk ass to her room," said Dante, coming out of the Blue Lagoon Lounge.

"What the hell are you doing, getting sloshed by yourself? I thought you were going to be with Brandon," Mia asked Megan, taking hold of her right arm as Dante took her left.

Megan said as if in a cloud, "After the show, brother Brandon went traipsing behind Nona Fox. Of course he picked the ivory portion of the Ebony and Ivory duo."

"And so you just decided to get wasted in his name, huh?" Mia asked.

"You don't need to be looking after me. You need to keep an eye on your man. We just saw him. He's a trip," Megan said.

Mia looked at Dante and then back at Megan and asked, "What do you mean?"

Megan responded, "I heard he's been on this ship before and was raising hell. What do you see in him?"

"What are you talking about? You're faded," Mia said, snatching Megan's purse to fish around for her room key.

"Ask Bianca. She knows," Megan added, leaning against the hallway wall with Dante at her side.

"What do you know about this?" Mia asked Dante.

"Don't look at me," he said. "You already got on me for that."

"Besides, Megan, what would Bianca know? She's been in her room the whole time," Mia said, opening the door and holding it ajar as Dante picked up Megan and carried her in like a sack of potatoes. "Just toss her," Mia suggested to him as he smiled, making his way toward Megan's bed. "Megan, go to sleep and rest your fanaticizing mind. Thanks, Dante," Mia said as he plopped her dumb butt on top of the indigo down comforter.

"No problem," Dante said, backing out of her room like Michael Jackson. "You've got a jammin' room, girl," Dante said to Megan. "How'd you get the . . . oh, never mind." Dante closed the door and left.

"Just be careful," Megan warned in a tequila-scented whisper as if someone could overhear. "Wear a condom. I've got a purse full," she said in slurred insanity as Mia walked toward the door.

"I don't need a condom with my man unless I'm worried about getting pregnant. We've been together for three years," Mia responded, turning her head in a circle with a don't-let-me-read-you attitude. She opened the door and stepped out. "Anyway, good night," Mia yelled without looking back as she closed the door behind her.

Mia walked right into her own room to digest the latest news. The topic of the recent conversation was missing in action. She took a long, hot shower, wrapped her hair and collapsed in exhaustion.

Miles came into the cabin at an ungodly hour, making his way out of his clothes from the doorway to his side of the bed. He tapped Mia on the back of her shoulder like a five-year-old who wanted to lick the spoon after his mommy poured the last of the yellow cake mix into the pan. Mia was barely half-awake. He slipped under the covers, lay down behind her, lifted up her purple satin nightie and manipulated his straight-on hardness into her pantyless semi-wet hole. Mia never even turned around to look him in the face. For all she knew, it could have been the captain stopping by to service an abandoned passenger. He, whoever he was, parted her cheeks and thrusted himself inside while sliding down to get under her ample ass for a full, deep grind.

Within seconds he was asking, "Are you cuming? Cause I am!" Before she could even answer him with a no, he shouted her name as if she had just run across the tracks with a train coming.

"MEE-YA, oooh shit, girl!"

They did not say a word. Within two seconds, he was snoring, still inside of her, while she lay in the same position she'd been in when he came into the room. Mia released him and went to the bathroom to clean herself up, took a blanket onto the veranda, and stared at the sunrise until suddenly, she was startled by sounds coming from Megan's room.

"Give me that white kitty," a man demanded in a deep, semi-familiar muffled voice. *Megan must be watching a porno movie,* Mia thought.

"You like the smell of that, don't you?" *That's no porno star, that's Megan,* Mia realized.

Megan continued to moan in pleasure. Mia could barely make out the sounds of a brother talking shit . . . down there . . . and sounding like he was growling.

"Right now it smells like Massengil. When I get through it will smell like kitty cat. Feel that tongue in your twat. You like that rock-hard tongue? How about if I suck you off? Oh, I feel you about to do it. Not yet, we're going to do it together," the instructional brotha demanded.

"Then you get on your back, now," Megan demanded just as forcefully.

"That's better," he said, followed by momentary silence. "This is sweet. Now straddle this big rod, girl. You're in trouble. It's time to ride the horse now."

Megan screamed as if a knife had pierced her back. Echoed sounds of spanking accompanied her pleas for continuance. Her squeals were repeated with increased intensity, rapidity and volume.

"This is some good stuff," he yelled.

"Faster, faster, baby," she demanded.

Suddenly she was quiet and he was moaning deeply and loudly. "I want you to take it all, all the way down to the shaft. This ain't no practice session."

His words again turned to moans as Mia heard Megan mumbling, "Um-huh, um-huh."

"Now ride it again. Get back on it now!" he said with force.

Within a couple of seconds, Megan replied in pleasure, "Ooh, it's harder than ever now. You like the way Mama does it, don't you? Show me you like it while I ride it."

"Oh, here I come, baby," he said as if he was about to burst from the pressure of his own swollen scrotum.

Suddenly, it was as if Mia's hands had a mind and memory of

their own from their old routine. It was like they had decided to polish her off from the one-sided screw Miles had managed to pull off. They independently made their way down to her pubic area to comfort her throbbing tiny muscle, which was producing a milky secretion between her legs. She touched herself, unsure if the warmth was from the eavesdropping or from the services of her own man. But just as she was sliding down into her lounge chair to pursue more of herself, Megan and her guest began screaming together in esctasy.

"Oh, uhh, umm, ahh!" they both moaned uncontrollably.

Finally Megan yelled, "Oh, Scott."

# COFFEE, MEN, AND SUN

It was already the morning of day four as the ship arrived in San Juan. Bianca and Mia joined each other for coffee in Starbucks on the Tawny deck. The smell of Colombian roast coffee beans and caramel macchiatto filled the air.

They sat at a small table as Mia massaged her temples and her forehead, taking in major swigs of caffeine-charged, ninety-two octane, tar-black coffee as if it would chase away her hangover and invigorate her from lack of sleep.

"Bianca, you must know that your man Omar describes oral sex as 'I tasted all of her—drank of her essence,' " Mia said, trying to paint a better picture for Bianca.

"And?" Bianca responded, unfazed as she sipped her vanilla latte with her hands wrapped around the heated cup.

"And, when you have an orgasm, he calls it cream de la cream."

"And?" Bianca said as she swallowed. "Darn, this is hot."

"And, when he has an orgasm it's a 'rumbling wave from the depth of his beast spilled forth like syrup' or something he said."

Bianca stopped before blowing her brew, enlarging her eyes. "What? He wrote that?"

Mia said, "He wrote that. I'll bet the sex with Omar is wild and nasty, and so did every other woman in that room so you'd better get on it."

"I'm not worried about those other women."

"Okay, then you'd better get to know him. You at least owe him a thank-you for saving Corey's life," Mia suggested.

"I thanked him already. Besides, he's too mysterious for me, girl."

Mia gulped more coffee. "He did sound like he was stuck on whomever it was he wrote that poem for. He talked about pain and dreams and hurt feelings."

"That just means I'd have to deal with him on the rebound. Not interested," Bianca said, placing her cup back on the glass table and picking up a newspaper.

"Bianca, your fun meter has been on low so far, right? Come on, girl. This man is fine, alone, interested, a hero and a freak."

Bianca put her newspaper down, totally uninterested in reading it, and put her hands up in surrender. "Enough said. I get it. I at least want to have a story to tell like Brandon was talking about, right? Right now all I have to tell about is how my kid had an asthma attack while swimming. That was scary as hell."

Megan walked up, keeping an eye on Brandon while she pulled up a chair. He was seated at a table near the window with Ivory. "I thought he wasn't getting any," she commented with a jealous look.

"Girl, those were just jokes he was telling," Mia replied.

"Well, I know I'm not," said Bianca.

"Megan sure is. Damn, Megan. You could have at least been cognizant of the freaking volume level. How the hell did you end up with someone in your room that early in the morning?" Mia asked.

"Who?" Megan responded with dumbness.

Mia looked her square in her eyes. "You know who. And it wasn't Olandi."

"Oh, girl, I heard a knock at my door when the sun was coming up. I needed it as bad as he did."

"I don't think either one of you needed it, but it sounded like you both wanted it pretty bad," Mia said.

"What did I miss out on?" Bianca asked, feeling left out.

Mia said, "Just Megan getting laid this morning. Her X-rated screams of pleasure, or pain, I'm not sure, went on for quite a while."

"Megan, you'd better slow your roll. Brandon seems like the type who would be searching for a nightly notch on this ship," Bianca warned.

"Who said it was Brandon?" Mia inquired, eyeing Megan to elicit a cleansing admission.

Megan still played dumb. "Who said it wasn't? I know one thing, Olandi is the one who has a thing like a cucumber. The tip was so damn wide I thought my mouth was going to split open."

"I can see the stretch marks," said Bianca, pointing in a circular motion around Megan's lips. "It's hard not to notice. Pardon the pun."

Megan gave Bianca a high five and said, "You know I think the tip is more important than . . ."

"The shaft?" asked Bianca.

"Shut your mouth," said Megan.

"I'm talking about the shaft," Bianca joked.

"Well, we can dig it!" Megan and Mia recited in unison.

"You're nasty, Megan," said Bianca. "Mia should beat you for keeping her up all night."

"When are you going to get your groove on? I didn't see you all day yesterday," Megan asked Bianca.

"I keep telling you guys, I did not come on this ship to freak my ass off and learn the importance of the scrotum and its neighbors. I'm trying to nurse my son and show him a good time."

Mia asked, "How is my baby anyway?"

"He's finally able to hang out at Club Ocean, where the teens go and play videos. And then they are going to play basketball on the Sports Court with the big boys."

A light bulb went off and Mia said, "Now that's a game we need to check out."

* * *

The captain of Corey's team, the Big Ballers, along with Brandon and Corey, was the infamous Omar Young. Miles was captain of the other team with Scott and Justin.

"How are you doing, young man? It's good to see you," Omar said to Corey, patting him on his back.

"I'm cool. I'm just glad to be out of that room," Corey said, dribbling the ball between his legs.

"I heard that, little man," said Miles as Corey shot the ball, making it from half-court.

Bianca and Mia were laid out along the deck surrounding the all-weather court with the cement surface and red, white, and blue basketball net. Bianca had on a cobalt blue paisley Gottex tankini, a tight, tight, tank top and bikini bottom combo, and Mia was sporting a yellow Pamela Dennis bikini with tiny purple and green seashells throughout.

"Girl, that sale we caught last week was the best investment we ever made. I could wear a different bathing suit every hour," said Bianca.

"Yeah, but too many different styles can screw up the tan lines," Mia remarked, pulling her strap away to check for effects of the sun.

Bianca said, "That's the least of my worries. I'll leave that up to you, with your light bright skin."

Tangie approached with a clipboard in hand and asked, "Would you ladies like to schedule a massage or a manicure and pedicure session for Ladies' Day?"

"Do they do hair?" asked Bianca.

"Yes, we have a salon onboard called Diamonds and Curls. Tookie is an excellent stylist. Do you need an appointment?" Tangie asked.

"Oh, *she* does," said Bianca, pointing to Mia.

"I can speak for myself. Yes, I need to book one," Mia said, running her fingertips across her hairline. "Hopefully this afternoon, before we get off the ship to hit San Juan."

Just then the basketball rolled under Bianca's chair. Before

Omar could scoop it up, Bianca snatched it as he leaned over her, resting his hands on each arm of her chair. He leaned in like Billy Dee Williams and asked, "Can I get that ball from you, or what?"

"Maybe. It's going to cost you, though."

Without missing a beat he offered, "How about dinner tonight? Will that do?"

"Okay, that would be nice," Bianca replied, shooting the ball into his hands. "Actually, I'm the one who owes you one, Omar. But I'll tell you more about that at dinner tonight."

"Deal. See you later," Omar replied with a Kobe-like strut, shooting the ball to Corey.

"Ooh, honey," Bianca said, waving her hand in a circular, stirring motion as Tangie was talking to Mia. "Add my name to the list of salon appointments, please."

Tangie said, laughing, "Okay, calm down. How about both of you at four this afternoon? I don't see anything sooner. One can start with a pedicure and one with the hairdresser and then switch off."

Bianca added, "And, please have her do my hair first. She'll be all afternoon sifting through Mia's head."

Mia teased, "With your TWA—teeny weenie Afro—there's not much she could do anyway."

"I'll have you know this curly, natural style takes time to clean and condition and set. What's your excuse?"

Mia begged, "Tangie, please put her down first. I'm tired of hearing her mouth about my head. I should have just gotten some corn rows like in *How Stella Got Her Groove Back* and called it a day."

"The only one getting their groove back around here is going to be me," Bianca said, shifting her attention to Omar's physique. "Look at that man's bowlegs. Now that's what I'm talking about."

"You have no game man. You're sorry," Scott said, taunting Miles, trying to mess up his concentration.

"Just worry about your skills. We already know you don't have the ability to jump," Miles said.

"Oh, that's cold, dude," Brandon said. "Clowning your White brotha like you're Snipes and he's Woody."

"It's cool. I'll show him. Let's get a slam-dunk contest going, with your trash-talking self," Scott dared.

"Let's do this," Miles said as Omar and Corey stood back, looking amused.

Miles took off running toward the basket and leaped into the air with a three-sixty slam to start things off. "Now what, Eminem? Top that."

"No problem, kid," Scott proclaimed.

Scott darted to the left side of the basket and propelled himself into the air with a three-sixty slam of his own that was even better than Miles's fancy slam dunk.

"Oooh," the guys on the sideline yelled, holding up ten fingers each.

Scott continued to taunt, "Give me something I can work with next time."

Now it was Scott's turn to start off. He took off again, but toward the left side of the basket, leaping into the air with a reverse dunk to the right side while airborne the entire time.

"Dang, Scott," Corey said, impressed.

"Not so fast. That was nice, nice. But take this," Miles said, taking off from the left side as he gained so much height that his head was above the rim, but his hand hit the basket and the ball bounced off to the sideline.

"Oh, you missed. I win," Scott said like a five-year-old. Miles left him hanging with a high five, acting like a four-year-old. He walked away to retrieve the ball, looking crushed.

"It's okay, baby," Mia yelled in support. Miles cut his eyes at her and dribbled to the free-throw line to shoot with his left hand and missed.

"What's his problem now?" asked Bianca.

"Who knows. I smell a funky ego problem, if you ask me."

"Can we get this battle of the testosterone stars over with and get our game on?" asked Brandon.

"Get your team ready," Miles demanded to Scott, pointing his finger within one inch of Scott's nose.

Omar and Corey high-fived Scott while Brandon and Justin lined up in a huddle with Miles. It's on now!

Later, on the beach in San Juan, Dante, once again the beach bartender for the day, tried to get Miles's attention, but it was obvious that he was not in the mood. His team had lost.

"What's dragging your chin down to your knees?" Dante asked, at least trying.

Miles said with a red light, "Man, just hook me up with a shot of Belvedere vodka."

"Drown that hurt with the good stuff, huh? That will surely make the pain go away, temporarily."

Miles reacted, "Look, Jerry Springer, don't try to earn tips as a therapist. I think you need to back up and mind your own business."

"Excuuuussssse me! How rude can you be? Shit, with an attitude like that you ain't getting no sympathy from me and no pussy up on this cruise either. You should have checked your bad manners in Fort Lauderdale," Dante said as he slid Miles's glass toward him. A bit of the vodka sloshed out of the glass and onto the bar.

Scott walked up just as Miles reacted, civilly: "Fill it up to the top. You spilled some."

"Say please," Dante nagged him further.

Miles stood up and tossed a ten-dollar bill toward Dante. "Fuck it. Here. Is this enough of a tip for your session?"

Dante snatched up the ten and said, "I'll take it. It's more of a tip than you'll be getting from anyone up in here—male or female."

Scott stared at Miles as if trying to figure out Dante himself. Miles said, pointing at Dante, "See, you've got to admit he's asking for it."

"Dante, chill out, man," Scott said. "Miles, what's really got you so fired up?" asked Scott. "Was it the game?"

"No. It's Rainbow Brite here trying to lecture me like he can tell me anything about life. I do not need his ear, but he's gonna need a new nose if he keeps pushin' up on me."

"Ooohhh, boyfriend, you need an enema," Dante said with further annoyance.

"I'll give you an enema all right," Miles said as he accidentally kicked over the bar stool while reaching over the wicker bar to go for Dante's throat.

Dante screamed like a child being chased by a rat. "Ahh, help!" he yelled as he flailed his arms and stumbled over his own feet, only to hide under the bar.

"Miles, what is your trip?" Mia asked, running up just as Scott grabbed him by the arm.

The top of Dante's head appeared over the bar followed by his peering wide eyes. "I was just kidding with you," Dante said with the word F-E-A-R spelled out across his frowning forehead.

"I was just joking too," Miles replied while picking up his bar stool, trying to play it off for a quick second. "I guess you can take a dick but you can't take a joke."

"Miles," Mia said with a motherly tone.

Scott laughed. "Mia, you must admit that was a good one."

Dante stood up, pulled down his brown shirt and proceeded to walk away, keeping one eye on Miles.

"No, I mean what is really going on?" Mia asked.

"Nothing, Mia. I'm fine," Miles replied.

"You're fine, huh?"

"Yes," he said again.

"How much have you had to drink?" Mia inquired, as if there must have been a reason for his actions.

"This is my first," he said, swigging the shot of vodka. "But not my last."

Mia gave up. "Well you sit over here and get wasted. I'm going to go for a walk along the beach."

"Good-bye," Miles said, as if dismissing her.

"Do you want to come with me?" she offered.

"No."

"Mia, we'll be over here chilling out, okay?" Scott said as Miles started to walk away.

"Okay," Mia said as she thought, *Damn, Scott has more success with him than I do.* Scott and Miles walked toward the lounge-chair area, where everyone else had staked out a spot. *I just need to stroll and think*, thought Mia.

# IS THAT BIG THING YOURS?

Mia kicked off her toe-ringed, metallic sandals and strolled along the white, clean beach as her toes lightly kicked the velvety virgin sand beneath her feet. She tiptoed along the rippling waters, whose waves made their way up and down the shoreline. She imagined what Miles's real intentions were and why he was so angry with her and with himself. She came to an old, rustic, tall stone staircase and climbed to the top, carefully taking each step up, hopefully toward a higher level of consciousness as to whether or not her shortcomings were contributing to this lack of harmony. She reached the top, short of breath and sweaty from the direct hit of the sun, and sat upon the top step, looking down upon the beautiful *Chocolate Ship* docked just a way out from all of the happy vacationers, who were surfboarding, hang gliding and snorkeling.

Down below, Brandon walked by with a distinguished-looking gentleman with a salt-and-pepper goatee. They momentarily stopped and glanced up at Mia and then Brandon continued to walk as the gentleman began to climb the stairs toward her.

He reached the top and stood next to her, looking like Ving

Rhames as they both faced the majestic waters of the Atlantic and looked toward the floating wonder.

"Beautiful sight. An ebony ship all our own," he said, sounding like Louis Armstrong.

"It is a thing of beauty, isn't it?" Mia agreed.

"It is indeed. It took a lot of blood, sweat and tears to get that branded with the *CS* logo." Mia looked over at his right calf muscle smack-dab in her face, and what a muscle it was. And etched into his leg was the same tattooed initials inked in three-inch dark brown scripted letters.

"You are the owner of this masterpiece?"

"Yes," he replied.

"Mr. Harrison?" she asked.

He answered charismatically, "Delmonte is what I prefer to be called. And you are?"

"Mia White," she answered, suddenly remembering he'd been so elusive. "You weren't at dinner the first night or anywhere else around since then."

"That was the captain's dinner. This is his ship. Why are you up here by yourself?" he asked.

"I am just seeking solitude in deep thought, trying to come to some sort of resolution as to how I could ruin the start of a vacation that you were creative enough to organize for our enjoyment."

"Man trouble?"

"I thought by now it would be fiancé trouble," she admitted.

"Is this your engagement cruise?"

"Sort of. I'm expecting to answer the big question."

Delmonte said, "Sounds like you're unsure of the answer more than the question."

"Believe it or not, I would say yes."

"Why?" he asked.

"Why not? My man, Miles, is my life. He is my best friend and he makes me happy. I do not believe it can get any better than this," she said, leaning back on her hands as she sat on the step.

"Then it won't," he advised.

"What do you mean?"

He informed her as though he had been there, done that: "If you limit yourself to this being as good as it gets, you're not allowing yourself the opportunity for true happiness. Is this true happiness sitting up here looking down on everyone else's pleasures and enjoyment?"

"No, but my true happiness is down there. I do know that," she said, looking toward the group of *Chocolate Ship* passengers.

"Then go get him. Just make sure you can look back ten years from now and like what you've built together."

"What makes you the expert?" she asked, wiping her hands off and rising to stand next to him.

"I've chased my dreams and caught them. Believe me, I know."

Mia smiled to herself at his healthy ego. She looked up at Delmonte and envisioned her African-American history teacher at Dorsey High School, Mr. Dangerfield, instructing the class on the Underground Railroad and the Last Flogging, teaching the basic rules for experiencing one's Blackness and the essence of one's true self. She admired his voice, as deep as the very ocean they'd set out upon, and the slightly graying goatee that framed his expressive mouth. He exposed his bleached white teeth as he rolled around a lucky Tic Tac with his thick, long, salmon-colored saliva-laden tongue that was tossing about. Mia was mesmerized as she zoomed in on his protruding taste buds, almost savoring the wintergreen flavor herself as he sucked and swallowed, sucked and swallowed, and sucked and swallowed.

She looked down at his massive hands. Each wide nail bed of each long finger looked Zestfully clean, with nails that were perfectly manicured with a coat of clear, high-gloss polish. The veins of his forearms were pronounced, as if the blood of the Amistad slaves was flowing from his heart to the tips of his enormous fingers. *This finger job would be an enormous ride,* she fantacized. *Look at him reaching out his finger, I mean his hand, gently touching mine, bowing his head in honor of my presence.*

He glanced at his gold and diamond Rolex on his other wrist as he held her hand and said, "I must go now and board the ship to take care of business. But, it was nice to meet you, Mia. Feel free to check in with me to keep me updated on your true happiness. Bless you."

"Bless you as well. Nice to meet you, Delmonte." He dropped her hand with grace and she left it dangling in place, with her lips framed from the completion of his name as if her tongue was frozen on the last letter.

As Mr. Harrison jogged down the stairs with vigor, Mia noticed his tan Bermuda shorts and brown cotton shirt. His big, thick, hairy legs carried him down the path with strength and precision in each and every step. As he placed his weight upon each foot, his pronounced calf muscles pulsated with the same blood that carried him down from the previous step, and all the while the branded *CS* waved at Mia like it was hula-dancing in satisfaction of being a part of his very being. His arms alternated as if he was a precision relay runner. He was no doubt just as powerful physically as he was mentally.

He flagged down the small passenger boat that had been keeping track of his whereabouts and climbed aboard to take himself to his baby, the *Chocolate Ship*.

# BEING A KID AGAIN

"I'm going to find my man so that we can enjoy our getaway," Mia said aloud, grabbing her sandals and jogging down the stairs just as Mr. Harrison had done. By the time she reached step number five she decided to walk, slowly and carefully so she would not tip over, only to plummet down the mile-high steps and bust her head open. And so she took each step gingerly until she reached the warm sand. She ran as fast as she could along the sand to find a seat on the lounge chair next to Miles and Scott.

"Hey, baby," she said out of breath. "I love you."

"I love you, too," he said, still with an air of resistance.

She reached over and kissed Miles and then took off her purple sarong so that she could join Kelly who was already frolicking about in the bathtub warmth of the water.

"It's time to get in some real fun," Mia said to Miles. "Kelly, wait up!" she yelled, bouncing her way into the clear blanket of wetness.

Winter and Captain Jim were positioned on two large peach-colored lounge chairs with their bodies glistening from the heat of the fiery sun.

Winter decided it was time to stand up. She was wearing her red, white and blue flag-print string bikini. She strutted her long, thirty-something body in front of the captain and kissed him on top of his head.

"I'll be right back, Big Daddy," she said, and then she sashayed her top-heavy, Taebo-toned stuff along in front of the row of male models, all lined up to enjoy the tall, tan, dark, lovely view. She strutted in slow motion, as if the song "The Girl from Ipanema" was playing as she walked.

She then made her way over to Scott and Miles and actually sat in Mia's chair.

"Mia, I say we totally vote her booty right on off the island," Kelly suggested, examining Winter's every move. "But she is fine," Kelly admitted, with non-adversarial admiration.

"How about voting her fine ass right on off the ship?" Mia asked, with willing intentions.

The captain looked over at Mia and she looked at him and then she looked back to see what Miles's reaction would be. They both awaited Winter's next move with bated breath. She whispered in Miles's ear and sashayed off to the bar to get something to cool her hot, pop-tart ass down.

She came away with two glasses of pink-umbrella-topped ginger coladas, one for her and one for the captain. *Smart move*, Mia thought.

Miles and Scott joined Mia and Kelly in the water. Scott darn near tackled Kelly just a few feet into the water, which splashed all over Mia and Miles.

"Hey, Scott, watch it," said Mia, wiping ocean water out of her eyes.

"Oh, sorry," he said, again jousting around with his wife until she ran back toward the sand. The couple continued their merriment around the lounging passengers, playing a game of chase like children.

"They're so silly," said Mia as she leaped onto Miles's back.

"Why is that?" Miles asked.

"They just are."

"They're just having fun," he said.

"And are you having fun?"

"Yes, I just have a lot on my mind."

"I thought vacations were for letting those things rest for a while," she said as Scott and Kelly traipsed over near them, falling into the water again.

"Sometimes we can shut ourselves off and sometimes it's not as easy," Miles said, watching Scott and Kelly jostle.

Kelly shook her drenched head of dreads from left to right, splashing water in Miles's face.

Miles quickly turned his head to the other side and remarked, "I see she's not worried about getting her hair wet."

Mia mocked him, "Oh, she's not worried about getting her hair wet? Kelly's little five-inch dreads? I'm sure that's not why they act like that."

"Then why do they?"

"I don't know, shoot. We never act like that because we never go anywhere together. I don't even think we've been to the beach in L.A.," Mia said.

"Well, we're on a beach now, smarty-pants," Miles remarked, tickling her arms, which were clasped around his neck.

"You know what? I'm going to dunk your big head like a basketball if you keep talking shit."

"Shit, shit, shit," Miles joked, like a child.

Mia propelled her body forward with all of her weight, leaning down toward the water as Miles lost his footing in the wet sand and slipped onto his side. Mia plopped down into the water next to him.

She rose from the warm ocean and pulled her drenched hair backward with her flat hands.

"My hair is jacked now," she said, squeezing the water from the ends of her gathered ponytail.

"You and your hair," Miles replied, shaking his head.

"Me and my hair are going to go swimming out further if you'd care to come with a sistah."

Miles walked farther into the ocean, pushing off with his toes from the bottom-packed sand and taking the first stroke, laying his body flat until his feet added momentum through his kicking.

Mia jumped in right behind him until they swam out a way. Hordes of snorkelers gathered near an instructor who gave them the full rundown on the proper use of their equipment.

Even without using eye goggles, Miles could look down into the clear water, and he was struck by the beauty of the marine life scurrying around their bodies.

"Baby, will you look at that?" Miles said in amazement.

A school of multicolored fish swam away just as Mia's treading feet fluttered near them.

"Look at that one," Mia said, pointing to a bright orange and electric yellow seahorse swimming slowly toward Miles.

"That looks like the knight to my chess set, doesn't it?" he noticed.

"It does, huh? I know you like that one," Mia concurred.

They swam out a little bit farther, treading water within inches of each other. Suddenly, purple and maroon ribbontail rays sprang from the water in pairs just to the left of Mia.

"Ahhh," Mia shrilled in surprise, making her way toward Miles and then retreating with a giggle, waving her hands under the water to stay afloat.

"Don't be scared," yelled the snorkeling instructor. "Just make sure you don't step on one. They have a mean, powerful whiplash sting."

"Okay, I'll make note of that," Mia replied. The instructor would not have to tell her twice.

The excellent visibility of the crystal-clear waters gave them a breathtaking view of a spotted eagle ray swimming around, being chased by a bold turquoise blue friend. There were pale red squirrel fish with giant black eyes. Along the bottom, two goldentail and green moray eels were swimming side by side in an S-shaped wave.

"That one has a big mouth and even bigger nostrils. I'm going in a little closer toward the shore," said Mia, leading with her left arm, waving the water past her torso and kicking her feet.

As they reached the waist-high water Miles made an admission.

"Mia, I might sing tonight at Karaoke," he said, coming close enough to hug her.

"You? Sing what?"

"Just don't be surprised. Knowing you, you'll look at me like I'm crazy."

"I would not. It's just that I've never seen your introverted butt sing anywhere but in the shower."

"I think it will be fun, if I can get up the nerve," he said, taking the initiative to dip both of their bodies in and out of the water.

"Maybe I'll sing too," Mia threatened.

"Sure you will," Miles replied with a chuckle.

"Hey, you two. Come on over to the other side of the pier and jet ski with us," yelled Megan, who was skiing with Lexi and Yanni. Yanni was looking cute in a lapis blue one-piece and this time it was Lexi who was barely wearing a Brazilian plum bikini with the bottoms creeping up in between her thick rear.

Mia replied, "That's okay. Not today." She said to Miles, "You can ski if you want. I'm going to dry off and get some more sun on that lounge chair."

"Those are your girls over there, tearing up the place. Where's Bianca anyway?"

"Oh shit, we have a four-o'clock hair appointment. I have to go. I'm late," Mia said, giving him a quick kiss on the lips.

She rushed off, running first to the lounge chair for her wrap and beach bag, and then trying to catch the boat in time.

As she checked out the scene from the boat, she noticed that Miles was indeed about to hop on that jet ski with Megan. Mia thought, *She'd better watch herself. She's having more fun with my man than I am. I'm not sure if I should be keeping an eye on Winter or Megan. I trust Miles. Shoot, I refuse to waste time keeping an eye on any grown person. Why the fuck is Megan, in her garnet tube-top body glove, squeezing him around his waist?*

* * *

"When are we going to go shopping again?" Winter asked the captain, lounging out while holding his hand.

"What do you need, Winter?" the captain asked.

"I want to get a suit for my closing report the morning we get back to Fort Lauderdale. I left one of my bags at home."

"Doesn't the station give you a wardrobe allowance?"

"Why do you ask?" she said releasing his hand and taking a sip of her colada.

"Because I know they write those types of deals into your contract."

"Jim, just go ahead and say you do not want to spend a little bit more money on me. Don't turn a question into a question. You owe me at least a damn two-hundred-dollar suit," she said as though she was being misunderstood.

"I owe you *what*?" he asked, taking off his shades.

"Oh, excuse me. This patriotic bikini is nice, but I hardly call this expensive," she said, pointing down at her bikini bottoms.

"So unless I buy you something expensive, I'm always going to owe you something?" he asked in amazement.

Winter began to squeeze her bountiful tits together, "Jim, if you haven't noticed, I am a woman."

"You are that," he admitted, glancing at her chest.

"Then what's the problem? You don't really have a problem, do you?" The question was more like a statement.

"Winter, I have a problem with any woman who asks for material things without even a subtle hint of humility."

"Oh, excuse me. Should I have waited for you to offer?"

"No, you should maybe get to know someone aside from their wallet," he advised.

"How about if you get to know me aside from my pussy? I am the MVP on this ship, Jim. I know you of all people know that," Winter said, sounding cocky.

The captain replied facetiously. "I'm not so sure about that.

Sometimes having the most valuable personality is worth much more than the most valuable pussy."

"Very good, Jim. You think you're pretty tuff, don't you? You know all I was doing was telling you what I needed. Remember that you don't know if you never ask."

"Remember this, you'll never get it from me if you do," he said, putting his sunglasses back on.

"Discussion closed. I'm going to soak up this beautiful sun for a while. Thanks for the swimwear," she said with sarcasm.

Winter pulled her blue block shades out of her bag, put them over her Cover Girl eyes and lay back, raising her chin to the sun.

"Can you spray me down, please?" she asked, as if the conversation had never occurred, holding out her bottle of cool tangerine shimmer spray without even opening her eyes.

The captain raised his muscular legs from his lounge chair with a swivel and settled his wide feet in the blazing sand. He took the tiny pale orange bottle into his titanic hand and reluctantly sprayed Winter's fit and curvy frame from her voluptuous chest area to her washboard midsection, to her thirty-four-inch legs and down to her perfect, pointed, powder blue creme toes.

"I've got to get back to work," he said. He placed the spray bottle in the sand, secured his toes into his black Nike thongs and took his white nylon sweatshirt and terrycloth towel from the head of his chair. He waved to his sunning passengers and took the small ship transport back to his unconditional ladylove. Winter remained silent, continuing to get her tan on.

# NOT SO HAPPY TO BE NAPPY

"Where have you been?" Bianca asked Mia as she sat in the salon chair, glancing up at the wall clock.

"Kicking it with my man, do you mind?" Mia replied, in no mood to be questioned.

"You'd better ask Tookie if she minds," Bianca said, looking at the hairdresser. "Tookie, Mia is why you call this place Roots."

"Shut up, girl," Mia said to Bianca. She then asked Tookie, "Do you? I'm sorry."

"Looking at your hair, no," Tookie replied in jest. "Sit down."

"This is Ashley," Bianca said introducing Mia to Miss Isley.

"I know who she is. Hello, ma'am."

Ashley was getting a pedicure. "Don't call me ma'am, please, call me Ashley," she said with a regal glow, sporting her hot orange nails with silver tips.

"It's a pleasure, Ashley," Mia stated with respect.

"I guess we women have one thing in common," said Ashley, "that's looking good."

"True, by any means necessary," Mia said. "What type of pedicure is that?" she asked, looking into the steamy tray of water as Ashley removed her golden feet.

"This is called a margarita pedicure. They use hot rocks, lime, and salt," she said while the pedicurist massaged her feet.

"I'll be damned. That must feel like heaven," said Mia.

"It is, honey," Ashley replied leaning her head back. "Like you said, by any means necessary."

"I'm getting one of those next," Bianca claimed. "But Ashley, you know Mia's real reason for coming on this cruise? She thinks her man is going to propose."

Ashley smiled. "That would be a beautiful thing. This is a lovely setting if you're going to pop the question. Looking out over the black evening water and the moonlight with the cool breeze."

"That sounds good," Tookie said while blow-drying Mia's hair. "Your hair is soaking wet. You know it's not a good idea to relax your hair just after your scalp has been wet."

"I'll take the risk," Mia replied.

"You should have had it done before you came," Bianca commented.

"I did. Anyway, about the proposal, I think he'd prefer to jump over the side of this ship than pop the question right now," Mia said. "He's just a little cranky."

"He's always cranky," said Bianca, as if she knew him well herself.

Mia replied, "Not like this. He's PMSing. Pre Male Syndrome."

"Pre what?" Ashley inquired.

Bianca responded, "More like pre-proposing syndrome. He's a nervous wreck."

"That's a good one," Ashley said with a giggle. "I'll have to remember that. I've given up on all of that engagement, wife, husband and family stuff. As you all say, been there, done that. I just perform and hang out with whomever, whenever, wherever, no strings attached. Now, don't get me wrong, I'm not irresponsible or loose. I've had a ten-year relationship with no strings that suits me just fine."

"To each his or her own. But, it's too dangerous out here in the Y2K. I'm looking to be a wife for life," said Mia.

"I'm starting to feel like Ashley," Bianca interjected. "My heart is in so many pieces it looks like a jigsaw puzzle."

"Oh, you're young, you'll be fine. At least you've got all the pieces. I've lost one or two and I'm not interested in turning back to look for them. I'm footloose and fancy free," Ashley said, looking up to the ceiling. "Hallelujah!"

Mia asked Ashley, "Are you going to the pajama party tonight?"

"No, I hope to have a pajama party of my own, if you know what I mean," Ashley answered with the devil in her eyes.

"Well, all right," Bianca replied.

Ashley said, as if from experience, "Just remember that there are no accidents in life. All is in divine order. You are where you are supposed to be in life at any given moment because it is part of your evolution. With or without a man, fiancé, husband, girlfriend, it's okay. Whether he proposes or not, just let go and let God. But if you want it, pray on it, claim it and ask that man yourself."

Mia said immediately, "No, I could not take control like that. He would say no, just because he'd think I was trying to take away his manly choices."

"If it was me, I wouldn't ask him *or* say yes," said Bianca.

"Well, it's not you," Mia fired back.

Tookie walked over to take Ashley to another chair. "I'm going back to get my hair fried. I'll see you two later," Ashley said as she walked away putting her weight on her heels, with baby pink foam cushions in between each toe.

"Why is it that wisdom comes with age and not desire? I guess I'll have to wait to become that content with life," Bianca said after offering her best to Ashley.

"Anyway, Bianca, I know when he's going to pop the question," Mia stated.

"Oh really?"

"Tonight during karaoke. He said he's going to sing and that is not like Miles."

"Sing what?" Bianca asked.

"Our song, *Here and Now*."

"Yeah, right. That boy has never been that sensitive in his entire life."

Mia said confidently, "Okay, you just watch. My baby is going to do it just before he sings like Luther Vandross. There's no better time than tonight."

"Don't hold your breath," Bianca warned.

Mia missed dinner because she let Bianca finish up everything ahead of her at the salon. Bianca had that important dinner date with Omar Young. Mia didn't get out of the salon until eight. Miles was sleeping like a baby but she noticed that he did take time to lay out his smoke gray pajama bottoms with a bright white crew-neck T-shirt for the pajama party.

"Wake up, Mr. Jet Ski Man," Mia said to Miles with a nudge.

"What," he said in a groggy, deeper-than-deep voice.

Mia turned to take off her sarong. "You got quite a tan. How long were you out there?"

"Just until about six, I think," he said looking over at the clock and then glancing at her. "Look at you. Your hair is *fresh*, baby." He opened his eyes wide as if he'd seen her for the first time.

"Thanks. That stylist did hook me up. I haven't had Shirley Temple curls since I was a little girl," she said shaking her head like she was in a Loreal commercial.

"We've got to go out and show you off," Miles said, as she lay on top of his stomach.

*I see he's feeling bette*r, Mia thought.

"What do you think would go better with my new 'do?" Mia asked, hopping off of him and making her way to the dresser. She turned and held up two choices. "This rainbow teddy with a long, red, sheer robe? Or this short, brown tie-dye nightgown?"

"I say anything long this time will work. That way you can cover yourself up, just in case," he said, forcing himself to sit up along the side of the bed.

"Just in case what?"

"Just in case no one else is wearing a nightie. I'm sure most of these women are going to be wearing pajamas."

"No one wears pajamas anymore," Mia said as if he needed to get with it.

"We'll see. But, you don't see me running around in my boxers or briefs. I'm going to play it safe," he said, heading into the bathroom.

Speaking at full volume, Mia quipped, "Everyone already saw you in your wet board shorts earlier. I'm sure you couldn't do worse than that. At least you'll be dry."

"Oh so I guess you should just wear a bra and panties, huh? There's an appropriate time for everything," said Miles, squeezing the toothpaste onto his electric toothbrush.

*I hope so*, Mia thought. *I suppose he does not want me to look like a hoochie when I come onstage as he sings to me.* "Okay, I'll wear the long robe."

Through the sound of the buzzing toothbrush came his muffled response: "That's my girl." He spit into the sink, humming an unrecognizable tune.

# SING ME A PROPOSAL

The Chocolate Bar had been transformed into a karaoke bar, complete with speakers, a huge, wide screen for the audience to sing along, three microphones (just in case there was a group of singers) and a viewing monitor for the brave soul onstage.

Omar sat close to Bianca at a front-row table with Mia and Miles and Scott and Kelly. They seemed much more friendly and familiar with each other than before.

"So, Omar. I was impressed with your poetry. You must continue to write and perhaps think about getting published," said Mia.

"Thanks, but I don't know if I can keep myself motivated enough to write a collection of poems. I write about what's happening at the time. Obviously I hope I never go through that one again."

"A broken heart?" Mia inquired. "We all know what that's like," she sympathized.

"Mia, why are you so nosey?" Miles asked.

"No problem, Miles," Omar said. "Yes, Mia. It was a broken heart." Bianca cut her eyes at Mia like a switchblade.

Miles changed the subject, looking around the room. "Grown people wearing lingerie and pajamas to a karaoke party. This is wild."

"I told you," said Mia. "I just wonder how sheer, how short, how tight, and how skimpy these outfits are going to be?"

"I just know that unless the women are wearing thongs, the only other option is no panties at all. That's got to be the magic combination to open the gate that will let the dogs out," Bianca commented.

Brandon finally got his chance to approach Winter, who was seated at the bar and for the first time, alone. Her lingerie of choice was a champagne pink, silk camisole with a pink pair of fishnet hot pants. She looked like Jessica Rabbit sitting at the bar with her extra long legs crossed to the side and her back as straight as a board, poking out her overpowering boobs.

He straddled the stool next to her and asked, "Can I buy you a drink?"

She looked him up and down, taking a gulp of Kahlúa. "Only if you have a Mercedes in your garage and a nine-inch dick in your pants," she said, still totally sober.

Brandon replied, "In my garage I have a 2003 five-hundred series, pearl white Mercedes with palomino interior and twenty-inch rims. In the other garage, I have a convertible candy-apple red Testerosa with blood red leather interior. But I don't care how beautiful you are, I'm not about to cut off three inches of my dick for nobody."

Winter looked stunned. Within two minutes and two seconds, Brandon and Winter were making their way out of the Chocolate Bar. The lofty Winter towered over his five-eight frame. Off they went to who knows where.

"No karaoke for them," Omar said as they walked away.

Bianca replied, "I'm sure they'll soon be making music of their own."

Tangie passed out the list of songs for all of the brave souls to view.

"Girl, I'm going to do this," Bianca said.

Mia shook her head as if Bianca was kidding. "No, you're not."

"Oh, hell yes, I am. This is my song right here." Bianca pointed to Sade's "Somebody Already Broke My Heart."

"Who's that for?" asked Mia.

"Girl, nobody. You know that's my cut off her *Lovers Rock* CD."

"Okay, then I'll pick a Sade song, too," Mia decided.

"Oh, no, Mia. Since when do you sing?" asked Bianca.

Mia answered, as if offended, "Since I'm on this damn ship trying to have some fun. Now don't you trip like you're the only one who can carry a tune up in here just because you took voice lessons back in middle school."

"Yeah, while you were lugging that cello home thinking you were going to actually do something with the symphony one day," Bianca reminded her.

"What's wrong with that?"

"Nothing. I'm just saying there's more to this than carrying a tune, or a cello."

"And? Like I said, I'm all about having fun. I'm doing it," Mia said with conviction.

Bianca toyed with Mia, "Okay. Having fun overrides common sense and eardrums. Let's go over here and reserve our place with Tangie. "Excuse us, gentlemen," Bianca said to Omar and Miles, who were deep into a conversation with Kelly and Scott.

Lexi, Yanni and Megan strolled in and took the three seats at the front table next to Mia's group.

Mia picked up the list from the sign-up table and said, "Girl, those three have put their names on this list for 'Bootilicious' by Destiny's Child."

"Hey, Tangie, can we get on this list, too?" Bianca asked.

"What do you want, girls?" Tangie asked. "Just tell me and it's done."

Bianca staked her claim to Sade's cut number four while Mia said, "I'll take cut number five, 'All About Our Love.' "

* * *

Several passengers had already gone real old school, performing the first few songs. One sang "Perfect Angel" by Minnie Riperton, another blew the hell out of "Gloria" by the Shadows of Knight and the third one got down with "Rock With You" by Michael Jackson. It was now time for Mia's girls, Yanni, Lexi and Megan.

"The next song is *Bootilicious* sung by Sisters Three," Tangie said with excitement.

Bianca looked at Mia with a question mark as the girls stood up. She asked, "Sisters Three?"

Lexi was at least covered up with white silk pajamas and strappy white slippers, while Yanni was barely covered, wearing a malted-milk-shake-colored sheer body suit and in her bare feet. Megan, the lead singer, had on a shortcake-colored baby-doll set with tiny strawberries throughout and four-inch raspberry T-strap heels. Her bare, tanned legs were dipping to the beat of the intro.

Megan, Lexi, and Yanni asked the audience if they could handle it, before answering in unison that they couldn't.

The men in the crowd started to hoot and holler, some standing up to get a better view.

The girls continued on and on until they got to the main chorus about their bodies being way too bootilicious.

Lexi and Yanni were shaking their asses like they were on fire while Megan was leading the pack with moves like Beyonce herself.

They ended in a stance much like the Supremes, each frozen in place in a different pose. The men clapped with reverence as the ladies returned to their seats.

"That was bootilicious!" Scott yelled, while Kelly took a sip of her pink champagne.

"That was for sure a lot of jelly, that's what that was," she said, acting like she was player hating.

Next up was Bianca. Omar lovingly let go of her hand from his protective embrace and she went up onstage. She arranged her mic as though she had done this for a living.

"That's a tough act to follow. Mine is a little more mellow than that," she said to everyone as she smiled sweetly in the direction of their table, particularly toward Omar. The music started with a slow, smooth beat and she bounced her head to the strum of the guitar and began crooning about needing a savior after being constantly disappointed in love.

She looked dead into Omar's eyes and continued on about already having her heart broken by someone, so she needed to be treated with kindness and care.

Omar leaned back in his chair, folding his arms across his abdomen as still as a mannequin, taking in every word. Miles nudged Omar, who was oblivious to Miles's elbow. Omar was now leaning onto the table with his elbows propped up. His attention appeared undivided.

The closing melody wound down and Bianca closed her eyes as though she was really feeling the words. She tapped her foot until the final note was complete.

She replaced the mic onto the stand and took a bow, rushing offstage just as Omar stood up. She took a seat while he and the audience continued to clap.

"That was really good," Mia said. "I knew you still had it."

Omar took his seat and hugged her, whispering in her ear. She smiled a Colgate smile and turned toward him for another embrace just long enough to come face to face for a brief kiss on the lips.

"Very good, Bianca," Miles said as Tangie called the next victim.

"Up next, we have Mia White, singing 'All About Our Love.' "

"Mia, you're really going to do this?" Miles asked with a combination of doubt, embarrassment and pity.

Without a word she stood up and walked the green mile as if here goes nothing, heading for the stage. Sisters Three whistled in support or in amazement. Mia was more amazed than they were.

Mia's first thought as she reached the stage was, *I wonder if the lights were this bright for everyone else.*

The music hadn't started yet as she stood in silence, not even the sound of a pin drop, not a clearing of a throat or the sound of faint whispers. She looked down at the monitor and noticed the words were lined up, but still there was no music. Suddenly, someone cleared his or her throat in the front row. *Uh-oh,* Mia thought, *it was just me.*

The intro started at a much slower pace than she remembered when she'd listened to the song in her car. In particular she'd never noticed the long, drawn-out beats and the extra loud, nerve-wracking sound of the base vibrating through the speaker. The first words lit up. She opened her mouth and nothing came out.

"I'm sorry, Tangie. Can I start again?" Mia said to a spotlight, with her hand shielding the glare.

She heard a voice. "No problem."

Again, an unbelievably annoying silence filled the room, but this time, the silence was iced with the internal sound of the rapid blinking of her own eyelids. Mia gave the cold, chrome microphone a good, firm squeeze, trying to release her own anxiety into the cylinder-like wand.

The beat began again and she sang the words about their love being everlasting.

Mia asked herself, *When will this end? I think I sound like shit.* She thought, through the thick air of silence, *Why is there so much dead time in between the choruses?* She could hear the sound of air being let out of a balloon, or was it Bianca trying to hold in her squeals of laughter? Nervously, Mia continued singing, admitting that while their love hadn't been ideal, they'd handle whatever came their way, now and forever.

*This was not a good selection,* Mia told herself. She looked in the direction of Tangie, thinking, *Please tell me I'm done.* Mia knew in her mind, her ass sounded awful. She thought someone was tapping his or her foot, or maybe it was Miles's heart beating from the shame. She said to herself, *There, I'm done.*

The intensity of the lights slowly subsided. She could see Miles, sitting in the silence of his amazement. His hands were parallel to each other as he began a slow clap, and then Bianca and Omar broke from their embrace long enough to join in.

Mia replaced the sweaty microphone on its stand and returned to the table feeling five inches shorter and fifty pounds heavier. Kelly said, "That was a really cool song. Was that Sade?"

"Screw you, Kelly," Mia said, crossing her legs at the knee.

"No, really. That was a totally good choice," Kelly said.

Mia replied, paranoid, "That's like when you see an ugly baby and you say, 'Now *that*'s a baby.' "

"What? Like, excuse me," Kelly said, looking over at Scott.

Miles commented, "Baby, you did a great job and that song was a hard one to sing."

"Miles, stop it," Mia snapped, knowing her insecurity was in overdrive.

Bianca joined in, "Okay then, if that's your reaction to everyone who said something I'm not saying anything."

"I guess you're a hard act to follow," Mia said to Bianca.

"Mia, look," said Bianca, pointing to Miles as he got up to sing. The crowd ceased with the weak-ass applause.

Mia was suddenly encouraged to sit back and focus on Miles's rendition of their Luther cut.

"He's about to sing our song," Mia told Omar.

"Okay," Omar replied.

"You're a trip," said Bianca as she watched Mia scoot her chair up, giving her full focus to Miles's every move.

The speakers bumped out the first few beats of his selection as Bianca said, "This couldn't be it, girl."

Of course it wasn't their song, not with the bass thumping and the singer chanting about her ass being so bad it'd make a nigga spend his last dime.

"Dammit, that's Juvenile," said Bianca, looking embarrassed for Mia.

"Yes, it is," Mia said with glazed eyes as she sank down into her seat. "That's juvenile all right."

Scott started bouncing and giving his *woo, woo* fist pump as Miles rapped "Back That Thang Up." He continued while

Sisters Three looked over at Mia, yet they hollered louder than Scott did.

Bianca stared at Mia instead of Miles. The look on Bianca's face told Mia that she was all up in her head, and reading it correctly.

"Girl," Mia said leaning in to talk to Bianca, "my man ruined this perfectly good chance to propose with our song. I think I'm going to be sick."

Miles exited the stage and approached Scott first, who stood up and gave him a pound.

"Man, that was funky. Your shit was smooth, bro," Scott said.

"Thanks, dude," Miles replied, wiping his forehead with a napkin. "Mia, we'll catch up later. We're going to check out that midnight golf tournament on deck."

"Bye, baby," Scott said to Kelly. Mia just stared at both of them as they walked out.

Kelly said, "Girl, I knew they were going to run off. I'm going to my room for some peace and quiet while he's out. Lord knows he'll be trying to get some when he gets in."

"Kelly, how do you deal with them being so into their boys and not their women? This is your honeymoon cruise," Mia asked in frustration.

"Don't forget we've already been married for one year. I knew he was like this when I married him. It's good clean fun, Mia. Plus, I like time to myself anyway. I'll see you later," Kelly said, picking up her purse and pushing her chair back as another trio was about to go onstage to sing "Zoom" by the Commodores.

"Mia, Omar and I are going dancing. Are you coming?" asked Bianca. "Just let a dog roam and he'll find his way home."

"Funny, but I don't think so."

"Come on, girl," Yanni encouraged her, slipping back into her shoes. "Lexi, Megan and I are going too. We're going to hit the dance floor on deck and shake our butts under the stars."

"Not me," Lexi said, just as Dr. Steven came over to claim her.

"Hey, everybody," he said, greeting the group. "Hey, baby," he said cozily to Lexi.

Lexi smiled. "I'll see you later, Yanni. I will be back tonight, so don't stay out too late."

"Don't worry about me. I'm a big girl too," Yanni assured her.

Bianca said to Mia, "So, we'll meet you over there at the dance, right?"

"Oh hell, why not," said Mia as Bianca and Omar walked just ahead of the girls.

"So, it looks like it's just the three of us singles," said Megan.

Mia thought, *I came on board as the other half of a couple in love, now I'm the third wheel in the Sisters Three trio.*

"Are you feeling better, Yanni?" Mia asked as they were walking.

"Better than what?" asked Megan.

"Nothing. I was just feeling a little hung over. I'm fine now. Where's Olandi?" Yanni asked Megan.

"He's probably working. You know he told me there's an underground strip club in one of these rooms."

"No way," said Mia. "I don't believe that."

"Why do the brothers always end up with the underground clubs with women who are willing to let them freak all night for tips?" asked Yanni.

"Where are all the men what will let us do that?" Mia asked.

"Everywhere," Megan said as they laughed.

Yanni continued, "That's the problem. I don't know of many men who wouldn't let you do that. Men love finding women who would be down with no boundaries and no strings attached."

"What is it that men desire in other women that they don't have in their own women?" Mia asked.

"New pussy," said Megan, again making them laugh.

Yanni responded, "No, I think it's just the variety. It's no reflection on us. I don't take it personally."

Mia said, "Megan, you can't even talk about why men who are taken sleep with other women, okay?"

"Believe it or not, just because I've been the other woman before doesn't mean I have to take responsibility for the men who screw around," said Megan.

Mia disagreed. "Yes it does, if you're part of the problem. Take a moment and think about the other woman who finds that she is suddenly not enough for the very man you're screwing around with."

Megan replied, "I don't think it's a reflection on her. It's a reflection on him."

"What are you guys gabbing about?" asked Bianca, who slowed up with Omar as they reached the dance area on deck.

"Just our normal debates," said Yanni.

Bo walked in.

"Hey, lady. Do you want to dance?" Bo asked Yanni.

Yanni looked at Mia and carefully responded, "Sure."

Mia tried to make a point by hinting. "Yanni. I thought we were going to just chill and talk tonight? You know, just the girls."

"It'll just be a minute. I'll be fine," Yanni said.

"Yanni?" Mia said.

"How can I say no when Mary J. is singing about getting crunked?" Yanni replied.

Bo took her by the arm and led her to the dance floor while a new guy swept Megan off her feet to dance as well.

"Okay, now I'm going to have to play baby-sitter," Mia said to Bianca.

"Girl, we are going to get to shaking things up and nothing else," said Bianca, holding hands with Omar.

"You go right ahead. I'm going to find my man, otherwise I'm not going to have any fun. Go ahead and shake your asses till they drop. And, Bianca?"

"Yes, Mia."

"Please try and keep an eye on Yanni if you can."

"She looks like she's having fun to me," Bianca said, running off to dance with Omar.

* * *

After a few songs, Bianca and Omar decided to take a seat at a nearby table and talk.

Leaning in close to chat over the music as they held hands, Omar asked, "What's up with Yanni? Is she the baby of the group, even though she's a twin?"

"You could say that. We all try to keep an eye out for her, especially on this ship," Bianca answered.

Omar stated, "I enjoyed our dinner."

"So did I," Bianca agreed.

"And especially your song. That's one of my favorite songs from Sade's last album."

Blood rushed toward Bianca's high cheekbones. "Every song on that album is just as good as all of her old music."

"Have you ever thought about singing professionally?" Omar asked.

"Oh, no way. I'm not the type to sing in front of people."

"You'd never know it. I thought Mia was pretty good too."

"Mia is never going to let me live down her own performance. She's a nut," Bianca said with love.

"Underneath it all, it looks like she had fun . . . So, if someone has to get hurt you don't want to play, huh?" Omar inquired, not missing anything.

"Did I say that?" Bianca asked with coy.

"Yes, you did. And I feel the same way. But the loving itself is so wonderful that you'd think it would all be worth it."

Bianca said, "I think when you see the hurt coming, you make a decision to stay for love or leave for your sanity."

"I never want to hurt anyone. Sometimes it's unintentional but it still happens," he said with an understanding tone.

"Yes, but each person can still make a choice to protect themselves."

"Sometimes there's no time to protect yourself. That's part of the risk and part of deciding to trust."

"You're right," Bianca admitted. "I think when you're so conscious of not being hurt, you get hurt in the process. The very thing you're trying to keep from experiencing, you experience."

"I've been through that," Omar said in agreement. "When was the last time you were in love?"

"Years ago," Bianca replied.

"And you've never fallen in love again?" he asked.

"No. I've dated but nothing serious came out of it."

"Is never falling in love again a choice of yours?" Omar asked, listening intently.

"I don't think it is. But sometimes I admit that I tend to run for the hills, almost to the point of looking for an excuse," said Bianca.

"That's no way to live, Bianca. You seem to be the type of lady who has so much to give. Why waste it because of fear?"

"Good question," she said. "What about you? I heard that your poem was pretty deep."

"That was written at a time when I was so in love that I was actually blind. If I hadn't been blind, I would have known what was going on. You don't want to hear about this."

"Yes, Omar. I really do."

"How about if we dance again for a while and then go for a walk later? I'll tell you about it then."

"Sounds really good to me," Bianca said as though looking forward to it.

After maybe ten minutes or so of grooving on the dance floor, Omar and Bianca were entwined in an embrace that resembled the vertical mambo when the captain intermitted.

"Excuse me, Omar. Do you mind if I interrupt?" he asked, standing with the purser at his side.

"Yes, actually, Captain. What do you need?" Omar asked.

"I need to talk to you for a minute in my suite. Will you come with me?"

"What's going on?" Omar inquired, surprised.

"I'd rather talk to you in private, if you don't mind. Excuse us, ma'am," the captain said to Bianca.

"No problem. Omar, are you okay?" Bianca asked.

"I'm fine," Omar assured her. "I'll meet you back in your room with the kids in an hour or so, okay?"

"I'll be waiting," Bianca assured him.

The captain, the purser and Omar all walked away without saying a word to each other. In deep thought, Bianca left the dance floor and proceeded on down the deck in reverie to Deborah Cox's "Nobody's Supposed to Be Here."

Yanni was still dancing with Bo.

# 30

## IS THAT A CIGAR IN YOUR POCKET OR ARE YOU JUST HAPPY TO SEE ME?

Mia checked out the bars, ballrooms, the gym, pool areas, golf course and coffee shop. She decided to give up. *Where in the hell is this underground strip club?* she wondered.

At one in the morning Mia decided to go to the Cigar Bar to look for Miles. Within minutes, she ordered a shot of Courvoisier and a slim clover Mexican smoke just like the ones she used to enjoy years ago.

She found a beautiful burgundy chenille sofa with black-and-white zebra-print pillows in the private Red Room. The mood was cozy, with flickering disco balls that threw off a kaleidoscope of dim light against the fire-engine red walls. Even though other passengers were all around her and the room was crowded, she had the sofa all to herself and she was loving it. She kicked off her sandals and stretched out her sunburned legs. It felt like she was finally able to enjoy some solitude, no Miles, Bianca or Megan. By the time the waiter brought her drink she'd forgotten who she was looking for in the first place.

"Mia, aren't you the queen of the Nile?" Delmonte commented, startling her from her train of thought. A clean-shaven Delmonte still had on his dinner attire, a grayish blue, double-breasted designer suit with a pale yellow silk tie. Even standing a few feet away from her, he smelled like he'd bathed in Curve bath and body soak. "Would you mind getting your pretty feet off of my sofa?"

Mia challenged him. "Maybe, or maybe you should make me. We paid good money to put our feet anywhere."

"I agree . . . that I should make you. I'll let the other comment go, with your feisty self. You're more ghetto than you look," he joked as he took two slow-paced steps toward the end of the sofa, wrapped his massive hands around her delicate ankles and lifted her legs as if he was lifting a feather. With direct eye attention, he bent her legs at the knees, placed his humongus body on the other end of the sofa and extended her legs across his lap. He stared at her feet for a moment, seeming to examine every toe as if deducing which grade he would give overall.

"What do you have, a foot fetish?"

He shook his head left to right. "Not at all. There are more important parts of the human body that carry more meaning. Like the heart and the mind."

Mia raised her eyebrows. "That's deep."

He placed the tip of his wide index finger against the soft brown skin of her ankle, admiring her tattoo. "What's with Felix the Cat on your ankle?"

"It's just my favorite cartoon, that's all," Mia replied.

"No other meaning?" he asked.

"No. And no kitty-cat jokes, I've heard them all."

"I wasn't going to go there. But, wasn't that cartoon way before your time?" Delmonte inquired.

She took her last swallow from her glass. "The Cartoon Channel. You should check it out."

"I must say I don't have time to be watching cartoons right now. What are you drinking?" he asked, keeping one hand around her ankle and the other hand in the air to get the attention of the waitress.

"Courvoisier."

"Have you ever tried Cristal, or better yet, how about a bottle of Dom P?" he offered.

"Yes, I've tried both and I'm drinking Courvoisier," Mia continued feistily.

"Courvoisier for the lady and a bottle of Dom P," he said to the waitress.

He leaned his two-hundred-fifty-pound-plus body back into the arch of the sofa and began rubbing Mia's toes, first the baby toe in a circular motion, pulling it outward and then on to the next. He held her heel firmly with one hand and moved the upper part of her foot in a circular, clockwise motion and then counterclockwise. "I hope you don't mind, do you?"

Mia leaned back, surrendering to pampered relaxation. "I don't, but I'm sure someone would."

"Are you referring to your Mr. Right?"

"Yes," she said, fighting the urge to close her eyes and enjoy.

He remarked, "Well, I'm not into gossip, see, so you didn't hear this from me . . . but he's observing the moonlit sky out on the deck with our roving reporter, Miss Winter Jackson."

"Oh, really?"

"Hard to believe?"

"Yes and no. Hard to believe you would be low-down enough to share that bit of information with me and not hard to believe that he's actually with her."

"Sometimes the truth needs to be told even though it's hard to hear," he said.

"I say what you don't know can't hurt you."

"Does he share that belief with you?"

"Probably so. But he's not the jealous type," Mia assured him.

Delmonte responded, "Obviously you haven't given him a reason to be. So, he won't mind your feet getting a little attention."

"I don't mind just as long as it's my feet, and nothing else," Mia said making clear her boundaries.

He looked at Mia as if to say, *Yeah right. You want this successful Fortune 500 dick, who you foolin'?*

He complimented her, "You do have pretty feet."

"Thanks."

They sat and drank for hours. As the room became more and more crowded and Mia's head became more and more cloudy, she removed her feet from his lap and scooted closer to him to share the sofa with the couple from the comedy night, the older man and younger girl. Mia and Delmonte laughed and shared stories and yes, they also shared that bottle of Dom P.

"What led me to this purchase of a cruise line is that I bought some rental property in Watts and Compton fifteen years ago and made enough money to pay the note on my own mortgage on my home. I partnered with a company that helped me buy, renovate and sell properties—the rest is history. Next thing I knew, thirty thousand turned to 300 thousand and then to three million and on and on. I'm an investor. I make money for a living. I'm diversified and I'm a smart Black mogul," Delmonte explained confidently.

"You're not very humble though," Mia joked. "So the whole inheritance, lottery-winner rumor is just that, a rumor?"

"Yes. Just good conservative spending and saving."

"Though I haven't bought a house yet, I am investing," Mia added.

"In what?"

"Stocks. I've got money on Intel and Crisco."

He corrected her, "You mean Cisco?"

"That's what I said." Mia reacted with attitude.

"Okay, right," he said, letting her think he heard incorrectly. "That's good that you're investing, but stay away from those fly-by-night Internet stocks and people who say they will manage your money for you. They want to get rich off of you. A good rule is to save thirty percent of everything you make. And buy some property."

Her long blink seemed to last for thirty seconds, as though she already knew to do that. "I plan on doing that next year."

Delmonte took a moment to examine the whites of her eyes. "Are you okay?"

"Yes, I'm fine."

He asked the waitress for some coffee for Mia. "I can get you in a home with no money down and it will be in your name if you want to know how. I have a real estate company and loan company."

"Yeah, and travel company, magazine, clothing lines and cruise line. Damn, just call you Mr. Big Stuff."

"Don't you forget it."

Mia teased through her haze, "But, you're never gonna get my love . . . even with the offer of a house."

"That would have to be some good lovin' for me to buy you a house. I'm not going to give you a damn thing just for letting me rub your toes—just a damn lead on some property," he said as Mia's coffee was served.

Mia picked up the cup, gave a firm blow and took a cautioned sip. "Oh, I'm sorry, I thought you were trying to make me an offer I couldn't refuse."

"No, just conversation. Actually, I'm going to retire to my cabin now. I think you need to check up on your other half."

Mia put her coffee down on the red lacquer sofa table. "I'd rather see your stateroom." She tried to lean into him as if she was smooth enough to follow her suggestion with a snuggle but she awkwardly bumped his arm instead as he steadied her, leaning her back onto the comfort of the sofa back.

In response to her comment, he arose to his feet and turned toward her, bent down on one knee like a shoe salesman, and slipped her sandals onto her feet.

"Let's go," he said, standing over her as he helped her up.

Most of the passengers in the room shook hands with him as he exited the room like he was Jesse Jackson. He gave a peace sign to the bartender and before Mia knew it, they were in the elevator.

# 31

## YOU LEFT THAT PART OUT

Mia stood in place, alternating her nervous bounce of each leg backward and forward in the all-glass-enclosed elevator, within inches of Delmonte Harrison. The chimed ring that confirmed the next floor and the slight abrading resonance of the rubber from the elevator doors opening were the only sounds as Mia and Delmonte stepped out of the elevator and turned the corner.

Then they heard a moaning sound near the stairway. It was nearly three thirty in the morning and Mia was still a little buzzed, so it was difficult to make out the dark silhouettes, but one thing was for sure, the person standing under the stairwell with his eyes closed was Justin, the cameraman. It appeared he was being serviced well, and loving it. Mia and Delmonte played it off as if they did not see the twosome and continued to walk toward the hallway of the Sienna deck.

Delmonte spoke. "That Dante is fired tomorrow."

He was truly serving his passenger of choice, on his knees. *Justin is into men?* Mia thought. *He'd better come on out of that closet.*

Speaking of closets, compared to Delmonte's two-bedroom executive stateroom, Mia's room looked like a closet. And everything was gold, bronze or platinum . . . everything. The furniture, carpet, drapes, lights, picture frames, candles, sofa, bedspread. The only contrasting color was the tinge of stop-sign red bleeding through the gold-and-charcoal-checkered bed pillows and the brick red piping on the platinum couches.

Each spectacular room left Mia speechless until she asked, "Where's the bathroom?"

"Upstairs," Delmonte said while popping the cork on some Krug champagne in the kitchen.

She steadied herself to make it to the top of the spiral staircase, where there was a major gold-and-platinum bathroom the size of most living rooms. The gold towel rings were lined with rhinestones. Gold and red hand towels hung from the rings with thin gold ropes tied into bows. It was obvious that Delmonte believed in living the royal life.

By the time Mia made her nosey way back downstairs to the living-room area, Delmonte had opened the balcony door for a private ocean viewing and placed two chilled glasses of champagne on the glass bar. He also managed to work his way out of his suit and into a red terry-cloth robe. Will Downing was softly serenading them in the background. Delmonte took three careful steps toward Mia in his bare feet on the plush, off-white outdoor carpeting, spilling his charmed whispers into her ear. His telephone began to ring in the background.

"Don't you want to get that?" Mia asked.

"Do you want to get comfortable?" he asked, as if her question was a thought. "There's an extra robe in the closet," he said, pointing to the corner of the room.

Without awaiting her response, he stuck his firm, hot, wet tongue into her left ear as Mia's eyes closed in unison. He delicately bit her earlobe and again inserted his tongue only to flick it in and out, flooding her consciousness with moist eroticism.

*That feels so right but so wrong,* she admitted to herself.

"Wouldn't you like this where it counts?" he asked as if ready, willing and able, running his fingers down her curvy spine.

Mia thought, *What did he say*? Her half-open, groggy eyes were suddenly as wide as walnuts in response to his question, and even though her willing body collapsed in surrender, her mind was fighting to stay sober. *He's really hitting me below the belt now*. Her eyes closed again, just for a second.

Through their slow grind and hot embrace, Mia opened her eyes, glanced over his shoulder, and spied a direct hit upon his family friggin' portrait over the fireplace. His woman, or young-ass mother, and two young girls, were watching them get their groove on.

Mia gave him a sudden push and shove. "You didn't tell me you were a member of a happy family."

"You didn't ask," he said, trying to pull her close again.

Mia squinted her eyes, trying to figure him out. "With all your success stories I thought that you would have been the first one to share the fact that part of your success included a spouse."

"They say behind every good man is a good woman. But, I do not have a spouse and neither do you."

Suddenly feeling sober, Mia backed away toward the front door of his suite. "Mr. Harrison, is this your *modus-operandi*—to find women on these cruises who are in doubt mode so you can share mutual stories of how the two relationships just aren't working out, hoping the answer would be to find comfort in each other?" Mia asked as she rubbed her ear and then crossed her arms.

Delmonte gave her a suddenly lifeless stare. "Mine is just fine, but my mate isn't with someone else tonight."

"Well hers sure is. Bon fucking voyage," Mia said loathingly.

"Oh, Mia, one more thing. That wasn't Dante on his knees tonight—guess who?" he asked with spite.

Mia stared for a minute. "You are such a dog."

He tried to correct her. "Dog? I was the number-one, richest Black man on *Forbes*'s top entrepreneurs' list for this year. Number one."

"Number one, huh? Well, there's no number lower than that!" she interjected with a piercing slice of the eyes.

"Good-bye," he said, handing Mia her bag.

She gave him scathing, loathing, up-and-down eye hate as if she wished she were a man so she could jack him in the face with a left hook. She ran out of the door just as she found herself face to face with Scott and Kelly.

"Oh, excuse me, you two," she said, attempting to regain her composure as the door slammed. *Oh, I know Scott is eating this shit up*, Mia thought. After all, the door reads, DELMONTE HARRISON.

Mia stood there like a deer caught in the headlights. A makeup-smeared deer with a wet ear, smelling like Dom P.

"Hey, Mia," Scott said. "I was just about to walk Kelly to our room and then join Miles at the Star Bar."

Mia asked in momentary distraction, "The Star Bar? Where is that?"

"It's right down the hall, in Brandon's room. We all go there to get drunk and play cards all night long."

"Will you tell him I've been looking for him?"

Mia said while summating to herself, *Surely he's thinking, "Yeah, right, looking for him." I know Scott cannot wait to tell Miles this shit so he can keep him as a running buddy*. Scott just stood there with his hat to the back and his Iceberg khaki pants with the waist hanging down to his upper thighs. Mia gave him a look that said now they both had stories to tell, and he'd better keep their little secret just that, a secret.

"Yeah, I'll tell him," Scott replied.

Kelly stated to Scott, "Go ahead and meet him, okay? Maybe Mia and I can talk girl talk for a minute."

"I think I need that," Mia admitted. The back of her neck itched with guilt. She reached back to scratch it.

"That's cool, ladies. Peace out," Scott said, pinching Kelly's thigh as he strolled off, walking like Snoop.

"I mean where are you coming from?" Kelly asked leaning into Mia while they walked toward the elevator. "I just know you are not fooling around with Mr. Harrison."

"Let's just say I was coming out of his room. That, I cannot deny. I actually could have taken some serious revenge out on Miles. I was saved by a moment of sensibility and a family portrait. I can't be with anyone's man. It'll mean bad karma, and before I know it, someone will be hobbing my man's knob."

"Mia, believe me. You've got nothing on him. That's for sure," Kelly warned.

"What does that mean?" Mia asked, stopping in her tracks.

"Mia, wake up. Miles totally has not been faithful to you."

"Oh really? And why have you decided to warn me now after all these years?"

"Because I have totally seen how much you love him. And Scott has like asked me to keep it to myself, especially now," Kelly said, giving half the scoop.

"What are you talking about anyway? Keep what to yourself?" Mia asked.

"Megan," Kelly replied.

"Megan?"

Kelly explained, "The second night we were here, Miles was out all night with Megan while Scott was like keeping you occupied so you wouldn't like run up on them."

"The second night I did not hang with Scott. Damn, he's got you trained but good."

Kelly turned to walk away and then said, "Mia, I knew you would just make excuses for Miles's behavior. Just forget it, okay?"

"Excuse me, but that was your man who was banging Megan that night, and from the sounds bouncing off my stateroom walls, Scott was giving it to her good," Mia blurted out abruptly.

"You're a darn liar. Scott was keeping an eye on you so you wouldn't try to get in Miles's way."

"Is that the best lie he could come up with?" Mia asked as though she actually had sympathy.

"It's the truth, and I for sure have no reason to doubt him."

Mia checked Kelly, "Kelly, Miles was in my bed, post-climax, when I heard that shit happening. So the next time you decide to go around spreading the news and sparing your befriended sister's feelings, think twice, just like I did when I thought about telling you. I didn't. I guess White men and Black men are just men. All that shit about once you go Black you never go back is bunk. He went back big time."

Kelly shook her head in disbelief and rubbed her eyebrows as if she was awakening to a reality she'd been dreading. "Miles was with you that night?" she inquired, with a bit less volume.

"Yes, Kelly. Plus, as much as I make it a point to always keep one eye on Megan, she wouldn't try to get with my man. We're tighter than that."

"That jerk is dead meat. A one-dang-year anniversary cruise and he stoops to this level. Oh, no, he did not!" Kelly said. Scott was in for it.

Mia said, "From what I know, Scott has been true up until now, Kelly. I have no doubt that Megan was hitting on him because she was pissed that Brandon was trying to play her. Scott was just convenient and he got weak. But, damn, hc could have kept it down knowing we were next door. He must have been faded."

"I'll fade his pale trick butt. Besides, where else was he going to take her? Our room? What exactly did you hear?" Kelly asked, seeking the entire truth.

"Kelly, I'm not the one to go into detail. I thought she was with Brandon so I was shocked as hell to hear her scream his name," Mia said, almost immediately mad at herself as she spoke.

"Hearing her scream his name? That witch is mine," Kelly declared.

"Kelly," Mia begged in frustration. "Calm down."

"Oh, heck no. That woman is going to have to swim her White self back to shore," Kelly said with certainty. She stormed off, sniffling and crying as if she'd been stabbed in the heart. Mia thought, *Megan had better lock her ass in her room, because she has nowhere to hide.* Now Scott really had one up on Mia. She knew eventually he was going to tell Miles about her hasty exit from Delmonte's room. Even if he wasn't sure that Mia overheard him that night, he was about to find out.

# A SECRET EXPOSED

On Wednesday morning, the ship arrived in St. Thomas. The only sound ringing in Mia's ear was Miles's snoring with his mouth wide open because he could not breathe through his nose that morning. She always thought he had that sleep apnea thing and it was getting worse. Sometimes he would stop breathing for a few seconds and it scared the heck out of her. It was always worse when he'd been drinking. Mia was not sure when he came in, but now he appeared dead to the world.

Just as Mia's foot hit the floor in a half-wakened state, Bianca called.

"Hey, Mia. Good morning," she said, sounding chipper.

"What's up, girl? How was your evening?" Mia asked, rubbing her mascara-smeared eyes and trying to keep her voice down.

"It was spectacular. Can you meet me on the main deck at the track? I need to jog off these excess hormones I've been producing lately."

"What did you get into? Or what got into you?" Mia asked.

"Nothing, but I do need to work off some energy. Can you meet me in thirty?"

"Thirty it is," Mia agreed.

Miles turned over to his left side and his snoring stopped. Mia hit the shower and threw on her maroon jogging shorts, sports bra, cut-off Reebok T-shirt and new running shoes. *I sure hope I don't work up too much of a sweat and get my roots to tightening up. My curls are still bouncing and behaving,* Mia thought as she laced up her shoes.

"Baby," she said, shaking Miles's shoulder. "I'm going to meet Bianca. I'll see you later."

"Uh-huh," he said, turning over onto his back and once again snoring like he was calling the hogs.

Bianca was lit up like a Christmas tree, glowing from ear to ear and wearing a loud-ass red-and-green workout suit, all zipped up with a hooded sweatshirt over her head. Her bright white teeth were fully exposed from her molars to her wisdom teeth.

"So tell me about the evening you had last night," Mia said, placing her towel around her neck.

"Omar is something else, I'll tell you that. He's sensitive and attentive and smart. But, there's a reason why he's been so elusive."

"What's that?"

Bianca explained as they began to stretch, "The brother actually took his kids on this cruise without her permission."

"Her, who?"

"His wife."

Just then, Delmonte came down the deck toward Mia and Bianca, walking slowly with a woman on his arm as he gave Mia a quick eye and then kept his sights straight forward.

"Hello, ladies," the woman said as they passed. "I'm inspired by your discipline to exercise. Enjoy," she said. The woman was Ashley Isley.

Bianca laughed. "Yes, we've got to stay ahead of all of this great food. Hello, Mr. Harrison."

Delmonte nodded.

Bianca stared in place as they walked away. "So that's her ten-year relationship? Now I bet that was a hell of a private pajama party."

Mia rolled her head and shoulders from side to side, stretching her upper back. "If that isn't something, I don't know what is. That man is busy."

"How do you know? We've barely seen him."

Mia bent over to touch her toes and bounced up and down for a few beats, reaching for her toes with each dip. "Bianca, Omar is married?" she asked, continuing the conversation.

"Mia, it's not what you think it is. It's not that simple. Let's go," Bianca said as they started to jog. "See, Omar Young, who is from Fort Lauderdale, has been estranged from his wife for the past three months. She served him with divorce papers last month."

"So like I said, he is still married."

"Yes, he's still married, okay? Omar went to her house to talk to her after she had the papers served and was surprised to find that she had moved her new man in already. Omar asked to see his wife and the dude told him she didn't want to see him and he couldn't come by again. He said he then asked to see his kids and the guy told him no. Well, any true man would have been upset and ready to tell the guy off, but Omar told me he just gave in and left."

Bianca continued, running one step ahead of Mia with her chest bouncing. "Within an hour after he returned to his apartment, she called threatening to file a restraining order and saying that he could only pick up and drop off the kids from school, and that she didn't want him coming by anymore."

Mia asked, "Why would she go to that extreme unless she was afraid of him?"

"I don't think it was because she was afraid. He said she moved this guy in and threatened to file the order because she had caught Omar in a motel room with an ex-girlfriend after he found out she'd been seeing another man for the past ten years."

"What a mess."

"The way Omar found out was that he discovered love letters in their garage from this guy that dated back to the time they got married. Omar confronted this guy last year and eventually she stopped seeing him, but Omar was so distraught by her betrayal that he started seeing the ex of his, who he ran into. She found out and that's why they separated. Now she's got some new man who apparently has been waiting for the right time to step in and put his shoes under the bed for good."

Mia asked, "Bianca, do you really want to get involved in something like this? This sounds like too much drama for anyone to get into."

"I can understand that he was hurt and that he turned to someone who he knew for comfort. People do that all the time."

"Yes, but what if that was your man who did that?" Mia suggested.

"If he'd found out that I'd had a lover for all those years, I wouldn't blame him. He said deep down, even with her adultery and his infidelity, he thought they could work it out after a separation. But, here's the real deal. He called her last month to tell her that the next time he picked up the kids, he was taking them on a cruise, but she said they couldn't go. He made a decision to just take them anyway, and here they are. So yesterday, the captain called him into his office to give him the rundown on what she's trying to do."

"Omar, we received a call from the Coast Guard that your wife has filed kidnapping charges against you," the captain said.

Omar replied with a frown, "That's ridiculous. I never kidnapped my own kids."

"Well, they sent us a fax of a letter you wrote that indicates that you requested her approval but that she told you they could not go. Why did you make the decision to just take them anyway?" the captain asked.

Omar explained, "That letter included detailed information of the conversation I had with her, that I had picked them up from school and that my intentions were to continue on with my vacation plans for them."

"Yes, but you neglected to tell her which cruise and where. She did not know where her own kids were. But as you can see, it is possible for port officials to locate someone if kidnapping charges are filed. Do your kids know what's going on?"

"No. They have no idea."

"That's good. Mr. Young, it is my responsibility to detain you. I have full jail facilities here to do just that. The only thing that is going to save you is if you prove to me that you have joint custody and that you did not violate any court-ordered visitation agreements. Can you do that?" Captain Douglas asked.

Mia rested near a railing. "So is this why he's been hiding from the cameras and stuff? It sounds like he didn't want her to know where they were so that she would worry—just to hurt her in return for his hurt. It sounds like he's still in love with her, Bianca."

"Well, he isn't."

"Bianca! You don't want to get involved in this, do you?"

"I'm already involved. I think he's a nice man who has been hurt."

"I think you're turned on by the fact that he's a bit of a mystery. You're missing the fact that this is a man who would use his own kids to get back at their mother for having a new man," Mia summated.

"I disagree. I don't think that's it," Bianca protested.

"Then what is it?" Mia asked.

Bianca leaned over the railing, looking out at the view as if she were reading her response. "This is a brave man who loved a woman for thirteen years and then found out she'd been unfaithful. She moved a new man into the very home her husband bought, the home he paid the mortgage on. And then she tried to hit him where she knew it would really hurt, with his kids. In spite of the fact that those two kids were about to go on a wonderful vacation, her ego got in the way so she wanted to control the situation by ruining his plans for them. He could not let her control him like that."

"But now he risks being detained and prosecuted, and perhaps he'll never see those kids again."

Bianca turned to Mia. "Lighten up, Mia. He was able to prove, through the divorce papers, that she was filing for sole custody as part of the proceedings next month. For now, he can take those kids anywhere he chooses as long as it's on his visitation time, and she can as well."

"So, the captain didn't detain him?"

Bianca answered, leaning side to side and front to back to stretch out her abs and back. "No. He cannot detain someone for moral reasons. Yes, she should have known but he documented the fact that he told her. He just didn't tell her where."

Mia inquired as though she already knew the answer, "Bianca, are you being blinded by the fact that Omar saved Corey?"

Bianca thought for a minute and said, "I didn't think about that, but subconsciously, that might be a part of it. He pulled my son from that pool when everyone else just stared at him. I watch him with those kids. They love him to death and he would never hurt them."

"But imagine what she's going to be telling them about him."

"He'll talk to them first," Bianca said with certainty as they walked back to their chairs.

"Bianca, I don't know," Mia said, grabbing her towel.

Bianca replied, "You don't have to know. I want to get to know him better. I think Omar Young is a very special man. And I want to make sure that the rest of his cruise is special."

"I'm sure it will be special," Mia said. "Sort of like a fantasy boat ride. But the reality will hit when you get back home."

"Mia, can I please have your positive blessings? That would really make me feel good. I think I've got enough common sense to not do anything that would hurt Corey and me."

"I trust you on that one, Bianca. I know I'm being pessimistic. I can afford to be. Just like you, when you warn me about Miles. But, all in all I just want you to be happy."

Bianca put her gym bag over her shoulder and replied, "I *am* happy. And I'm going back to my room to take a shower and just think."

"Don't you want a cappuccino or something?" Mia offered.

"No, I just want to wash all of this sweat off of me. I'll see you later," Bianca said, walking away.

Mia walked to the bow of the ship, to nearly the highest point on the top deck. It was the Peek-a-Boo bridge over the observation area. Mia simply leaned upon the chrome railing and stared at the view of land and water all around the seemingly never-ending island of St. Thomas. The emerald hills were sprinkled with white and pastel houses, and the calm waters with multicolored sailboats and filled-to-capacity party boats. The eye-catching apple green foliage and casuarina trees and flowers of every color, like cherry blossoms and papaya-colored snapdragons, graced the island's rich countryside. The scene tantalized her senses and mesmerized her mind as she took in the wonder of the beautiful world she lived in.

Snapping out of her mystic reverie, Mia decided to head back to her room to continue her cruise experience. She stopped at Starbucks to grab a banana muffin and white chocolate latte, totally ruining the effect of all of her jogging but feeling more refreshed mentally than she had in years.

Upon reaching the cabin, she found a note from Miles saying he was playing chess and that he'd catch up with her for lunch or dinner.

*Since everyone else is doing their thing, I think I'm going to do what I like to do best: gamble,* she told herself.

# A REAL FIND

The Safari Casino was unusually crowded for an afternoon. The sound of the silver dollars, quarters, dimes and nickels falling from the paying slot machines was music to Mia's ears.

Miles knew she liked to play the mega-bucks machines with the red, white, and blue patriotic stripes. Mia stopped by a huge Wheel of Fortune machine and flagged over a change person so that she could exchange a twenty-dollar bill for a roll of silver dollars.

"Good luck," the waitress said as she handed Mia the roll.

Mia pulled off the paper and threw it to the side of the machine. Holding onto her twenty silver dollars, she maneuvered half of them into her other hand so that she could put in three at a time more easily. She slid one, two and three into the slot and pulled the handle. In return she got a smiling picture of the lovely Vanna, a picture of a brand-spanking-new red car and a picture of a crisp dollar bill. She wondered, *Why the heck do they have Vanna and not Whoopi staring at me? That's it for me on this one.*

There was an older couple who resembled Ossie Davis and

Ruby Dee playing a mega-bucks machine across from her. The woman was seated and the man was standing next to her, handing his woman the money and entertaining her with jokes.

Mia thought, *Now see, here's an older couple who has been through all of the things that Miles and I are going through now. They understand what it means to spend time together having fun, because life is too short.* There was an empty seat next to them, with the red, white and blue machine just calling to her. She took a seat.

"Hello, little lady," the older man said. "That machine has been hitting all day. That's a good one."

Mia was wondering why if it's so good, they were not playing it.

Mia replied, "That probably means it's empty now or it will be in cold mode for a while."

"Now, that's no way to think. You've got to be positive. When you hit and there's no money in there, they'll come over and fill it up," he assured her.

"That's a good attitude," Mia said to his wife, admiring his irrefutable certainty.

His wife replied, "Yeah, my husband knows these slot machines like the back of his hand. He's got it all figured out. Dammit," she said, hitting the side of the machine with her open hand and grimacing at the sight of two red sevens and a cherry. "That looked like it was going to be a good one."

"You got six dollars," her man said.

"Yeah, that was close," Mia commented, preparing to put her coins in the slot. *Pling, pling, pling.* She put in three and pulled the handle. Nothing.

"See, I don't pull the handle," the lady said. "I just push spin and let her go."

"Yeah, well it feels more like a slot machine if I can reach back and pull the handle down," Mia informed her.

"I agree. I keep telling her to do that," her man told Mia.

"Well, honey, I don't think we're doing so bad. Do you?" she asked.

"No, dear," he agreed.

She said, "We've been winning every day since we got here. I cannot tell you how much luck we've been having." She asked him, "How much have we won all together, Vincent, eighty-five hundred or so? Somewhere close to that. Don't ask how much we had to spend to win that much."

"I know it goes fast," Mia replied, once again putting in three dollars. She got a mega dollar, a bar and a seven. Nothing.

Mia was now down to eleven dollars, which, in her conservative mind, meant eleven more spins at one coin each.

She put in one—*pling*—and hit nothing.

"Oh no, don't do that," the man warned. "When you hit, you're only going to have in one, and see"—he pointed to the window of the machine—"If you have in three and you hit the red sevens you get ten thousand, but if you only have one and get all red sevens you only get five thousand dollars."

Mia replied, "I know, but the way I see it, at least I'll be able to spin ten more times instead of three."

The woman said, "But if you hit the mega and don't have in three, you win nothing."

"Good point," Mia said, putting in three again just because of her audience. She hit a cherry and won two dollars. Now she had nine dollars.

*Maybe I should try a different machine. This one is cold*, she thought. *But I'd better not say the word* cold *to them.*

She put in three dollars again and hit two bars and one cherry. She won two dollars again.

She put in three again, nothing. And three again, nothing.

She said to herself, *I'm going back to my room after this. I dare not pull out another twenty if my luck is running like this. These are my last two, so I'll try my one at a time again*. She put in one and got two cherries, four more dollars.

The man said, "See, if you'd had in three you'd have won twelve dollars."

*I know, dammit*, Mia was thinking.

"I'm going to try another machine. I'll see you both later."

"Okay, young lady," the woman replied.

"Can I get you a drink?" the waitress asked Mia.

Mia ordered her usual gambling drink. "Yes, I'll have an Absolut and cranberry."

"You need to stay right where you are and pull out some more money," the man said, handing his wife a hundred-dollar bill.

"No, I'm not a big risk-taker when I'm on a budget. I just do this for fun," Mia explained.

"You don' look like you're having fun," the man said.

Mia turned back to the same machine and put in three dollars. She got a red seven, a bar and a bar.

"That looked good for a moment there," said the woman.

*One last time*, Mia said to herself. *No, two more times, one dollar each.*

One dollar, nothing. *See, if I'd put in all three I still would have won nothing*, she said to herself, almost mimicking what the older couple would have said. She put in her last dollar and pulled the handle. One blue seven, two blue sevens, three blue sevens.

"Aahhh, look. I got sevens. I got three sevens!" Mia yelled as the green light went off and alarms sounded like the machine was on fire. She jumped up and down, hugging the old man, while his wife stood up to hug her too.

"How many did you have in there?" he asked.

"One. My last one," Mia replied grinning.

"See you would have won seventy-five hundred dollars. But you still won twenty-five hundred. That's no chopped liver," he admitted.

"Twenty-five hundred," Mia said, lining up her finger along the chart above the machine next to the three blue sevens.

"Red sevens would have been better but blue pays more than white. Congratulations, young lady," the woman said.

The waitress brought Mia's drink and congratulated her too. The attendant came over with a million keys and opened the machine.

"Just like I thought," the old man said, "the damn thing was empty. They're going to have to have you fill out paper for anything twenty-five hundred or more, and then they'll pay you in dollar bills so you need to put it away or wire it to your bank or something."

"No, I want these bills in my hand so I can touch them and show my man. Dammit, where is my man?" Mia wondered, looking around the room. "He's not going to believe this."

The attendant counted out the hundreds as a crowd formed around her. She stuffed the loot into her waist belt and said her good-byes.

"You're not going to put money in to spin it off?" the lady asked, surprised.

"No, I'll let the two of you handle that. I'm satisfied."

"Okay," the woman said as she put in three dollars and got three bars. "That's sixty dollars!" she yelled. The money started coming out, clanging into the tray.

"Congratulations to you both. I hope to see you later," Mia said running out to head off to find Miles or someone.

She stopped at the main desk to get a key to the room safe.

The front desk attendant informed her, "It's no problem, just sign here and show me your room key."

Miles was not in the room and it was already after three o'clock, so Mia assumed lunch was not going to happen.

The safe was behind the picture over the nightstand. There was actually a button she pushed next to the picture and it just opened up. It was funny to her that the combination was Miles's birthday. She turned the lock left, right and then left again. She turned the knob and opened the small door with one hand, reaching into her pouch with the other. She placed the stack of twenty-five one-hundred-dollar bills into the safe just as her knuckles hit something way back to the right. She pulled the money back out and then reached in again to take out what she thought might have been someone else's property from the previous group of passengers.

There was a business card wrapped around a large envelope with a rubber band. The card read JUSTIN COOPER—CAMERAMAN KMIA.

She took the rubber band from the envelope and turned over the card. Justin's home number was written on the back in pencil. She reached into the envelope and pulled out a small, rounded red satin box with a tiny gold latch. *Okay, now what is this that I've stumbled upon?* Before she could even put herself in the position of doubting whether or not she should take a look, the box was open.

Staring back at her was a fancy, vivid, natural yellow emerald-cut diamond solitaire in a platinum raised setting with two tapered, triangular white baguette diamonds on each side. The solitaire was huge. She thought, *Miles must have spent fifteen to twenty thousand dollars on this ring.*

Mia closed the box just as quickly as she opened it. She replaced the box into the envelope and, in a stupor, put the rubber band and the card back just as it was. She took her winnings back out so Miles would not know she had been in the safe and closed it. She replaced the picture and ran out of the room and down the hall, finding herself frantically knocking on Bianca's door.

"Bianca, I need to talk to you, now!" Mia yelled, knocking like she put the *C* in crazy.

"Girl, what are you banging about? What's wrong with you?" Bianca said, opening the door and thinking there must be an emergency, looking like she was interrupted from a much-needed nap.

Mia stepped inside and took a seat on Bianca's unmade bed. "I found the ring that Miles bought me."

"That's what all of this commotion is about? Miles bought you a ring? Please."

"He did, Bianca. And it is the most beautiful ring I have ever seen in my entire life. He had to have spent thousands on it," Mia said, breathing heavily.

"Where was he keeping it?" Bianca asked, making her way to the coffee machine.

"In the safe in our room."

"And what were you doing in the safe? I didn't even know we had one."

"I won twenty-five hundred dollars in the casino after we went running."

"Damn, Mia. You must be Miss Lady Luck on this cruise. You won thousands of dollars, and you now have a bomb-ass ring to go along with it. What did it look like? How big is it?"

"I'd say a few carats, maybe a little more. It is a yellow diamond, Bianca, and the setting is platinum, just as I mentioned to him a couple of years ago. He remembered," Mia said, almost in tears.

"I'll have to say that you deserve at least three carats for putting up with him. But why hasn't he remembered to pop the question?"

"That's why I'm so confused. We only have two more full days and he hasn't even asked me to go for a moonlit stroll along the deck or gone out with me for a private dinner. He's not even in the room long enough to make love to me and slip it on my finger while we're getting down."

"Now that's kinky," Bianca said, pouring water into the coffeemaker.

Mia fell back onto the bed and asked, "Bianca, what the hell is he up to?"

"With Miles, you never know. Maybe he just picked up the ring out here but he's going to ask you next year or something, or maybe it's Kelly's and he's holding onto it for Scott."

Mia quickly sprang up from the bed and stared at Bianca with an evil eye. "It had better not belong to her. Anyway, she already *has* a rock. Damn, I'm confused. The way he's been acting, I'm not even sure he's still going to ask, or if I'd even say yes."

"Where is he now?" Bianca asked.

"I don't even know. He said we'd meet for lunch or dinner or something, but I haven't even seen him. He doesn't even know that I won this money yet."

"Are you going to tell him you found the ring?"

"No way. He would freak out if I ruined his surprise."

"Now wait, if he said he'd meet you later, maybe he's planning on asking you tonight."

Mia said for clarification, "He didn't ask me specifically to meet him anywhere. He just said he'd catch up to me."

"Are you sure you want to be the wife of the Invisible Man? Like you said, after the way he's been acting, I'm not so sure he deserves to be your husband."

"I'm going back to our cabin to leave him a note asking him to meet me at seven o'clock in the room. No excuses this time," Mia said.

"That sounds like the best way to do it," Bianca replied, pouring a cup of black coffee. "And Mia? What are you going to do with all of that money? Maybe we should head over to the Black art exhibit and then over to the bookstore."

"I'm not going to give Delmonte Harrison back all the money I just won. He's a trip."

"He's a fine-ass trip, though," Bianca stated.

"Anyway, where's your man, and where's Corey?"

"Omar took Corey and his kids to play miniature golf. That was Corey's idea. You know, he's in heaven. They'll be back in time for dinner and then Omar is going to get some rest just like I was."

Mia stood up, making her way toward the door. "Let's say we hang out until dinnertime. Maybe we could go pick up a new novel to read on the island in Nassau on Friday."

"Hold on, I'm going to need a minute," Bianca said, taking a test sip from her butter yellow coffee mug. "I still need to get dressed."

Mia turned up her nose. "I'll just run over and leave that note for Miles and meet you in the bookstore at, let's say, four," Mia said, glancing at Bianca's digital clock on the nightstand.

"You paying?" Bianca questioned with hope.

"I'm paying for you to buy an eight-dollar paperback. How's that?"

“That’s cold. All that money and that’s all I get. You are one cheap woman.”

“At least if I come home without a man I’ll come home with a little bit of money. I’ll be back,” Mia said, leaving Bianca to her coffee.

# 34

## SHOP UNTIL YOU DROP

The Little Black Bookstore was the cutest store Mia and Bianca had ever seen. It was not like the airport bookstores you see with all of the big-time author's books showcased in the front. The front-line books were those written by new authors, some self-published, some making their debut with big publishers, but they were mainly fresh, new voices just starting out.

There was a children's section with a tiny little Hershey's chocolate table and four preschool-size chairs. There was a teen section with books about African-American role models like Condoleezza Rice and Oprah Winfrey, and then there were the authors who had already carved out a niche, like Terry McMillan and E. Lynn Harris, to name two, and some who had founded, nurtured, and paved the way for Black contemporary fiction, like Toni Morrison and Alice Walker, along with poets like Maya Angelou and Gwendolyn Brooks. Each shelf was made of little porthole stand-ups representative of the ship, and the latest titles were propped up in each porthole in alphabetical order by author names. And along the walls were pictures of Black novels that had been made into movies, like *Roots*, *Amistad* and *Waiting to Exhale*.

This store was more like a museum than your typical bookstore. There was even a section related just to African-American inventors, with outlined posters that gave examples of their contributions.

"Now this was a great idea," Bianca said, pointing to the inventors' shelf.

"What are you getting?" Mia asked Bianca, looking over the books by new authors.

"Any of these authors written a book about meeting an X-rated poet aboard a Black–owned cruise ship who has kidnapped his kids?"

"And is there one about a marriage-phobic man who is afraid to give up his freedom, yet buys a ring and then avoids the proposal?"

"Yes, check out this one. It's called *Phobic Miles Returns the Ring.*"

"Shit, girl what are you buying, really?" Mia asked.

"I'm getting *Raising a Black Boy to be a Black Man.* That's a great topic. Somebody had a brainstorm," Bianca said, turning the book over to read the back cover copy and check out the price.

Mia said, "I'll get *How to Raise a Black Man to be a Grown-Up Black Man.*"

"That's not the title. What is that?" Bianca asked, trying to take a peek.

"It's called *Love Don't Love Nobody.*"

Bianca quickly replied, "I heard that."

"It takes a fool to learn that," Mia said as if she could have written the book.

"Girl, but what? Tell me something I don't know," Bianca said, making her way to the cash register. "Where's my eight dollars?"

The art exhibit was just as beautiful and just as informative. There were handouts that reviewed the history of the Black art ancestral legacy as far back as the 1800s. It was like an African marketplace—it was possible to pick up everything from handcrafted gifts and angels to incense to soaps and clothes and jewelry and sculptured African pieces.

"Okay, now get me out of here. I'm about to buy one of everything," Bianca said, touching each item she passed.

"I knew you would. You're as weak as water."

"Hello, ladies," said Delmonte, suddenly appearing before them at the cashier's counter in his faded jeans and blue crocodile cowboy boots. He signed some sort of receipt and pushed it across the counter to his employee. "Here you go.

"Are you ladies finding what you what?"

Bianca stepped up to reply, "Yes, we are finding everything we need. You had a brainstorm in coming up with all of these shops and events and games that represent our heritage. You've done a great job, sir."

"Thanks for the compliment. And you?" he asked, looking to Mia, "How's everything with you?"

"I'm just fine, thank you," Mia said wondering why she hadn't told Bianca about the incident with him and wondering why he was playing it off like nothing happened.

"How long did it take you to organize all of this from start to finish?" Bianca inquired.

"I'd say about two years. This ship was going to be built for one of the other cruise lines but I bought it and redesigned it, along with two others."

"Where are the other two?" Bianca asked, wide-eyed.

"They will set sail next spring for fourteen days each from Kenya to Cape Town. That's our *Chocolate Ship* South African cruise. And then next summer we christen the *Chocolate Ship Hawaii*, which departs from Los Angeles for the Hawaiian Islands."

"I didn't know that," Mia blurted out in groupie-like wonder. She quickly remembered, *He's just trying to look like he's still got it going on even though he's a dog.*

Bianca responded, "So this Caribbean cruise is like the premiere cruise?"

"Oh yes, these seven days are nothing compared to those two-week-long cruises. But we will sail this ship every week during the season like clockwork. When you disembark, hours later another group will set sail again."

Mia looked at her watch to detach herself from the conversation and said, "We'd better get going if we want to get back to the room in time to get ready for dinner."

"That's right, excuse me, sir. Mia, first let me pick up this bad jeweled picture frame. I'll be right back," Bianca said, walking back to the shelf where she saw the glass figurines and crystal frames.

"So," Delmonte said to Mia, seemingly glad to have her one on one, "I heard you won some money. Congratulations."

"Thanks, yes, I did," she answered, looking down at a crystal Nefertiti paperweight.

"It's yours if you want it. Just my way of saying I'm sorry," he offered.

"No thanks, actually I do want it but I can get it myself," she said, looking down the aisle. *I don't want this thing*, she thought, picking it up.

"Where's your other half?" he asked as she took a step closer to the counter.

She stopped and turned toward him. "Just don't you worry about it. Where's yours?" she said over her shoulder.

Delmonte said to the cashier, "Lauren, whatever they buy is on me," and then walked out before the reverberations of his deep voice could subside.

"Yes, Mr. Harrison," she said, taking the paperweight from Mia and placing it in a bag.

"What did he say?" asked Bianca, looking like she heard incorrectly.

"He said, whatever you want is on him," said the cashier.

"Well actually, I did have my eyes on these lovely Sugar and Spice glycerin brick soaps. Not to mention this leopard-print cinnamon-scented candle and this sugar-cookie-scented candle too," Bianca said greedily.

"Bianca, please. We can perfectly afford to buy those. There's always a trick involved in an offer like that. Just get the frame and let's go."

In spite of Mia's instruction, Bianca rushed back to get the frame plus more, gathered everything into her arms, and ran back over to the cashier. Leaning against the counter, she placed it all in a neat little row.

"I don't even know you right now. I'm going. I'll see you at dinner in a little while," Mia said, shaking her head.

"Whatever you said to him, thanks," Bianca remarked as though she'd struck gold.

Mia waved her hand above her head as if she was too through. *I have enough to deal with just catching up with my man, and Delmonte knows that as well as I do.*

At around seven o'clock, just as Mia was stepping out of the shower, Miles walked in and threw his tired, weary body down on the sofa.

"Hey, Miles. I see you got the note I left."

"Yeah, I was in here a couple of hours ago looking for you," he said.

"Where have you been?" Mia asked.

"Playing basketball. And you?" Miles asked too, as if she was the absent one.

"Bianca and I went shopping. Baby, do you think you and I can hang out a little bit more since we did come here together?" Mia suggested nicely, shifting from a body wrapped towel to her silk robe.

He adjusted the sofa pillow under his head and placed his hands over his eyes. "Mia, there's so much going on, it's not like we have to be connected at the hip, especially if there are different things we like to do."

"I agree, but come on now, you must admit that for you to stay out that late last night when I was here sleeping was a bit much."

"I am sorry about that. I just lost track of time. Being on this ship is like being in Vegas. Twelve noon is no different from twelve midnight." He crossed his legs at the ankles.

"But you've got to remember, Miles, we came here together. You've got to be more sensitive than that," Mia said, rubbing papaya lotion on her arms.

"Now wait a minute, I did come by here a couple of times last night looking for you. Where were you?" Miles asked, sitting up.

Looking through the closet for a dinner outfit, Mia said, "I went out with the girls after you left karaoke and then went looking for you."

"We just got our lines crossed, Mia. It's no big deal. We've got three more nights to kick up our heels together, okay?"

"Okay, baby. That sounds good to me," Mia replied cooperatively. Thoughts of that yellow diamond seemed to make her a lot more agreeable. "You know the island party is until twelve tonight. Do you want to go over there?"

"We could do that. I'm about to get in the shower. Can you make me a drink? Just Bacardi and Coke is cool," Miles asked, standing up.

"All right, baby," Mia said, making her way out to the veranda bar. *I'm going to make sure I add very little rum. He's not going to conk out on me tonight.*

# I HAD NO IDEA YOUR MOUTH WAS BIGGER THAN YOUR FOOT

Yanni showed up for dinner unescorted, and there was no sign of Megan. Mia hoped Kelly hadn't stuffed her butt in a lifeboat. Perhaps Kelly was still mad at Mia, because Scott was flying solo, sitting next to Miles. Omar and Bianca were like happy bookends to the three kids between them.

"Mia and I had a good time this afternoon," said Bianca. "We went shopping, and Delmonte was nice enough to tell us to get anything we wanted from the Black art exhibit kiosk."

Yanni's eyes popped. "And you did, right? I would have been stocking up."

"I did, but Mia was trying to be all conservative," Bianca replied.

"Why would he offer to be so generous?" Scott asked, looking at Mia like he just ate a worm instead of a bite of his dinner roll.

Mia looked down at her menu. "I don't know. Maybe he does that for lots of people."

Bianca said, "Oh Mia, I know why. I think it's because you won that money in the casino and it's his way of congratulating you."

Miles jumped into the conversation. "You won money today? You didn't tell me. On what?"

"The dollar slots. Oh, look, they're serving gumbo tonight." Mia pointed her index finger to page two of the menu. "I am so hungry."

"You didn't tell him yet?" Bianca asked.

"How much, Auntie?" inquired Corey.

"Quite a bit," Mia answered with reserve, not wanting people to know how much darn cash she had on her that she could not put in the safe.

Miles did not catch on to her discreetness: "Where are you keeping it? Did you get it all in cash?"

"Miles," Mia said under her breath.

He paused and then spoke from the corner of his mouth. "Just give it to me and I'll put it in our safe in the room. Okay?"

"Okay," Mia replied, wanting to change the subject and looking at Bianca as if her mouth was as big as her foot.

Omar asked Mia and Miles, "What are you two getting into later?"

"We were talking about going over to St. Thomas to check out the island tonight," Mia said.

"Why don't we all hang out together?" Omar suggested.

"That sounds good," Miles answered as Scott spoke up.

"There's that bid whist game at midnight on the main deck, you know."

Mia's squinted eyes urged Scott that he needed to cut the cord connected between him and her man. "Yeah, we know. Maybe Kelly would like to go with you."

"Kelly doesn't play cards," said Scott, refusing to look at Mia again, instead taking a quavering swallow of water.

"Maybe she could just be with you and watch you and cheer you on," Mia suggested.

"I think maybe we'll all go over there after we get back from the island. How about that?" asked Miles.

*Ain't that nothing?* Mia said to herself.

Yanni added, "I'm going to be wearing my dancing shoes again, that's for sure. I am having a ball."

"So, everything was cool last night after I left the bar on deck?" Mia asked Yanni.

"Yes, I had a great time."

Mia looked at her in disbelief. "Are you sure?"

"I was fine, Mia," Yanni repeated.

"Yes, she was. We saw her kicking up her heels just before we left. She was just plain old having fun," Bianca said with certainty.

Mia asked, "Where has Lexi been, anyway?"

Yanni help up her fluted glass for one last sip of her Calypso Cooler and then replied, "She's so far up the doc's nose, who can tell? I don't know how he gets any work done with her around."

By the time Mia, Miles, Bianca, Omar, and Yanni made it over to the sparkling beach on St. Thomas, Virgin Islands, it was late into the evening. The enormous sky of eternal, deep darkness was captivatingly beautiful, with accents of hundreds of bright stars that sparkled like diamonds against the depth of the moonlit sky. The air was still, warm, and fresh.

The picturesque scene of the evening beach was illuminated by flickering tiki-lights, heat lamps, flames from the wicks of lanterns, small bonfires at every other lounging area, and tiny, blinking white lights hanging atop each bar area. The reflection of the lights twinkled along the powdery, sandy shoreline as far as the eye could see.

Megan had probably been on the island all day, because she was knocked out in a lounge chair looking like a red lobster. The sun had done a real job on her.

The DJ was bumping major sounds. The barefoot partygoers exuded an air of energy and exhalation that filled the island. Each and every beat of the music invigorated their bodies from the top of their heads to the tips of their frolicking toes as their feet stepped in and out of their own sand-laden imprints.

Yanni started dancing in place as they approached the dance

area. "That's what I'm talking about. Who wants to shake their booties?"

"We're with you," said Omar, who grabbed both Yanni and Bianca by the hand and galloped over to groove to "Shake Your Booty."

"Are you game?" Mia asked Miles, expecting him to be the party pooper.

"How many times can one say they are standing on the beach in the Virgin Islands, in the romantic night air, with the one they love, dancing to KC and the Sunshine Band?" Miles posed a look that urged a smile upon Mia's face. "Let's do this."

The group of nighttime partygoers contained many new faces, mainly because other ships had docked as well. There were people of all ages, races and colors, just partying and getting down in their bare feet to the beat as one cut after another played for more than an hour.

Bianca's lungs were doing overtime to regulate her breathing. Panting, she yelled to Mia, "We're going to find a place to chill for a minute. We'll see you two later."

Bianca and Omar surrendered to two waiting cedar lounge chairs. The flames emanating from the barn fire flashed intermittently along their silhouettes as they laid upon their backs, looking up at the magnificent sky.

Omar's arms dangled along the fine grains of sand as she sprawled out in submission. "The sight of this place is calming and exciting and invigorating and renewing and captivating and amazing, all in one."

Bianca sighed. "It makes me anxious for more and it makes me want to savor each and every moment, almost freezing in time and space."

"Man, am I glad I decided to do this. Thanks for sharing your time with me."

"No, thank *you*. I'm sure I would have been trying my best to be the third wheel to Mia and Miles. You did them a favor, actually."

Omar's capitulation was obvious. "And you did my kids a favor.

They've actually gotten rid of me and they've made a new friend in Corey at the same time."

"I know that's right."

Omar gazed over at Bianca for a moment. "You look so relaxed. Would you like something to drink?"

"No, I'm fine. Thank you."

Omar smiled. "I can't get you a screaming orgasm?"

"I've never tried one of those, but no thanks."

"You've never had one?"

"I've never tried the drink." Bianca look down at his muscular bowlegs, admiring his sex appeal and his attempt at not so sly X-rated conversation. She smirked.

"Okay. I'll back away from that one."

"Yes, Omar. I've had one of those. It's very overrated."

"I disagree with you on that one. It can be most memorable if it's done right."

Bianca asked, "What makes you the expert on it?"

"I've found that men seem to have no problem achieving them, over and over again, actually. It's women who have difficulty."

Bianca turned to her left side, toward him, being careful to make sure her right breast was covered as it gave way to gravity. "I've had my share."

Omar shifted his long body toward her too. "Which way was that?"

She played dumb. "What do you mean?"

"The aided kind or the unaided kind?"

Bianca looked at him like she was lost, so he tried to be more descriptive by asking, "The direct hit or the internal type?"

Bianca nodded her head. "The direct hit, definitely."

"And why not the other way?"

"It just never happened. I've never really thought about it."

"Okay. That's good to know."

Bianca repositioned herself onto her back again. "Oh, like you're ever going to get a chance to do anything about it."

"So," he said, again looking up at the stars from his side. "This will be one vacation you will never forget. I'm going to get myself a Screaming Orgasm. Are you sure you don't want one?"

Bianca took a few seconds to organize her thoughts, noticing droplets of sweat forming upon her upper lip. "I want one. Thanks."

Mia sat at the Cloud Nine beach bar with her man, looking at the impressive sights and taking in the sounds all around.

She glanced at the abandoned heliport at the other end of the beach. "I'll bet that daytime helicopter ride is exciting. It looks like there's so much to see. We'll have to come back on our own."

Miles gave his attention to a half glass of Remy Martin and asked, "I'm ready to join in that card game with Scott. What do you say?"

"Sure, I'll be a spectator. I'm right behind you." *At least it's doing something together*, she thought.

Somehow, Yanni had disappeared from sight. Mia noticed, but grabbed hold of Miles's hand, taking tiny, fast steps to synchronize with his pace as he led the way back to the ship.

The bid whist tournament was in the Five Heartbeats card room on the outer deck. There were only three teams of four each, and they were deep into the game.

Scott noticed Miles approaching. "It's about time. This gentleman was kind enough to stand in for you."

"Oh no, you cannot change players midstream," said one of the opposing team members.

"It's cool, because we won anyway." The teammate of the other member declared victory, stood up, and said with a trash-talking tone, "Now-den!" He slammed down his cards.

"Come on, Miles. You've got next," Scott said as Miles took a seat across from him.

Mia approached Kelly, who lay on a chaise nearby, reading a *Vibe* magazine.

"Mind if I sit here?"

As Kelly looked up into Mia's downcast eyes, Megan walked by, returning from the beach looking whooped.

Kelly opened her mouth as if to say something to Megan instead of Mia and then talked herself out of it.

"Feel free to sit here but I'm like concentrating," said Kelly.

*Concentrating on fashion and rap music,* Mia thought. "Thanks." Mia stepped along each side and then placed the weight of her hips on the chair, looking into her bag for something to distract her attention. All she could find was a bottle of Evian. She leaned her full weight back, uncapped the half-full bottle and took a long swig followed by a deep breath, replacing the cap slowly and deliberately. She stretched out her legs.

Mia and Kelly lay within inches of each other's elbow. One was reading the same magazine over and over again and the other was watching twelve people play cards from afar. Mia took her last gulp of water. She never understood bid whist and definitely could not tell what was going on from where she sat, so she decided to pull up a chair next to Miles.

"I'll be right back," she said to Megan, who gave no reply.

Miles smiled and gave Mia a peck on her cheek as she sat down next to him. "Now my luck is going to start. I've got my good-luck charm. This lady is always in my corner."

Mia looked over at Kelly, who shrugged her shoulders as though communicating to herself, and then peeked over the top of her magazine at Mia, shaking her head back and forth.

Mia dared not look at Scott, even when he said, "Yeah, that's one heck of a lady you have there, Miles."

Bianca joined Omar in his quad after he made sure the three kids were sleeping the night away, dead to the world.

"How'd you luck up on a Jacuzzi on your balcony?" Bianca asked as they stepped into the tepid water, both wearing T-shirts and shorts. "There are probably only a few rooms that have this."

"I did pay a real premium for it," he said, pressing the button to release the jets after he took off his shirt, exposing his pectoral muscles and bulging triceps. "So Bianca, you mean to tell me you've never had an orgasm vaginally?"

Bianca's eyes were stuck on how gorgeous his physique was and amazed that he wasted no time in getting back to their previous topic. She stepped back out of the water to take off her shorts, revealing her lime bikini bottoms. "I knew you'd get back to that. No."

"Oh, you just didn't have anyone who knew what they were doing," Omar interjected as his eyes focused on her thighs.

She tossed her shorts onto the chair and lowered her body. "You think so, huh? Maybe it's me. Maybe I just can't have one that way."

"Every woman can have one that way. A man just has to know how to hit the right spot, repeatedly," he stated as though he were a gynecologist.

"I suppose I've been just fine with the other way."

"What, with oral sex?" he asked.

"Yes."

He stared. "That's cheating."

Bianca said, "By any means necessary, is my answer to that."

"You don't know what you're missing," Omar informed her as he pulled her in closer. Bianca straddled him to permit his lower torso to connect with her belly. "And it has nothing to do with size. They say sex is like football. Skill is always more important than size."

"Is that good or bad?" she asked, wondering where that came from.

"You'll just have to see," he said, to peak her interest.

"So are you saying I'll be missing out on one of those two, skill or size?" she asked, curious.

"I'll say you'll just have to see. You smell so good," he said, taking in a whiff of her Kerasilk-conditioned hair. "And, you feel so good too."

Bianca rubbed her more than ample chest against his as her protruding nipples made themselves known through her wet T.

She rested her head on his shoulder while Omar started to grind in a slow, circular motion, putting one hand behind her back.

"Are you relaxed?" he asked.

"Very. This feels good."

Omar pulled her in even closer, making certain to place Bianca's opening just at the exact location of his penis.

"Wow, you must feel good too," she said as she felt the width and length of his excitement.

"I suppose I cannot hide that."

"I see I'll be getting both size and skill, huh?" she asked, pleased.

"Good observation," Omar said with confidence.

Omar continued his grind even with the fabric of their swimwear between them, until Bianca started to respond.

"Ooh, Omar. I must say you've hit a pretty good spot there."

"That's not quite the spot I was talking about," Omar said. He stirred his hips in a circular motion, pressing Bianca closer and closer and tighter and tighter until she raised her head to look him square in the eyes. With a one-quarter turn of her head, she kissed his mouth, inserting her tongue under and around his until he stopped.

"Okay. Now here we are talking about what you've never experienced and I'm the one feeling like I'm about to lose my way in this Jacuzzi if we don't stop," he admitted.

Bianca moved her body away from his torso and slid around to allow her back to rest against the side of the tub next to him.

She stated, "I think that if and when we decide to go all the way, it's going to be very special, Omar."

"Good observation. You are one hell of a kisser, I'll say that much."

"I cannot imagine any woman desiring more than you," Bianca said.

"Neither can I imagine any man hurting you. But I know one thing. I'll try extra hard next time I get involved."

"Extra hard, huh?" she asked.

"Extra hard, Bianca." Omar put his defined, long arm around her and they talked deep into the early-morning hours, finally deciding to each fall asleep in separate beds with their respective offspring.

"Good night, Omar," she said to him from across the room.

"Good night, Bianca. Sleep tight."

She thought, *I always do*.

# WHAT'S HIS PROBLEM?

The next morning Mia thought she could use a nice, brisk walk. She stood on deck as the clouds gave way to the power of the king-size sun, and then decided what she needed instead was a good, stiff, early-morning drink and then some more of that sun.

Bianca and Omar were already snuggled up enjoying each other's company at the Stingray Bar while Corey and his new friends were playing Ping-Pong at a nearly table.

"What are you two drinking?" Mia asked as she approached.

Omar answered, "Bacardi Limon and Cristal. Would you like one?"

Mia accepted. "I think I need two."

"Girl, you know what? If I see you by yourself one more damn time I'm going to have a talk with Miles myself," Bianca confessed as Omar ordered for Mia. "Where is he anyway?"

"He's still sleeping. Give him a break."

Bianca looked fed up. "Oh, please. And what will his excuse be today?"

"Maybe he'll sleep in late, I'm not sure. Why are you so worried about it?"

"Sleeping in? This should be a day of activities and swimming and going to seminars together, Mia. Come on now, you cannot possibly be that understanding."

"It's early." Mia turned to Omar. "Omar, I know Bianca told you about the ring."

He looked at Bianca, who answered for him. "Yes, I did tell him. I think you should tell Miles to shove that damn ring up his butt."

"He's not that bad," Mia said, waving her hand at Bianca in a swatting motion.

Bianca said what had been on her mind. "Mia, yesterday at dinner you two looked fine and I thought everything had been worked out. It seemed as though you two were having a damn good time in St. Thomas last night and then you guys were playing cards together. Then he turns around and doesn't show up for breakfast?"

Mia replied, "Okay, you're making too much of this. We did not have breakfast plans. Besides, you know Miles has never been a *we*–type person or a morning person. He is a loner and he doesn't like being together every minute of the day. He's always been that way."

Bianca continued to make her point. "But Mia, he's not being a loner. He's spending more time with Scott than with you. You two are not casually hanging out on Santa Monica beach. You're in another country on a once-in-a-lifetime cruise."

Omar interjected, "Mia, let me ask you this: Have you ever thought that maybe he's being distant because he's about to pop the biggest question of his life? He could actually be so fearful of taking this step, that he's just staying busy, trying to distract himself, enjoying his last bit of freedom. That's how some men are."

Mia took in what Omar said and then asked, "Freedom? Omar, he's not going to jail. He's just proposing."

"Just proposing. Do you know what it's like for a man to propose?"

"So you say he's freaking out because he's about to pop the question?" Bianca asked.

She added, "That makes sense, Omar, but I don't think Miles deserves that much credit. This man grew up in a family much like the Huxtables. I don't know what his problem is when it comes to how a man should treat a woman."

Mia said, "I think it's because of the way women have tripped on him."

Bianca shook her head in disagreement. "I say he's tripping. I'll bet he's with Scott right now."

The bartender brought Mia a drink and she and Bianca argued back and forth until late morning, debating some topic as they often did. Omar sat back and enjoyed the view with a calm look on his face.

"Hello all," said the captain, who approached wearing his tan uniform shorts. "How is everything going?"

"Hey, Captain. We're fine," replied Omar.

"Bianca, I wanted to tell you that we are refunding your money for you and your son, because of what happened in the pool the other day."

Bianca looked stunned. "No way. It was not your fault."

The captain explained, "We're just glad everything turned out okay. There's no amount of money you can put on that. It's our pleasure."

"Thank you so much, Captain. I really appreciate that," Bianca said, grinning from ear to ear.

"No problem. And, what do you have planned for today, Mia?" the captain asked.

"Just sun, sun and more sun," Mia said as she took her drink from the bar and put her bag over her shoulder. She decided to head over to a chaise lounge near the sky-dome pool. "Thanks, you two. See you later tonight at the rap concert, right?"

Bianca looked Omar up and down. "I don't think so. We've got a late-night date of our own."

"Okay, now. You two watch yourselves. Let me know if you need me to keep an eye on those young ones, okay?" Mia offered.

Bianca said, "You just make sure you have all the fun you can." Then, turning to the captain, she said, "Thanks again, sir."

Omar echoed her: "Yes, sir. That was very generous of you."

* * *

"Yes, that was quite a nice thing to do," Mia said as she and the captain stopped at two chairs.

"We want her to come back."

"Oh, she will. So, Captain, how have things been going with you?" Mia asked, stepping out of her jean shorts and sitting down on a lounge chair near the pool.

He smiled a pleasant smile. "I'm doing fine. Just keeping an eye on things to make sure everybody's happy."

Mia took off her shoes. "Yeah, that's what my friends are trying to do, make sure I'm happy. We were just talking about the fact that I should be spending more time with my boyfriend."

"What do you think?" he asked.

"I agree with them," Mia admitted.

The captain pulled up a chair to sit closer to her. "So, what are you going to do to make yourself happy?"

"I'm going to enjoy the rest of this African-American cruise with all of my people. I'm just happy to be here," Mia said, stretching her legs out, lounging in her gray-and-white faux snakeskin two-piece.

"What conclusion did you come to for why your man is spending so much time without you?" he asked.

"That he's just not the type to be all up under me."

"Or, he's not the type to have you all up under him," he said.

Mia said with an open mind, "Maybe so. What are you saying?"

"I'm not saying anything. Now see, earlier you asked me about Winter and said you weren't trying to be nosey, so I want you to know that I'm not trying to be nosey either."

"Go ahead and say what you're thinking. I'm sure I need to hear it," Mia said, playing with a lock of her still curly hair.

"I think your man is just immature. He does not understand the importance of treating a lady like she's the priority, that she comes first and that his main mission should be to make you happy," the captain said, like a pro.

"That sure sounds good," Mia responded, taking a sip of her mimosa.

"Not to say he will never get to that point. Perhaps he's taken you for granted and will not learn until he feels there's a risk of losing you. You've obviously proven that you only have eyes for him."

"Ahh, yeah. You could say I've been pretty focused," she said, thinking, *Other than playing Lick My Face with your boss.*

"Just be patient, Mia. If you love him, you'll find that he'll come around."

Mia shook her head and asked, "What makes you so sure? What's your story?"

"My story as far as what, knowing women?" he asked.

"Yes, you sound like you have a mature understanding as to what a woman needs."

"If I had all the answers, I'd probably be in a relationship myself," he admitted.

"So why aren't you?"

The captain explained, "Because I don't believe it's fair to put any woman through the rigors and demands of my job. This is not the type of job a spouse should have. It would be hard for any woman to be able to trust me and deal with the amount of time we'd be separated. That's why a lot of employees' spouses work on the same ship. Eventually, I'll take some time off and maybe change professions in order to have a family."

"That makes sense," Mia agreed.

"I was in the navy and then moved right into working on cruise ships, doing anything I could to get to be captain."

Mia informed him, "My father was in the military, and it was as if he was just always expected to be away. I don't think I ever got a chance to get to know him, so I can imagine how it was for my mother. Some marriages survive and some do not."

"Most do not," the captain said.

"That's too bad. So, you've never been married?"

"No, never been married. And as for now, the prospect of Delmonte's storybook dream becoming a reality just blew me away. That is a powerful man with a hell of a story to tell. I just had to be a part of it," he said, showing no regrets.

Mia agreed just for the heck of it. "Yes, he is a hell of a man."

"Hey, Mia," called Yanni, walking by arm in arm with Bo.

"Hi, Yanni," Mia replied.

"Hello, Captain, did you meet Bo?" Yanni asked, as if she was showing off a new sports car.

The captain said, "Who doesn't know Bo? Bo's going to be in the Football Hall of Fame one day."

Bo just waved his hand at the captain as they walked away. They then stopped to talk to Winter and Deshaun.

Mia commented, "That Winter has been one busy lady on this cruise, huh?"

The captain concurred. "Yes, she has. She's what we men call a female Mack. And to think I was really willing to give her some serious time and energy. She's something else."

"She's going to have to figure out why she has to have so much variety. That could prove to be dangerous for her," Mia summated.

"I think Winter is just here to play, like so many other people. There are people like her on every cruise. At first it's hard to tell them apart. But now I see she's a prime example," the captain said, leaning back in his chair and looking her way.

"You deserve better than that," Mia complimented him.

He replied with equal sincerity, "And so do you. You know something, Mia? Some people say all the good ones are taken. I'm here to tell you they're not. Except for you."

# BLOW THE MIDDLE RIGHT OUT OF THAT SUCKER

"Mia, where have you been? We've been looking all over for you," said Miles, standing over Mia and the captain, with Scott and a distant Kelly standing behind them.

Mia replied, startled, still focusing on the captain's last comment, "Hey, you guys, what's up?"

"Hey, Captain," Miles said without looking at him. "Mia, we're going to go skeet shooting. Do you want to come, or are you busy?"

"No, that sounds like fun," Mia said, standing up to gather her belongings. She stepped back into her jean shorts as the captain stood up too, still keeping one eye on Winter.

"Enjoy yourself," the captain said. "That skeet shooting is addictive. I hope to see you all at dinner later tonight." He turned to walk away in the opposite direction of Winter and Deshaun.

Mia replied for the group as she picked up her drink, "Okay, Jim. Take care."

"Jim, huh? Is that what you call him?" Miles asked, taking her bag as she slipped on her Gucci flip-flops.

"That's what he asked us to call him ever since the second day."

Miles remarked, "That looked pretty cozy."

"Oh, Miles, don't worry about Mia with the captain," Kelly said, as if he should be worried about her with someone else.

The foursome walked toward the observation deck. Mia waved good-bye to Omar and Bianca at the bar. Bianca was shaking her head instead of waving back, looking at Mia like she told her Miles would be with Scott. Omar yelled, "What's up, dude?" to Miles.

Miles gave him the raised head brotha signal.

Corey hopped, skipped, and jumped over to Bianca and Omar, out of breath and holding a green Ping-Pong paddle in his hand. "Mom, we're going to go over to the Cookie Bar. Is that okay?"

Bianca's eyes perked up. "Why are you breathing like that? Are you okay?"

Corey popped his tongue from the roof of his mouth. "Yes, Mom. I just ran over here. I'm fine."

Bianca held up her hand as if to wave the white flag. "Okay, sorry for asking. That's fine. Thanks for telling me."

"You're quite a responsible young man for checking in. I'll be right back," Omar said, patting Corey on his back as he left to go check on his kids.

"What's going to happen after tomorrow? Are we going to see him again?"

"Do you want to?" Bianca asked.

Corey turned his head slightly to the left for a second. "I want to see all three of them. But only if you do."

"You know Omar lives in Florida, so he and I would have to travel back and forth quite a bit to see each other."

"Would they be coming too?" Corey asked looking over at Omar's kids.

"I'm not sure, Corey. I'll talk to Omar and we'll see what can be worked out. But I'm glad you approve. It means so much to me to know that."

Omar returned to his bar stool. "Hey, you two. They're ready, Corey."

"We'll see you in a minute. Bye, Mom. Bye, Omar," Corey said, starting to walk away and then turning around again. "Hey, Omar?"

"Yes?" Omar answered, giving his full attention to Corey.

"Thanks for saving me in the pool that day. I really appreciate it, man."

"Corey, no problem. Thanks for taking the time to say that. I'm glad everything turned out okay."

Corey said, "I'm glad too. Keep an eye on her, okay?"

"We can both do that," Omar replied pointing at himself and then Corey.

"Cool, " Corey said, hurrying off toward Omar's kids. The three of them ran off toward the dessert bar.

"One thing is for sure, on this ship you don't have to worry about handing out any money to your kids, huh?" Bianca said.

"I've thought about that. This is the life," said Omar. "You've got quite a special young man there. Any man would be proud to be in his life."

"I totally agree with you on that one," she said, pulling down her sunglasses to get a better view of the kids standing in line at the dessert bar.

Miles signed in as Mia picked up the rifle. It was lighter than she thought it would be, but with a longer barrel. Mia pointed it out into the ocean and aligned the shoreline with the focus guide. She handed it to the purser, who went over a few safety instructions with them and then asked who wanted to go first.

"You go first, Miles," said Scott.

"Okay," Miles said, taking a rifle from the purser and mounting it over his shoulder.

He yelled, "Pull!" as if he'd done this many times before. He missed the first skeet and quickly yelled, "Pull!" again. He hit the second one with precision, as it broke apart just as quickly as it appeared. The third skeet flew through the air, but Miles could not even get a grip on the trigger in time.

"This damn trigger is stuck," he said as he handed the rifle to Scott.

"Oh, brother, stop making excuses," Scott said, taking the rifle. "Pull!" he said in a commanding voice. He hit the first one.

"Not bad," said Kelly." You always *were* good at shooting your bullet into the middle of someone, I mean some*thing*."

Then Scott managed to miss both of the next two.

"Kelly, you are not allowed to talk. You blew my concentration," he said irritably.

Miles retorted, "But I thought you said stop making excuses."

Scott handed the rifle to Kelly, who pulled it to her chest, placed the barrel on her shoulder, closed her right eye and yelled, "Pull!" Kelly smacked the shit out of the first skeet. "Pull," she said again quickly, blowing the dead center out of the second one. "Pull!" she yelled again, as if she had Scott's face on target, tracing its path like a markswoman. Damn if she did not blow the middle out of the third bright orange skeet as if it were standing still.

"Is there anything you can't do?" asked Scott.

"Yes, get you to keep your thing in your pants, but that would for sure take an act of God," she said, pointing the rifle at his crotch. The purser took it from her with a glaring eye and handed it to Mia.

"Okay, now, let's go. Pull!" Mia shouted, squeezing the target so slowly that the skeet landed in the water before she even got off a shot.

"Baby, you're just a little off-key," Miles said. "Like her singing," he mumbled to Scott.

"I heard that. You didn't do much better. After all, rapping and singing are two different things. Pull!" Mia yelled again, just barely snipping the side of the next one. "Pull!" she screamed in frustration at the top of her lungs, hitting the target so that it disintegrated into a million pieces.

Blowing on the mouth of the barrel as if it was smoking, Mia said, "So, we're all up at least one, except for Kelly the sharpshooter there."

"Totally cool job, Mia," Kelly said, keeping an eye on Scott. "I just had one heck of a visual when I aimed. Slow and steady and let her rip."

They continued to play another few rounds until the next group came up looking impatient, so they quit at four rounds each. Kelly remained the winner by a long shot, and it was apparent that Scott's ego just could not handle the loss.

"Let's shoot pool or go bowling or something else," Scott suggested, not wanting to be outdone.

"Scott, you'd need to get on the driving range or the basketball court to beat your wife the way she's going," Miles teased.

Scott replied, "She's good at golf and basketball too."

Kelly informed Scott, "You cannot play a game on a player. So like, remember that, okay?"

It seemed as if Kelly was starting to warm up to Mia a little bit, being that the game being played was suddenly the testosterone versus the estrogen. While they walked toward the bowling alley, Big Mack walked by with Brandon.

Brandon asked, "Hey, you all. How's it going?"

"We're fine," Mia answered.

"Yeah, I can see that," said Big Mack, staring all up in Kelly's round mound. Kelly strutted her big-boned self around in a red glitter dental-floss bikini covered by a tattered, paper-thin, white T-shirt that left little to the imagination. He told Brandon, "Damn, man if that came in six-packs I'd be turning tricks to get me a case."

"What the hell is he looking at? Did he say something?" Scott asked as Brandon and Big Mack proceeded through the Tawny deck double door and on around the corner, still half looking.

"I think he was admiring your wife," said Miles.

"Yeah, but he can do that without the comments," Scott remarked, stepping back and looking at Kelly and then in the direction of the two departing men.

Kelly said with attitude, "You need to be flattered that other men still find me attractive. Or is this a male ego thing again, for sure?"

"Kelly, don't try to figure it out. It's just disrespectful," Scott explained.

She continued, "Oh, so other men cannot want me, but it's okay for you to want other women."

"Where did that come from?" Scott asked, as if in the dark.

"Scott, I'm going to the room to get ready for dinner and the rap concert. I'll see all of you later. I'm tired of playing games."

"Bye, Kelly," Mia said as Kelly walked away heavily along the deck.

"Damn, what's gotten into her?" asked Miles.

"Who knows," said Scott.

Mia asked, "Do you two still want to go bowling?"

"I do," said Miles.

"I'll take a rain check. I think I need to go to our room and check on Kelly. You guys have fun, dude," he said, giving Miles the frontal hug with the break-away daps.

"I'll check you later," said Miles.

"Yeah, we'll check you later," Mia added.

After a tie-breaking third game of bowling in the main arcade, Miles was elated to declare himself the winner, scoring two hundred sixty-two, almost doubling the score of his previous game.

Mia replaced her purple bowling ball in the rack. "What game would you like to play now?"

"Pin the tail . . . doggie style?"

She rubbed her aching thumb on her right hand. "Oh, you're full of yourself now, huh?"

"And you should be too," he suggested.

Mia dipped her head as though suddenly shy as she spun her body into Miles's chest. "Damn, you're nasty. But, that sounds like a plan."

Miles added, "And after that, I think I'll take a nap."

# RAP ON, BABY!

The Egyptian theater was the setting for the rap concert with Ebony and Ivory and Big Mack. Bianca and Omar were nowhere to be found. Obviously, they had business to take care of.

Delmonte strolled in with Ashley on his arm, both dressed to the tenth degree. They proceeded to their front-row seats next to the captain and Tangie.

Ebony and Ivory came onto the stage with outfits so small they looked like they were wearing Garanimals. The necklace of one matched the hot pants of the other, and they were each wearing the other's boot or something because they each had on two different color shoes, one lime green and one cotton-candy pink. Each one's left tittie had a silver beaded tassel matching the tassel of the other's right tittie. It was freaky.

After an hour of the ladies' rap songs, Big Mack came onstage and busted out with "Hypnotized," sounding just like Biggie himself.

Mia and Miles bounced in their seats, clapping and having a grand old time. The next cut he performed was Tupac's tribute to his mom, "You Are Appreciated." Suddenly, he sounded like Tupac.

"That's amazing," said Miles.

After that cut, Big Mack announced, "And now, ladies and gentlemen, I have a new vinyl release entitled, *Two All-Beef Patties.* This is the title cut I'd like to premiere for you here."

As he began to perform, it was obvious from the words that he was singing about a vagina.

"That's worse than the song 'Peaches and Cream,' " Mia said, but still feeling the beat. "I'll never eat a Big Mac again in my life."

"Don't you, of all people, act like you're not down with that," Miles said, snapping his fingers.

"Yeah, but the way he's describing it, it sounds like shredded cow. Besides, I'm into receiving, not giving."

"We know that—"

"Miles, man, you've got to come to the main deck," interrupted a frantic Scott. "Kelly is about to kick Megan's ass."

"Why is she doing that?" Miles asked as he sprung to his feet.

"Mia told her about the night I screwed around with Megan," Scott said, glaring at Mia like she had made him do it in the first place.

Miles gave Mia full-on, unblinkable eyes of amazement and disappointment. They ran off, with Mia chasing behind them.

"You dang tramp!" Kelly yelled, running up behind Megan, who was leaning over a pool table, exposing her cellulite-less thighs.

"Who are you calling a tramp?" Megan replied with volume. She raised her pool stick in the air near Kelly's head.

"Ladies, now cut out this madness," said Miles, taking a step in toward Kelly.

Brandon echoed Miles's sentiments, "Yeah, both of you need to back off and show some class up on this ship."

Kelly replied to Brandon, "Oh, my God. Maybe you should have been keeping an eye on this pussy-cat running-amok tramp. Maybe then she would have been sucking your rod instead of doing my husband." Kelly ranted and raved.

Disappearing into the background, Scott turned his head to the side, rubbing the back of his head in discomfort, without even saying a word.

"You are one nutty woman if you think I'd want to screw that puny thing you call a man," Megan said, pointing to Scott who was suddenly paralyzed from head to toe, except for a slight glance down at his own zipper.

"It must not have been too puny the way you were apparently yelling his name in pleasure. The stroke was pretty darn good, huh?" Kelly asked with fury.

Miles looked at Scott. "Aren't you going to step in there?" he asked, pointing toward the two of them.

"Let them talk this out," Scott said, now poking his chest out as if they were two women fighting over him on Springer.

Mia moved in closer behind Kelly and said in a calming tone, "Come on now, this will not solve anything. Let's all sit down and talk about it."

Kelly rcsponded adamantly, "Oh, yeah, I'm sure. You don't talk about a physical act like what they did. You fuck someone up over fucking."

*Oh hell, she finally cursed. It's on now*, Mia thought.

"Then fuck up your man over there," Brandon said, pointing at Scott. "Why are you mad at her?"

Kelly answered him without a second thought, "This is a woman-to-woman thing. I'm going to teach her to think twice before she goes around spreading her legs to permit entry of OPP—Other People's Penises."

"That's old, Kelly," Mia whispered from behind her. "Come on now, let's go have a drink with the guys and talk about this."

"Yeah, we should talk about it," said Megan with a bold cockiness. "We shouldn't be adversaries, we should be friends. After all, we have something in common. We both know what he looks like naked. Now you'd better back up before I decide to let him tap it one more time. Oh, and another thing, I love the way he growled while eating me out."

"You slutty bitch," Kelly yelled, dodging in front of Megan, shoving Brandon's little ass out of the way as Megan tried to run away. "You're not going anywhere other than over the side of this ship."

Kelly grabbed Megan around the throat with both hands, scratching her lip and neck. Megan struggled to pull Kelly's arms away and started to gag, gasping for air, when suddenly Brandon pulled a kicking Kelly away.

"Let go of me," yelled Kelly, flailing her feet toward Megan as he managed to move her back for a moment.

"Yeah, let go of her, dude," said Scott, standing behind Miles, who stood behind Brandon.

Megan rushed Kelly as Kelly was being held and yanked her hair so hard that she pulled a tract of dreadlocks right off the side of Kelly's head. Kelly freaked out, grabbing her head while her eyes started to bulge.

Everyone stared at each other for a few seconds, anticipating the next moment or thinking that they didn't know Kelly wore a weave.

"The only thing getting tossed over the side of this ship is your tired-ass weave," said Megan. With a burst of boldness, due to Kelly's being restrained, she rushed over to throw the tract over the railing.

Brandon stopped in his tracks. "Oh, shit," he said. "No, she did not pull the weave out of a Black woman's head. You're on your own now," he admonished, letting go of Kelly.

Kelly ran up and beat Megan straight in the face and then backed up with a stance like a professional prizefighter. Long overdue, Scott intervened and pulled Kelly back, but she was too strong and she pulled away. Miles joined in, each of them taking one arm and pulling her back.

"Damn, we've got Ali and Frazier up on my cruise," joked Brandon.

The captain and Dr. Steven suddenly arrived, running up to Megan, who had fallen to the ground. "What is going on?" asked the captain as the doc helped her up and checked out her wounds.

Brandon looked at Megan and said, "You were talking a lot of shit there girl." Megan stuck her tongue out at him. "And to think I was trying to get some of that loony pussy," he said to Mia as he walked away.

The doctor and captain took Megan off to the side, where a waiter brought ice packs and cold drinking water.

Kelly simply rushed off, saying, "If anyone is looking for me, I'll be in my cabin."

"Oh, no, you're both coming to my office," said the captain.

Miles approached Mia with a look of frustration and asked, "Why did you tell her Scott's business? That was not for you to get involved in. What's wrong with you?"

"What's wrong with me? Scott screws someone other than his wife on the same damn ship and something is wrong with me. I'm not a guy, I didn't take the brotha oath of silence."

"You're one to talk, Mia." *Oh, shit, here it comes,* Mia thought. "Maybe you can explain why you were coming out of Mr. Harrison's room at four in the morning the other night," said Scott.

"What? She was coming out of where?" Miles asked, first looking at Scott and then focusing on the sight of Mia. "Mia! When was this?"

Mia stared at Scott in silence, as if she could stick needles in his eyes.

Scott peered over Miles's shoulder. "Tell him, Mia."

"Mia, is this true?" Miles grunted, frown lines getting deeper on his forehead.

Mia's mouth went dry. She answered in a hushed, cottonmouth tone, "Yes, Miles, I was coming out of his room, but nothing happened."

"Mia!" he said in guarded disbelief. He stared and stared, looking right into her as if he suddenly saw another side of her, with his mouth open and without even blinking. He seemed to be sizing up the situation, giving her a malevolent gaze of disappointment as his jaw tightened. After a few moments of looking her up and down, he said to Scott in a lowered voice, "I'm about to break, dog."

Suddenly, he backed up, keeping both eyes on her, turned around and scurried away toward the observation deck. Scott looked down the same aisle Kelly and the captain had taken and then in Miles's direction. He looked down at his own feet, too ashamed to look Mia in the eyes, and proceeded to follow Miles.

*Trifling boy didn't even go to see about his wife.*

"First of all, what are your names?" the captain asked, sitting in his executive chair while the girls sat at his conference table.

"Kelly Stevenson."

"Megan Barnes."

"Okay. Now, please tell me what happened out there," said the captain.

"This madwoman jumped me, that's what happened," said Megan.

Kelly tried to explain. "Captain, I totally know what happened was wrong, but this woman slept with my husband within the second day of this cruise. I mean, she knew he was married and then she absolutely had the nerve to give me attitude about it. It's women like her that enable our men to be unfaithful."

"Enable him? It's my fault that he can't keep his dick in his pants?" asked Megan.

"Ladies, that's enough. What I want to know is who struck the first blow," the captain asked with authority.

"She did," they both said, pointing at cach other in unison.

The captain tried to make sense of it. "Okay, let's just say Megan did. Do you want to press charges?" he asked Kelly. "If you do, Megan will be detained in Florida and booked. Once she's released on bail, you both will have to come back to court for the trial. Do you understand that?"

Kelly nodded her head yes.

"Then what do you want to do?" he asked Kelly.

Kelly replied, "If she presses charges, then I will press charges too."

"Megan, what do you want to do?" he asked.

"I cannot stay in Florida," Megan said, starting to yell at him. "I have to get back to my life. But maybe I should press charges. She should have thought about all of this before she decided to bum rush me."

The captain ran it down. "First of all, do not raise your voice at me," he demanded as Megan turned to look at the wall. "Secondly, if you both decide that you are not going to press charges, then we can blow this off as an inconvenience and a misunderstanding. But if either of you so much as look at each other crooked, I will detain you myself for the rest of the cruise. And if you fight on a Harrison Cruises ship, destroying our property, we have the right to press charges ourselves. This is not a joke. You cannot just walk up to someone and put your hands on him or her without repercussions. That is called battery. Do you understand?" he said to Kelly with no nonsense.

"Yes," Kelly replied, looking down at her lap.

"Now what do you want to do?" he asked them both.

Kelly answered, "I'm willing to let it go. I'm going to enjoy what time I have left on this ship, without worrying about her or my soon-to-be ex-husband."

"He really is the one you need to be dealing with, peacefully. And you?" the captain asked, looking at Megan.

Megan looked at Kelly with disgust and said, "I cannot believe you came up to me and punched me out. Look at my face. How am I going to have any more fun after this?"

The captain spoke up, "Megan, the type of behavior you engaged in is just what I train my staff to look out for. Your decision was made without regard for the outcome. You only looked at the immediate gratification without looking at the possible consequences. I suggest that you both learn from this and consider yourselves better for the lesson."

"Thanks, Captain. My revenge is about to take place. And I don't mean physical harm to anyone. It's on now," said Kelly, this time looking him square in the eyes.

He made a suggestion. "That type of attitude will only make the problem worse. I suggest you go get a massage and maybe take in a movie and get your mind off of what happened. Is that clear?" he asked, looking toward Megan.

"Yes," Megan responded, touching her lip to check for blood.

He reiterated, "Now this is the last I want to hear of you two getting into it. I mean it. You are grown women, not children, I suggest you act like it. Help me make this first Black cruise a success."

"Thanks, sir," said Kelly.

"Good-bye," said Megan as the ladies stood in unison.

The captain sat back as they exited with a crewmember escort, each in a different direction. He rocked in his chair and then placed his elbow on his maple desk, bracing his chin with his flexed palm. He could not help but chuckle and shake his head in disbelief. He leaned back and closed his eyes as if in prayer.

# GUILT COULDN'T LOOK ANY DARKER IF I HAD MY FACE UP MY OWN ASS

Mia had been seated on the velvet sofa in her room for nearly three hours, thinking about how she and Miles had become so disconnected just when it had seemed everything was going so well. Surely this man had intended to propose, and now she thought it would never happen. Mia wondered if she would have even wanted it anyway, if it meant she'd have to deal with his absent ways for the rest of her life.

At nearly five in the morning, while Mia was sitting on the couch staring into the darkness, the door opened and Miles stepped inside. He turned his back to close the door, totally ignored her, and stormed outside onto the veranda, violently slamming the sliding glass door shut. Mia sat still for a moment and then sprung from the sofa, marching off toward the door and sliding it open.

"What do you think you're doing?"

"I'm trying to go to sleep. And you should too," Miles replied in ominous retaliation, curling his body into a fetal position on the chaise lounge.

"Miles, get up and talk to me," Mia demanded in a sharp, high-pitched tone.

He said nothing. The loud, annoying silence in the air could have shattered lead crystal.

"Miles," Mia bellowed, tapping him on his back as if to wake the dead. "Get up and deal with this. Now," she demanded.

He abruptly stood with his back to her as if the sight of her sickened him. Miles took a step toward the bar and leaned his elbows onto the black granite top with his hands to his face.

"Miles, talk to me, please," Mia requested again, as if willing to make nice.

"Mia," he said turning in her direction while simmering in his skin. "Did you sleep with Delmonte?"

"No, Miles," Mia said, sounding disbelieving even to herself.

He turned away again, looking down at his hand. He balled up his fist and banged it down onto the bar. "What the fuck happened?" he asked, turning to her again with his eyes fully open, fast losing patience.

Mia struggled for words. "I . . ." Mia said nervously as if trying to remember herself, stunned by his wrath.

He looked askance at her. "You're stuttering, Mia," Miles said with extra pressure for her to speak up.

"I went to his room but nothing happened," Mia hissed in auto-defense mode.

"Then why were you in there?"

Mia struggled. "Because I couldn't find you," she replied, sounding as if she wanted to shift the blame.

He challenged her reply in a flat tone. "Oh, you thought I was in there?"

"No, Miles," she answered, not appreciating his sarcasm. "I had been looking for you all night and I had been drinking."

"Now you're going to use the excuse that you were drunk?" he asked stiffly, as if he was no fool.

"No, it's not an excuse," Mia said, lowering her voice in surrender.

"Then why were you in there?" he asked with a direct, disconcerting stare.

"I was wrong, Miles. I thought you were off playing with Winter or who knows who. I just needed some attention," she said in a demure voice, looking over the balcony and off into the darkness.

Miles replied with a disappointed face, "I thought you said you were not going to be insecure because of what your last man did. But I see you're unsure as to whether or not I would screw with your friend or anyone else for that matter."

"It's just that you've been so damn absent on this ship," she commented, becoming defiant again.

Miles looked to his side as if to recall a thought and stated, "Oh, so now we're back to if you can't be with the one you love, just love the one you're with, huh? So you went into the room of the man who I paid good money to get you on this ship?" he asked with volume and depth to his voice. "Did I pay him to fuck my woman? You made me look like a damn fool."

"Miles, I did not do anything with him, you have to believe me," she begged, moving her body to meet his glance.

"Did you kiss him?" he asked suspiciously, taking a step backward.

"No. I did not kiss him," she answered firmly, biting her lip.

"My best friend saw you coming out of that room, Mia. I want a woman with virtue. Not a woman who makes bad choices like that," he said, wagging a finger in her face and then cringing away from her.

"Oh, so now I'm the only one who makes bad choices," she said, as if this was an example of the pot calling the kettle black.

He flailed his hand about for emphasis. "Mia, like you told me, don't choose the behavior if you can't live with the consequences."

She sighed for a minute and then crossed her arms, shifting her weight to her left leg. "Miles, you know what? Okay, I was wrong. I made a mistake. But dammit, where the fuck have you been for the past three days? You are so damn selfish and such a loner that even when you come on a cruise with your woman you still run off to play with the boys. Scott can kiss my ass. He gets more time with you than I do," she said, wanting to spill these words for a long time. "And if you think I'm just not virtuous enough for you and you can't forgive me, fine. Then this trip was not in vain," she yelled again, sighing and resigning herself to the worst.

Miles stared for what seemed like forever. His chest expanded more intensely with every breath. He screwed up his face like he was having a hot flash and took one heavy, forceful step through the doorway into the room, and then another, and then another until he reached the front door.

"Miles, don't you dare walk out on me," Mia forewarned with a furious, desperate barrage of words, following his every step. "You are going to work through this with me and face this. You had better not walk out of that damn door. I am not playing with you."

He stopped at the door with one hand on the knob and the other hand on the wall as if he was frozen. "Maybe I should go and do whatever it is you think I've been doing all along, Mia," he threatened with his back to her.

"Miles, no!" Mia said with a sinking feeling in the pit of her stomach as she placed her shaking, sweaty palms on his back.

"Mia, get the fuck away from me," he replied, immediately pulling forward with a snarling edge.

He stood with a blank stare.

"Do not leave me, Miles," Mia begged at full volume as if Daddy was about to go off to war.

Miles took each breath with deep intent, so much that you could see his expansive shoulders rise to inhale and lower to exhale, over and over and over again. He suddenly let out a long, forceful exhale, released the doorknob.

He turned around toward Mia, grabbed her from under her arms and lifted her high above him so that her back slammed against the wall. He then languidly lowered her to the floor. He pressed his hands flat against the wall over her head and stood still, one millimeter of an inch from her wide-eyed, disbelieving face. Her continual, mile-a-minute blinks from her long lashes gave Miles full appraisal that she was in fear of losing him.

On the other hand, his eyes did not blink even one time. The glow from the whites of his eyes was blinding as if every other tinge of light in the room paled in comparison. The pupils of his eyes pierced through her with a look that was disapproving, disappointed, discontented, and disbelieving. His eyes delivered the message. Miles was hurt and scared.

Mia, feeling defenseless, was the first to interrupt eye contact, shifting her glance downward. He pivoted away from her, walked over to the bed, snatched the comforter and headed off to the balcony, walloping the door shut behind him.

Mia stood in place, out of breath from her racing heartbeat, hyperventilating respiration, the buzzing in her ears, and the shattering of her heart.

The clock read eleven thirty in the morning. Mia was lying flat on her back, wondering if all of the drama was a nightmare or reality. She parted her lids, turned her head, and looked out onto the balcony to see Miles, tucked into his lounge chair with the comforter over his head. There was her answer.

Feeling like it was the crack of dawn, Mia covered her head with a blanket to shield herself from dealing with what was out there in the cruel world. She turned her back to him and hoped that if she dozed off again, at least her brain would be shut off from the reality of the situation.

The telephone rang but she did not have the energy to answer it.

A couple of minutes later as she began to doze again, she heard the sound of the sliding glass door opening and closing as Miles headed to the bathroom. She expected to hear the sound of the bathroom door closing. But she noticed that the light from the balcony window was blocked for a moment by a shadow of darkness over her bed. She turned and peeked from underneath the covers, only to see Miles standing over her with his hand extended.

"Come with me, Mia," he said with swollen eyelids.

She immediately raised her naked body from the bed, taking his hand and following him into the bathroom, where he leaned in to turn on the shower. He took off his tank top and boxers and stepped inside.

She stepped in behind him as he faced the spray of the water from the showerhead, rinsing his face and chest from the awfulness of his hurt. Mia took the bar of spring-fresh soap and reached to the front of him to wash his chest and stomach. He took her hand and the soap and turned around to her.

Miles moved Mia around to trade places with him, working the soap into a lather and washing her breasts and pubic area. The hot water rinsed the soap down the front of her body and Miles pulled her toward him, lowering himself to below her navel, raising her leg to rest along his shoulder. He kissed her middle split with soft pecks one after the other, all lips for about five minutes.

"This is my pussy, Mia," he stated, as if she'd forgotten.

"I know, baby. I know it's yours. No one has had it but you," she said with a moan while looking down at him.

"You did not hear what I just said," he repeated with emotion.

"Yes, I did," she said as if she was becoming weak.

"I don't think you did," he insisted as he parted her lips with both hands, taking her clit into his mouth as if it belonged there twenty-four hours a day. He gently pulled on it with his lips as if he was sucking a hard nipple until she could feel her blood pumping toward his face. This was the most intense make-up sex session ever, in her mind. To her it was fueled with love, emotion, forgiveness, desire, yearning, passion, and belonging.

"Miles, I'm sorry!" she yelled as her warm, salty tears started to flow from her eyes, mixing with the water from the shower and dripping down into her wide-open mouth. She felt the powerful, pulsating wave of her muscle throb in response to his lips as she released and sighed.

He then removed her leg from his shoulder, stood up, wiped his mouth with the back of his hand, and moved her around so that he could once again rinse his body with the direct spray of the showerhead.

"Miles," Mia said, standing behind him with more teardrops

trickling from her cheek to his back. He did not answer. She hugged him around his fine-ass waist and said, "I love you."

He still said nothing and continued to wash under his arms and between his legs, turning around to wash his back without taking a moment to catch a glimpse of her.

Mia stepped out sniffling, not yet satisfied because of her guilt and the fact that she had let him down.

"I love you too," Miles mumbled, turning again to rinse his chest. Mia wrapped the towel around her body after blotting her eyes, suddenly managing to crack a smile as she left him to his solo shower. He began humming the song "Lifetime" by Maxwell.

# 40

## FUNKY NASSAU

Stepping into his black cotton boxers, Miles asked, "What do you want to do today?"

"Miles, I just want to be with you. Especially after all that's happened. I think we're in Nassau already for our last full day."

"I say we go eat," he suggested.

The Freedom Café was deserted on this early Friday afternoon. Either everyone was still sleeping in, or they had already made their way over to the island.

"What are you in the mood for?" Mia asked as they lined up at the buffet.

"It looks like breakfast is over, so lunch it is. I'll have a little of everything," Miles said, loading up on steak, ham, salmon, Monte Cristo, pasta, potato wedges, macaroni salad, greens, okra, corn on the cob, and dirty rice.

"Dang, Miles. You are hungry."

"I think we both worked up an appetite," he said.

Miles walked over to pick out a table by the window to enjoy a view of the beautiful island of Nassau. The sprawling beach area was packed with vacationers already one step ahead of Mia and Miles.

"Hey, Mia," Tangie said, walking up with Delmonte. "You are going over to the private island, right?"

"You mean the nude beach?" Mia asked.

"Yes," Delmonte answered for Tangie, raising his eyebrows.

"No, I don't think so, but we'll be over to hang out on the beach in Nassau after we eat."

Mia looked over at Miles, who was coming back, maneuvering past the tables to join in. *Oh, shit*, she said internally.

"Hey there, man, what's up?" Delmonte asked.

"Hi, Tangie," Miles replied, ignoring Mr. Harrison's greeting.

"Are you two having a good time?" Delmonte asked, this time directing the question to Mia.

Miles answered for her. "I see that you make it your private responsibility to see to it that all the ladies have a good time, don't you?"

"I make sure all of my passengers are satisfied," Delmonte replied with a smile.

"I'll bet you do. Just make sure you stick to the single, available ladies up on this ship. Us men would appreciate that," Miles requested with a scrap in his voice.

"Excuse me, sir, but I'm not even going to dignify that comment with a reply," Delmonte said, catching on.

Miles responded, "You don't have to. As long as you know where I'm coming from, that's all I'm saying."

"Aah, Mia," Tangie interjected uncomfortably, "we'll let you go ahead and finish getting your food. We'll see you later."

Mia turned toward their table with her plate in one hand and a tall mug of black coffee in the other. "Okay, girl. Thanks for checking on us," she said, looking back as Tangie and Delmonte walked away.

"Yeah, Delmonte, thanks for checking on us," said Miles, walking to the table behind Mia.

"What was that all about?" Tangie asked Delmonte as they departed.

Delmonte shrugged his shoulders as if he was in the dark as to why Miles was tripping.

Miles looked across the table at Mia as he sat down, shaking his head from side to side. "That's the last time I check some brother for fucking with you because you let them, that's all I'm going to say."

"I hear you. How's your food?" Mia asked, seeking a new topic.

"It would be better if I didn't have this bitter taste in my mouth."

"Miles, can we move on from this, please? I'd really like to enjoy our last day."

He stared out of the window at the parasailers and waterskiers and jet-skiers in silence.

Mia suggested, "How about we go over there and lay out, drink, party and have the time of our lives?"

"I'm with that," he said reservedly, taking an offered bite of barbecued chicken from Mia's fork.

"How's that?" she asked.

"Let me get some of that," Miles said, standing up to go back to the buffet line. She saw this as a good sign, but she could tell he was still pissed. That ring was sure to be returned now.

# FANTASY ISLAND

This island of Nassau was so beautiful, with its fine, pristine, pearly white sand beaches, picturesque tropical splendor, tall leaning coconut trees, and turquoise blue waters. Just in from the shore a little way Mia and Miles could see the special Old World charm and ambience captured by the colonial buildings, wooden chalets, and straw markets as well as the New World luxury hotels. The abundance of people enjoying the splendor of the island was amazing. There were people everywhere, from other ships as well as vacationers who had booked hotel accommodations. Just beyond the front line of hotels was a city with gigantic casinos, sidewalk cafes, open-air markets, an eighteen-hole golf course and world-class entertainment, all just a bus ride away. The spectacular vision was the essence of the intoxicating spell the Bahamas is known for.

Mia was finally wearing that white string bikini with the tiny pineapples all over it that Bianca had bought her. Miles was not complaining, since he was serving as her bodyguard for the day. Miles was wearing bamboo-colored Fubu trunks, brown flip-flops and a tan bandana on his head.

At the circular Island Bar, Lexi and Steven sat at one end and Megan and Olandi sat at the other.

"Hey, Lexi. How was your night?" asked Mia as she and Miles approached.

Looking over at Megan, Lexi replied, "Fine. I heard there was a commotion with Kelly and Megan."

"Yeah. The two of them got into it," said Miles.

Lexi commented, "Dang, Kelly really tore into her, I guess," glancing at Megan's face.

"Megan will be fine, she just has a bruise near her chin and her lip was cut, " Steven said.

"What's up, Doc?" asked Miles.

"Hey, man. I'm just having the time of my life with this young lady," he replied, rubbing Lexi's back.

The bartender walked over and asked, "Can I get you two anything to drink?"

"I'll have a Bahama Mama," Mia answered.

"Make that two," said Miles.

Mia asked as the new bartender walked away, "Where's Dante?"

"Who cares," said Miles.

Steven replied, "Delmonte fired him yesterday."

Miles blew air from his nose and let out a faint chuckle. "I'm not surprised."

"For what?" Mia asked Steven.

"I don't know," Steven answered, as if maybe he really did know.

"I'm thinking I do," said Mia.

"Well, he's over there," Lexi stated, pointing out toward the shore. Dante was laid out on top of his official *Chocolate Ship* beach towel, which was the size of a blanket. He was chilling under a topaz-and-teal-striped umbrella. He sat up briefly to rub suntan lotion on his legs, and who leaned up next to him to rub some on his back, but Justin.

"Oh, my goodness," said Miles. "Justin is gay?"

"Either that or they just really like that big beach towel," Mia said.

Lexi admitted, "I've noticed them flirting with each other the entire week."

"I missed that," said Steven.

"I say we go grab one of those blankets ourselves and get some sun," said Miles just as the bartender placed their drinks on the bar.

"Can we join you?" asked Lexi.

"Let's roll," said Mia as the four of them grabbed their drinks and vacated the bar.

Megan gave them a half-baked wave as they walked by.

"Hey, Megan," Mia said as the four of them waved.

Her response was a cold shoulder.

Walking closer to the shore, Mia noticed four people lounging, soaking up the rays, and laughing. One of them reached into a cooler for a bottle of Evian and handed it to her man. It was Yanni and, of all people, Bo.

Lexi stopped and stared as though the scene was a mirage, just as Yanni stood up with the other female who was with Deshaun. They headed toward the bar. The other female was Winter.

"Hey, everybody, hey, Lexi. What's up?" Yanni asked, stumbling from the effects of her obvious alcohol intake, trying to secure her footing in the sand and leaning into Winter.

"Hi, everybody," said Winter.

"Yanni, what are you doing with him?" Lexi inquired.

"Him who?" Yanni answered, with her eyes half closed.

"Bo. And even that other guy, Deshaun. What's up with that?" Lexi asked.

Yanni replied, "What's up with you? I don't ask you what you're doing with the doctor here."

"Yes, but the doctor did not try to force a train on me."

"What?" Steven asked in surprise.

Lexi said, "Tell him, Yanni. Tell him what those two tried to do to you."

Slurring her words in confusion, Yanni said, "No, I was to blame for that, and thank you very much for sharing my private information with everyone now," she said, flailing her hands outward in a wide-open wave.

"Those guys are harmless," said Winter. "We're just having a good time. Lighten up, sister."

"You stay out of this, sister," Lexi stated, cutting her eyes at Winter with a long blink and then focusing on Yanni.

Yanni said as if she thought she was running it down, "Lexi, first of all, you are not my mother, so don't come comforting me like I'm in trouble or some shit. And second of all—well, just first of all is enough, so butt out."

Mia intervened on Lexi's behalf: "Yanni, she's just concerned that those two tried to take advantage of you."

"Maybe that's not really how it happened, okay?" Yanni said, leaning forward with a stumble. "And if it did, and I still decided to kick it with them, what business would it be of yours, Lexi?"

After a minute of a deep stare and one single blink, Lexi said, "You are my sister."

"Ahh, isn't that sweet. And you are mine, but you don't see me all up in your business with the good doctor here. You've had your head so far up his ass all week you haven't even had time for me. Now on the last day you're going to try to act concerned. You never even come back to the room. Shit, I don't even know why you wasted Daddy's money," Yanni said, pointing in Lexi's face.

"Is that how you feel, Yanni? You feel that I have been ignoring you?" Lexi asked with a squint of her eyes, simultaneously gritting her teeth.

"I don't really care what you've been doing, and I'd ask that same respect. Now excuse us while we go to the bar for some more Screaming Orgasms," she said, bumping into Lexi and reeling past.

"I'll see you all later. Good-bye, Miles," Winter said, brushing by him and then running after Yanni, only to catch up with her and hold her up by the arm.

" 'Good-bye, Miles'?" Mia repeated, taking one step as if she was ready to trace Winter's footsteps. Instead, she just shook her head, considering the source. Miles took her hand and headed toward the shoreline.

"When did all of this happen?" asked Lexi, looking back at Yanni.

"I don't know, but I did see them together at the club the other night. Lexi, maybe she is right. Maybe these two guys just followed her lead incorrectly," said Mia. "Come on."

Placing her hand over her forehead, Lexi stated, "I am not ready for the world. I need a beach blanket."

Lexi and Steven found a spot near Dante and Justin while Miles and Mia took up a spot right next to Bo and Deshaun.

"If those two so much as look your way, Mia, I'm going to roll up on the little punks," Miles said as if he wished they would.

Mia dared not even look over at the roving Casanovas. She just laid her already exhausted self down on her towel and fell back in surrender.

"Okay, everyone who is ready to go over to the Fantasy Island nude beach must board the boat now. No one under twenty-one allowed, and no cameras of any kind either," Captain Jim announced while assisting Tangie in loading the boat.

Of course Bo and Deshaun immediately jumped up, as well as Winter and Yanni, who ran back to get their belongings so they could get in line. Captain Jim stared at Winter and her now third new friend, Deshaun, as if he must have lost his mind to have been so taken in by her.

Megan got in line, leaving Olandi to his work, just as Kelly showed up from out of nowhere to stand behind her. Megan quickly got out of line and returned to the bar by herself. Scott strolled by the line as if he didn't even notice that Kelly was going and headed straight for Megan at the bar. He was obviously asking for trouble.

Dante and Justin grabbed their lavender insulated cooler and lined up behind Kelly.

Delmonte and Ashley were already on the boat. The captain and Tangie stayed behind.

* * *

"Baby, this is the life, but it is hot out here," Miles said after an hour or so. He sprayed himself down with a handheld water fan. "I'm about to get baked on this towel. I need some shade for a minute," he said, springing to his feet.

"Miles, this is the most still you have been all week. I knew you'd have to make your way into something."

"No, I just need some shade and another drink. Do you need anything?"

"No, I'm fine. I'll just lie here in heavenly splendor."

Lexi and Steven focused their undivided attention on themselves, each facing the other with their hands on the other's hips, stretched out flat on their sides upon the enormous beach blanket. Lexi's eyes were closed, and Steven watched her breathe as he had so many nights before. The position seemed familiar and comfortable, even on their first night together.

Steven could no longer contain his concern. "Are you okay with Yanni's comment?"

Lexi's eyes remained shut. "No, I'm not okay."

"Do you think you two should talk about it one on one?"

"No, Steven. This is not the first time we've disagreed about something."

"I think she believes you're having a wild, mad, passionate sex rendezvous with me and that's why you're not coming back to the room at night."

"And if I was, what business would that be of hers?" Feeling him stare, Lexi opened her brown eyes.

"It would be the wrong impression."

"I'm sorry if she thinks that just because you sleep with someone you have to have sex with them. That's her misconception about men. Not all men are trying to hit it and quit it."

"That's true. But I think that years of being so close and years of subtle, subconscious competition can breed jealousy."

Lexi moved her right hand up toward his face and traced the

outline of his perfect lips with her index finger. "Steven, I am happy. How can anyone be jealous of their sister's happiness?"

"Maybe she wanted to spend more time with you on this vacation."

"If Yanni had met a decent man like you she would be doing her own thing too. Actually, she *is* doing her own thing, so I'm not even going to trip it. I'm just enjoying getting to know you and enjoying my personal time on this land, far, far away." She repositioned her hand on his chest, covering the circumference of one pectoral muscle with her palm.

Steven's words ceased and he shut his eyes in response to her touch. He paused and then regained his breath.

Lexi's fingers played twirl and pull with his six or seven chest hairs; a few of them were graying. "I appreciate you trying to play devil's advocate. I'm fine, really."

He regained his sight and placed his left-hand index finger under her chin, directing her vision to connect with his. "Lexi, I will never pressure you. We can sleep in the same bed again and again and it will not happen until you're comfortable."

"Steven, I just want to make sure that I don't get caught up in the moment. The sex can wait. It will be the bloom if we nurture the root."

"Enough said." They resumed their blissful relaxation, shut off from the world.

Charming Fantasy Island was just what the name described, a fantasy. It was carefully hidden from the outside world along a stretch of glistening secluded beaches lined with crystal clear water and the natural wonder of sun, sea, and sand. It was totally uninhabited, except for the bartenders at the Hut Bar who lined up to greet the tender of passengers. The soft, white stretches of sandy beach, clear sparkling aquamarine water, and sultry, luscious, green tropical forest met all of the requirements for a perfect beach holiday. The palm trees towered high above the skyline. Everything was some shade of green, from the beach towels to the lounge chairs to the beach umbrellas—even to the serving glasses and beach rafts. It was the ideal escape. There was no snorkeling here, no parasailing, no scuba diving, and no shopping. No inhibitions, no reservations, no expectations. It was serene and untouched, as if it was waiting to be explored. Just a massive, remote beach at the visitors' disposal, with calm bathlike waters to float upon, in the nude.

"You are all welcome to remove your clothing if and when you choose," said Delmonte as the boat pulled up along the shore.

This day the weather was beautiful. Delmonte stepped out of the boat, turning for a moment to assist Ashley as she took her first step onto his island of paradise. Bo, Deshaun, Winter, and Yanni exited next with their jaws dropped, without saying a word. Winter ran ahead like a preschooler to stake out her spot.

"This is the place for us. Come on, you guys," Winter yelled, leading the way.

"This feels like a dream," said Yanni, turning in circles with her arms extended, looking up at the tall trees and blue skies. She toppled a bit, still feeling uneasy from her previous intake. Bo grabbed her by her arm.

Kelly stepped out next, looking stunned and speechless. She proceeded to take a seat at the bar in silence, plopping her red beach bag onto the seat next to her.

A few more boatloads of Chocolate Ship passengers arrived. Within no time, there were a few dozen other passengers quickly mixing into the available chaise lounge chairs. Twenty minutes later, the beach was full.

"What if that boat never comes back to get us?" asked Yanni in a declarative tone as the tender made its way back to Nassau, almost as though she wished it would not.

"Then we'd have our own soulful Gilligan's Island going on," Winter said, looking over at Kelly, alone at the bar. "And there's Ginger right there. Come over here," she yelled to Kelly while lowering her Sunpearl glasses to the tip of her nose to get a better view of Kelly's response. Kelly grabbed her bag and started walking over to the group.

Deshaun got up and offered his chair as Kelly strolled over, taking barefoot steps on the soft, warm sand, twisting her heels and leaving wide imprints along the way.

"What's your name again?" Winter asked, patting the palm of her hand on the chair that Deshaun vacated.

"Kelly."

"Kelly, I'm Winter and this is Yanni."

Kelly replied, "I know Yanni," straddling the chair. She was sporting a white halter bikini with gold trim.

"Kelly, huh? I love the way that name just rolls off my tongue. Kelly," Winter said, giving extra attention to extending her tongue on the two l's.

Deshaun stared at Kelly, smiling as if to welcome the new addition to the family.

Winter inquired, "Why are you alone?"

"I have a jerk for a husband and I wish I'd like never gotten married, to be honest with you."

"Wow, that's to the point," said Yanni.

"Why should I tone it down or lie about it? I was better off single for sure," Kelly said bitterly.

"That's enough to discourage me from getting married," Yanni said, laying her head back for stability.

Bo and Deshaun excused themselves and went to check out the scene on the other side of the bar, where there was a group of women who were literally sunbathing and obeying all of the rules.

Winter looked over at them and said, "What do you say, ladies? Should we shake these bikinis or what?"

"I say we do it," said Yanni, as they all lay flat upon their backs.

"Okay, so here we go with our tops first," Winter said, leaning up to reach around her back to untie her translucent opal bikini top.

"Count to three," said Yanni.

Kelly said, "One, two, and three," and raised her top up from below her breasts, pulling it off over her head. Yanni pulled her jade green tube top down to her waist.

"Oh, my goodness. That sun feels good," said Winter, tossing her top onto the sand. "Nice boobs, ladies," Winter said, her award-winning Anna Nicole Smith jugs separating to each side as she lay on her back. Winter lifted up her rear end and wiggled her way out of her bikini bottoms. "You ladies are on your own for this one," she said. Winter's bald pubic area was fully exposed as she bent her knees upward, placing her feet flat on the chair with her legs spread wide apart. "I say let it breathe."

"That's a bit much for me, I'll just go topless," Yanni said, drawing the line.

"Okay, you're going to go home with a major tan line," Winter warned.

"Tan line? As dark as I am it will not be a problem," Yanni said.

"Well, I totally do not want a tan line, I know that much," Kelly said as she stood up and turned her back to Winter and Yanni. She stuck her thumbs into the sides of her bikini bottoms, and from the hips, bent all of the way forward as if to kiss her toes. She pulled her bottoms on down inch by inch, to her knees, to her ankles, and then she stepped one foot and then the other out of each leg. Winter's eyes were full on bugged and almost without noticing that she was licking the side of her lip, she said, "That's what I call getting nude."

Winter leaned back as Kelly took her seat in the raw. Winter proceeded to spread Hawaiian Tropic dark tanning glitter gel on her chest without looking at anything but Kelly.

"Do you need help with that?" Kelly offered, already leaning over with her palm extended for the tanning gel.

Winter acquiesced, "Well, actually, could you rub it on my back once I turn over?"

"Yes. Your entire back?" Kelly asked almost with warning.

"Please. Every place I cannot reach would be fine," Winter clarified.

Kelly squeezed globs of clear gel onto both hands and massaged Winter's back in large circles, making her way past her butt to her legs, her feet and then back up to her rear. First she rubbed the left cheek with a deep tissue pressing motion, and then the right, using her fingers as she added pressure, and then lightening up with a soft, subtle, almost tickling rub. The rays of the sun accented the tiny specs of silver glitter that sparkled over Winter's butter-pecan skin.

"Wow, that feels nice. You're very good with your hands," Winter meowed.

Kelly replied, "That's what I've been told. But I suppose it went unappreciated."

"Not anymore it won't," acknowledged Winter. She turned over and asked, "Can I do you?"

Without a verbal response, Kelly lay flat on her back. Her tiny brown nipples were standing straight at attention as Yanni watched with her mouth open.

"You two are really making the most of this excursion," Yanni remarked. "I'm either drunk or dreaming."

"We just want even tans, that's all," Kelly said as Winter rubbed her neck, chest, stomach, thighs, and toes.

"Well, Yanni, this is the Fantasy Island. Do you want some?" Winter asked.

"Oh, no thanks. I'm just fine," Yanni said, turning onto her stomach and placing a towel over her butt just in case.

Bo and Deshaun walked back over, drooling, and gave each other a high five.

"Oh, control yourselves, boys. You've seen more tits and ass than this in a tittie bar," said Winter.

Bo took his seat, removing his T-shirt but keeping his deep blue trunks intact. Deshaun, who realized he had no place to sit, headed back to the bar.

For the next few hours, Winter and Kelly talked and turned their sun-toasted bodies from front to back, all the while keeping a steady flow of peach daiquiris and cherry blossoms at their disposal. Yanni was stretched out, talking to Bo, and Deshaun had moved on to a woman who had decided to strut her nakedness along the shoreline.

* * *

Delmonte and Ashley never seemed to pull themselves away from their horizontal chaise lounge and steady flow of Remy Martin. Neither of them went for the nude idea, but Ashley was sporting a bubble-gum-colored thong that left little to the imagination.

Dante and Justin went full-out nude. They moved their chairs back toward the shade of the Hut Bar.

"I still think you should say something to him about firing you," Justin suggested to Dante.

"No, Justin. He let the captain do his dirty work. I would have thought a successful Black man who has experienced so much of the world wouldn't be so homophobic," Dante said, glaring at Delmonte.

"Do you really think it's because you're gay? Or because he caught us having oral sex in the companionway?"

"It's both, Justin. And don't you think for a moment it's not."

"I'm really sorry, Dante. You really liked your job, didn't you?" Justin asked.

Dante sounded angry and regretful. "I love traveling and getting paid for it. This was a dream job, and I get fired the first time the ship sets sail."

"What if you hadn't gotten the job? We never would have met," Justin said in reflection.

Dante just continued to look banefully at Delmonte and Ashley. "That bastard," he said. "Yes, you're right about that. At least I met you," he agreed as he placed his hand on Justin's arm and squeezed.

Within what seemed to be no time at all, Mia opened her eyes to the realization that she must have fallen asleep. It was already late afternoon on the island and the pre-setting sun reflected off the ocean in a blaze of deep orange like the color of peach cobbler. Mia could hear the subtle rush of the waves along the shore, the sound of the steel drums echoing through the cobblestone streets nearby and the sound of people giggling. The laughing and giggling female in the water near the pier was Megan, and the man in the water with her was Scott. Mia thought, *I hope that boat doesn't come back too soon from that nude beach, or else hardheaded Megan will get served up round two.*

Mia looked back toward the bar and saw Miles, sitting and drinking and talking to Tangie. *What's up with that? I'm going to just close my eyes again and shut down. This scenery* is *too much to take.*

# THE SCREAMING ORGASM

"Mia!" Bianca yelled enthusiastically. She came running toward her, hard nipples and all, wearing a red-and-white bikini top that read ONE WAY and a white, ankle-length wrap skirt. Her firm, brown legs were exposed through the long slit with every step. Bianca's clay red ankle-wrap sandals crunched against the grains as she came closer, moving much too quickly to stop herself from kicking sand on Mia's lower body. Mia turned away, bracing herself for more flying sand as Bianca plopped down on Miles's towel. "Just wait until you hear what happened last night," Bianca said as if she had the scoop of the century.

Mia asked, brushing sand from her legs, "Where have you been?"

"Omar and I took the kids swimming on the ship this morning. They're still over there."

"You trust him alone with Corey in that water again?"

"Well, if anyone can save him, Omar can. But, girl, Omar gave me my first intercourse orgasm last night."

"Oh, no. Let me sit up so I can hear every detail of this one," Mia said, crossing her legs under her.

Bianca sat with her legs to the side, leaning in toward Mia just in case someone would overhear her.

"The kids went to sleep in his room, so he came back to my room just so we could get away for a few hours before they woke up and found us gone."

"They've been spending the night in each of your rooms too?"

"Just the last two nights. Now listen, damn," Bianca said, still sounding out of breath.

"Damn, what happened?"

"He wouldn't let me touch him at all. Even when I tried to start at his neck and work my way down, he said no. 'I want this to be your night,' he said after he sat me on the bed and stood right in front of me, removing his clothes. His long, dark body was perfect, Mia, and his thing was curved."

"Thing? Curved?" Mia asked with a snicker.

"Yes. It had a hook to it and it was long and thick. He looked like a Greek Black God as he laid on his back on top of my bed and told me to sit on him.

"Did you?"

"Oh, yes, I had to. He was just lying there ready to go to work. I said to myself, 'Oh, he knows this is the way for me to get off and he is going to just get me wet this way so that he can get his.' I took off my shorts and midriff top and removed my panties and proceeded to straddle his face, when he said, 'No. No oral for you, baby. You are going to cum with one hundred percent dick tonight,' " Bianca said, reenacting his exact words and the depth of his voice.

"Girl, I knew he was a freak!" Mia said, bringing her knees in to her chest.

"I thought I was going to die. He guided the width of my body with his hands by moving my hips to straddle his penis while he laid on his back. He parted my legs like the sea, and raised me up to take it in for what seemed like five minutes. He called it Cobra."

"Cobra?"

"Yeah, like the snake? Anyway, his tip kept hitting something along the side of my wall, deep inside that kept making my body jump involuntarily. Right away I knew that had to be the spot, although it's never been hit before, I knew that it was a different sensation. He kept hitting it over and over again and my ass was getting dizzy quick. I knew I was in trouble."

"Damn, Omar," Mia said with a new respect.

"He raised my hips according to how he moved so that he was leading my grind, holding my hips in his hands for guidance. I tried to work him kind of like bucking, but he kept making me stop, asking me to follow his lead. He pulled my torso down upon his and kissed my nipples, sucking my hanging breasts. I felt the lubrication just exuding from my walls like never before.

"Then he turned me over to my back, still inside of me and raised my legs straight into the air so that my feet were parallel to the ceiling with the backs of my legs along his chest and shoulders. He turned my hips slightly to my left and hit another spot that made me scream in pleasurable shock. Again, he did it faster and faster until I got lightheaded and my mouth was just hanging open with this, *uuhn*, *uuhn*, *uuhn*, sound, like I had lost my mind."

"Omar's a pro, girl." Mia almost cheered. Hearing about his prowess made her happy for Bianca.

"Calm down now. I haven't gotten to the best part yet. First of all, he told me the rule was that I could not kiss him. He said my kisses would surely interrupt his focus. Instead, he bent my legs back toward the headboard and told me to breathe, slowly, in through my nose and out through my mouth. I thought I was in a Lamaze class again. But just when he laid his body down, his chest upon my chest, he started breathing slow and deliberate and whispered in my ear, 'Follow me. Breathe with me.' And so I did. I felt his chest expand and I followed his every move. By the fifth or sixth deep breath, I felt something tighten in my hips and then his face was a blur. I just went into another world, Mia. He asked, 'Is Cobra getting it done?' I answered in a scream through my orgasm, 'Yes, I . . .' Mia, I almost said I loved him. So I said, '*Eye-yai-yai*,' just as I snapped back from the zone I was in. I've never in my life felt anything like that, girl. I looked at him like he was from another planet and told him to get the hell up—him and Cobra."

"Cobra," said Miles, walking up to give Bianca a hug.

She replied as though he was dumb, "Cobra. King Cobra. I cannot find any King Cobra beer for Omar."

"He comes all the way to Nassau and has you looking for King Cobra beer?" Miles asked.

"Yeah."

Mia jumped in, "Ah, Miles, what's up with you coming over here trying to get all up in our stuff? What were you up to over there?"

"Just talking to Tangie," he said matter-of-factly.

"What's up with that?" Mia asked.

"Nothing," he said looking over at Scott and Megan.

Bianca asked, "Are those two still at it?"

Mia said, "Miles, Scott is really screwing up. Kelly is going to hurt both of them."

"Mia, I'm going to go back and check on Omar and the kids and then get ready for dinner. It's almost early evening already," Bianca noticed.

"Hold up, I'll go with you," Mia said.

"I'll be in the room soon to get dressed," said Miles. "But first, I'm going to keep an eye on Vanilla Ice over there."

"All right now, don't be late. This is the African-American attire night and you haven't even tried on the outfit I bought you. I want to get an early start," Mia said to him, giving him a kiss on the lips.

Miles whispered in her ear, "Omar let her have it, huh?"

"Uh-huh," Mia replied on the down low as Bianca skipped along ahead of them with a pep in her step like Mia had never seen before.

Bianca and Mia headed back to the ship just as the first boat was returning from the Fantasy Island. Mia wondered what types of fantasies occurred over there. She noticed one thing for sure. Winter was sitting next to Kelly, all but licking Kelly's armpits as the tender stopped along the beach. There was no sign of Deshaun and Bo, or Yanni. Winter helped Kelly out of the boat and they continued holding hands as they walked away. Winter had moved on again. Perhaps Kelly didn't notice what Scott was doing, but it was a fact that he noticed *her*.

"Scott, get your ass over here," demanded Miles as Scott was talking to Megan.

Scott walked toward him, turning to check out Kelly and Winter as they walked by. "What's up?" he asked Miles.

"What is your problem? You know Kelly kicked Megan's ass and you're still flirting around with her. What do you expect her to do next? You cannot continue to push a woman like that."

"Oh yeah, don't fuck up on your woman, otherwise she'll start pushing up on another woman."

"I'm not even going to go there with you," Miles said with rawness.

Scott pointed toward Kelly. "What's she doing all hugged up with Winter? That's shady."

"I don't know, Scott. But maybe you can start controlling yourself now that we only have one night left. Do you think you can?" Miles asked.

Scott replied, "Why should I? She just straight walked by me with the tritest ho' up on this cruise. I wouldn't touch Winter's ass for a million dollars. She's tapped out."

Miles said, "You said earlier that you would hit that like a baseball. But now, Winter is ready to take advantage of a vulnerable woman who is playing the 'Men are dogs' role. Kelly is a prime target for someone like her."

"All this tells me is that Kelly is bisexual. A woman doesn't just turn to another woman unless she's had those tendencies," Scott stated, as if he were an expert.

"Maybe. Or maybe your wife is just trying to make you jealous and give you a taste of your own medicine."

"I wasn't on that ship giving head to a dude. She's gone too far," Scott declared, nodding his head and looking down at the sand.

"Scott, all you can really do is focus on yourself. Have you tried to apologize yet?"

"Man, she's not even saying a word to me. She's got me sleeping on the couch. I might not even be able to get in my own room tonight. Or maybe she'll decide she won't come back until the sun comes up. I'd have to hurt her then," Scott threatened.

"What about the night you didn't come home until the sun came up?" Miles asked.

"Dude, I just got caught up in the moment. Kelly is my wife. I'm losing my wife."

"And it was her husband who was sleeping with Megan that night. You have a lot of work ahead of you, Scott," Miles told him.

"Man, this isn't the first time I've fooled around. You know that."

They walked toward the shore. "Yes, but you did it on a ship that your wife was on too. Maybe this is just what you need to get you to slow your roll, bro," Miles said, placing his hand on Scott's shoulder.

"Slow my roll. You mean to tell me I should just sit back and let her have a rendezvous with a woman? Now you know you would lose your mind if it was you," Scott stated.

Miles reminded him, "I have lost my mind over that. What I know now is that you have to decide if this is the type of woman you want. Can you forgive her, and can she forgive you? But the first step is admitting you were wrong and acknowledging her feelings and her right to be hurt. You have a lot of work ahead of you."

"Miles, man, I love Kelly. She's a good wife and she's already put up with a lot. What I like about her most is her independence and her ability to just go on about her business when I'm going about my day. She never sweats me about anything."

"And now that's the very side of her you're going to have to deal with. She's probably not going to sweat you either. She's going to go on about her business and now you're really going to get a taste of her independence. Are you going to be all right, man?"

"Yes, I'll be all right, Miles. I'm just spent. That's my girl, though," Scott replied with his voice sundering.

"Come on, dude," Miles said as they continued to walk. "You'll be fine. You're going to be going through it for a while. Just make sure you don't get near Megan again for the rest of the time we're here. Promise?"

"Promise," Scott replied sincerely.

"You are my dog, right?" Miles asked, giving him daps.

"Yeah, I'm your dog."

Scott and Miles walked back toward the tender to return to the ship. Miles noticed Delmonte standing near the captain and Ashley.

"Excuse me for one minute, Scott. I'll catch up with you," Miles said.

Miles approached the group and stood nearby, awaiting an acknowledgment. The captain said, "Can I help you?"

"Mr. Harrison, can I talk to you for a minute?" Miles asked.

# OUR AFRICAN HERITAGE

Mia realized that Miles was off keeping an eye on his boy as she removed her beautiful gold-and-ivory Nigerian wrap set from the closet. The classic, rich, handwoven cotton Asooke fabric looked like it was fit for a queen. It had a princess neckline and drop waist. Mia held the dress in front of her, looking in the closet mirror, imagining herself as a regal heiress, standing on a flower-laden balcony high above her subjects, gracefully accepting her appointment to the throne. Her slippers were gold leather, thin-strapped sandals with round, two-inch crystal heels. The matching headpiece and wrap were pure solid cream linen with embroidered gold detail outlined by piping.

Mia had bought a matching outfit for her elusive king. "Perhaps I should send my royal subjects to track him down and return him to my lair," she said out loud just as there was a knock at the door.

Mia peered through the peephole and saw the same attendant from the casino who had counted out her money peering back. She opened the door.

"Hello, can I help you?" Mia asked upon opening the door.

"Yes, Ms. White. I neglected to have you sign this tax statement so that we can report your winnings."

"Yippee, isn't that great? The government always gets theirs, don't they? In all of the excitement, I forgot."

"No problem. Just sign right here," the attendant said, pointing to the shaded space with Mia's name typed below.

Mia took the pen and scrolled her John Hancock. "Shall I date it?"

"No, we'll date it back to when you won the money. I'm sorry to bother you."

Mia handed her back the pen and shook her hand. "It's cool. I'm just getting dressed for that African event we're having. Check you later."

"Take care and enjoy the rest of your cruise." The young attendant walked away as Mia shut the door.

Mia hung Miles's outfit outside the closet so he could get to it without delay. It was a Khemetic ensemble with a gold ankh embroidered on the front and a brocade lapel. "I hope he wears this headpiece," she said.

Within no time, Mia was dressed and ready to go. She opened her tiny leather jewelry bag and picked out her eighteen-carat gold chain with the diamond horseshoe charm that her mom had given her when she graduated from college. Holding it to her neck, she decided to leave on the puka-shell necklace that matched Miles's, who, by the way, there was still no sign of.

The Egyptian Ballroom looked even more elegant than before, its round tables draped with ivory cloths and brass centerpieces filled with freshly cut purplish pink geraniums and vibrant yellow and white tulips.

Mia approached her table and saw Delmonte Harrison, wearing white snakeskin cowboy boots, taking his seat next to Ashley. His Nehru collar shirt was a bold combination of red, green and black plaid, and his pants were made of simple white cotton. Perhaps he was shooting for Afrocentric, but he just barely missed his mark.

Her lost King Miles suddenly walked through the theater door with Scott, who made his way over to his own table with Kelly, wearing a plain black suit and an attitude. Kelly, wearing a simple white pantsuit, turned her back to him, still shining him on.

"Damn, Mr. Lewis. You look very handsome," Mia complimented Miles.

He stated, "You picked out a good one. I'm just not sure about the dress part of this outfit. I feel naked."

"Miles," Mia said, looking down at his feet. "You were supposed to wear pants underneath." He looked at Mia like he wanted to do damage. "I say you should go back up to the room and put on some simple black dress pants. And why aren't you wearing your puka shells?" Miles just shook his head and ignored her suggestion.

They stood next to their table, where Bianca, decked out in a purple-and-silver outfit with a purple headdress, was making sure to save four seats from the table of ten for Omar and the kids.

"Where are your pants, Miles?" she asked with a snicker, placing her silver purse in the chair next to her.

Miles said, catching on, "You overheard us talking. You wouldn't have noticed on your own."

"Yes, I noticed, but just barely. You have great ankles," Bianca teased.

"Hey, everyone. We clean up pretty well, huh?" Omar asked, sporting his dark sienna tux with a tiger print cummerbund. Bianca looked at him from top to bottom, like she was ready for more orgasm lessons. "Hey, baby," Omar said, embracing Bianca around her tiny waist as she stood up. "You make Tyra Banks look like a scag."

Corey laughed and gave Omar a high five. Omar's son's dark blue and green outfit was actually similar to Corey's, and Omar's daughter was wearing a tangerine dress with lemon yellow trim.

Speaking of yellow, Megan quietly took her seat wearing the hell out of a yellow stretch-knit minidress with matching shoes.

"What's African about that swap-meet dress?" asked Bianca.

"Yeah. Where's the skirt that goes with it?" Miles joked.

"Wherever your pants are," Megan replied right back.

Miles said, "That's it, I'm going back to the room. I'll be right back." He looked at Megan and warned, "Don't let me call Kelly over here to check you." Megan cut her eyes and turned her back to see what was going on around the rest of the room.

Somehow, Winter made her way next to Kelly for a moment as Scott sat across from them, looking over at Megan. Megan turned back in an instant, rubbing her forehead and then digging through her miniature yellow satin bag for a mirror. Her tiny shiner near her lip was barely noticeable, what with all the makeup she was wearing.

"Hey, Yanni, you look beautiful," Mia said as Yanni walked up with her sister, barely saying a word in response. Even though Lexi and Yanni were a little distant with each other, they still wore their matching outfits. Their pale magenta suits with matching turbans were the hit. Lexi was wearing her blazer and pants and Yanni was wearing a pair of linen shorts with a waistline blazer, only she was wearing panty hose, unlike Megan.

"Thanks," she mumbled as she took a seat next to Megan.

"I'll be right back," said Lexi, touching her seat back while catching a glimpse of Steven. She headed toward his table. He stood when she approached and embraced her.

As everyone took their seats, except Miles, the waiter, Olandi, approached.

"May I 'ave your menu cards, please?" he asked, grinning at Megan.

"Here you go, baby," Megan said with a wink. "I'll have the catfish with white rice and a salad with Italian dressing."

"Okay, and you, madam?" he asked, looking at Bianca.

Omar spoke up and ordered for her, "The lady will have the smothered steak and yams and greens and I'll try the neckbones, dressing and gravy, and macaroni and cheese."

"And for the kids?" Olandi asked, writing.

"Two orders of BBQ ribs, one with French fries and one with

potato salad, and one cheeseburger, no onions and no tomatoes, with fries."

Bianca smiled at Omar, who had obviously taken over as head of the Black Brady Bunch.

"I'll have oxtails and red beans with rice, please," said Yanni.

"No problam. And you, ma'am?" He turned to Mia.

"Can my other half order in a minute? He'll be right back."

"Okay," Olandi obliged.

"I'll just have the Jack Daniel's salmon with the country mashed potatoes and fried okra, please. And you know what, give my man the smothered pork chops with the same side orders. He'll just have to live with it," she said, handing Olandi her cards.

Olandi looked over his chart and said with a deep, resounding bass to his Jamaican voice, "I tink I've got everya-ting. Your drink server will be right-ova."

"Thanks," Omar said for all of the ladies and children, even as he was distracted by what he saw at the captain's table. "Baby, do you see what the captain is sporting up in here?" he asked Bianca.

"I see him," Bianca said as they all turned around in admiration.

"That suit had to have cost him at least a grand, easily," Omar said, referring to the captain's jet black tuxedo and white button-down shirt with a kinte-cloth bow tie and matching pocket handkerchief. "And I know his kicks are Ferragamo black patent leather."

"I guess they're paying captains well nowadays," Bianca commented.

Everyone ordered drinks from the server just as Tangie walked over, taking her stance behind Mia as the server exited. "You all look like you're enjoying your last night on the ship."

Mia turned around with a smile. "Yes, we are. Thanks for asking."

"Yeah, it seems like we just started yesterday, and here we are, one week later," Lexi remarked as she returned to the table. "Did you order for me?" she asked Yanni.

"No," Yanni remarked without eye contact.

"I'll be right back," Lexi said to the group, stopping to talk to Olandi.

Bianca stated, "I don't want this week to come to an end. I'd like to turn right back around and spend another week. Tangie, you are so lucky to be able to sail for weeks at a time."

"Yes, it's nice, but sometimes we'd like to be getting off the ship right along with you. We just turn back around and take off again, week after week."

"Well, I want your job," said Yanni.

"Your sister just might stay if she plays her cards right," Tangie added. "It looks like she caught one of the biggest fish in the ocean."

"What do you mean, 'if she plays her cards right'?" asked Yanni.

"Oh nothing. I'm just saying I've never seen Steven this enamored, and I've worked with him for over a year," Tangie said as Lexi returned to take her seat.

"What?" Lexi asked as Yanni and Tangie simply stared at her while the main course was served.

Winter walked up and interrupted. "Mr. Young, can you tell us about the accusations your wife has made against you?"

Omar did not answer.

Justin was standing behind Winter shooting film and Winter had the microphone to her tiny tape recorder primed under Omar's chin.

Omar stood up and politely said, "Excuse us, but we are trying to have dinner here. Do you mind?"

The captain came over to take Winter by the hand, "Shouldn't you be making your way over to your table or someone else's table other than this one?"

She snatched her hand from him.

"Come on, Justin, let's go," she ordered, leading the way.

"Good-bye, everyone," Justin said. "Sorry, man," he said to Omar as he followed behind Winter.

The captain winked at Mia and pulled out Omar's chair for him to take his seat again.

"Please continue to enjoy your farewell dinner. You will have no more interruptions," the captain assured them.

"Thanks, man," Omar said, shaking his head as he took his seat and placed his napkin back on his lap.

The captain walked away as Bianca said, "That woman is busy. I don't know what he saw in her the first few nights."

The group proceeded to dig in. The conversation faded down to near silence. The only obvious sound at the table was the repeated clangor of silverware. Within no time at all, the courses were devoured.

"Sometimes we women don't even take the time to see a good thing coming. It seems to me that Winter is trying to fit in all she can with whomever she can," said Lexi.

"Well, he can do a whole lot better," Mia stated, as if it were a fact.

Yanni said, "Oh, Winter's not so bad."

"It doesn't look like the captain has been too successful this cruise with anyone," said Bianca.

Mia remarked almost out of the blue, "Yes, but he is a good catch. That's for sure."

"Yes, I am," said Miles, returning just as the waiter prepared to take away the main course plates and serve dessert.

"Uh-huh," Mia said in agreement, looking over toward Bianca as though she was growing tired of humoring him.

Scott came over to take Miles away again, "Excuse me," he said, putting down his fork just after cutting into his barely warm pork chop. He stepped away to talk to his jilted friend.

Mia took a double sip of her Chardonnay. "That crap is getting old," she said to Bianca.

Bianca surprised Mia by saying, "Oh, chill out."

"What's gotten into you?" Mia asked as the waiter brought the lemon sock-it-to-me cake with lemon sherbet. Mia took a bite, swallowed and then remarked, "The day you start supporting Miles will be the day that—" Her sentence was interrupted by the sound of a loud microphone being powered up.

"Testing, testing," a deep voice blared over the speakers through a loud tapping on the head of the microphone. The squealing of the high-pitched setup forced some to cover their ears.

"Hello. My name is Miles Lewis and if you don't mind, I'd like a few moments of your time."

Mia gagged at the same time her swallowing reflex took hold of her sherbet. She quickly dropped her spoon, picked up her napkin and wiped her mouth. She looked behind her to see Miles standing onstage with the captain and Delmonte Harrison standing behind him.

All at once, Bianca, Corey, and Scott got up from their seats and took the trail along the plush carpeting from their table to the stage, standing beside Miles.

"This is a very special evening for me. I'd like all of you to kindly share this moment with my lady, Mia White, and me."

Tangie emerged to stand behind Mia and the crowd began to sigh at the realization of who Mia was. But all Mia could hear was Miles's comforting voice.

"Mia and I have been together for three and one half years. She has been patient, understanding, supportive, and loving. Mia, my parents and your mom have given us their blessings. They are here in spirit and they send their love to us both."

Corey then took the red satin box from his suit pocket and slowly opened it. He took the ring and handed it to Miles. The crowd gasped.

"Mia, will you please come to me?" Miles asked, looking at her with hope on his face.

Mia's hands were shaking and her feet were numb. Tangie stepped back and Omar stood to gallantly move Mia's chair back. He extended his hand and raised his palm upward, motioning for her to stand. Mia placed her napkin on the table, mindfully raised her hips from the chair, and joined her hand in his. He waved his other hand for her to proceed onto the stage. She forced her rubbery legs to take each step toward Miles in slow motion, scared and stunned. Her eyes spied Bianca's simpering expression. *Bianca is crying either out of sentiment or fear that her ass is mine*, Mia thought, with a look that could kill. Scott smiled at Mia and motioned for her to continue to the stage.

Just as she reached Miles face-to-face, Ashley came up to the stage with another microphone and began singing "Here and Now." Miles took Mia's trembling hands in his. They embraced as if they were one, both shaking as their chests met. He took her right hand into his left and they began to slow dance. Ashley backed farther away and began to sing at a lower volume as Miles stopped and asked, "Mia, will you marry me?"

The crowd gave way to a simultaneous "Aaaahhh," as if to answer his question. But Mia was blind to anything but Miles's dark, deep, serious stare. He took her hand and gingerly held out the square, elegant, huge yellow diamond ring. Her ring finger wobbled its way into its perfect fit. She gazed down at her hand and up at Miles's face, and down at the ring again.

She fixed her tear-filled eyes upon the many faces around the room, taking in the encouraging stares. Is this the way she thought it should happen, or was this taking things a bit further than she said she wanted? Mia felt paralyzed, as though in a trance or in the middle of a dream. She gazed at the many passengers staring back at her. Some of them she knew, some were complete strangers.

Mia then leveraged her focus upon Miles, who almost seemed to stand in front of her in a different light. The light of a man who was ready to take on the responsibility of someone other than himself. A man who had realized that this phenomenal surprise was something he felt was necessary, without prodding and without coercing. Mia formed her lips to answer his fervent question. "Yes, Miles, I will marry you."

Everyone applauded aggressively while Ashley switched her selection to "For You" by Kenny Lattimore. Mia and Miles walked toward the captain, who had a white robe draped over his left arm. He was holding a Bible in his hand. Delmonte took the Bible while the captain put on his robe. Delmonte handed it back to him, walked by to shake Miles's hand and kissed Mia on the cheek.

Bianca stood beside Mia. Scott stood beside Miles as the couple faced the captain. Tangie handed Mia a bouquet of dried dark blue and purple chrysanthemums.

"Dearly beloved," the captain said, "Mia and Miles have agreed to be married, here and now, on this big, Black boat, in front of all of you who will witness this celebration of their marriage."

He continued to speak to the onlookers. "We've come together not to mark the start of a relationship, but to recognize a bond that already exists. Miles has decided to surprise his lady with a proposal that shocked and elated all of us. The confirmation of that bond is a love force that will become the foundation for their union now and for evermore."

He directed his words to the couple. "Stand fast in faith and confidence, believing in your shared future as strongly as you believe in yourselves and in each other today. In this spirit, you can create a partnership that will strengthen and sustain you all the days of your lives."

The captain looked at Mia. "Mia, will you have this man to be your husband, to live together in the covenant of marriage? Will you love him, comfort him, honor, and keep him, in sickness and in health, and forsaking all others, be faithful to him as long as you both shall live?"

"I will," said Mia.

The captain repeated the same vows to Miles and the captain paused for a moment as someone in the room cleared their throat.

"I will," Miles said, without missing a beat.

Miles repeated after the captain, "I, Miles, take you Mia, to be my wife, to have and to hold from this day forward, for better, for worse, for richer, for poorer, in sickness and in health, to love and to cherish, till death us do part."

Mia repeated the same, with him as her husband, ending with a loud and confident, "Amen," as Bianca leaned in to brush up against Mia's left arm.

The captain continued, "May the source of your love touch and bless you and grace your lives with color and courage. The circle of the ring has been a symbol of an unbroken end to completeness and continued love. Since Mia already has her ring on her finger, we will proceed. By the power vested in me by the Bahamas, I declare that you are husband and wife. You may kiss the bride."

Miles took the lead, pulling Mia toward him and gazing at her, without blinking, almost as if he could examine his own reflection in her eyes. He proceeded to tongue his bride for a second, and then he switched to a more conservative lip lock to seal the deal.

"I present to you, Mr. and Mrs. Miles Lewis," the captain said to the room full of onlookers.

Mia and Miles pivoted to face the crowd and everyone stood to cheer, clap, and whistle.

As the applause subsided, the captain explained, "Dating back to slave days, jumping the broom was a way of jumping into holy matrimony together and it has been a part of African-American tradition." Tangie handed the captain a beautifully handcrafted wheat-colored broom with pistachio green and white dried flowers joined together with a gold bow. The captain placed the broom on the floor in front of the couple and said, "Jump the broom from one life into another."

Scott, Bianca, and the captain counted together, "One, two, three, jump," and Mia and Miles jumped over the broom. The captain picked it up and swept behind the couple, saying, "May all evil influences be swept out of your life." He handed it to Bianca as Ashley sang again.

Yanni and Lexi rushed Mia, "Girl, congratulations! We had no idea."

"Yeah, right," Mia said in disbelief.

"No, really. Bianca must be good at keeping secrets," said Lexi.

Bianca shuffled up and hugged Mia tightly.

"You've got a good man, Mia. He came through at the last minute after all."

Mia warned Bianca, "Yes, he did. But your ass is mine. You knew the whole time, didn't you?"

"No, I just found out tonight when Miles came to my room

after we left the beach earlier to ask me to participate. I could not believe that he planned all of this to surprise you. Let me see your ring, girl." Bianca took Mia's hand into hers and examined the rock with a dropped jaw. "Damn, this is huge, Mia. Where did Miles get all of this money?"

Mia glanced over at Miles where he and Scott stood nearby, shaking hands. "I don't know where he got any of what he's been using lately. I'm just glad he did," Mia said with pride. Miles walked over, with Corey at his side.

"Corey, my ringbearer," Mia said. "Thanks for being such a handsome keeper of the ring."

Corey hugged her. "That was nice, Auntie M. Can I go back to the table?" he asked, looking at his mom, sounding like he'd had enough of all the fuss.

"Yes, you may," Bianca answered.

Omar approached to bring Bianca back to the table too, saying to Miles, "Congratulations, brotha. That was what I call first class."

Justin walked up and said, "Don't forget to call me so that I can get a copy of the video to you next week." Miles gave him a Black hand five.

"How long did you know about this?" Mia asked Justin.

"I plead the fifth," he said, zipping his lip with his finger in allegiance to Miles.

"Okay, all you single ladies. Line up for the tossing of the bouquet," said Tangie, who pulled Mia from Miles's clutches and handed her an alternate bouquet for her over-the-head toss, making room for the small group of women who came forward.

Mia turned her back to Yanni, Lexi, Megan, and about six other bachelorettes. Their faces were childlike as they arched their backs and stretched their arms upward, giggling to one another as though they really did not mind who made the catch of the day.

Mia caught a glimpse of Ashley Isley backing as far away as possible. Mia laughed to herself.

"Here we go," Mia said. She leaned forward and bent down to

gather enough momentum to really get some distance. She raised her right hand above her head and threw the bouquet of dried red roses high into the air behind her, turning quickly to get a look at the efforts of the lucky recipient.

The bouquet tipped off of Lexi's fingers and bounced over to the left, straight into the hands of Tangie, who was standing nearby with her mouth wide open.

"Oh, no, I cannot participate. This is for the passengers."

"No, it's for every single lady in this room. You're single and you caught it," said the captain, standing less than two steps behind her.

Mia approached Tangie and congratulated her with a hug. "He's right, Tangie. It looks like you're next."

# 44

# THEIR LAST DANCE

"Who planned this whole thing, and the wedding reception?" Mia asked Miles while they stood waiting for the captain's instructions.

"That's why I've been talking to Tangie so much," Miles explained. "At the last minute, I had to confirm it with Delmonte too."

"What? Even after you checked him?" Mia asked while chuckling.

"Yes. Tangie convinced me to swallow my pride."

"That's some convincing."

The captain announced, "Now, to celebrate the first wedding aboard the *Chocolate Ship,* Tangie had our chef make a beautiful cake. Tangie, will you bring that out?"

She wheeled out a five-layer chocolate cream cake with a brotha and sistah on top wearing African attire, while Olandi and three other waiters poured champagne by the case.

"Before you both cut into your cake, I'd like to give a toast. Everyone please raise your glass. By the way, these libations symbolize expressions of good wishes taken in to honor Mia and

Miles's future together. May you share a lifetime of love and happiness. And if one of you acts up, read those vows to each other again and again until one breaks down and surrenders. May you never lose love. Here's to you."

"Here, here," Miles said as they interlocked arms and tipped their glasses to each other.

"And now, it's time to cut the cake," said Tangie.

Delmonte Harrison was still standing toward the back of the stage when Ashley came over to whisper in his ear, handing him a glass of brandy. He stepped up to the microphone and said, "I'd like to propose a toast as well."

Mia slid her arm under Miles's as they faced Mr. Harrison.

"To our first couple to be wed on our first ship. Miles, you have a beautiful lady there, man, and Mia, you have one hell of a man. He came aboard this ship and talked me into a last-minute wedding. That man really loves you. So, in spite of what anyone ever tells you in life, know each other based upon what you've shown to each other. Stay true, and congratulations." Delmonte raised his glass, particularly toward Miles.

Miles looked at Mia. His eyes were dreamy and hopeful as though in his mind, he was preparing to bury the thought of the two of them entwined in some sort of assignation. Miles shifted his focus to Delmonte and with a look only one masculine man could appreciate from another, raised his silver goblet to Delmonte and took a sip of the bubbly.

"Now, we were given a list by Miles himself, asking us to play some of their favorite songs. This is one romantic man, Mia," announced Tangie. "So after the first song, which is for the couple only, feel free to get up out of your seats and dance with the bride or the groom, or both. Whatever floats your boat, pardon the pun. The first song is "Always," by Atlantic Starr." Tangie signaled the DJ to begin.

Miles looked at Mia and extended his hand. She stepped to him and they began to slow dance. As the song played, Ashley started to sing the chorus out loud while standing next to Delmonte. "Ooh, you're like the sun, chasing all of the rain away. When you come around, you bring brighter days. You're the perfect one for me, and you forever will be."

Miles sang in Mia's ear, "And I will love you so for always."

As the next song started, Scott got up enough nerve to ask Kelly to dance.

"No," she replied bluntly. "Would you like to dance?" she asked Winter, standing and extending her hand.

"Yes, I would," Winter answered as she stood.

Kelly and Winter walked to the dance floor next to Mia and Miles and began to hug. Kelly delicately rested her head on Winter's voluptuous chest, being that Winter was about five inches taller, and closed her eyes.

"I've seen it all now," Miles said to Mia.

With anger and frustration seething from his aura, Scott approached Mia and Miles. "Man, do you see that?" he asked, pointing at the same-sex couple.

"Sorry, you're on your own, man. I've got my own wife to see to," Miles replied with a lack of sympathy.

Scott looked back at his wife dancing with Winter and stormed out of the ballroom.

"Oh, well," Miles said.

The DJ then played "Spend My Life with You," by Eric Benet and Tamia.

Mia's ears perked up. "You remembered that I wanted this song played at my wedding. Miles, you are too much," she said, her voice filled with emotion.

Captain Douglas stared at Winter, giving a quick, subtle laugh, and then lowered his gaze to the floor. He looked at Tangie and asked, "Would you like to dance?"

"Aye, aye, sir," she said, saluting him with a flexed hand over her right eye.

Before long, the *Let's Get Married* remix by Jagged Edge was playing, as Omar and Bianca joined in for a dance. Lexi and Dr. Steven managed to pull a resistant Yanni onto the floor to dance with them. Brandon was even getting his groove on with both Ebony and Ivory.

Dante sat alone at the table as Justin worked his camera magic. Corey raided the cake table with Omar's kids.

"Are you ready to start our honeymoon, Mrs. Lewis?" Miles asked his bride.

"I'm ready, Mr. Lewis," she answered.

Without further delay, they abandoned their own reception, but no one seemed to notice.

"Captain Douglas, you did a great job," Delmonte Harrison said as the captain and Tangie headed to a table to rest their aching feet.

"Yes, you did," Ashley confirmed.

The captain held Tangie's hand. "No problem. This was the icing on the cake of this great cruise. Thanks for making it possible."

A thought came to Ashley. "So, is this wedding legal while we're on the waters, or will they have to get married again?"

The captain explained. "Oh, no. We have not actually set sail yet. We are still considered to be on Mr. Harrison's privately owned island. This will be recognized in the States."

Tangie added, "We had Mia sign a marriage application, which she thought was a government tax certificate for her casino winnings. Pretty slick, huh?"

"Yes, I'll say that for sure. It's a good thing she said yes," Ashley chortled, her hand on Delmonte's shoulder.

The captain said, "I knew that early on. Mia really loves that man. We'll be over here if the two of you need us." The captain and Tangie grabbed two seats at their table and leaned in toward each other in discussion.

Ashley thought for a minute. "That surprise wedding was so romantic, baby."

Delmonte gave a stern, straightforward stare. "Yes, it was. I say save all of that romantic stuff for the young ones. After all, a player can't change his game in the ninth inning. I need another drink." He turned his brandy glass completely over without spilling even a drop.

"No, you're going to dance with me," Ashley insisted, taking his empty glass and putting it on a nearby table as she led him to the dance floor.

Cool Delmonte Harrison stood stiff, only scarcely moving to the left with a side step, and then to the right with a side step, barely popping his fingers while Ashley lit it up, dancing in circles all around him to the tune "I Get the Job Done," by Big Daddy Kane.

Steven and Lexi took a seat at his abandoned table as he inquired, "Baby, you know that I have the authority to hire people?"

"No, I didn't. Hire who?" Lexi asked.

"A nurse," he responded.

"You need a nurse?"

Steven dabbed his sweaty forehead with a cloth napkin. "Yes, I do. And being that you're already licensed and certified, you could sign a contract for four months on a trial basis just to see if you'd be able to live this type of oceanbound life. What do you think?"

Lexi smiled. "You're asking me to stay?"

He looked at her with his deepset, sad puppy-dog eyes. "Yes, I'm asking you to stay. We'd mainly deal with a bunch of people with motion sickness and sunburn. Not very exciting, but there's free room and board, free food, traveling to faraway places, and me. I might be a little old for you, Lexi, but I haven't felt this good about someone ever before."

"But what about my job back home?" Lexi reminded him.

"That's something you'd have to work out. If you want to stay in touch and come back later after you've handled all of your business, that's fine too."

"Can you give me until the morning to think about it?" she asked.

"I can give you all the time you need," he complied.

"And can I get more time on the other situation we discussed as well?"

"I will continue to give you all the time you need, Lexi," he said, letting her know that the sex could continue to wait.

As soon as Mia and Miles hit the door of their room they noticed that Tangie had left a basket of fruit and candy at their door.

"Oh, look at that," Mia said, picking it up as Miles picked her up and carried her across the threshold. He immediately locked the door, and as soon as he turned around, Mia was down on her wifely knees, pulling his pants down to his ankles. Mia was now the giver, sucking him down like he was a Popsicle. She took him in her mouth and stroked with one-handed precision. Before she knew it, she swallowed.

Miles lifted her to the bed fully clothed and pushed up her dress. He pulled down her white silk panties and climbed on top like a twelve-year-old grinding for the first time.

Finding himself at full attention again, Miles entered her in a thrust synchronized with her own. He muttered in her left ear, "I love you, Mrs. Lewis." The throbbing of his emotions consumed her. Soon, Mia was full from his second powerful release.

At three in the morning, Mia woke up to realize they'd collapsed on top of the bed. Miles was still on top of her, snoring like he was calling the hogs. This had been their wedding night, or maybe it wasn't. Mia could not get her thoughts straight.

"Was that a dream?" Mia mumbled aloud.

Their hands were clasped together as Miles raised her hand to look at her ring finger. They both focused upon it in silence for a second. "We got married, baby. It was not a dream," he said, turning over to lie on his back.

"You did a beautiful and loving thing," she said, still half groggy.

"Knock, knock."

"Who is it?" Miles asked loudly from the bed.

"Your bellman. We need your bags outside the door in one hour. We will dock in Florida by eight this morning."

"We will, man," he said, sitting up while rubbing his head. "We're on our honeymoon," he yelled.

"Sorry, man. But rules are rules."

"No problem, one hour it is," Miles acquiesced, making his way to the bathroom, stumbling to each side with every step.

"What a trip," Mia said, lying back, sprawled out in the middle of the oversized bed. "I only expected an engagement ring and fiancé. Instead, I got a wedding ring and husband."

# DISEMBARKATION

"We will announce the times of disembarkation via deck and room number. Please either stay in your room, feel free to have breakfast at one of our cafes, or lounge around any other areas of the ship, but please try to keep the aisles clear so that we can continue the process more smoothly," the purser announced over the P.A. system.

"How much of a tip do you want to leave in this envelope for the stewards?" Mia asked Miles, holding the tip chart with one hand and clutching her wedding bouquet under her arm.

"What does it say?" Miles asked, tying his tennis shoes. "You're not letting that bouquet out of your sight, are you?"

"Nope. The chart says three dollars and fifty cents per room steward per day. That's almost twenty-five dollars per person."

"I say leave them fifty each. They were on their job. I hooked up the dining room maitre d', headwaiter and busboys. Plus they dealt with the whole reception setup and cleanup."

"You spent a lot of money for this getaway, not to mention the cost of the wedding. I really appreciate it." Mia conveyed her appreciation, placing the money-filled envelopes on the pillow.

"It was worth it, baby," he said looking around the room. "This room was really something." He checked to make sure they did not leave anything behind.

"Did you get my cash out of the safe, Miles?"

"Yes, dear. And it's going straight into the bank, too."

Mia smiled. "In a joint account?"

"Yes, in a joint account."

Mia looked out onto the veranda. "Hey, baby. We never got a chance to do it out here on the balcony. Come on, let's get in a quickie."

"Mia, you still remain the freak in the family. Now go," he said, holding the front door open with his foot, weighed down by the heavy shoulder bags. He looked back at the room as Mia walked through the door and shook his head in awe of the amazing week they'd had. Room S224 was where they'd spent their honeymoon night.

Bianca, Omar, and the kids were walking down the hallway toward the atrium to await the departure announcement. Mia and Miles joined them.

"What's going to happen to Cobra now?" Mia asked Bianca, referring to Omar as he and Miles chatted amongst themselves.

"Very funny. I never should have told you that little story. I just know that I'm not going to let him out of my sight for the next week. He's coming back with Corey and me."

"Good. For how long?"

"Just for a week. He booked a room at a hotel. And, by the way, his ex is supposed to pick up the kids at the dock."

"Do you think she's going to trip?" Mia asked.

"I don't really care. As long as her man doesn't start any crap with Omar everything should be fine," Bianca stated.

Megan walked right by Bianca and Mia as if she didn't even see them.

"Girlfriend is tripping," Bianca commented, with her nose in the air.

"I really should not have told on her. That was not for me to tell," Mia admitted.

"She's the one who made that bed. I say let her lie in it," Bianca remarked with conviction.

Mia pulled Miles's sleeve hard upon seeing the approaching couple. "Oh, no, where is Scott?" she asked.

"Why?" Miles replied.

"Because his wife and Winter are at it again."

Kelly and Winter walked by hand in hand, just as the purser announced the next section of cabins to line up to exit. Kelly and Winter jumped to the front of the line upon hearing that their deck was called.

"Do you see that crap?" Mia asked Miles.

"You women have lost your minds nowadays. That's cold blooded," said Miles.

The captain and Tangie walked over. "There's the couple of the cruise. Mia and Miles, how was your last evening?" the captain inquired.

"We didn't get much sleep," Miles said with a yawn.

The captain did not look surprised. "I can imagine you didn't. Miles, you really kept that a big surprise, man."

Miles said, "Yeah, it was a last-minute surprise to me, too."

"You looked beautiful, Mia," said Tangie.

"Thanks," Mia replied. "And Captain, you've got a first-class cruise director in Tangie. She's awesome."

"I've heard that quite a bit over the past week. We made a good choice. She comes to us with a lot of experience. Well, I wish you all nothing but the best. Maybe you could send me one of your wedding photos. I'd like to frame it and hang it in our library as our first wedding ever."

"I'll make sure I send you one. Thanks again," said Miles.

"And was everything else satisfactory for you all?" he asked Omar and Bianca.

Omar replied, "No complaints at all."

So, everything is copacetic?" the captain asked with sly concern.

"It's all good," Omar assured him.

"You too, son," the captain asked Corey. "How'd it go?"

Corey broke away from Omar's kids long enough to reply. "I had a ball."

Tangie said to Omar and Bianca, "You two look like you made one of the true love connections this week. That is, other than Dr. Taylor and his new love. That's a pretty high percentage."

"Where are they, anyway?" asked Bianca.

"They've got a lot of work to do what with inventory and getting set up for the next group of passengers. No more play for her now," said the captain.

"So Lexi is staying?" asked Mia.

"Yes," said Tangie.

Mia nudged Bianca and commented, "I knew it."

"She's in good hands," the captain assured them. "Don't forget that picture, now."

"We won't," Mia said.

The captain and Tangie turned, stopping to say farewell to another group of departing passengers. The captain had his hand on Tangie's back.

"I think they need to hook up," Mia said to Bianca.

Bianca remarked, "That girl is too young for him."

Mia assured her, "Neither one of them has anybody. I guarantee you by next year they are going to be a love connection statistic."

The line moved slowly as everyone departed from the ship, using the gangway ramp toward the luggage area.

"How are we going to find our bags amongst all of this stuff?" Bianca asked Omar as they walked with the kids, looking around at the many rows of luggage.

"Just look for what's familiar and I'll check the tag numbers," suggested Omar.

"That's a great idea," Miles said. "Mia, let's do the same."

"Hey, newlyweds, how are you?" asked Delmonte, who was leaving with only an attaché case in hand. Ashley was walking just behind him.

"Hello, Delmonte," Mia said.

Delmonte reached into his inside jacket pocket and removed a Harrison Cruises envelope. "I just wanted to give you two a little wedding gift, since you really didn't have the full honeymoon you deserve. Feel free to be my guest to come back for my two-week South African cruise next year. Inside this envelope you'll find two fully paid voucher tickets in your names."

Miles took the envelope and then attempted to hand it back. "Mr. Harrison, you don't have to do this. You've done enough."

"It's just my way of thanking you for being the first couple to wed aboard my maiden ship. I think you both deserve a real getaway," Delmonte said, waving his hand to indicate that he rejected the return.

"Wow. I don't know what to say. Thank you so much. We will indeed be looking forward to that," Miles said, looking at Mia as if the gesture was too much.

Ashley interjected, "You'd better take those tickets. He's normally not that generous."

"Daddy!" two young girls yelled, running toward Delmonte. And walking behind them was the same woman Mia had seen in the picture in his room. A beautiful, classy, sophisticated, Chanel-wearing Black woman sporting a blinding, pear-shaped diamond ring. Delmonte hurried toward them, picking up his young daughters in his arms and kissing the woman on her ruby red lips.

"Take care," he said to Mia, Miles and Ashley, turning to walk away with his family.

"Well, it was nice to meet you both. Congratulations, and I plan to see you next year on that Cape Town cruise," Ashley said. "And Mia," she said, touching Mia's shoulder and squeezing her trapezius muscle with her long, sexy fingers, "One thing my mother always told me. Remember to love like you've never been hurt and dance like nobody's looking. That's my wedding gift to you both."

"Thanks, Ashley. Aren't those great words to live by? Now I know where you get your wisdom. I look forward to seeing you again too," said Mia.

Wheeling a small, black, compact piece of luggage, Ashley walked through an adjacent door like a stewardess, humming a barely audible tune to herself as she exited onto the dock.

Mia stated in amazement, "That's one strong woman. I don't think I could handle that."

"You'll never have to now," said Miles. "Delmonte is married?"

They made their way to the dock parking lot and stood in a short line for a cab. A brand-new steel silver 500SEC Mercedes pulled up and honked at Winter. Winter was oblivious to the sound of the horn as she was standing nearby getting up close and personal with Kelly.

The driver, a Creole-looking gentleman, maybe in his fifties, honked again and motioned to Miles as he got out, "Hey will you tell my wife, the reporter, that her ride is here?" The heavyset man popped the trunk, made room for her bags and said, "Thanks, man," as he got back into the car.

Miles cooperated. He walked over to Winter, tapping her on the shoulder. "Your ride is here."

Winter gave a half turn and replied, "Thanks, Miles. I'm coming." She faced Kelly again and kissed her with enough tongue action to resuscitate a corpse. "Good-bye, baby. I'll call you at your office next week. Have a safe trip home," Winter said.

Kelly gave her a close hug and said, "Okay. You too."

Winter saw Justin and Dante coming down the stairs to line up for a cab as well. "Hey, Justin," she said, walking toward the Mercedes. "I'll see you at the office tomorrow. Keep an eye on all of that great video you've got."

"I will," Justin replied as both he and Dante waved good-bye.

Winter sashayed off to the Mercedes and leaned into the driver side window to place a big pluck on her husband's lips.

"She's pretty," her man said loudly through the window, browsing Kelly with his eyes as Winter placed her own bags in the trunk and closed it.

"I'll tell you about her later," said Winter, walking around to the passenger side. She waved again as Kelly flagged down a Delta Airlines shuttle bus.

"Well I'll be damned. I've seen it all. Looks like he's a swinger too. Kelly's in for some real fun," said Mia. "She's got to be traveling on the same flight as Scott. Where is he, anyway?"

Miles replied, nonplussed, "I have no idea. He might still be in that room crying."

"Omar," a petite woman belted out as she stood beside a white Toyota Celica. It was Vivica, Omar's wife, with open arms as her kids ran toward her.

"Momma, Momma," her young son yelled. Vivica hugged them and then opened the car door and pulled the driver-side seat forward so they could get in the backseat. The front passenger door opened and Vivica's intimidating hunk of a boyfriend got out and leaned against the door with his arms crossed.

"What's up, man?" Omar asked calmly.

"Yo, brotha. Why were you tripping like that?" the man asked with much attitude.

"Dude, I've already apologized to Vivica. This is between her and me," Omar said. The man needed to see his way out of the situation.

The man came around toward the front of the car. "Her stresses are my stresses. You're going to have to deal with the two of us from now on, do you understand that? So, if you ever think of pulling any more dirty tricks, you'll have to answer to me."

Omar replied as if unaffected. "Like I said, this is between Vivica and me."

"Mommy, can we go now?" Omar's son asked from the backseat.

"Yes, baby. We're leaving," Vivica said, keeping one eye on Omar as she turned to get in the car at the same time as her man.

"Good-bye, Daddy. Good-bye, Corey and Bianca," Omar's daughter called out as Corey waved.

As Vivica started the car she peered through the window and

yelled, "Bianca, huh? You brought a woman with you too. Oh, I'll see you in court."

"Good-bye, woman," said Omar, flagging down the next cab. Vivica screeched off. "Are you two going to the airport too? Do you want to ride with us?" Omar said to Miles and Mia.

"Okay. I'm down for anything to save money," Miles said. "And it sounds like you're going to need all the money you can get too," he joked with Omar.

"You would think so, huh?" Omar remarked with a laugh.

Miles and Corey hopped in the front seat after the cab driver put the luggage in the trunk. Omar closed the door after Bianca and Mia got in one side and then he went around to the other side to get in the backseat.

"We're on United," Miles said to the driver. "What about you, Omar?"

"I'm on United too. I'm on the same flight as Bianca and Corey," Omar said with a huge grin.

Corey turned around and smiled at Omar.

"You cool with that, my man?" Omar asked Corey.

"I'm cool with that," Corey answered.

Bianca rubbed the back of his head.

"Mom," Corey said with an irritating tone. He reached back to pat his hair back into shape.

Mia thought it strange that there was still no sight of Scott and no sign of Yanni.

"What an adventure this has been," Mia said, turning back to admire a final view of the colossal ship.

# 46

## CAPTAIN'S LOG

Five hours after disembarkation, a motivated, reflective, and inspired Captain Douglas sat down in his room with his numerous plaques, awards, commendations, and framed photographs surrounding him. The many staterooms and various areas on the ship had been cleaned up in preparation for thousands of newly arriving passengers. Linen and towels had been cleaned and restocked. Due to the mass weekly consumption of fresh meat, dairy, vegetables, and beverages, the restocking delivery was already complete. And the captain had had his crew meeting about an hour earlier. Mr. Harrison would not be making the trip this time.

After every cruise Captain Douglas entered the happenings and accomplishments in his journal. This entry would be no different. This entry deserved a new log, one specific to the *Chocolate Ship* and his experience at the helm of Delmonte Harrison's first ship.

***Dear Journal:***

***This particular cruise, I've added a new employee, a nurse who will assist Dr. Taylor in more ways than one, and terminated an em-***

*ployee for the very behavior that I constantly warn the crew about. The next one to go just might be Olandi with his smooth self, but he is a damn good waiter. We had a near drowning, a legal incident with border officials, a fight that nearly resulted in assault charges being filed, a couple of testosterone-filled athletes who thought they received a green light to get freaky and are banned from returning, and I married my first couple aboard my new ship.*

*All in all, my staff did an excellent job. The christening and all of the events were successful, and the cruise itself was a fantastic voyage.*

*This sailing soap opera is just one of many more to come aboard this big, brown Hershey's bar. Surely, I will always be able to supply you with stories about couples who see this escape as an excuse to act up. There will always be singles who come aboard looking for love. There will always be those who break up, stay together, find love, lose love, some who experiment and some who just chill. For some, their only purpose is to get a magnificent suntan. For others, their purpose is to have sex on the high seas, with whomever. Even I got "my freak on," as they say.*

*The whole term Black–owned breeds an expectation of low standards and less than stellar behavior. But, similar to any of my previous posts, human beings are just that: human. The romantic factor alone on a cruise is a test of one's fidelity and self-control. Every now and then, passengers are expected to live for the moment and deal with it later. The owner himself has his chick on the side and more opportunities thrown at him on a daily basis than you could shake a stick at. Surely his woman knows the deal. Perhaps the advantages outweigh the alternative.*

*This was a week of real-life emotions, scantily clad bodies, the feeling of experiencing the magnificence of the constant direct hit of the generous sun, beautiful, blinding white suede sand lining exotic tropical beaches with beanstalk-like palm trees, imbibing in fancy island drinks with names like Banana Boat Margarita and Jamaican Sunrise, music that takes you back to a place in time that included your first grind back in middle school, and all of the rest and relaxation you can handle.*

*So journal, each week for six weeks at a time, I will be back to spend a little time with you before moving on to the next.*

*But until next week, when a similar update will be entered, I must get back to my duties as captain of the* Chocolate Ship. *The first and only Black–owned cruise ship in the world. I love the life I live and I live the life I love, because after all, ocean water is in my blood, just as the essence of my very Blackness is in my soul. For now, this ship is my lady, my baby, and my love. But maybe next time, I'll have a story to tell of how I too found true romance aboard this ship of love. I'm out.*

Closing his journal and placing his Harrison Cruises ink pen back into the brass penholder, Captain Douglas rose from his gold studded, diamond patterned, black leather executive chair and again stood in the full-length mirror, cut to fit his ten-by-ten closet.

"I salute you, Captain Douglas. Good luck," Captain James J. Douglas said to himself, upon releasing a stiff right-handed salute to his own full-length mirrored image.

Over the P.A., once again he heard his previously recorded captain's bulletin, which would be repeated many times over the next couple of hours.

> *Ladies and gentlemen, Harrison Cruises and I would like to welcome you aboard the maiden voyage of the new and pioneering superliner, the* Chocolate Ship—Caribbean. *I am your Captain, James Douglas, and I am honored to have you as a guest on this magnificent floating hotel, as I like to call it. You won't find shuffleboard on this ship . . .*

# THERE'S NO PLACE LIKE HOME—OR IS THERE?

"Hey, Mom. How are you and Dad doing? When he gets back, ask him to call us. We've been missing each other since we got back. I know we cheated you out of a ceremony, but we plan on having a reception here too. We're sending pictures. I know, Mom. Well, thanks so much. She's right here, hold on one minute." Miles handed Mia the phone.

"Hi, Mrs. Lewis. Okay, I'm sorry. Hi, Mom. Thank you so much. No, it was a total surprise. I had absolutely no idea. Sounds like you knew about it before I did. The best I'd hoped for was a proposal. He is something else, you're right. I'll make sure to get the pictures in the mail. We'll plan the reception together, okay? All right, Mom. Good-bye." Mia pressed the talk button.

"I think she might have been a little disappointed that she didn't get to participate," Miles commented.

"That's surely understandable. My mother felt the same way, but she was so excited for us that she understood."

"I say within the next few months, we have a big party and show the video that Justin is going to send us," Miles suggested.

Mia took her seat at the dining-room table to resume their game of chess.

What a difference a cruise made. Mia was now a full-time resident in Mile's twenty-five-hundred-square-foot home. No more showing up and knocking at the door. Mia had a key of her own. The only change décor-wise was that she added a few Pier One accents here and there, like dried flowers, chenille throws and fancy pillar candles. And of course, their ten-by-thirteen photo of the first day of their voyage was strategically placed over the fireplace just to convey her presence to each and every person who walked through the door. Next to the picture was their framed marriage license.

"Checkmate," Miles said with his usual competitive glow. "See, I don't know why you try to act like you are the chess queen herself, Mia. You can't beat the king at his game."

"Oh, really?" Mia asked.

"Really."

"Well, I think I already have," she said, rising from their beveled glass dining-room set to take their empty soda cans and popcorn bowl into the kitchen.

"Yeah, you got me on that one. But I let you win to check this mate. I'll never let you win from across the board. Chess is a game of skill, concentration, intelligence, and strategy."

"It's a game of luck," Mia said.

"Oh, you're tripping," Miles confirmed as he stood up from the table.

"And how do you know I haven't let you win all of these times, Mr. King?"

Miles replied, "You never know my next move."

The telephone rang just as Miles grabbed the TV remote to stretch out on the couch.

"Hey, Scott. How are you? Hold on." Mia gave Miles the phone with a reserved hand-off and returned to the kitchen.

"Yo, what's up? Just chillin', " he said, looking at Mia like she needed to get out of his business.

"Just chillin', " she mimicked under her breath.

"Okay, but just for a couple of hours, man. You need to get yourself together. See ya." Miles hung up, placing the cordless on the leather sofa next to him in silence as he stared at the TV.

"Is Scott coming over here tonight?"

"No," he answered as if that was ridiculous.

Mia sprayed Windex on the table. "Good, because I thought we could just hang out and have a Blockbuster night. I'd planned a nice, quiet evening alone with you. And plus I wanted us to just talk. I have something to tell you."

"I'm just going to meet him for a drink. I'll be right back."

"Tonight?" she asked, stopping to give him question marked eyes.

"Yes, Mia. Should I have asked you first?" he inquired with sarcasm.

"Maybe not ask me first, but check with me first. That would have been nice. It is the two of us now. You know what I mean?" She rubbed the tabletop with fast pressure.

"It's only going to be for a little while. I'll be back before you know it."

"Miles, ever since Kelly left him he has been the true example of misery loves company. He's doing this on purpose to start trouble between you and me, and it's working."

"You're being paranoid. That man's wife is seeing a woman, Mia."

"He should have thought about that before he decided to stick Megan," Mia said, throwing the dish towel onto the counter.

"Maybe so, but he is paying the price, and I'm worried about him. Shit, the man barely has enough energy to take a shower, let alone get up and go to work."

Mia sat at the opposite end of the sofa and said, "Yeah, but I see he can muster enough energy to sit up at a club and drown his sorrows. He's looking for a woman to help him forget about her and you're just allowing yourself to get caught up in his web."

"We are not going to a club. We are going to Delmonico's for a couple of beers."

"Well, while he's out there trying to prove to himself that his dick still has value, you'll just be sitting next to him as his pussy magnet," Mia replied with aversion.

"Mia, come on now," Miles said, moving in closer to spark some understanding, "I know you trust me. We've come too far for all of this."

"We've come too far for you to still be hanging out with Scott. Maybe you need to get a new best friend."

"He didn't kick me to the curb when he got married and I won't kick him to the curb either. What's up with you? Are you about to start your period?" Miles asked as he stood up, buttoning his blue-jean shirt.

"I wish. Maybe that would be a good excuse for why I'm feeling so adamant about this. This is not about emotions, this is about reality. You need to detach from Scott."

"Mia, do you realize what you're asking me to do? You're asking me to give up my good friend. Would you give up Bianca for me?" Miles asked as he went into the bathroom with Mia on his tracks. "You really should be nicer to Scott. After all, he was the reason I got that ring you're wearing. He worked out a deal with the owner of a jewelry store. Otherwise you would not be sporting a rock like that."

She'd reached her limit. "That's not fair. I appreciate the fact that he hooked you up." Mia tightened her jaw. "But, I'm just asking you to grow up."

Miles stared at her with an acrimonious look of revisited doubt. He walked past her, turning off the light and exiting the bathroom as if he forgot why he walked in to begin with. He stood at the front door with his back to her.

"I just know you are not going to leave," she said with the sound of a dare.

"I'll be back in a little while." Miles walked out, closing the door behind him.

"I told you I knew your every move. You're so damn predictable!" Mia yelled through the closed door, kicking it with her foot. "Damn," she said, as she hopped to the window. She separated the black horizontal blinds with her fingertips and watched for a moment as the garage door opened. She watched Miles pull off in his pale yellow vintage Corvette.

*What just happened? Am I overreacting, or is he just always going to need time and space away from me?* she wondered. She snatched the phone as it rang. "Hello. Hi, Mom. Just, ah, getting ready to take a shower. He's gone to run an errand, he'll be right back. Okay, I'll catch you tomorrow. Yes, being a wife is wonderful. Talk to you later. I love you. Good-bye, Mom."

Mia made her way to the shower. She couldn't figure out if she'd lied to her mother again or not, about how wonderful it was to be a wife, but she noted that this incident was the third time since they returned from the cruise that Miles had been out alone with Scott. He would never just come right back, and he'd never ask her to go with him. Maybe he just wanted to hold on to a bit of his bachelorhood. *Well, maybe I'll just hold on to a bit of my bacherlorette-hood,* she thought just before she stepped her wet, still half-soapy body out of the shower. Without even drying off, she went to pick up the cordless and dialed.

"Yanni, what are you doing tonight? Let's go hit the *Spot.*"

Megan was hanging out with a new group of Black girls, shining Mia on when Mia greeted her.

"Hey, Megan. How have you been?"

"Just fine, Mia. How about you?" Megan barely turned around to reply. She was wearing her usual colorful attire: This time the skinny mini was baby blue.

"I can't complain," Mia said, lying.

"Where's Miles? I thought your club-hopping days were over."

"So did I. He's hanging out with Scott tonight."

Megan stepped closer to Mia. "Oh, my goodness. I see. Well, I'm glad you're out. Just sit down with your girls and chill. There's no harm in that."

Mia replied, "Yes, but my supply of girls is dwindling down quite a bit."

"Excuse me, Neecee. I'll be right back," Megan said to one of her new buddies. "This sounds like a Long Island evening. Come with me."

"That's cool, Megan, but I'm not drinking tonight. I'm driving and I won't be here long," Mia said, following behind Megan.

"That's cool too, but damn, Mia, that fucking ring is blinding me. Would you mind putting your hand in your pocket or something?" Megan remarked.

"I know. I just keep looking at this stone every now and then to remind me that I'm actually a wife for life now. Sometimes, it just doesn't feel like it, though."

As they walked hand in hand to the small bar table, Mia asked, "Megan, why did you sleep with Scott?"

"Oh, Lord. I knew you'd been dying to bring that up. It's because he'd been flirting with me earlier that night. When I was sober, the fact that he was married seemed to matter. But as the night went on, I remember him asking me for my room number and I gave it to him. Maybe I thought he was someone safe because you knew him, I don't know. But I answered the knock at the door and turned around to return to my bed, almost without looking to see who was standing there. The next thing I knew, I was in the heat of the moment and did not want to turn back."

"Why were you so angry with Kelly?" Mia asked.

"Maybe because I felt guilty enough. I'm not sure. But I know one thing, I think that girl really loves him," Megan said, spotting an empty table.

"Yeah, well they're history now, Megan. You really should think about why you drink so much. Being in an altered state to that extreme can end up tragically for everyone."

"Thanks, but can we cut all of the dramatic advice and focus on you tonight?" Megan motioned to Yanni to come over to the table as she sat down. "Come on, girl," she said as Yanni approached and they took their seats. "Mia needs a little girls'-night-out time. No men tonight, no catching, no dancing, just focus on . . . damn, who the hell is that?" Megan asked, easily distracted as usual.

Megan's head spun around like she was going through an exorcism. Her body swiveled off her bar stool, propelling her directly into the arms of some Morris-Chestnut–looking brotha with black leather pants and a see-through burgundy muscle shirt.

"Some things never change, Yanni," Mia said as Megan traipsed off to the dance floor.

Yanni took her seat, wiping her forehead with a napkin as she remarked, "My, my. Don't we dress conservatively now that we are actually someone's spouse?"

Mia wore a casual sage pantsuit with a camel turtleneck and tan ankle boots with not an ounce of skin showing.

"I just threw on whatever I could grab to get out of the house. I am not trying to be cute," Mia said, pulling her turtleneck collar up closer to her chin.

"I'm going to keep on going the scantily clad route just to keep them coming," Yanni said, taking off her sweater to reveal a black-beaded bustier, which stopped just above her perfect belly button. "One day I'll meet Mr. Right."

"You'll catch him wearing that. What ever happened to you and Bo, anyway?" she asked as Yanni ordered a drink.

"You're not drinking?" Yanni asked, ignoring Mia's question.

"No, not tonight," Mia answered.

"I had to drop bad boy Bo after he told me that Winter ended up doing him and Deshaun. That woman puts the *T* in *tramp*. He was way too fast for me. But he looked good."

"He was fine, with his perfect black head."

"Yeah, he was. I was just trying to stay as busy as Lexi. I guess I was wrong."

"I'm glad you came to that conclusion. Have you talked to her?"

"That girl had me ship her things to her already. She didn't even take a moment to breathe—just cruising back and forth like she's lost her mind. My parents are happy for her, though. She caught her a doctor. She'll be back in a couple of weeks. By the way, she told me she finally found out that his pecker works just fine."

"They hadn't gotten it on all that week? Good for her. Who'd've thought less than two months ago that her cruise would end up being permanent?" Mia reflected.

"Not me. But Lexi's always had all the luck."

"Hey, Brandon, how are you?" Mia asked as he appeared out of nowhere, offering a hug.

Brandon was sharp as usual in a dark brown, three-quarter-length suit with a mustard-colored tie. "I'm cool, ladies. I'm just here promoting an event at the Atlas next weekend."

"No more cruise promoting?" Yanni inquired, standing to hug him as well.

"I've had to get on a list to even book a date on that ship, it's so popular now. Maybe next year. This year I'll have my own television show called *The Wicks*."

"Congratulations, Brandon. That's great." Yanni beamed.

"Yeah, I think that phone call from Mr. Harrison didn't hurt either," Brandon admitted. "You know, friends in high places."

"Brandon, you are very talented. You earned that all by yourself, if you ask me," said a complimentary Yanni.

Jay-Z's latest cut started playing. Yanni snapped her fingers to the beat.

"What I will ask you is, Would you like to dance, lady?" Brandon inquired.

"I'd love to," Yanni answered, taking his hand as they hurried to the dance floor.

*How'd they miss hooking up on the ship?* Mia asked herself. *I should have asked him what was up with the supposed underground strip club in his cabin. Oh well.*

Mia watched the two of them get down like they were on *Soul Train*, but this time she was not joining in. She focused on her wedding ring, swirling the platinum band back to the left and then to the right, over and over again, holding her hand away to bask in its brilliance. She still felt disappointed in Miles for leaving her at home on a special Saturday night. Tonight was the night she was going to reveal her secret to him. He blew her chance to watch him open his belated wedding gift. She had used the money she'd won on the ship to buy Miles a platinum wedding band, since he hadn't had one during the ceremony. She'd wrapped it in newspaper and put it in a fancy box with a big yellow bow. Included in the box was the positive home pregnancy test she had taken that morning. In spite of being on the pill for years, she'd conceived on one of those wild nights on the ship. Perhaps he'd finally have that son to carry on his name. God only knew what his reaction was going to be.

"Would you like to dance?" a tall gentleman asked Mia, startling her from her thoughts.

"No. I'm just waiting for my friend. Thanks anyway," she replied with appreciation.

"Just let me know if you change your mind," he said respectfully.

As he walked away, a handsome Hispanic man approached. "Hey, lady. Can I buy you a drink?"

"No thanks, I'm here with someone," she replied as he tipped his head and walked away.

*Yeah, right, I'm here with someone*, she thought, sipping on her glass of ice water.

"Hey, miss. You'd better be careful. You know I read an e-mail today that warned of cyanide-laced drinking glasses served to Black patrons by some nightclub owners." It was Miles, sneaking up behind Mia and whispering in her ear.

She smiled. "Oh, really?"

"Yes," he said, coming around to take Megan's seat. "You really should ask for a straw."

"I will try to remember that." She blushed from his charms.

"Maybe I should take you home to your husband so that he can make love to you all night to keep you up just to make sure," Miles suggested.

"Maybe you should." This was one move Mia did not predict.

Mia took Miles's hand as they stood up. She grabbed her purse and started looking around for Yanni. "Hold on one second. Let's go tell Yanni I'm leaving."

Yanni yelled at Mia from the dance floor, "Mia, where are you going?"

"This guy is taking me home so that I can do my husband. Do you mind?" Mia teased.

"Excuse me. You go ahead, girl," Yanni shouted.

The words to the next song blasted over the zillion watt speakers. "Got you working with some ass, yeah, you bad, yeah. Make a nigga spend his cash, yeah, his last yeah."

Miles said, "Oh, no, they are not playing our song."

"Oh, is that our new song now?" Mia asked with surprise.

"Girl, you'd better back that ass up. Move over, ladies," Miles said, making his way in between Megan and her dancing king, and Yanni and Brandon.

Miles leaned in toward Mia's left ear, trying to talk over the music. "For your information, I did not go to meet Scott. I drove around for a while and thought about what you said about growing up. You're right. The *we* has to replace the *I*. It's no longer just Miles. It's Mia and Miles now. I turned my car around, called Scott to tell him he was on his own, and raced back home to you but when I got back you were gone. Thanks for leaving a note."

"You're welcome," Mia said, shaking her head in amazement and pleasant surprise.

"But I don't want you here anymore," Miles said, half dancing. "The only hot spot I want to hit is yours. And I don't want to end up like Scott and Kelly. I want to be around for our one-year anniversary cruise next year."

"I thought you said Scott needed you," Mia reminded him.

"You need me more. Now can *we* get out of here and go home?" he asked, standing still.

Mia continued shaking her butt to the music. "But we didn't finish dancing to our song."

"That's my song," he said, pulling her away from the floor by her ring finger. "It's time I started listening to our song. What did you want to tell me earlier?" he asked.

Just then Yanni yelled out, gyrating her hips like a belly dancer, "You two go home and start that family!"

Mia waved her hand over her head to her friends, answering Miles's question, "Just that I have a present for you when *we* get home. That's all."

# EPILOGUE

The good-looking, dapper, redheaded, Caucasian lead anchor for Sunday night's eleven-o'clock news resumed the telecast after the final commercial break with an entertainment news segment lead-in for Winter's story. "Now reporting in studio is anchor-reporter Winter Jackson, who just returned from a Harrison Cruises one-week-long adventure to the Caribbean on the *Chocolate Ship*. Winter," he said, sounding like Ted Koppel.

"Thanks, Harold," she said with copy pages in hand, turning toward the lead camera to read the prompter. She sported a powder blue blazer with gold buttons. "Yes, the *Chocolate Ship* was not only a spectacular cruise in general terms, but this particular cruise was the first of its kind. It was the first Black–owned, luxury-liner cruise ship ever to sail in the history of the United States. And what a week it was."

Winter continued to roll her piece, which included video from the christening, the captain's dinner, the luau, and the final morning's disembarkation. She included sound bytes of interviews with the captain, the crew, numerous passengers, footage of the wedding, and Delmonte Harrison himself. She closed her story by outlining the details of the next cruise.

"So, Harold," she said, looking toward the anchor and his female, blonde, conservatively dressed co-anchor, "This is an exciting and entertaining adventure that I guarantee you will never forget. I know I never will."

"Thanks, Winter. And the owner has his own travel company?" Harold asked.

"Yes, call 1-800-HARRISO for more information."

Harold commented, "Sounds like it was quite relaxing."

"Oh, no, not much resting on this one, Harold," Winter informed him, giving first-hand advice.

"Thanks again, Winter. You get all of the good assignments," he joked. "And on to our final story."

Winter participated in the closing shot from the set as the final credits rolled and the director yelled, "Clear." She proceeded to her news desk to gather her belongings in preparation for going home for the evening.

"Winter, line one is for you," the assignment editor said.

"Hello. Hi, baby. Yes, I'll be there in about thirty minutes. Did you call Kelly to see if she was coming by tonight? She is? Good. I'll stop and get some of the bubbly. Good-bye, honey." She grabbed her black leather Coach purse and matching briefcase. "Hey, Justin. What are you doing here so late?" Winter asked as she walked past his desk.

"I'm just preparing to send this wedding video edit off to Miles. It turned out pretty good," Justin informed her as he placed the video into a padded envelope.

"Oh, shoot. That reminds me," Winter said as she walked back to her desk and opened her top drawer. "Here, catch," she said to Justin, making an awkward toss. "Stick this in that package with the video."

Justin stretched his long, lean frame off center, catching the white puka-shell necklace that had belonged to Miles.

Winter said, "I'm sure the addressee has been looking for it."

He eyed Winter with a look that indicated he knew her well. "How did you get this?" Justin inquired with subtle curiosity.

"He left it—well, let's just say he left it. Good night, Justin. Tell Dante I said hello."

"Good night, Winter, I will tell him. See you tomorrow," Justin said, watching Winter wiggle her way down the hall in her short skirt while he tossed the necklace high in the air and then caught it.

He remembered how Miles had treated Dante and then he thought about how nice Miles was to him even after he found out he was gay. He shook his head and exhaled sharply, placed the shells deep in his ROCAWEAR jeans pocket, sealed the video envelope and placed it in the outgoing mail bin. He placed a call on his cellphone while marching down the narrow hallway.

"I'm on my way," he said. "Can't wait to see you."